THE
UNLIKELY
CANDIDATE

A Novel of Politics, Religion, and the Media

Stephen Palmer

ISBN: 9798638399351

www.sdpalmer.net

To my wife Jennifer and daughters Avery and Haley. Thanks for being so amazing.

Author's Note

This novel is a work of fiction. More precisely, it is a work of political fiction. Because of the subject matter, I've found it useful to incorporate references to actual historical figures. All other characters are fictional, and any resemblance to any real-world person is coincidental. The same is true for newspapers, television stations, websites and the like that appear in my novel; these are fictional and not intended to refer to any actual institution. One exception here is the excellent and informative Powerline Blog found at www.powerlineblog.com, whose owner was kind enough to give me permission to refer to his site in the novel.

I confess that I vacillated on the dates and timing aspects of this novel. I used the 2016 election for the framework mainly because I began writing this book in 2013. At that time, a 2016 date seemed safely in the future. But life intervened, the writing took longer than anticipated, and the political landscape certainly didn't stand still.

Donald Trump was merely a real estate mogul and reality television star when most of this book was written. His shocking election in 2016 was encouraging to me in the sense that it made the unlikely candidacy of the fictional Jeff Ackerman seem a little less far-fetched. But Mr. Trump's rise to the White House also forced me to rewrite parts of the book. For example, in early drafts, Jeff Ackerman pledged to "make America great again," years before Donald Trump made this his campaign slogan. But because I'm fairly certain that most readers would find it hard to believe that I thought of this phrase before Mr. Trump made it famous, my fictional candidate does not use this slogan in the final version of the book.

I considered removing all date references, as well as moving the dates a decade or two into the future. But neither of these alternative approaches would really solve my problem, which is that, at some definite point in time, the narrative must move from actual historical people and events to fictional people and events. Accordingly, in order to minimize frustration and confusion when reading this novel, I humbly request that the reader set aside his or her knowledge of actual historical events from and after approximately 2008.

The facts and figures cited by the Ackerman campaign (such as tax rates and the percentage of the African-American vote that typically goes to Democrats) are, to the best of my ability, accurate as of the dates in which they appear in the novel. The biblical and theological material is also accurate, rather than fictional. However, Jeff Ackerman's achievements as governor of Mississippi are wholly a product of the author's imagination: Mississippi still has eighty-two counties and has not, as far as I know, enacted merit pay for teachers or the other reforms attributed to Governor Ackerman in these pages.

On the topic of Mississippi, let me be clear: I am a native Mississippian, and I am extremely proud of that fact. Although the state has had and continues to have its problems, it is a beautiful state inhabited by warm, wonderful, kind, humble, hardworking people. To my fellow Mississippians, please know that all negative references to our home state in this novel are intended to be the stereotypical, thoughtless, and uneducated views of outsiders, rather than the opinions of the author.

Finally, this is a story of ideas. In an effort to have this book be something other than a cure for insomnia, I use fictional characters to convey those ideas and the arguments for and against certain political and theological positions. Accordingly, the bulk of the material relates to those ideas, rather than minute physical or emotional details about the characters. If you're wondering about the color of a particular character's eyes, or if another character likes his steak prepared medium rare, I can only say that the answers are whatever you want them to be.

Chapter 1

The White House
March 2015

President Upton Landers breezed into the Oval Office at the crack of ten, ready to spend a tough four-hour day working to transform the United States of America. He wasn't really sure exactly how—or into what—America should be transformed. But the promise of national transformation had played well in his speeches on the campaign trail, and he knew better than to question what his teleprompter told him. After all, he had smart people writing those speeches for him. At least, he assumed they were smart. He'd never actually spoken to most of them. But nothing good ever happened when he went off script.

One White House staffer took the president's suit coat while another handed him a cup of coffee. Heavy with cream, no sugar. Neither received a word of thanks or even a glance. These little people were lucky to be so close to the seat of power. That was thanks enough for them. Landers would start being nice to people again months from now when he launched his re-election campaign, but now was the time for governing. And governing was hard.

After all, it wasn't easy to transform a nation. But transformed it must be. Because America had been racist. Still was, of course. And some rich people hadn't paid enough in taxes. And the Indians! Or Native Americans . . . or whatever they were calling them this week. Couldn't forget about America's shameful exploitation of the Indians/Native Americans/indigenous peoples.

As president, Upton Landers would fix all of that. Somehow. He'd leave the details to Richard Jordan and all the minions that Jordan had scuffling about. What did all those people do all day? He'd let Jordan worry about that. He, Upton Landers, needed to focus on the big picture, needed to project an image of working hard.

President Landers rolled up his sleeves as he strode confidently to the big desk in the Oval Office. This gesture, he had recently determined, projected an image of hard work, dedication, manliness, and seriousness. Of course, one casualty of this new habit was the fact that he could no longer wear French-cuffed shirts, but even he was intelligent enough to understand that removing gold cuff links in order to roll up one's sleeves was a bit over the top.

The first time Landers tried the roll-up-the-sleeves-and-get-to-work routine, he dropped one of his cuff links. He then confounded the situation by accidentally kicking the offending cuff link under the desk as he lowered himself into the leather desk chair. An over-eager female staffer hurried to his side of the desk, bent low, and reached under the desk to retrieve the missing cuff link. As her head popped up on Landers' side of the desk, some fool made a wise-crack about it being too early in the Landers administration for this president to have his own Bill Clinton/Monica Lewinsky moment.

Everyone had laughed. Everyone, that is, except the president. Upton Landers didn't laugh at the expense of Upton Landers. Couldn't have some underling think that he had the right to denigrate the presidency. Anyway, Landers was the only one allowed to be funny around here. *Hope that former staffer and would-be comedian is enjoying life in the ranks of the unemployed*, the president thought to himself as he finished rolling up the left sleeve of his expensive, hand-tailored—but non-French-cuffed—dress shirt. He made a mental note to have Jordan remind everyone out there in the Democratic Party establishment not to hire that wisecracker for anything. Not even the mail room. Some people had to learn lessons the hard way. And sometimes a leader had to send a very clear message to his subordinates.

Richard Jordan entered the office just behind Landers and examined the chair across the desk from his boss. Finding it satisfactorily dust-free, he lowered himself into it, careful not to risk undue wrinkles in his navy-blue worsted suit. The thirty-eight-year-old Yale graduate was the perfect White House operative. He wanted power but not fame, and lusted for control but not adulation. This made him the ideal chief of staff for Upton Landers, who wanted fame, applause, and adulation, and was perfectly willing to let someone else exercise power as long as Landers got the credit for the results.

Unmarried, childless, and seemingly hobbyless, Jordan lived for politics. Specifically, liberal Democrat, left-wing-as-you-can-get-away-with-while-still-winning-elections politics. He was a doctrinaire liberal and could cite chapter and verse from the Democratic Party platform. But he was smart enough to know that much of the current liberal doctrine was worthless at best and harmful at worst.

As a high school junior with dreams of political power, Jordan had carefully analyzed the American body politic. He determined at the ripe old age of seventeen that liberalism might not be great for America but that it had the potential to do great things for his favorite American—himself. Nothing had happened in the intervening twenty-one years to alter that analysis. He smiled inwardly as he relished, not for the first time, the power that he wielded from what others considered to be the wrong side of the presidential desk here in the Oval Office.

President Landers and his chief of staff began each day with a quick chat. They covered the day's schedule, what mischief Congress was up to, and the latest political gossip. Although conversations like this marked the beginning of Landers' workday, Jordan had been going strong since five a.m., sipping robust Colombian coffee and wielding power in the name of President Landers.

Today was no different. Jordan had selected Juanita Henderson-Kohn for an open judicial seat on the 9th Circuit Court of Appeals and prepped his media contacts accordingly. Now, due to a quirk in the U.S. Constitution that grants the power of judicial appointments to the president, rather than to his chief of staff, Jordan had to go through the tedious exercise of convincing Landers to do what Jordan wanted. Life would be so much simpler if this moron didn't bother coming to the Oval Office at all.

"So what's on tap today?" the president asked, a trace of boredom in his voice.

"Nothing major." Jordan glanced over the agenda in his leather-bound notebook. "Glad-handing with the New England Patriots at eleven to celebrate their Super Bowl win. They'll give you a jersey and cap, you make a few jokes about liking the team even though their owner is a Republican, the usual crap."

"Can you make sure the damn jersey fits this time?" Landers grumbled. "They usually swallow me whole. Makes me look like I'm wearing a muumuu."

Jordan worked hard to keep from rolling his eyes as he pretended to scribble an item in his notebook. He decided that now was the time. Might as well get it over with. "Then,"—Jordan continued to describe the schedule for the day—"you've got a Rose Garden news conference at noon to announce Henderson-Kohn for the 9th Circuit."

"Henderson-Kohn? I thought we were going with Andrews."

Jordan shook his head with disdain. "He went to a public school, remember? Probably a closet conservative. Henderson-Kohn is Harvard undergrad *and* Harvard law." Few things swayed his Harvard-graduate boss like Ivy League elitism, especially if it involved Harvard.

Landers sighed. "She probably got in through affirmative action both times."

"Probably so, but what do we care? She's perfect. She's solidly liberal—"

"Like that matters for the 9th Circuit," Landers muttered. "That bunch is so granola they're almost too liberal even for my tastes. One more liberal judge won't make any difference in that West Coast freak show."

"True." This wasn't going as smoothly as he'd anticipated, and he'd already told D.C.'s leading newspaper, the *Washington Chronicle*, that Henderson-Kohn was the pick. Better play the trump card. "Keep in mind, though, that Henderson-Kohn checks all the boxes. She's a woman, first of all. And then think of that name: Juanita Henderson-Kohn. It gives the Hispanics, the WASPs, and the Jews all something to smile about." Jordan was rolling now and picked up speed in his presentation. "Plus, she's got one of those ambiguous skin tones. You can't look at her and determine whether she's black, white, Hispanic, or some combination. We can't lose on this one, boss. Gotta go with Henderson-Kohn."

Landers was tired of arguing but not thrilled about giving in— yet again—to his young chief of staff. "Okay, okay. We'll go with the mixed-race, hyphenated Harvard grad. She certainly won't be the first person appointed to the federal bench based on her race—whatever it might be—and lack of a penis. But"—Landers wagged an authoritative finger at Jordan—"I want Andrews for the next open seat on the Court of Appeals. He raised a lot of money for me in 2012, and I want him taken care of."

"Duly noted, Mr. President." Jordan again pretended to write something in his notebook.

Landers would quickly forget about Andrews, so Jordan didn't bother explaining that Andrews' fundraising prowess was exactly the reason why he *wouldn't* get a coveted judicial appointment, at least not yet. Landers would need Andrews to raise money again for this 2016 re-election campaign, and Andrews couldn't do that from the federal bench. At least, not without severely bending numerous canons of judicial ethics. The Landers administration would string him along, let him keep earning millions each year at his Wall Street law firm, milk as much campaign cash as they could from him, and then finally reward him with a judgeship once the president was safely re-elected and didn't need any more campaign funds.

"Anything else on the schedule after I enthusiastically announce my selection of Henderson-Kohn?" Landers' sarcasm wasn't lost on Jordan, who shook his head as Landers continued, "It's supposed to be a nice day today, a little bit warmer. I'd like to get in some golf this afternoon."

"No problem, sir." This was a blatant lie, and this time Jordan actually wrote in his notebook. A last-minute presidential golf outing would, in fact, be a huge problem for a rather large number of people. The Secret Service would have to scramble to make security arrangements, traffic would have to be re-routed, golf course personnel would have to spruce things up to the president's liking, and members of the golf club would be turned away in order to keep the course clear for the president.

Jordan finished his golf-related notes on his pad and began to stand.

The president stopped him with a question. "One more thing, Richard. Do we need to be doing anything to get ready for the 2016 election?"

"I don't think so, Mr. President." That was Jordan's second lie of the morning to the president of the United States. Did this idiot not realize that everything he did during his first term was geared toward getting re-elected for a second term? Maybe Landers actually believed that the presidency was about running the country or something equally ludicrous. But Jordan's political instincts quickly kicked in, causing him to realize that the president was simply looking for reassurance that all was well for 2016. "I don't think re-election will be much of a problem," he went on to soothe his boss. "The economy is okay,"—this was a generous assessment—"the world is relatively peaceful,"—who cared about a bunch of savages slaughtering each other in various wars in Africa?—"and your approval rating is fifty-eight percent." But down from 63 percent a year ago, and likely to fall further soon.

"Fifty-eight? Can't we do something to get it back into the sixties?"

Never having faced the voters with his own name on the ballot, Richard Jordan had no patience with questions like this. Politicians craved approval and adoration like the human body craved oxygen. This was especially true for those sufficiently narcissistic to run for president of the United States. No level of public approval was ever high enough, even though at least 35 percent of the voters viewed the fact that it rained yesterday as sufficient reason to dislike the president. But Jordan knew that a lecture along these lines would be useless. Instead, he tried to give Landers the assurance he needed.

"Mr. President, anything above fifty percent is more than sufficient at this point. Your solid approval rating will keep the main competition on the sidelines in 2016. No rational Republican with any national name recognition will want to risk running against a popular incumbent during a time of peace and prosperity. A candidate is only going to get nominated by his party one time to run for president, so those who are serious about winning will sit out 2016 and get ready for 2020. The Republicans will nominate some dried-up, boring, moderate elder statesman to take the bullet and run against you. Think Bob Dole, John McCain, Mitt Romney, someone like that. If they get really creative, it will be a moderate woman like Senator Hollister, but she's the last person the Republican base wants. You'll win with something like fifty-three percent of the vote and then spend the next four years cementing your legacy."

President Landers suspected, but didn't know for certain, that similar thoughts were being entertained in the offices of Republican governors and senators around the country. Their aides would research historical precedents, check the temperature of big donors, and wisely advise their bosses to stay relevant, stay in the public eye, but not push too hard for the 2016 nomination. *2020 will be your year, Boss,* Landers could almost hear these nameless, faceless functionaries saying to their benefactors, *so just sit tight for now.*

"Thanks for the reassurance, Richard, but I've got to say that this talk about 'rational Republicans' has me a bit uneasy. If they were rational, they wouldn't be Republicans."

Jordan grinned at that observation. For all of his incompetence with, and disinterest in, actual public policy, Landers was a fairly solid political analyst and strategist.

"I agree with you that the Republicans will likely run a moderate, someone who will try to distance himself from those crazies on the right and be the voice of reason," Landers continued. "We'll win a race like that in a cakewalk. Nobody is better than me at governing as a leftist but then talking like a centrist at re-election time. But what if they nominate a true, hardcore conservative? One of those Bible-thumping boobs from the South who wants to turn back the clock on all the progress we've made? I want to be sure we're ready for a challenge like that."

Jordan gave a devilish grin. "Mr. President, I'd like nothing better than to work with you in a race like that. It would be all-out war, no holds barred, the forces of sweetness and light against the hordes of evil and darkness. And if the Republicans are dumb enough to go down that road, we'll use the power of the presidency and the overwhelming force of the media to make that guy wish he'd never been born."

Considering this, Jordan started to really relish the prospect of a campaign between polar opposite ideologies. "And the best thing about that scenario, Mr. President, is that you'll win that race in a landslide, with something like sixty percent of the vote. A margin like that will crush conservatism for all time. You'll be the one to put Democrats in power for generations to come. We'll be in an era like the one described by that FDR aide in the 1930s: 'We'll tax and tax, spend and spend, and elect and elect.'"

Upton Landers leaned back in his leather chair and smiled for the first time that day.

Chapter 2

Jackson, Mississippi
March 2015

G overnor Jeffrey Clinton Ackerman sat behind the cheap, pathetic pressboard desk. Every few minutes, he wandered aimlessly across the threadbare industrial-grade carpet to the window and watched the sparse pedestrian traffic on Capitol Street below, strangely envious of the folks who were pressed for time because they had so much work to do.

Although people still addressed him as Governor Ackerman, he had actually been the former governor of Mississippi for the past two years. Pursuant to some obscure line item in the state budget, the taxpayers of Mississippi paid for this useless office on the eleventh floor of what passed for a skyscraper in downtown Jackson. Few people were aware that the state paid for office space for its former chief executives. Even fewer knew what a former governor was expected to do or accomplish from such an office.

Admittedly, the space had been somewhat necessary for a few months just after Ackerman's second term in the Governor's Mansion had concluded. During that brief interlude, his opinion had mattered. Lobbyists and reporters and his fellow politicians had been eager to meet with him. Ackerman's political endorsements were important at the time, and his views were cited by candidates and media outlets as arguments in favor of this policy or that one.

He would sit behind this same desk, assume a thoughtful expression, and offer his learned opinion on all manner of things, charming his visitors all the while. Now he had suddenly become the washed-up elder statesman. He wasn't particularly useful to anyone. At this point, no one seemed to care about his views on public policy—or anything else, for that matter.

Ackerman thought back to all the advice and input he had received, first as a candidate and then as governor. Everyone had been eager to tell him what he should do and how and when he should do it. Much of the advice had been bad. Some of it even bordered on political malpractice. But these would-be advisors were mostly sincere, and Ackerman had appreciated their efforts to help him. Unfortunately, no one had prepared him for the empty, useless feeling he had now that his political career had come to an abrupt end.

"Why do I even bother coming in to the office?" he muttered.

No one was present to hear him. The state provided funds for the office, but Ackerman would've had to pay for a secretary out of his own pocket. He was far too frugal for such extravagances, not that he would say that aloud. Asking himself questions was moderately acceptable, but it would be a bit much to answer them, even with no one else around.

In truth, he knew the answer. He came to the office purely out of habit and because he had nothing else to do. He had been going to some sort of office five or six days a week since graduating from law school twenty-five long years ago. It was who he was and what he did. He couldn't seem to break the habit now.

The former governor rose at five thirty a.m. every day. This used to be a point of personal pride, as he would slap the offensive alarm clock into submissive silence and then bound out of the bed, ready to attack the challenges of a new day. But now his days offered no challenges other than fending off boredom. He would gladly sleep later if he could. Unfortunately, now that he was fifty years old, he woke up at this ungodly hour entirely on his own, knowing that further sleep was impossible. The alarm clock had been relegated to a corner of the garage with other used and useless household items awaiting disposal.

He would shower quickly because he had always showered quickly, even during his days in the Governor's Mansion when he wasn't paying for his own hot water. He continued his lifelong habit of dressing briskly, wasting no time in his morning routine even though time was no longer a precious commodity. Ackerman typically wore some version of a gray or navy-blue suit, mainly because that's what was in his closet. The thought of buying a new wardrobe never occurred to him.

Occasionally, Ackerman's eyes would flitter about his closet to take a quick inventory. Dark suits, most of them conservative pinstripes or solids. White dress shirts with mostly button-down collars, two or three with a tab collar and French cuffs for dressier occasions. Staid, boring wingtip shoes in black, burgundy, and brown.

Governor Ackerman's one sartorial indulgence was his tie collection. Here, he strayed from the conservative dress code and tended to wear bold, striking colors and patterns. Electric blue with tiny white polka dots one day, a repp tie with orange, purple, gold, and white stripes the next. He'd briefly flirted with bow ties but discarded the idea and the bow ties when he decided they made him appear too academic, too theoretical. Governor Jeff Ackerman was a man of action and had to dress the part, he'd decided. No more nerdy bow ties for him.

Except that now he wasn't a man of action. There was no particular reason for him to dress the part, and he didn't really have a part
for which to dress. But he stubbornly clung to the routine of rising
early, suiting up, and heading to the office just as if he were a worthy
individual with some laudable goal to pursue.

Jeff Ackerman was self-aware enough to understand that he
continued to show up at the little-used office in downtown Jackson
because he really didn't have any other ways to occupy his time.
He was tired of golf. A weekend round with friends provided more
than enough frustration to last until the following Saturday. A creaky
knee and distinct lack of talent ruled out tennis. And, unlike the
majority of male Mississippians his age, he didn't particularly enjoy
hunting or fishing.

Accordingly, he found himself here in the Capitol Street office
each weekday. Today, a Tuesday in Mississippi's all-too-brief spring-
time, was no different. Governor Ackerman was the ultimate creature
of habit. He'd quickly settled into a routine for these boring office
days soon after the flood of visitors, well-wishers, and favor-seekers
slowed to a trickle a few weeks after his second term ended and
then ceased completely. He typically arrived in the pre-dawn darkness, telling himself that he got up early to beat traffic, but really
because he was physically incapable of sleeping past five thirty. He
drove into downtown Jackson from his home in Brandon, a suburb
of the capital city. And then the routine kicked in.

Park in designated space in garage, walk across empty floor of
garage to elevator vestibule, ponder why he didn't just park in one
of the hundreds of other empty spots closer to the elevator. Greet
sleepy, surly security guard. Take the elevator up to the eleventh
floor. Stumble down the dark hallway, since the hall lights were
set on a timer and didn't flicker on until eight. Unlock office door
and start flipping on light switches and lamps. Hit switch on coffee

maker and wonder how people live without coffee. Shed suit coat and hang it on the back of the office door.

Boot up desktop computer while coffee perks. Raise venetian blinds to watch the sun rise over Jackson. Ask himself who closes the blinds each night and why they do so. Mutter to himself that this mysterious person should clean the blinds every now and then.

Listen for newspapers to be dropped in mail slot in office door and grab them seven seconds later. Stack the *New York Daily Ledger*, the *Washington Chronicle*, the *Wall Street Post*, and the *Jackson Daily Dispatch* on the credenza for review later in the morning. Pour first cup of coffee.

Plop down in leather swivel chair behind desk. Nearly fall over backwards when chair reclines suddenly. Curse to himself, reach down below seat portion of chair, and engage locking mechanism for chairback. Breathe sigh of relief that coffee cup was on desk and not in hand and that no one saw him nearly fall out of a desk chair and scald himself with hot coffee. Silently accuse whoever closes blinds each night of screwing up his chair. Wonder briefly if a clever assassin had ever killed a politician by sabotaging his office furniture.

Check voicemail. No new messages. Not surprised but still disappointed. Check email. Nothing but spam offering highly questionable stock market advice or the latest in penile enlargement technology. Wonder how long it will be before he sees an email combining the two: a stock tip touting a company that makes a penis enlargement pill. Fight off brief feeling of uselessness while waiting for caffeine to kick in.

Turn to computer and take quick tour through his standard diet of websites and blogs covering news, politics and sports. Nothing new under the sun. Something causes cancer. Something else that was previously thought to cause cancer turns out to be good for you.

Senseless murder in Detroit. Another shooting in Chicago. A federal government program is wildly over budget, while the problem that said program was designed to address is getting progressively worse. Local politician jailed for embezzlement. Movie star seeking publicity rails against conservative policies. Strangely, people pay attention to her even though she's an admitted drug addict with an IQ not much higher than her dress size.

Pour second cup of coffee and stand before office window. Watch sun creep into the eastern sky. Quick prayer of thanks to God for His beautiful creation. Feel depressed and washed up. Then feel guilty for being so whiny and pathetic when he's been blessed with so much. Pray silently for forgiveness and guidance for future.

Walk back over to desk to read newspapers. See no new information that wasn't on the websites he just browsed. Same material, but newspapers are a day behind the blogs. Republican senator makes the mistake of speaking off the cuff about race relations. Pretty bland remarks, but gets roasted in the press as a racist. Apologizes for misspeaking, gets accused of being a racist again, and this time with demands for his resignation. Clear violation of the first rule of holes: when you find yourself in one, stop digging. Doesn't that fool know that no apology is ever enough for the left? They don't want apologies; they want scalps. Toss newspapers aside in disgust. Quickly get disgusted with his own messiness, so gather papers and lay them gently in trash can.

Third cup of coffee. Gotta cut back on this stuff. Pull out legal pad and fancy Cartier pen, a gift from a wealthy campaign donor. Perhaps words written with a two-hundred-dollar pen would prove more valuable than those written with a thirty-nine-cent Bic. Rip a few pages of doodles and illegible scribblings off a yellow legal pad. Literally, a fresh start.

He drew two lines vertically down the page, dividing it into three columns and then labeling the columns *Charity*, *Academics*, and *Business*. In these columns he scribbled out plusses and minuses of a future career in each category. Charity would make him feel good. He might actually accomplish something worthwhile. Perhaps he could travel a bit to press the flesh and raise money. But asking other people for money feels really tawdry. And traveling because you have to, instead of because you want to, gets old really fast.

Teaching would be fun and would keep his mind engaged. Law professor? Teach business? Political science? Some combination of law, business, and politics? Maybe he could design his own course instead of having to fit into some preconceived box. Being around young people might slow the aging process a bit, but being tied to a particular class schedule wouldn't be any fun. Did he want to be one of those guys who counts down the days until summer vacation? Every day should be a vacation at this point in life. A flexible schedule was crucial.

A business role would be lucrative. It would be nice to make some real money for a change. First-year attorneys in big law firms made more than he made as governor. He could get paid to be a figurehead at an investment bank, for example. His title could be *Senior Vice President in Charge of Doing Nothing but Having Expensive Lunches with Other Useless Do-Nothings*.

He smiled to himself and decided that such a title wouldn't look good on a business card. Did people even use business cards anymore? Anyway, he would eventually need to produce something of value in order to justify a salary. He couldn't imagine having to sit in on endless conference calls and boring budget meetings. The thought repulsed him.

Ackerman drew lines through some ideas on the pad, underlined others, and circled a few for no good reason. After standing up, stretching, and strolling back to the window, he glanced at his watch.

Eight forty-seven a.m. He had accomplished nothing and had no idea how to fill the rest of the day.

As he turned back toward the desk, the newspapers in the trash can caught his attention. The headline from the *Politics* section of the *Washington Chronicle* on top read Who Will Republicans Pick to Run Against President Landers?

He snorted with derision. Who would the Republicans pick? Probably some loser to be the sacrificial lamb. No one who was halfway intelligent would run against a somewhat-popular incumbent president, even one as inept as Upton Landers, with the economy in decent shape. Politicians only got one real shot to seek the presidency. After that, they were a retread. So the big names on the Republican side would be sitting this one out.

They'd half-heartedly nominate a half-wit candidate who would run a half-competent campaign. Half the country wouldn't even notice. They'd lose 53 percent to 47 percent, maybe worse depending on the economy in the fall of 2016. Following the loss, Republicans would form a circular firing squad and commence firing, whining and pointing fingers for a few weeks, and then they'd get busy speculating on who to nominate in 2020 when there would be a real shot to take back the White House. Must've been a slow news day for the *Chronicle* to start speculating this early.

Hmmm. Who *would* the Republicans pick? Probably not a sitting U.S. senator, as the party wouldn't want to risk losing that seat. Maybe Senator Hollister from New Hampshire, since she was barely a Republican anyway and her seat would be no big loss. Congressmen had a notoriously bad record in presidential races, so probably not a member of the House of Representatives.

Current governors usually made the best candidates, as they had an existing platform and political operation in place. But they had to walk a fine line, because running a state and running for the presidency were both full-time jobs. Too many candidates did a poor job on both fronts and ended up losing the presidential election and tarnishing their gubernatorial legacy at the same time.

It would need to be someone with good experience but who was still young enough to be somewhat energetic. It should be a fresh face, someone undamaged by prior Washington political wars, but it couldn't be a kid either. What was the word the pundits liked? *Gravitas.* That was it. Gravitas.

Ackerman got a notion, laughed silently at himself, and pushed the thought out of his head. Then he looked out the window again and tried to think of something else. But the thought came back. *Why not?* He strode purposefully across the room to brew another pot of coffee. After sitting back in his chair, he ripped the pages of scribbles off the legal pad for the second time that morning and checked his watch.

Eight fifty-one a.m. on Tuesday, March 18, 2015. Not a second to lose. He began scribbling furiously on the legal pad.

Chapter 3

Brandon, Mississippi

March 2015

Michelle Ackerman moved briskly through the den of her home, dusting a table here, picking up a piece of lint from the carpet there. Married for twenty-eight years now, Michelle and Jeff had purchased the house when his second term as governor expired two years ago. They had each grown up and lived most of their lives in Jackson, located a few miles west of their current home in Brandon. But crumbling infrastructure, increased crime, and failing public schools had triggered an exodus of middle-class white families out of Jackson and into the surrounding suburbs.

Now that Jeff was retired, it didn't much matter where they lived. Both were happy that there was no longer a political element to which neighborhood or school district or city they chose to live in. Michelle had picked out the subdivision of Castlewoods, an upper-middle-class neighborhood with a golf course and tennis courts. Jeff deferred to her on this selection, knowing that in the past she'd lived in more than her share of undesirable locales in order to advance his political career.

Michelle played neither golf nor tennis, but her parents and best friend lived in the subdivision, and she enjoyed being able to walk to their houses when the mood struck her. She also enjoyed taking long walks around the golf course in the evenings, brazenly ignoring the signs proclaiming *Golfers Only! No Joggers, Walkers, Bicyclers, or Skateboarders*. She was normally a stickler for following all laws, rules, and regulations, no matter how insignificant, but she figured no one would mind too much as long as she stayed out of the way of the hopeless hackers flailing their way around the course.

The Ackermans' two daughters, Ansley and Holly, were in high school. Michelle was enjoying Jeff's retirement. And, although she loved being a full-time mom and spending time with her children, she was secretly looking forward to the next stage of being an empty-nester with the girls heading off to college in the next few years. She and Jeff would have plenty of time to themselves to read, travel, take walks, and otherwise make up for all the time they'd spent politicking and governing over the past twenty years. The idea of grandchildren in seven or eight years made Michelle tingle with excitement.

Jeff's dual career path as an attorney and politician had been difficult for both of them. He'd worked sixty to seventy hours per week at his "real job," as they called it, as an attorney at a mid-size Jackson law firm. Another fifteen to twenty hours per week was spent wading through the perilous swamps of Mississippi politics. Most of Jeff's remaining waking hours were spent preparing for and teaching their couples' Sunday-school class at a local Baptist church, along with a few other community service projects that ambitious politicians were obliged to undertake.

Michelle had played the role of the supportive and adoring wife brilliantly. This wasn't overly taxing for her because, unlike so many political wives, she actually did support and adore her husband. She couldn't imagine how the others faked it for so long.

Jeff was a great husband and father who never missed a soccer game, cheerleading competition, or youth choir concert. He had served his time coaching his daughters' youth league teams and dutifully attended the father-daughter dances sponsored by their Girl Scout troops. But his demanding schedule left little time for the day-to-day grind of raising children. Accordingly, Jeff was the big-picture guy who set the overall course for the family, and Michelle was in charge of executing the plan and managing the details.

She had handled the carpool duties, arranged the playdates, overseen the science-fair projects, and enforced the limitations on cell phones and texting boys. She juggled all of these tasks while also attending fundraising dinners and galas and ribbon cuttings that she and Jeff both detested but had to pretend to love. The fifty-year-old version of Michelle Ackerman got tired just thinking about what the thirty-year-old version of Michelle Ackerman had accomplished.

She often told herself that she had been a good political wife, but not a great one. Michelle was private, shy, and didn't particularly like meeting new people. She enjoyed small gatherings of friends but detested functions where she was expected to work the room. Public speaking terrified her to no end. She easily identified with the old joke that people feared public speaking more than death, and thus would rather take on the role of the corpse at a funeral than be the person delivering the eulogy.

In short, she was satisfied with her accomplishments as First Lady of the State of Mississippi, but she certainly didn't miss it. She much preferred her current role as Mrs. Former Governor Jeffrey Ackerman. In fact, for the first time in twenty-something years, she felt like she was developing an identity of her own. People in the community were beginning to know her as Michelle Ackerman, rather than the wife of the state legislator/state senator/governor.

Michelle smiled with satisfaction as she surveyed the now-spotless main level of their two-story home. The second floor was also in good shape, with the notable exception of the girls' bedrooms.

Each of those looked as though the proverbial tornado had crashed through them, and she was tired of nagging them to clean up their rooms. She resolved to sic their father on them in order to address that issue.

Despite Michelle's efforts to the contrary, Ansley and Holly had been spoiled by eight years in the Governor's Mansion, with full-time domestic support to clean up after the family. Michelle and Jeff were now working to reintroduce their daughters to the real world, where people washed their own clothes and made their own beds.

Thinking of Jeff caused Michelle to glance at her watch. Four forty-five p.m., and no sign of her husband yet. He normally came home no later than four. Not for the first time, she wondered what exactly he did at that office in downtown Jackson every day.

Chapter 4

Gulfport, Mississippi
March 2015

Art Morgan startled awake from dozing.

Sitting up at his desk, he looked around his cramped office. From his chair he could see Gulfport's harbor. The tidy, efficient port facilities and the diligent labor of the dock workers contrasted starkly with his musty, stale office and its occupant's distinct lack of productivity. "I can't sleep at home and I can't stay awake here," he grumbled. He did a lot of that these days, but he felt entitled to it. After all, he had just turned sixty-five.

He tried to wipe the drool off of the messy pile of papers he'd been lying on, then swiped the whole lot of them into the overflowing trash can beside his desk. "With no job—and no prospects, for that matter—to occupy my time, you'd think I could keep this dump a little neater." Shaking his head, he sighed. He was talking to himself again.

He was getting old all right. First he couldn't sleep at night, then he couldn't stay awake in the daytime, and now he was talking to himself like a loon. Next thing he knew, he'd be answering his own questions.

Why not? There wasn't anyone else to talk to.

The phone on the desk rang, somewhat muffled by the week-old newspaper on top of it.

He backhanded the paper to the floor and stared at the phone, contemplating whether he should answer it or not. Although caller ID was now a standard feature throughout Western civilization, Morgan had little need and even less money for such an extravagance. He'd only recently upgraded his rotary dial phone to a push-button model.

Oh well. It wasn't like he had anything better to do. He picked up the phone and snarled, "Hello. Art Morgan here."

"Good morning! Did you know that you can receive home delivery of the *Sun Daily* for only pennies a day? If you'd like to subscribe, please press one now."

It was an automated sales call, but that didn't stop him from screaming a profanity-laced tirade into the phone for twenty seconds. He cursed newspapers, telemarketers, and unsolicited phone calls in general before slamming down the phone. *Guess I showed that robot/ computer a thing or two.* But it was a good thing no one else was around. They'd have him committed for sure if they knew he was yelling at a robot.

Morgan wasn't accustomed to solitude and was even less used to silence. He had been one of the most sought-after political minds in the State of Mississippi for three decades, helping numerous candidates get elected to posts ranging from constable and county coroner at the low end all the way up to the governorship and U.S. Senate seats at the high end.

But after helping Jeff Ackerman get re-elected as governor in 2008, his career had fallen off the proverbial cliff. Morgan couldn't identify a particular reason for this. The candidates had simply stopped hiring him. Even long-shot types whose calls Morgan wouldn't have taken a decade before refused to even meet with him now. At this point, he couldn't give away political advice, much less get paid for it.

The political world had apparently decided that Art Morgan was too old, too crusty, too grouchy, and too "yesterday" to operate in today's political environment. He didn't own a computer, much less a smartphone. How could he help this generation's political wannabes who were determined to campaign via email, Facebook, and Twitter? It seemed that Morgan's forty-something years of political wisdom had become irrelevant overnight.

He wasn't taking it well and he knew it. Divorced and childless, he had lived and breathed politics for over four decades. Now, nearly broke and with no prospective clients on the horizon, he simply lived and breathed. He didn't hunt, he didn't fish, and he didn't play golf or tennis. He didn't go to strip clubs, although mainly because he couldn't afford them. He drank to get himself through the day but didn't drink for fun. *Fun* to Art Morgan was the campaign trail. It was winning elections.

But he couldn't campaign or win elections without a client to manage.

With nothing else to do, Morgan showed up at this office six or seven days a week. His lease had expired two years ago, but the absentee landlord apparently hadn't noticed. No one had thrown him out, changed the locks, or asked for rent, so he continued to take advantage of the opportunity to escape his ramshackle rented bungalow two miles away.

The dust had barely settled back on the telephone when it rang again. Morgan didn't hesitate. This time he'd really give that telemarketer a piece. "Listen, here, you dumb sumbitch. I told you not to call here again—"

Laughter came from the other end, followed by, "Is this how you usually treat people who call to offer you a job?"

He sat up straighter. "Who is this? Ackerman, is that you?"

"That's Governor Jeffrey C. Ackerman to you, Art. I'm surprised you're still able to hear the phone ring at your age."

"I'm still young enough to read a calendar, which is evidently more than I can say for you." A smile crept onto Morgan's face and into his voice. "You haven't been governor for two years now, yet you still cling to the title that you'd never have sniffed in the first place if it weren't for my brilliant efforts on your behalf."

"We both know a campaign manager is only as good as his candidate," Ackerman said. "You're just lucky I took you along for the ride and let you get paid for the privilege."

Morgan chuckled, then got serious again. Jeff Ackerman wasn't the type to call just to chat. Even if he was, he'd call someone more chatty and cheerful. "So what can I do for you, Mr. Former Governor Jeffrey C. Ackerman?"

Ackerman took a deep breath. "Well, Art, I want you on my team again. I'm thinking about running in 2016."

Pause . . . pause . . . pause. Morgan's head spun. There were no U.S. Senate seats in Mississippi coming up for election in 2016. And no former governor would even consider running for the U.S. House of Representatives. Such a post was a step down in rank and deemed beneath them.

Finally, Morgan had to ask the question to end the awkward silence: "Running for what?"

"Ouch." Ackerman exhaled. "Now there's a lesson in humility for me. I'm thinking of running for president."

President? Really? "Uh, Jeff, I gotta tell you, I hope you don't have your heart set on winning. If you're in such dire need of an ass kicking, there are much easier and cheaper ways to accomplish that. Couldn't you just challenge a ten-year-old kid to a golf match?" Non-golfer Morgan had always loved teasing Ackerman the Hacker about his golf game.

"I'm running for president in 2016, Art," he said seriously, "and I want you on my team. I want you to be my campaign manager."

"How much you gonna pay me?" Morgan asked, cutting to the chase. He might be willing to make a fool of himself along with this has-been who thought he could be president, but he wasn't gonna do it for free.

"More than you're making now."

Well, that had a certain undeniable logic to it. "Sold. Let's get to work right away."

Ackerman laughed. "Glad to hear it. Do you need a day or two to let your other clients know you're dumping them?"

"Now I guess it's my turn for a lesson in humility. The fact is, I don't have any other clients right now. According to the prevailing political wisdom in these parts, I'm a washed-up old drunk with nothing to offer the modern candidate. And just so you know what you're getting into, I've never run a national campaign. You ever been to Iowa or New Hampshire in the winter?"

"I've never been to Iowa or New Hampshire at all," Ackerman responded.

That made two of them. "Me either."

Ackerman chuckled. "Well, what could possibly go wrong with this little venture?"

"Lots," Morgan said. "But I've got a feeling that you and I are going to find new, exciting, and innovative ways to screw up. Let's have some fun with this."

"Agreed. Let's meet in Jackson day after tomorrow."

Stunned, Morgan hung up the phone. Was it possible for a man to run for president and no one else notice? Not wanting to find out the hard way, he reached for a legal pad and began scribbling out some ideas.

Chapter 5

Brandon, Mississippi
March 2015

Michelle Ackerman paused halfway down the driveway to take in the perfection of the day. Seventy degrees, brilliant sunshine, no clouds, a slight breeze. The oppressive summer heat and stifling humidity would arrive soon, so she resolved to enjoy central Mississippi's fleeting spring while she could.

The buzz of her cell phone in her jeans pocket interrupted her thoughts. As she withdrew the phone and glanced at the screen, she exhaled the deep honey-suckle-scented air she had breathed in on the way to the mailbox. "Hello, Mrs. Baxter," she said with mock formality.

Kara Baxter had been her best friend since high school. Michelle had a special place in her heart for the friends who preceded Jeff's political success. She never fully trusted those who had befriended her just as Jeff's career took off.

"Hello, Mrs. Former Governor Jeffrey C. Ackerman," Kara responded, giggling. "How's my favorite former First Lady of the Magnolia State?"

"Still very glad to be able to put *former* in front of that *First Lady* title." She opened the mailbox with one hand, pulled out the mail, and closed the box. "I like being able to go to the grocery store and be mostly anonymous. And the girls are finding it easier to fit in at school now that they aren't known as the governor's kids. But enough about us. How are the Baxters?"

They continued their chat as she strolled back up the driveway to the garage and into the kitchen. Dropping the mail on the kitchen island, she began the type of multitasking that only a veteran mom could accomplish. Talking on the phone, sorting the mail, putting the final touches on dinner, cleaning up her daughters' latest messes, and unloading the dishwasher. She accomplished all of these simultaneously and without much in the way of mental effort.

Instead, her mind wandered to other topics while her hands accomplished multiple tasks. *Remember to get that recipe from Kara while you have her on the phone. I sure hope the girls make it to their youth group meeting at the church on time and safely. Time to get going on a grocery list before the weekend rush kicks in. Where's that new spatula I bought last week? Need to call Mom and check on her and Dad. What's keeping Jeff? The last two weeks, he's been late getting home. It would be nice for all four of us to sit down at dinner together again.*

"The girls are doing great," Michelle said as she sprinkled the chicken breasts with parmesan cheese and oregano and determined that they were nearly done. "They left about an hour ago for a youth group function at the church." As she slid the chicken back into the oven, the garage door opened. "Hey, I'm sorry to have to cut this short, but Jeff just got home."

"Sure. How about we talk tomorrow?"

"Definitely. I'll give you a call." Michelle set the phone on the counter and ran one hand through her hair, then turned when the door to the garage opened. "Welcome home, Mr. Former Governor."

"Hi, honey. Dinner smells good." Jeff pecked his wife on the cheek.

Michelle noticed that he seemed a bit tired and distracted as he carried his briefcase to his study. Why was he tired? And what did he carry in that briefcase, anyway? He hadn't done any real work in two years.

Jeff drifted back into the kitchen, peeked into the oven, lifted the lid on the two pots on the stovetop, and glanced at the microwave. She had never told him that this habit bothered her. Why couldn't he just wait until dinner was ready and on the plate? It always made her feel like he was conducting some sort of surprise inspection and that he didn't trust her to prepare a decent meal without his input. But he never complained or criticized her after these little kitchen tours, so she let it pass.

"So what did you do today?" Michelle asked, more out of habit than any real desire to know. She continued to flit about the kitchen, moving quickly to get dinner on the table so they could eat together.

He loosened his tie and unbuttoned the top button of his dress shirt. "I thought about running for president."

"President of what?" Michelle's words popped out before her mind was fully engaged on the topic.

Jeff's jaw dropped. *Damn, I've got to get better at this announcement thing. I've told two people that I'm running, and neither one of them could figure out that I'm running for president of the United States.*

"Please don't tell the media what your reaction was when I broke the news to you. I'm running for the presidency of the United States. You know, big house in D.C. with a huge lawn? I seem to recall that the house is painted white. What did you think I meant?"

Michelle nearly dropped the pan of baked chicken breasts but managed to recover just in time. She faced him, her eyes narrowed and her head tilted to one side. Then she set the pan of chicken on the stove and placed her right hand on her hip.

Danger, danger! Jeff thought, recognizing these signs of anger in his wife. *She's mad at me and I don't know why.*

"And just when were you planning to tell me about this little venture of yours?" she asked through clinched teeth.

Now it was Jeff's turn to speak before thinking. "I'm pretty sure I just did."

Bad move, man. He knew right away it was the wrong thing to say. This conversation was going off the rails quickly. Then his own anger kicked in. *"President of what?" What kind of a question is that? She couldn't even figure out that I was talking about running for the White House?* Did she not believe in him? He was an excellent governor, so why wouldn't he be a great president? And what was with her reference to "this little venture of yours"? It had taken her less than ten seconds to start belittling his candidacy. *Thanks so much for your confidence in me, dear. Feels so good to have the full and enthusiastic backing of my loving, supportive wife. Please excuse me while I pull this knife out of my back.*

"So let me get this straight," Michelle said, the anger and sarcasm still heavy in her voice. "You're gonna be the candidate with no money, no national reputation, and who, by the way, just happens to be from a small, unpopular state that the rest of the country views as racist and backward. Have you lost your mind?"

Jeff was stunned. While he didn't know what he expected her to say, he certainly hadn't expected this vitriolic reaction. And by the look in her eyes, his heretofore supportive and adoring wife wasn't finished twisting the metaphorical dagger.

"Don't people usually mention the likely candidates in the news? Forgive me if I've missed it, dear husband, but I don't think your name has come up."

Jeff opened his mouth to return a cutting remark, but then thought better of it and stalked out of the kitchen. He hated fighting with his wife. Over the years, he had developed the habit of saying nothing at all when he was angry with her. As a politician, he had learned from experience the difficulty of undoing the damage caused by a careless statement. Walking back words spoken in anger was even harder. Remaining silent, on the other hand, had never caused him any political trouble, and he carried this approach over into his marriage.

In the master bedroom, Jeff strode into the walk-in closet and sullenly changed into comfortable clothes. He then went to his study, barely resisting the urge to slam the office door behind him. There, he plopped heavily into his desk chair. *She'll show up in here in three, two, one . . .*

Michelle eased the door open, not entering but leaning into the room with her head and shoulders. "Dinner's ready."

"I'm not hungry," he replied, his eyes never leaving the computer screen he was pretending to read. He was starving, of course, but she didn't need to know that. He was still silently congratulating himself for predicting the exact timing of her foray into the office.

"Okay. I'll fix your plate and leave it on the stove for later." Michelle eased the door shut.

This was her way of trying to apologize. Jeff knew the grown-up thing to do would be to jump up, kiss her as a sign of silent forgiveness, and walk hand-in-hand with her into the dining room to eat a delicious dinner with his wife of twenty-eight years. But something in his heart wouldn't let her off the hook so easily. His conscience was clean, and she knew she was wrong. *I told her about a big new project and she attacked me for no reason. If she wants to make up, she's gonna have to serve up a real apology.* "This little venture of yours."

Jeff conveniently glossed over the fact that he had used the same phrase in his conversation with Art Morgan. He continued his internal rant as he recalled her sarcasm. *"Forgive me if I missed it, but your name hasn't come up." That's my loving wife, ladies and gentlemen. She's always in my corner, through thick and thin. Except when she's not.*

Michelle knew that she had wounded Jeff. She wasn't as good at holding her tongue and measuring her words as he was. While she had been truly shocked by his news, it was more than shock that plagued her. The idea of being dragged into a national political campaign, one that her husband would lose in a manner that gave new meaning to the term *landslide*, horrified her.

She'd willed herself to endure Jeff's two stressful statewide campaigns for governor. Being the wife of the governor was one thing, but she hated being the wife of a *candidate* for governor. She was quiet, somewhat shy, and hated gossip and hypocrisy. This made her particularly unsuited for a life in politics, especially during campaign season. She'd lived in that fishbowl before and thought she'd escaped for good. Now she was being pulled back in without warning, without consent or consultation, and she had lashed out at her husband before thinking better of it.

Now she needed to do two things. The first was apologize to her husband. No matter how crazy his idea was, he didn't deserve to be spoken to like a child. The second was to talk him out of this madness before it went any further.

After preparing a plate for Jeff and setting it on the stove, Michelle went back to the office at the front of the house. She dropped into the guest chair opposite his desk while Jeff typed on his laptop keyboard, avoiding her gaze. "I'm sorry I snapped at you. Your news was just so unexpected, and I didn't think before speaking."

"It's okay." His eyes met hers for the first time. Relieved that their fight was over, he looked forward to hashing out some ideas for the campaign with her. Now, it was time for Michelle to close the loop by telling him what a great candidate and outstanding president he would be. He turned the computer screen toward her so she could see the initial strategy he had mapped out.

"When we've discussed your future before, you've made it clear that you want a flexible schedule," she said. "You've mentioned how much you want to avoid meetings, budgets, and conference calls. You don't like to travel. Dealing with the press frustrates you, and you hate raising money."

Alarm bells sounded in Jeff Ackerman's mind. Where was she going with this? Did she think he hadn't considered these things? Then it hit him. *She's trying to talk me out of this. She doesn't believe in me!* "And?" he snapped when Michelle paused.

"And all of these things you don't like and say you want to avoid … well, that's exactly what you'd be doing in a campaign for the presidency."

He grit his teeth. "Don't you think I've considered those things? Believe it or not, I know a thing or two about what a political campaign is like." Jeff bristled at how she had accurately identified all the negatives that he'd listed on the business/charity/academics chart that he'd scribbled out while brainstorming about his future two weeks earlier.

"I'm sure you did consider those things," she said softly. "At least as far as how they affect you. But what about the girls? Have you given a single thought to how this might impact our daughters' lives?"

"Of course I have. I think they'll have a blast living in the White House."

"Honey, they can only live in the White House if you win. And let's be honest here. Doesn't that seem just a tad bit unlikely? Think about how our kids will be attacked during the campaign. And think about how I'll be attacked."

Jeff shook his head. "They won't be attacked. The press has a hands-off policy with respect to the candidates' children." This unspoken policy only held true for the children of the Democratic

Party's nominee, but he didn't mention that. Republicans, even the children of Republicans, were fair game in the eyes of the media and must be destroyed at all costs. And Jeff wouldn't insult his wife's intelligence by trying to convince her that she wouldn't be ripped to shreds by a hostile press corps. He simply let her statement that she'd be attacked during the campaign go unchallenged.

"Listen," he said, trying hard to sound reasonable. "I've given this a lot of thought. I've prayed about it extensively." That was an exaggeration. While he had prayed about it, *extensively* was hardly the right descriptor. But it sounded good and he needed to win this argument. "I think I've got a lot to offer the Republican Party. I think I've got a lot to offer the country. This may be a long shot, but I think I'll be a good candidate. Yes, an unlikely candidate, but a good candidate, a qualified candidate nevertheless. And if things fall into place the way I think they can, I can win this thing."

Michelle's expression softened, and he knew she was slowly coming around to his point of view. Time for the clincher.

"And if I do win, I'll have the best First Lady in American history by my side." He stood up and walked around the desk.

She smiled, accepted his hug, and then squeezed him in return.

Although it had been much harder than he anticipated, Jeff celebrated having his wife on board with his dream. Well, if not exactly on board, at least she was no longer overtly hostile. And he was hugely relieved that their little spat was behind them. Still embracing her and rubbing his cheek against the top of her head, he said, "Me running for president isn't really as crazy as it might seem at first. Art's got a few ideas that sound promising."

Michelle ripped herself out of his embrace and fixed him with the angriest glare he'd ever seen. "Art? You've talked to Art Morgan about this? Before talking to me? I can't believe you! Who else have you discussed this little venture with?"

And there she went again with the belittling phrase "this little venture."

"Honey, I just—"

"You just nothing! You waltz into the house and drop this bombshell on me, tell me that you're upending our lives, make me think you've completely lost your mind, but I forgive you for it because you obviously haven't thought too much about it and will come to your senses eventually. But now I find out that you've been going down this road for God knows how long and discussed it with God knows who, but you haven't even bothered to mention it to me!" Michelle stalked out of the room, slamming the office door behind her.

Jeff could only stare at the door. This time, he was wrong and she was right. He absolutely should have talked it over with her before saying a word to anyone else. With a sigh, he took a quick mental audit of the state of his fledgling campaign for the presidency. *I've told two people that I'm running: my wife and my campaign manager. But I told them in the wrong order. Even worse, neither one of them understood that I was running for president of the United States. And my wife might not even vote for me. Man, I'm really kicking ass so far.*

Chapter 6

The White House

March 2015

"Get Jordan in here, right now!" President Upton Landers barked into the intercom system on his desk in the Oval Office.

"Yes, Mr. President," came the reply from the gray box on the corner of the desk.

Landers dropped the thick report onto the desk with a thud and rubbed his eyes as if he were weary from a long session of reading, thinking, and laboring to shape the future of the nation. In fact, even though it was almost ten a.m., he'd been at his desk for only a few minutes. Landers had decided long ago that early mornings and long work days were for the little people. If he were interested in actual work, he would've gone into some field other than politics. Finance, accounting, law, banking, whatever it was that all those people who wore suits and carried briefcases did in tall office buildings all day.

Richard Jordan bustled into the Oval Office with his fourth cup of coffee of the morning in one hand and a legal pad in the other. He was ready, if not eager, to pretend to scribble notes at the direction of his fearless leader.

Landers began snarling at him before the fussy Jordan could get comfortably settled in the chair opposite the beautiful executive desk fashioned out of timbers from the H.M.S. *Resolute.* "I've told you to tell these people to keep these reports, these memos, whatever they are, short and sweet! I don't have time to read a hundred pages of academic doubletalk each day from every employee in my administration! And tell them to dial back the jargon! I can't be expected to know all the slang and acronyms of each cabinet department."

Jordan sighed. He knew his boss wasn't actually frustrated by the length of any memo or report that reached his desk, because each one contained an executive summary. By order of the chief of staff, these summaries were subject to a hard limit of one page, preferably less. Landers never even pretended to read beyond that short summary.

What had Landers riled up today, Jordan knew, was the content, not the length or complexity, of the latest forecast of U.S. federal tax revenues and their impact on the nation's budget deficit. It was not good news. The executive summary bluntly stated that total tax revenues would increase slightly in 2015 and then decline precipitously in 2016. Even the good news regarding the increase for 2015 was significantly tempered by the fact that the increase was much smaller than the initial projections made by the Congressional Budget Office when Congress narrowly passed a tax increase bill championed by Landers.

The full report made the case for all of this in excruciating detail, complete with charts, graphs, a regression analysis or two, and various other mathematical contortions that no one would ever read. This projected decrease in tax revenue would cause a significant expansion in the annual deficit run by the federal government, which was already more than half a trillion dollars.

Jordan had received the report from the Treasury Department three days prior but waited a bit before sharing it with the president. He knew that Landers, like any president, could only digest so much information at any one time, and a problem with a U.S. peace-keeping mission in Africa had held the full attention of the White House for the past two days. Jordan had placed the report on top of the president's pile of daily paperwork this morning only because the information was likely to leak to the press soon. The president would need to be ready to respond in case a reporter shouted a question to him about it.

"How can tax revenues be going down?" the president demanded from his chief of staff. "We passed the biggest tax increase in U.S. history just two years ago! In case you've forgotten, I caught a mountain of criticism on that from our good friends in the Republican Party, but we responded that we needed the extra revenue to help out the less fortunate. This report makes it look like those lunatics were right all along!"

That's because they were *right, you imbecile,* Jordan thought but didn't dare say aloud. Instead, he answered, "Not exactly, sir. You'll see there in the summary, about the middle of the page, that tax revenues were significantly higher in 2013, the year we passed the tax reform package."

Jordan mentally patted himself on the back for three things. One, he quoted the executive summary and gave his boss precise instructions on where to find the relevant passage, all from memory. Two, he used the phrase *tax reform package*, which was the euphemism dreamed up by Democratic congressmen and their consultants for what was, in fact, the largest tax increase in the history of the Republic. It sounded so much better than "taxing you rich, selfish bastards back to the Stone Age," which was a much more accurate assessment of the sentiment behind the bill but politically unpalatable.

And three, he omitted the fact that the tax increase was signed into law in November 2013, the president's first year in office, but was effective retroactively for all of 2013. Thus, no taxpayer had a chance to adjust his behavior in response to the higher marginal tax rates. This contributed greatly to the 2013 tax windfall.

"Additionally," the chief of staff continued, "tax revenues went way up in 2014 and will go up a bit more in 2015. The only reason they won't go up again in 2016 is that the rich are expected to dial back their economic activity in response to the tax increase. Evidently, they'd rather work less and earn less instead of paying their fair share."

"But we sold the tax increase to the American people—remember them? the voters? the people who decide if I keep my job for another four years?—on the idea that this tax increase would help us pay for new social programs to help the poor. Those programs are now firmly cemented in place and are costing billions of extra dollars each year. Now I'm learning after the fact that the tax revenue that's supposed to pay for all of these new programs isn't going to be there! Somebody screwed up in a major way here, Richard."

By *somebody*, Richard Jordan knew that President Landers meant someone other than himself. Maybe the Secretary of the Treasury, Malcolm Denton, would need to resign in the next few weeks in order to "pursue other interests" or "spend more time with his family."

Now Jordan was angry at himself for letting the president see the report. Landers was much easier to manipulate when facts didn't get in the way. He scribbled something on his pad. The boss probably assumed it was a note to take some sort of corrective action. However, it was actually a reminder to himself not to share any bad economic news with Upton Landers for the next several weeks.

Jordan almost never gave up on an argument, however, and he wasn't quite ready to abandon his attempt to mollify his boss. Capping his pen, he looked at Landers. "With all due respect, Mr.

President, I really think you're blowing this out of proportion. The tax increase legislation did exactly what we said it would do: it increased tax revenue. Remember, this forecast showing a decrease in revenue for 2016 is just that: a *forecast*. Forecasts and projections regarding tax revenues change constantly. Who knows. The social programs you've put in place might just stimulate the economy a bit. It might even be enough to offset the loss of tax revenue from the wealthy slackers who decided to play a little more golf instead of making money and paying it over to us in taxes."

"So what you're telling me, Mr. Jordan," the president snarled across the desk, "is that people actually change their behavior in response to tax rates."

Jordan knew that being addressed as *mister* by Upton Landers was not a good sign. "But, sir, you have to understand—"

"Don't interrupt me!" Landers roared. "I'll let you know when I want you to speak again!"

Richard Jordan meekly leaned back in his chair, putting as much distance as possible between himself and the outraged chief executive.

"You're telling me that, at the margins, folks work more, earn more, and pay more in taxes when tax rates *decrease*," President Landers continued in a calmer but no less menacing tone. "Conversely, they work less, earn less, and pay less in taxes when tax rates *increase*. Is that a fair statement?"

"In certain circumstances, that's possible, sir, but there's no way to know for sure—"

"I'm going to take that as a *yes*, Mr. Jordan."

Mr. Jordan again. The chief of staff groaned to himself. *What's got him so riled up today?*

"So the Republicans were right all along about that Laughter Curve thing. I can't—"

"Uh, sir, I believe that the correct term is *Laffer Curve*."

"I told you not to interrupt me!" Landers screamed back.

The Secret Service normally left Landers and Jordan alone in the Oval Office, but an agent eased into the room at this point—probably just in case the confrontation became physical. The agent had to know there was a greater risk of the president assaulting his chief of staff rather than vice versa, but he didn't get paid to make such assumptions. Besides, it was really fun watching the president—whom he didn't like—yell at that sniveling twerp Richard Jordan—whom he *really* didn't like.

Landers continued his diatribe. "Laughter Curve, Laffer Curve, whatever the hell it's called, doesn't really matter, because they were right and I was wrong! And I was wrong, Mr. Jordan, because I listened to your advice!"[1] He wasn't finished venting his anger but

---

1   The Laffer Curve is an economic theory named for Art Laffer, the economist who argued that lower marginal tax *rates* can actually produce higher tax *revenues* than high tax rates. The reason for this is that the lower tax rates provide greater incentive to taxpayers to work, save, and invest, leading to increased economic growth and job creation. This increased activity, in turn, produces a surge in tax revenue. Thus, a top marginal tax rate of, say, 20 percent, can actually produce more tax revenue for the government than a top marginal rate of 40 percent.

In 1974, Art Laffer famously drew a rough version of what became his namesake (a graph of the amount of tax revenues produced by differing tax rates) on a napkin in a Washington restaurant to illustrate his argument in favor of lower tax rates. The idea became a touchstone of supply-side economics. Ronald Reagan's tax cuts in 1986 proved that Laffer was correct. Reagan convinced a Democratic Congress to slash tax rates and simplify the tax code. The economy boomed and federal government revenues increased accordingly. Unfortunately for Reagan and supply-side proponents, that same Democratic Congress rejected the spending cuts that Reagan wanted to offset his higher spending on defense that eventually bankrupted the Soviet Union and won the Cold War. This higher spending led to a ballooning federal government budget deficit. Moreover, it provided Democrats with political cover to claim that the tax cuts—not the massive spending increases—caused the deficit to explode.

was starting to move toward seeking a solution. "The right-wingers said the tax increase would increase the deficit, and we laughed at them for it. Now, unless we can do something to turn this around, the world will know that we were wrong, and I'll look like an idiot. So we need to get to work on fixing this, right the hell now. And in case there's any doubt in that scheming little brain of yours, when I say *we*, I mean *you*."

"Of course, Mr. President."

Landers nodded and picked up another report from his desk, indicating that Jordan was dismissed. As the young staffer walked toward the door, the president called after him, "One more thing, Richard."

Jordan turned around. At least Landers was done with the *Mr. Jordan* thing for now.

"Are there any other policy positions, any other arguments, we've made publicly that will come back to bite us?"

Richard Jordan knew there were times in every politician's life when he wanted his staff to lie to him. Now Jordan had to decide—quickly—whether this was such an occasion. One second of contemplation was all that was needed. He answered with great conviction, "No, sir. Of course not." The remainder of the answer went unsaid: *Not that you need to know about right now, anyway.*

Chapter 7

Jackson, Mississippi
April 2015

Jeff Ackerman's campaign staff gathered for the first meeting with their candidate on a windy, pollen-encrusted Thursday afternoon. *Campaign staff* was actually a generous term, since the "staff" consisted solely of campaign manager Art Morgan and the heretofore unemployed Scott Williamson. Ackerman referred to the gathering as a "staff meeting" partly out of custom but mostly because it sounded better than "a couple of has-beens with nothing better to do who are plotting a hopeless little venture with a modern-day Don Quixote."

Scott Williamson was a twenty-seven-year-old native of Pascagoula, Mississippi. A rabidly righteous Reaganite, he never missed a chance to quote his hero, President Ronald Wilson Reagan. Williamson insisted on referring to Reagan using his first, middle, and last name, as if anything less was a sign of disrespect. He had somehow become infatuated with the former president even though he was too young to remember Reagan's presidency from personal experience. But he devoured every book dealing with the Gipper, and was a particular fan of Steven Hayward's two-volume opus, *The*

Age of Reagan. Williamson had also watched hours of video of the former president and could recite Reagan's "A Time for Choosing" speech from memory. A hard-charging, type-A personality, Williamson shared the optimism and love of country epitomized by Reagan.

But what set Scott Williamson apart from the tens of thousands of other young Republicans and Reagan fanatics was his skin tone. He was black. African-American Republicans were a rare breed in the United States and even more rare in the Deep South. Blacks tended to vote overwhelmingly for Democratic candidates, often well in excess of 90 percent in favor of the Democrat over the Republican in any given election.

He was the middle-class son of a union welder at Ingalls Shipyard and an elementary school teacher, so nothing about Williamson's background indicated he would deviate from the Democratic stranglehold on the black vote. But unlike most of his peers, he had conducted his own review and research of the political landscape. He concluded that conservative ideas worked and that liberal ideas did not. Accordingly, he had proudly proclaimed himself a conservative Republican, shocking his family and friends in the process.

Williamson's background and personal story fascinated Jeff Ackerman. He wanted to know more about how Scott escaped the ideological plantation that trapped so many blacks in a leftist mindset that didn't serve their interests. But he was hesitant to talk to Scott about it very much. In this age of acute racial sensitivity, Ackerman worried that he'd say the wrong thing and somehow offend his young subordinate, even though Williamson had not demonstrated any inclination to be unjustly offended.

Art Morgan had hired Williamson as a driver and gofer for Ackerman's first gubernatorial campaign. Scott's work ethic and enthusiasm generated a steady stream of promotions and increased responsibility, and the former low-level grunt eventually attracted the approving eye of the candidate himself. After winning the governor-ship, Ackerman retained Williamson as an advisor, and Scott continued to distinguish himself.

But Ackerman's Republican successor as governor apparently viewed Williamson as an "Ackerman guy" first and foremost, and had not offered Scott a post in his administration. Thus, Williamson had immediately accepted Ackerman's offer to be the senior policy advisor for his nascent presidential campaign. The title of senior policy advisor implied, albeit falsely, that there were at least a few additional, presumably junior, advisors. Ackerman hoped no one would notice this situation until he could remedy it by adding a few more bodies to his staff. For once, he took a bit of comfort from the fact that no one had thought of him as a candidate at all to this point.

Jeff Ackerman bustled into the conference room, full of energy and optimism. "Good morning to the best campaign staff in the history of presidential candidates from Mississippi!" he boomed and then exchanged warm handshakes with Morgan and Williamson. As the three settled into their seats at the conference table, Ackerman continued, "Gotta like the leanness and meanness of this group. Don't have to waste money on nametags and don't have to waste time on introductions."

Crusty, grumpy Art Morgan rolled his eyes. He flipped a page on his legal pad and kicked off the business aspects of the meeting. "Let's talk about the most important item first."

"Our platform?" Ackerman asked. "Theme for the campaign? Media strategy?"

This time Morgan couldn't resist snapping at his boss in addition to rolling his eyes. "No, you moron. Money. Money, money, money. Nothing else matters if the money isn't there to fund the campaign. Without money, there is no platform, no media strategy. Hell, there's no media, much less a media strategy, if there's not enough cash to get your name out there."

Ackerman had almost forgotten how blunt Morgan could be, but was only momentarily deflated. He'd thought about this issue, of course, and he wanted to keep an upbeat tone for this first meeting. "Well, Art, I don't think money will be much of an obstacle. You see, the only problem I have with respect to campaign funds is that I don't have any. So, if you geniuses, you gurus, can solve just that one small problem, we're good to go and you can check all money-related items off of your to-do list."

To Ackerman's left, Scott Williamson sank a bit lower in his chair. He had been thrilled to get the call from his former boss but hadn't appreciated just how slim their chances were until now. Political campaigns, even smallish ones at the state and local level, burned through money at a rapid clip. And Williamson correctly assumed that national campaigns required exponentially more funding. He'd simply assumed that a smart, successful politician like Jeff Ackerman had a plan for funding his campaign, and he was horrified to learn that this wasn't the case.

Art Morgan shook his head and muttered to himself, scribbling furiously on his pad. The silence grew awkward, so Williamson offered a timid suggestion. "Governor, perhaps you could infuse some personal funds into the campaign to get things started?"

Like most people, Williamson assumed that anyone who had a law degree and had served as governor must have some serious money squirrelled away somewhere. Morgan knew better though. He shook his head some more and muttered louder.

Ackerman smiled. "Thanks, Scott. Two things. First of all, you can call me Jeff in private. No need for formality among this small group. Second, I'm proud to inform you that I have two hundred thousand dollars of my own money to spend on this campaign."

Morgan snorted. "Aren't you missing a digit? Hell, Jeff, you're missing at least two digits if you actually want to make a difference."

Williamson sank even lower in his chair.

"I can easily add two digits to that number," Ackerman responded, "but unfortunately, they both come after the decimal point." He looked from Morgan to Williamson. "Look, money is obviously a problem. We don't have much and don't have any obvious means of getting more. Now, excuse me for being blunt here, but you guys were both unemployed a week ago. I can assure you that you'll get paid for at least the next several weeks. If the money situation doesn't improve quickly, that means the campaign never got off the ground, and we'll shut it down and go our separate ways. No one gets hurt, other than my pride, and you each make a few bucks in the process. Fair enough?"

Morgan and Williamson nodded, but the mood around the conference table was now decidedly sober. The candidate sought to move the meeting forward with a lighter tone. "Art, what's the next item on that high-tech legal pad of yours?"

Morgan cleared his throat. "Jeff, I don't really know how to ask this politely, so I'll just ask it." He sounded uncharacteristically reticent. "What's your ultimate goal for this little venture?"

Ackerman was really starting to hate the phrase *this little venture*. He wasn't sure at first what Art meant by the question, but the light bulb came on soon enough. "Oh, I see. You're asking me if there's some hidden agenda here. Otherwise, why would I tilt at this particular windmill? Why launch a hopeless campaign unless there's something else in it for me?"

He leaned forward, knit his brows, and removed all traces of the smile from his face and voice. Speaking slowly, clearly, and slightly louder than normal but not yelling, Jeff Ackerman informed his staff in no uncertain terms, "I want to win. Period. I'm not in this for some sort of moral victory. Second place is no different than fifth place or eighth place. I'm not using this campaign to land a book deal, a cable TV show, or paid speaking engagements. I'm not trying to raise my national profile so that the eventual winner will appoint me as ambassador to Bulgaria or special assistant to the deputy secretary of the interior. Everything we do in this campaign, every speech, every interview, every advertisement, will be designed for me to get the Republican nomination and then win the general election. Are we clear on that, gentlemen?"

Morgan and Williamson nodded again. He didn't show it, but Morgan was relieved that his boss was serious about winning. The veteran politico had worked for his share of candidates whose goals were something less than winning the election at hand. None of those campaigns had been fun or resulted in a victory—moral or otherwise.

Now it was time for Scott Williamson to ask a tough question. "Jeff, what's your vision for this campaign? To be blunt, why you for president? There's not exactly a huge groundswell of people begging you to run, and we've got to give voters a very clear reason to pay attention to you when you announce. Otherwise, they'll just write you off right away and never give you a second look."

Ackerman had nodded along as Williamson spoke, signaling that he wasn't offended by the question. Now he responded, "I should be president because I'll focus on reversing the decline of America from the greatest nation in the history of the world into merely an above-average one. I'll concentrate on making the country stronger, more competitive, and more united, rather than making myself a great president. I'll accomplish things for the country, not for Jeff Ackerman. I'll get government out of the way in order to help Americans build a legacy for themselves, their families, and their businesses, rather than a legacy for myself. I'm not a great man, but I think I'm a good one. In short, I'll be a good man who helps America get back to the top once again."

Morgan had already asked one question he hoped he already knew the answer to and had been correct. Now it was time for the second. "Okay, boss. The next step is for us to decide on a big-picture strategy. As I see it, we could take either of two general approaches in the campaign, and it would behoove us to choose one or the other up-front and stick to it." Art stood up and paced the length of the conference room, then looked out the window. Arthur J. Morgan, Political PhD, now took over the room. Art Morgan the Curmudgeon faded into the background. "First of all, we have to commit to a consistent approach," he began. "Pundits talk all the time about a candidate being liberal or conservative in the primaries and then moving to the center for the general election.

"No! No, no, a thousand times no!" Morgan shouted, as if refuting the advice of some unseen political advisor. "That simply doesn't work. We've got to pick a path for the primary and, if some miracle occurs and we win the nomination, we've got to stay on that same path for the general. Are we clear on this?"

Neither Ackerman nor Williamson challenged him on this point, so Professor Morgan turned around and continued his lecture. "So, as I mentioned, we have two options. Let's call them the moderate approach and the hardcore approach. I'll lay these out for you now, in no particular order. With the moderate approach, you play the role of eloquent elder statesman. You're wise, calm, and measured. No childish name calling and little in the way of attack ads. Surrogates can go after the opponent hard, but the candidate stays above the fray, tsk-tsking about negative advertising and calling for an adult conversation about the issues that Americans really care about. With the moderate approach, we avoid the polarizing issues as much as possible and take a middle-of-the road approach to the ones we can't avoid. You'll be some combination of Bob Dole, John McCain, and Mitt Romney.

"The goal of this moderate approach," Morgan went on, "is to attract independent voters and soft Democrats, while still getting the Republican base to the polls. This is the low-risk, low-reward path. In my view, this path leads to a respectable loss in the general election, something in the range of fifty-two percent to forty-eight percent.

"Of course, this assumes you can get past Senator Hollister in the primaries. As you know, she's already staked out the moderate ground and is the only Republican candidate out there right now. She has more money, a better organization, and better name recognition than you. Trying to run as a moderate in the primaries borders on political malpractice. If you take the moderate road, you'll almost definitely lose to Hollister and not even get the chance to get your teeth kicked in by Landers in the general election. Hollister is the epitome of a RINO, and it will be very hard to out-RINO a veteran RINO."

Ackerman twitched involuntarily upon hearing this acronym for *Republican in name only*. This was a mostly pejorative term, frequently used by true conservative believers to mock Republicans who abandoned conservative principles in order to win favor with the press. Ackerman and Williamson each wanted to speak up at this point, but neither of them dared to interrupt Morgan's presentation.

Professor Morgan continued to stride up and down the length of the conference table. "The hardcore approach, on the other hand, is exactly what it sounds like. You pound the table and go balls to the wall on every issue. You never settle for half a loaf. It's all or nothing, baby. Attack, attack, and attack some more. If we go this route, the campaign's worldview is that we're the force of sweetness and light in a battle against darkness and evil. We'll never retreat and never surrender. We're right and they're wrong, and the voters can take us or leave us. Pat Buchanan, Newt Gingrich, folks like that are the model here."

Morgan's goal was to present the two alternatives in a neutral manner. But his tone and mannerisms mirrored the approach he was discussing at the time. When presenting the moderate path, his voice was soothing and calm. He still paced, but did so slowly, methodically, and thoughtfully. Consciously or not, Morgan's manner changed when he lectured on the hardcore approach: he repeatedly punched a fist into his palm, and his volume increased. He paced faster and with greater purpose and energy.

Ackerman and Williamson each sat straighter in their chairs, fighting the urge to inch away from the highly energetic politico lest Morgan's spittle land on his two audience members.

"It won't surprise you to hear that the hardcore approach is high-risk and high-reward." The switch had flipped back to the *off* position, and Morgan's demeanor calmed as he gave his analysis and made his prediction. "The base will be fired up and ready to go to war for you, but the media will portray you as Hitler and slaughter you with independents. You've got a much better chance of winning the primary against Hollister and getting the nomination if you run to her right."

Morgan stopped pacing. "But that's where the good news ends. You've got a better chance of pulling the upset against Landers with this approach, but you've also got a much greater chance of getting embarrassed. And when I say embarrassed, I mean a Mondale/ McGovern/Goldwater type blowout loss in the general election. My best guess is that you lose in a landslide, something like fifty-nine percent to forty-one percent, with Republican congressional and gubernatorial candidates also getting smashed across the board, thanks in large part to your scorched-earth tactics. So, those are the two options that I see, each with plusses and minuses. I suggest we pick one of these approaches as our first item of business today before we find ourselves taking inconsistent actions."

The three were silent as Morgan returned to his seat, the day's lecture having come to a conclusion. Each had a preference between the two approaches but none wanted to speak first. For his part, Scott Williamson was ready to charge down the hardcore path. Damn the torpedoes, full speed ahead! But his name wasn't on the ballot. Of course, neither was Ackerman's at this point, but nevertheless this had to be Jeff Ackerman's decision. And the candidate needed to make the choice without passion or prejudice.

Art Morgan also preferred the riskier approach, especially in light of Ackerman's clear statement that his only goal in the race was to win it. Morgan saw no path to victory along the moderate road. Besides, he knew from experience that Ackerman's policy stances were more suited to the hardcore conservative method.

Campaigns in which the candidate was free to be himself—within reason—were relatively easy to manage. And those in which the candidate had to mask himself or hold back his true thoughts always seemed to go off the rails at some point. A candidate who displayed his true beliefs, rather than playing a different character, was much easier to sell to voters. However, Morgan was hesitant to push his boss in either direction.

After a few moments of silence, Ackerman realized that the other two men were waiting for him to speak. "Thanks, Art. That was a helpful summary, and I agree with you that we need to choose one of these two approaches and stick with it for both the primary and the general election." Now it was Jeff Ackerman's turn to pace the conference room. Holding a pen and twirling it in his fingers as he walked, he continued, "I don't think the moderate path will work for us. It didn't work for Bush I. He got elected as a conservative heir to the Reagan legacy, mainly because he promised 'Read my lips: no new taxes.' But then he governed as a moderate, caving to the Democrats on spending and even raising taxes in violation of his promise. The result? He loses re-election. Remember that lame way he tried to justify it? He said, 'You didn't send us to Washington to bicker.'

"Oh, yes we did, Mr. President!" Ackerman went on, raising his voice a bit in rebuke to the former president, as if the elder Bush was there in the conference room. "In fact, we sent you there not just to bicker with the Democratic Congress, but to *win* the bickering." He took a deep breath and continued, speaking more slowly now. "Likewise, moderation failed for Bob Dole and John McCain. It didn't work for Mitt Romney, although he was somewhat in between the moderate and conservative wings. These guys lost not because they were conservative, but because they weren't conservative enough.

"Also, Art is right. I see no way to win the primary against Hollister unless I can motivate the conservative base. We'll have to find a way to convince them to vote for me over Hollister even though she has a better chance than I do in the general against Landers. The best argument is probably that a Hollister presidency won't be much better than a second term for Landers, so they might as well roll the dice with me. Besides, I'm a conservative at heart, as you both know. Even if we won on a moderate platform, it would be an empty victory because I wouldn't be able to govern the way I want, the way I think is best for the country. There would be no mandate for it."

Ackerman ceased his pacing at this point and stared through the window overlooking downtown Jackson, his back to his staff. "But Art is also correct that the flame-throwing, hardcore conservative approach is the best way to get obliterated in the general election.

The left is very good at demonizing opponents, and it wouldn't take long for the Hitler comparisons to kick in if I run as a true conservative. I'm willing to risk losing, but I'd like to avoid a landslide."

"I don't think you can avoid the Hitler stuff either way, Jeff," Scott Williamson said. "The Republican nominee automatically becomes Hitler in the eyes of the media. Even Mitt Romney, the nicest guy in the history of politics, got slandered like that."

"You're right, Scott." Ackerman spun around and began walking the length of the room again. "What we need is a conservative message with a reasonable tone. Right-wing politics with a smile and handshake rather than a punch in the gut. Newt Gingrich, Pat Buchanan, even a moderate like John McCain, they were all easy for the left to demonize because they snarled more than they smiled. We've got to be conservative warriors, but happy, smiling conservative warriors."

"You want to be Ronald Wilson Reagan!" Williamson exclaimed, nearly coming out of his chair as he did so. He couldn't contain his excitement.

"Yeah, Reagan without the name recognition, the financial backing, or the Hollywood good looks." Morgan brought his younger colleague back down to earth. "In other words, you'll probably be Barry Goldwater."

Ouch. Art Morgan the Curmudgeon was back in full force.

"Yes, that's the risk, but I think it's one we have to take," Jeff said thoughtfully. "What we have to do, and what we have to do better than previous Republican campaigns, is explain the *why* behind our policy positions. We want lower taxes not for the sake of having lower taxes, but to spur economic growth. We want fewer government employees and less bureaucracy not because we hate government but because government doesn't produce anything and inherently impedes those who *do* produce things.

"And instead of shouting from the rooftops, we'll do this all in a calm, measured tone. We'll say conservative, even controversial, things and won't hesitate to be extremely blunt. But we'll say it all with a smile. We'll be friendly to the Democrats and the media— the latter include the former. We'll joke with them and poke fun at them. We'll mercilessly mock their policies, biases, and blind spots but with satire and teasing rather than fire and brimstone. In short, we try to get the best of each of the two paths Art described earlier. Moderate tone, conservative message. Friendly expressions but tenacious on policy. Most of all, we've got to give the voters the *why* behind our positions. This won't be easy in today's soundbite world, especially with a hostile media, but it's our best shot to pull off an upset for the ages."

Williamson and Morgan nodded and grunted their agreement. Each had reservations but instinctively knew there wasn't a better strategy that would reduce the risk but increase the reward.

With the overall strategy of the campaign now in place, Ackerman sought to move things along. Turning to Scott Williamson, he asked with a smile, "All right, Mr. Senior Policy Advisor. Got any senior policy advice?"

Williamson handed Ackerman a memo and slid a copy across the table to Morgan. A dozen additional copies in a neat stack next to his laptop went unused, as Williamson had wrongly assumed that the "staff meeting" would include, well, an actual staff.

The three men talked through the afternoon and into the evening about how to launch, and then wage, one of the most unlikely political operations in recent history.

Chapter 8

Jackson, Mississippi

April 2015

The disheveled, wrinkled, and sleepy-looking media contingent assembled itself, under the gruff and grumpy direction of Art Morgan, a few feet from the podium near the front steps of the Mississippi Governor's Mansion.

Morgan had put in calls to all of his contacts in the Mississippi media, telling them only that former Governor Jeff Ackerman had a major announcement to make. The media turnout wasn't what Morgan had hoped for, but it was respectable. Fortunately, it was a beautiful spring day in the capital city, and a few minutes on the lush grounds of the Governor's Mansion promised the reporters a more pleasant experience than a dingy conference room in the state capitol building or a cramped media room at a local courthouse.

Most media members in the Magnolia State were as uninquisitive and unintelligent as their more recognizable colleagues around the country. They had fallen into the habit of simply taking whatever information was spoon-fed to them by political insiders, adding their own leftist slant, and regurgitating it on the front page. Thus, none had bothered to ask Morgan or Ackerman the nature of this so-called major announcement. They probably assumed that Acker-man was forming a new law firm or lobbying group. This was the traditional career path of other former governors of Mississippi and their primary means of cashing in on their remaining political clout. But at least the reporters had shown up for the event, even if most of them had rolled out of bed only minutes before.

Jeff Ackerman peered out a front window of the Governor's Mansion, analyzing the crowd outside. *Crowd* was a rather generous term, really. Perhaps *gathering* was more appropriate. Ackerman had invited a hundred or so friends and family members to attend the event, and like Morgan, he didn't provide any specifics about the nature of the occasion. Only about half of these folks were present, and Ackerman mentally crossed the no-shows off of his list of candidates for jobs in his administration and invitees to his inaugural ball.

He shook his head. *I can't even generate a decent crowd for the announcement of my candidacy. If a guy announces that he's running for president and no one notices, can he avoid the humiliation of losing? Maybe it doesn't count as a loss if the public isn't actually aware that you're a candidate.*

But it was too late to back out now. He considered tossing aside his prepared remarks and instead announcing that he was opening a new business venture: Jeff's Bait Shop, Hair Care, and Tire Center.

It was almost time to go outside. Michelle Ackerman eased over to her husband and straightened his already perfectly straight tie. "You'll be great today," she said with a smile.

Jeff's mood immediately improved. He knew she didn't want to be here, didn't want anything to do with "this little venture," but she was putting that aside and standing by her man. *Maybe my wife will vote for me after all.*

Time to walk outside and address the public—all fifty or sixty of them. Ackerman wore his best politician attire: charcoal-gray suit with muted pinstripes, a heavily starched white shirt with button-down collar, and a red pin-dot tie. A conservative black leather belt—no braces or suspenders today—and freshly shined black wingtip shoes completed the ensemble.

Ackerman felt nervous, but he had delivered thousands of speeches before, and he recognized this as the good kind of nervousness. When he felt relaxed and confident, he tended to give a lazy performance. On the other extreme, when gripped by real fear before a speech, he usually spoke too fast, letting his mouth get ahead of his brain. Today's emotions were in that sweet spot between fear and confidence, a good sign for the soon-to-be-announced candidate.

James Clayton, the current governor of Mississippi and Ackerman's successor and occasional friend, spoke for a few minutes to kick off the festivities. Clayton was one of the few who knew the purpose of Ackerman's upcoming presentation, and he appeared to have done a surprisingly good job of preserving the secret. Ackerman had been forced to tell Clayton, in strictest confidence, the whole story in order to get access to the grounds of the Governor's Mansion for the event.

Art Morgan had hoped that Clayton would leak the purpose of the announcement, thereby increasing the media buzz. *For the first time in the history of U.S. politics, a sitting governor simultaneously keeps both a secret and a promise,* Morgan groused to himself, *at the very time when loose lips and promise-breaking would help my guy.* He didn't consider this a good sign, as it indicated that Clayton wanted as little to do with the announcement as possible. *Ackerman hasn't even announced yet and Clayton is already waiving the white flag. What an ungrateful little wimp.*

Governor Clayton's speech did little to allay Morgan's concerns, and it certainly didn't boost the spirits of Jeff Ackerman. Clayton read directly from his notes, speaking in a monotone as if he were announcing the latest set of soybean farming regulations that his administration had fearlessly enacted. When he finally welcomed Ackerman to the podium, he did so with such little fanfare that those assembled weren't sure if applause was appropriate or not. A few clapped timidly, and this led to a small ripple of enough additional clapping to qualify—barely—as polite applause.

No cheering throng for Jeff Ackerman today, Ackerman thought as he took his first public steps toward his candidacy. Jim Clayton obviously had no interest in a cabinet position or ambassadorship in the Jeff Ackerman administration, probably because he knew damn well that there wouldn't be a Jeff Ackerman administration. *Well, forget him. I'll deal with him later.* For now, he needed to walk across the stage with energy and purpose, and for God's sake, avoid tripping over the microphone cord. Firm handshake and a plastic smile for the backstabbing Clayton. *Good. Now, a deep breath but not so deep that the audience can see it. In through the nose and out through the mouth. Let tension flow out with the breath. Final peek at the notes on the podium before a big smile for the audience. Let's do this. God help me.*

Ackerman fought back a rueful smile as he took his final glance down at the text of his speech, which Scott Williamson had written. It was annotated with instructions to the candidate in bracketed words, the first of which was [WAIT FOR APPLAUSE TO DIE DOWN.] *Wishful thinking there, my man.*

"Good morning, and thank you for coming out today. Thank you, Governor Clayton, for that warm introduction. It's a beautiful day and, as always, 'it's a great day to be in the great State of Mississippi.'" Ackerman recycled this phrase that had served as his theme during his time as governor.

His friends and family in the audience smiled in recollection but didn't applaud. The media just looked bored.

"As you know, as governor of our amazing state for eight years, I worked for the benefit of the wonderful, kind, hardworking people of the State of Mississippi. And when I spoke to you during that time, I focused on the unique problems we faced here in the Magnolia State and how we could improve things by working together. But today, I'd like to speak to you for a few minutes about our great country.

"Yes, our country is indeed great, although many Americans either don't like that fact or are embarrassed to proclaim it for one reason or another. But, unfortunately, America isn't as great as she once was. Our economy is limping along, hamstrung by high taxes on both individuals and businesses. Our military is adrift, suffering from an acute lack of leadership from a commander in chief who couldn't lead a Boy Scout expedition without a gaggle of staffers and advisors to read his compass for him."

The media perked up at this criticism of President Upton Landers, for whom each of the assembled reporters had voted in the previous election.

"Our children are trapped in public schools that are designed for the benefit of administrators rather than students, schools that consume more and more tax dollars while producing worse and worse results," Ackerman rolled on. "Similarly, college costs continue to skyrocket while producing graduates in useless majors who leave college with less practical knowledge than they had when they entered.

"Our health insurance system is an unmitigated disaster, hampering the heroic effects of the world's greatest doctors and soaking up a larger and larger slice of each worker's paycheck.

"Worst of all, the United States is on the verge of sinking to the level of so many other countries around the world, in which ethnic, racial, or other tribal groups fight each other for a larger share of an ever-shrinking pie. Groundless lawsuits, government giveaways to favored industries, and so-called affirmative action for whatever group whines the loudest have led us to this point.

"Because President Landers and the Democrats in Washington can't deliver significant economic growth, there's presently no hope of expanding opportunities for the benefit of all Americans. We're forced to pay more and more in taxes, more and more for health insurance, more and more for college for our children. All of this while our paychecks stagnate or, worse, disappear altogether because American businesses can't compete against firms in other countries with lower taxes and less regulation."

Even the reporters, by far the least intellectually capable members of the audience, figured out by now that Ackerman wasn't here to announce the formation of a new law firm or lobbying shop. He was definitely building up to something bigger. But no one guessed what it was.

"Ladies and gentlemen, America can do better. America has done better in the past. And America can most definitely do better in the future. With competent leadership, with common-sense policies, and with a smaller, less intrusive government, we can revive that spirit of growth, pride, and optimism that are so sorely lacking in our country today.

"Yes, it is very easy to criticize our nation's leaders, especially in recent years when Upton Landers and his minions have done so much damage to our country. Criticism from the sidelines is easy, but it's not effective. Even enlightened criticism backed by wisdom and prudence won't be enough to turn our nation around. What's needed is action in addition to words, courage in addition to wisdom.

"And so, my friends, I am resolved to act. With your help, with your support, with your prayers, and, yes, with your votes, you and I together can make America into a nation of which we can once again be proud."

The audience just stared. *Votes? What's this guy leading up to? Surely he's not about to announce that he's running for—*

"I'm Governor Jeffrey Ackerman, and I'm running for president of the United States of America!"

What followed was perhaps the most awkward silence in the history of American politics. In crafting the speech, Ackerman, Morgan, and Williamson had all assumed that this line would lead to enthusiastic applause. Maybe even a roar of approval. This was a reasonable assumption, and Ackerman had delivered his speech perfectly.

But none of Ackerman's invitees made a sound. A few lifted their hands to clap but paused when no one else applauded first. The media scribbled in their notebooks and elbowed their colleagues, trading looks of haughty derision with each other. *Who does this guy think he is?* they seemed to wonder.

The candidate soldiered on, completing his speech with boiler-plate language that was well written but immediately forgotten. He spoke about not having made the decision lightly, knowing that he was an underdog, and being thankful for the love and support of his family and friends. Ackerman's pace was a bit too quick in the final few moments of the speech, mainly because he just wanted to finish and get off of the stage before he died of embarrassment.

The audience members felt the same way. They liked Jeff Acker-man—and in some cases loved him—and now realized that their lack of enthusiasm had ruined the event and humiliated a good man. They hurt for him and wished for a do-over, but it seemed best to wrap this up quickly and let everyone get on with the business of pretending it never happened.

Ackerman and his meager staff had not adequately anticipated what they would later dub the "Mississippi Effect." Mississippians love their state, but they are painfully aware of its poor reputation—sometimes deserved—in the country as a whole. Mississippi ranks last or next-to-last among the fifty states in many important statistical categories, and its strengths are in hard-to-measure categories such as friendliness, hospitality, and personal warmth. The national media never misses an opportunity to publicize her faults while ignoring her virtues, and comedians and pundits mercilessly mocked Mississippi without fear of contradiction or retribution.

As such, Mississippians had an unspoken dread of having one of their own thrust upon a national stage. Even if he or she did well, criticisms of the state as a whole were inevitably included in news stories about that individual's success. Authors, musicians, athletes, and business leaders all received the "he's great even though he had to overcome growing up in a poor state full of fat, ignorant rednecks" treatment.

The crowd at the Governor's Mansion today knew that Ackerman and Mississippi would be portrayed the same way even if he did well in his pursuit of the presidency. Even worse, the nation was at peace (except for a few police actions in backwater places around the globe that no one could find on a map), the economy was okay (although growth had slowed dramatically in recent months), and Ackerman was taking on a sitting president who was moderately popular. Thus, Ackerman would likely fail in his quest in spectacular fashion, giving media members in New York and California just that much more ammunition with which to smear Mississippi.

A Texan, a New Yorker, or a Californian would not recognize anything like this Mississippi Effect. Residents of these more-reputable, less-maligned, more-confident states assume that their former governors have a God-given right to the White House after having run such an important state. At a minimum, their guy would run a strong race and be chosen by the eventual nominee as his vice-presidential running mate. But Mississippians, having been whipped down by the rest of the country for so long, couldn't see anything good coming out of Ackerman's candidacy for national office.

No foundation had been laid to get the crowd fired up. No national media outlet had floated Ackerman's name as a possible candidate, and the Ackerman team had done an outstanding job of keeping the purpose of the speech a secret. Too good of a job, it turned out. If the attendees had known what to expect, they could have at least been ready to cheer at the appropriate time. As it was, the only memorable part of the event was the extremely uncomfortable silence following his big announcement.

Ackerman, Williamson, and Morgan left the Governor's Mansion soon after the speech ended and slunk over to Ackerman's office to assess the damage from the disastrous start to the campaign.

Chapter 9

Russell Senate Office Building
April 2015

Productivity grinds to a halt in many office buildings around the country on Friday afternoons. This is especially true on Capitol Hill in Washington, D.C., as most of the congressmen and senators flee the nation's capital on Thursday or Friday to go back to their home states for fundraising dinners, ribbon cuttings, and similar events. Their slew of staff members left behind, mostly young interns who aren't needed on the junket back to the home district, barely pretend to work while the boss is away.

Senator Olivia Hollister was an exception to the rule of traveling back home. She had escaped rural New Hampshire for Washington, D.C. twenty-four years earlier and went back only when absolutely necessary. Interacting with constituents was for the less-accomplished members of Congress who weren't shoo-ins for re-election. Senator Hollister preferred appearing on Sunday morning political talk shows and giving interviews to national media pundits to pressing the flesh at elementary school bake sales. As a third-term senator who had also served for a decade in the U.S. House of Representatives, her re-election every six years was assured so long as she maintained her current national reputation as a calm, reasonable voice in the middle of the two warring political parties.

But Senator Hollister's suite of offices in the Russell Senate Office Building was not immune to the rule of Friday-afternoon slowdowns. This particular Friday was no exception. As a steady rain soaked the gawking tourists outside, the senator stood in a corner of the conference room just down the hall from her office. Her staff huddled around a laptop computer at one end of the long table, gleefully watching the now-infamous YouTube video of Jeff Ackerman's disastrous announcement of his candidacy. They replayed it again and again to ever-louder peals of laughter.

"Go back to the awkward pause," one of the interns suggested.

Earlier that afternoon, Hollister's chief of staff needed to quiet a noisy gathering of younger, louder staff members in order to start a meeting about a pending budget bill. Clearing his throat hadn't worked, nor had rapping his knuckles on the conference room table. Finally, he stood up and yelled, "I'm Governor Jeffrey Ackerman, and I'm running for president of the United States of America!" Understanding the joke immediately, the staffers did their part to re-create the scene by falling completely silent for ten seconds. During this silent pause, they smirked at each other around the table and mentally congratulated themselves for working for a sensible woman like Hollister instead of a hopeless Baptist boob like Jeff Ackerman.

The senator wanted to join in the fun around the laptop that was now replaying Ackerman's embarrassing scene for the fifth or sixth time. However, she felt that a third-term senator should always strive for decorum. The last thing she needed was for some video to leak out showing her laughing at a fellow Republican—even if he was a Southern Bible-thumping fool like this Ackerman guy. Her carefully crafted reputation as a moderate, sensible, prudent, and well-grounded member of the United States Senate was her greatest political asset, and she guarded it carefully.

Olivia Hollister was unique among the one hundred members of the Senate in that she was the only one who lacked an urgent desire to be elected to the presidency. This made her an extremely unlikely frontrunner for the Republican nomination for the 2016 election cycle, but that's exactly what she was. One by one, potential Republican candidates had quietly signaled their intentions to remain in their current roles as senators, governors, generals, CEOs, etc., foregoing what was almost certain to be a losing battle in a November 2016 matchup with President Upton Landers.

The much-maligned but ill-defined Republican establishment was nearly in a panic. *Someone* had to run against Landers. Normally, the party establishment worked to "clear the field" for its preferred candidate, but this time, the field was clearing itself, with no establishment candidate in sight.

After a few discreet dinners and conference calls—the twenty-first-century equivalent to a meeting in a smoke-filled room—the party elders landed on Olivia Hollister as their preferred candidate. The Republican establishment knew they needed to nominate a female candidate at some point. Might as well get that silliness out of the way now, they grumped among themselves. The men who ran the GOP didn't particularly care about how cynical and transparent this maneuver was, for no one would have ever thought twice of nominating a male version of Senator Olivia Hollister.

If by some miracle she happened to win the presidency, the GOP establishment concluded, at least she wouldn't be a pain in the ass in the Senate any longer. In a perfect world, she would run for president and lose respectably, tiring herself out in the process and deciding on a swift retirement from the Senate. That would give the party a chance to elect a real, reliable Republican to replace her. RINOs such as Hollister consistently caused more trouble for their fellow Republicans than they did for Democrats, and thus one less RINO in office was always a good thing for conservatives.

The senator was flattered yet intimidated by the attention as phone calls rolled in from major Republican donors, former Republican presidents, and retired cabinet members, all urging her to run for president. "You'll be an outstanding candidate," they all said. Hollister didn't miss the fact that none had predicted that she would be a good *president*.

The other 99 senators, all 50 governors, and most of the 435 members of the U.S. House of Representatives would have said a quick *yes* to such strong appeals from the party elders, especially with such an empty field of competition in the primaries. But Senator Hollister hesitated. She cherished her role as one of only two or three true swing votes in the closely divided Senate.

Nothing gave her greater pleasure than to stand in front of a huge crowd of expectant reporters on the steps of the U.S. Capitol. With misty eyes and a sad, solemn voice, the senior U.S. senator from New Hampshire would announce that she simply couldn't support this or that piece of legislation sponsored by her more conservative colleagues. The bill gave the military too much power; or it cut taxes too much for the rich, who already failed to pay their fair share; or it didn't have sufficient protections for minorities or women or children. Or all of the above.

Her stated reasons never really mattered. Regardless of her rationale, the Democrat-dominated media would shower her with approving editorials lauding her statesmanship, wisdom, maturity, and strength in the face of mean-spirited Republican efforts to "turn back the clock on civil rights" or enact the latest round of "tax cuts for the rich."

Truth be told, Senator Hollister was one of the most intellectually lazy members of the U.S. Senate. She had no real political principles, but rather sought always to split the difference between the extremists on both sides. In one of the few good lines of his announcement speech, Ackerman criticized her for always wanting to build half a bridge. His point was that sometimes a politician has to take a stand—that there are good reasons for building a particular bridge, and good reasons for not building a bridge, but building half a bridge as a compromise makes no sense at all.

Senator Hollister was cold, standoffish, and generally dislikable in the eyes of the few normal, non-political people who had a chance to get to know her. But she was smart enough to understand these downsides of her personality and thus let few such people into her inner circle. And the dislike went both ways. If she had preferred the company of common people, she would have stayed in New Hampshire and not fought her way to the top of the Washington political summit. Her true political base was the media, especially the left-leaning types who dominated the major networks and newspapers. Among actual voters, her base consisted of elderly folks who voted for her because she "wasn't as mean as most Republicans," women who voted for her because she had ovaries, and weak-willed men who wanted to impress said women.

With each thrust of the knife into the metaphorical back of the Republican Party, Senator Hollister bought herself an additional round of invitations to the best social events in Georgetown and appearances on the major political talk shows. These dinner parties and interviews gave her additional opportunities to bemoan the hyperpartisan and divisive atmosphere of Washington politics. No one seemed to notice that no Democrat ever strayed from the left-wing reservation to defy his or her party on an important piece of legislation or in a major confirmation battle. In fact, the same perks that came to Hollister for being a contrarian to her party would be denied to any such heretic on the other side of the political divide. She was every Democrat's favorite Republican.

In short, Olivia Hollister was quite content to remain *Senator* Hollister and wasn't particularly eager to become *President* Hollister, especially since the effort was so unlikely to pay off. Running for president required work, effort, and strong positions on the issues. It was so much easier to sit on the sidelines and throw the occasional hand grenade into the Republican tent.

The senator knew that she'd be able to hold her seat in the upper chamber even if she ran for and lost the presidency, but even a half-hearted campaign would require her to take real positions on real issues that would cost her precious political capital. She feared that her media admirers wouldn't continue to adore her after an almost-certain-to-fail presidential campaign. Nonetheless, she eventually relented to the repeated requests of the party elders and announced her candidacy for the White House.

Thus far, Hollister had enjoyed an easy path to the Republican nomination, just as the party elders had promised. The idea of slogging through state fairs and snow-covered farm communities in Iowa repulsed her. So many lower-class people wearing overalls and John Deere hats; so much fried, fatty food; so far from her favorite editorial boards at newspapers in Washington and New York. She'd made a few desultory appearances in the Hawkeye State just to let folks know she wasn't completely mailing it in, each time quickly returning to the more sophisticated environs of D.C.

Jeffrey Ackerman's entry into the race would force her to make additional treks to Iowa, which for some odd reason held the first primary in each presidential election cycle. Iowans insisted that presidential candidates conduct retail politics: meeting folks one-on-one at PTA meetings, Rotary Clubs, garden clubs, and Wednesday-night church gatherings. Senator Hollister had avoided these events thus far, sticking to larger gatherings such as speeches and rallies in Des Moines and Cedar Rapids.

This would have to change now that she had a primary opponent. She resented Ackerman for compelling her to interact with the corn and pig farmers more than she did for his having the temerity to run against such a highly esteemed U.S. senator. Hollister shuddered at the thought of tramping through some cornfield in God-Knows-Where, Iowa.

Well, Ackerman wouldn't last long, especially given the disastrous announcement of his candidacy. Who in their right mind would give this guy a dollar's worth of campaign contributions? Besides, even if Ackerman somehow got his act together and became a real threat, her friends at major media outlets such as the *International News Network*, the *New York Daily Ledger*, and the *Washington Chronicle* would dash his hopes with brutal efficiency.

Senator Hollister smiled to herself at this thought and quietly slipped out of the conference room, enjoying the laughter of her staff as they watched the video of Ackerman's announcement yet again.

Chapter 10

Air Force One

April 2015

P resident Upton Landers dozed in one of the many soft leather chairs on board *Air Force One*. Of course, this one had the presidential seal on it, was slightly larger than the others, and was in the front of the cabin. The little people in his entourage could sit in undecorated, smaller seats farther back, although there was no such thing as a bad seat on board the presidential aircraft.

Landers deserved this higher class of first class because . . . well, just because he did. He wasn't only the president of the United States. He was Upton Landers, president of the United States. Many men had left the White House with a giant ego, but few had entered it with the self-confident, selfish sense of self-importance and self-love that enveloped Upton Landers.

He had put in at least an hour's worth of work on behalf of the taxpayers earlier today and had therefore fully earned a nap. And not just any nap, but a presidential snooze in a presidential reclining seat bearing the presidential seal. There was certainly no interesting scenery to distract him. They were flying over one of those flat, boring states in the middle of the country whose only purpose seemed to be to get the number of states up to a nice, round number.

Why did anyone live out here in the middle of nowhere? The money, the power, the smart people, and the beautiful people were all located along the coasts. There wasn't anything in between other than rusty factories and gritty farms. Chicago was a bit of an exception, but it was a major metropolitan city mainly because those yahoo pig farmers had to sell their meat somewhere. Landers was glad that they at least had the decency to do so somewhere other than more-important, more-upscale cities like New York, Washington, or San Francisco.

He didn't feel any guilt over this elitist attitude. After all, everyone on board *Air Force One* felt the same way, especially the reporters snoring away in the back of the plane. They were too dumb or too naïve to realize that the politicos up front looked down on the reporters in the same way that they all looked down on the denizens of flyover country. But they were all on the same team here on *Air Force One*—the enlightened, progressive few who would drag the unwashed masses into the twenty-first century and away from their Bibles, guns, and spacious suburban houses with wasteful lawns. They would do so by persuasion to the extent possible, and then by force if necessary. It was for the little people's own good, after all. Those backward hillbillies just weren't smart enough to realize it yet.

The purpose of the trip was ostensibly for the president to attend the funeral of a former governor of California. Thus, the taxpayers thirty thousand feet below Landers' seat had the privilege of paying for the junket. The actual purpose of the trip was for Upton Landers to conduct a few fundraisers and give a couple of speeches on the West Coast, which he would do both before and after mourning the loss of his dear friend Governor Whatever-His-Name-Was. The irony—or injustice—of enriching his campaign coffers at taxpayer expense was lost on Upton Landers, just as it had been lost on the past dozen or so presidents of all political stripes.

Landers had just entered a fairly deep sleep when his shoulder was gently shaken by Chloe MacKenzie, his political director. She was stunningly beautiful, reasonably intelligent, and at least thirty years younger than the president. Chloe had shaken more than Landers' shoulder on several previous occasions, although it had been several weeks since they had retired to a private spot for "an urgent campaign strategy session." Landers' instinctive anger at being awakened was mostly ameliorated by the sight of Chloe's face and the memory of the last time she had touched him on *Air Force One*.

"I'm sorry to wake you, Mr. President," she began, "but Ackerman just announced that he's running for president. I thought you'd want to know immediately."

Landers rubbed his eyes in an effort to buy himself a moment to think. He soon gave up and asked a very reasonable question. "Who is Ackerman?"

Chloe was simultaneously relieved and concerned by the president's reaction. She was relieved because she herself had been forced to do some quick research on Jeff Ackerman after seeing a short news blurb about the announcement of his candidacy. Her job was to know all the important political players in the country, and Jeff Ackerman was nowhere near her radar screen. The president's question proved that the same was true for him, so it wasn't like she had missed some obvious threat to her boss's re-election.

However, she was also now concerned because she had just interrupted a presidential nap for no good reason. Upton Landers would fire a less attractive, less sexually available staffer on the spot, but Chloe had earned a deep reserve of what might be referred to in the trade as "political capital." She cleared her throat, stood up straighter, and did her best to give Landers a quick brief on Ackerman.

"Jeff Ackerman is a former two-term governor of Mississippi. He's been on the sidelines the past couple of years and probably decided to run for president because he got bored. Typical good ol' boy who's been cleaned up a bit but not enough for polite company. Baptist, Bible-thumping gun owner, believes the federal government is the devil incarnate and that the Constitution literally means what it says and nothing more, yada yada yada."

Landers nodded impatiently and gave her a wry smile. "I stopped listening when you said the word *Mississippi*. We won't have to worry about this guy. The late-night comedians will kill his candidacy the minute they notice he's running, if things even get that far. The jokes practically write themselves."

"So no need for any opposition research on Ackerman?"

"No, not at this point. If anything, maybe this will force Hollister to have to spend a little money instead of just waltzing along to the Republican nomination completely unopposed. For that matter, she might even float the idea that he's a religious extremist. That would open the door for us to criticize Christian conservatives more aggressively in all races going forward. You know the drill: 'Even some Republicans are worried about the far-right Christian conservative leanings of the party,' et cetera, et cetera."

"Got it. I assume there's no reason to have any of our friends back there,"—she tossed her head toward the sleeping media contingent—"to take him down a notch?"

Landers, MacKenzie, Jordan, or any of a dozen other operatives in the Landers campaign/administration could get a front-page hit piece on Ackerman in the *New York Daily Ledger* or *Washington Chronicle* with a quick word to a friendly reporter. Blogger Glenn Reynolds often referred to the mainstream media as "Democratic operatives with by-lines" for this very reason.

The president didn't need long to ponder this idea. "From what little

I know about this guy, he can't get any lower on the totem pole. Let's not waste any bullets or favors with the press on this bozo. But"—a gleam came to the president's eye as he shifted in his seat—"perhaps we should continue this conversation later tonight? You could provide me with some additional background and we could, uh, explore the issue a bit deeper? The First Lady wasn't able to accompany me on this trip due to a scheduling conflict." Landers didn't bother to tell Chloe that he had personally engineered said scheduling conflict so he could give his ears a rest from his wife's constant nagging.

Everyone aboard, from the lowliest staffer up to the leader of the free world himself, appreciated the absence of First Lady Abigail Landers. Although both had been born to wealthy families, Abigail Landers' money was more plentiful and, more importantly, much older than that of her husband. She somehow managed to treat the White House staff and the Secret Service with even more contempt and arrogance than Upton Landers. The only thing she had in common with the hundreds of servants and staffers who surrounded the Landers family was that she, like each of them, thought her husband was an idiot.

Chloe MacKenzie was far too intelligent to miss the president's signals. Upton Landers wasn't particularly subtle on this or any other such occasion. She was also flattered by the presidential attention, especially so now after worrying recently that she had fallen out of favor with her boss. And she was far too practical to be concerned about the feelings of Abigail Landers. After all, if the president didn't cheat on his wife with Chloe, he'd cheat on her with someone else. "Of course, Mr. President. I'll swing by your suite tonight. Sorry to have awakened you for nothing."

Landers reclined his chair as she walked away, knowing that he really needed a nap now. He and his favorite staff member had a long night of vigorous policy discussions ahead of them.

Chapter 11

New York Daily Ledger
Headquarters Building,
Manhattan

May 2015

Austin Brant marched purposefully into the immense skyscraper on Seventh Avenue in Manhattan. As he did every day upon entering the building, he congratulated himself on reaching the pinnacle of his profession. For the past six months, he had been an opinion columnist for the *New York Daily Ledger*, the most famous newspaper in the world.

He maintained an outward modesty, but knew that he was widely respected by readers and media critics alike for his immense talent with the written word. Austin Brant could say more in a fifteen-hundred-word column than others could say in twice the amount of space. But his skills weren't confined to pounding out a weekly column, as he had demonstrated with several well-received appearances on radio and TV talk shows to give his views on the issues of the day. Brant knew that his peers respected him, but he really enjoyed the fact that his peers were jealous of him.

Landing any job at the *Daily Ledger* was difficult. Even the lowliest grunts in the mailroom at the paper had called in favors from connected friends and relatives in order to obtain their positions. But being a writer for such a prestigious paper was more difficult still, and obtaining a by-line as a political columnist for the *Daily Ledger* was rare air indeed. Austin Brant had achieved that rarest of positions: he was a *conservative* political columnist for the *New York Daily Ledger*. In fact, he was not just *a* conservative columnist for the *Daily Ledger*; he was *the* conservative columnist for the *Daily Ledger*.

The *New York Daily Ledger* was clearly a liberal publication, and the paper barely even tried to deny its leftist leanings at this point. But the paper retained just enough journalistic integrity to keep one conservative voice on its editorial page, and Austin Brant was now that voice. As he mentally patted himself on the back for his successful career while striding toward the elevator, he fought off a nagging sense of shame over how he had obtained his dream job half a year earlier.

Brant's predecessor, the former token conservative at the *Daily Ledger*, had humiliated himself and lost all credibility among the paper's dwindling number of Republican readers when he fawned over "the perfectly knotted tie" of a Democratic presidential candidate, using this as evidence that said candidate would—and should— be elected. The paper's management had quickly reached out to Brant, who was then a leading columnist for the *Wall Street Post*, to gauge his interest in working for the *Daily Ledger*.

A native New Yorker, Brant had dreamed of writing for the *Daily Ledger* ever since he was a young teenager, when he and his father had engaged in good-natured political debates while devouring the *Daily Ledger's* thick Sunday edition. He had envisioned an older, wiser version of himself with a small portrait next to his latest column, which would inevitably be read and discussed by millions of eager readers all over the country. He was more than qualified to be a *Daily Ledger* columnist, as he could write circles around anyone else who had written for the paper in the past twenty years. In a perfect world, Brant would have jumped at the offer to move to the *Daily Ledger*.

But Austin Brant was a true ideological conservative, which was a seemingly insurmountable obstacle to achieving his boyhood dream. In recent years, it had become clear even to casual readers that the main purpose of each so-called conservative columnist at the newspaper was to provide just enough cover for the paper's editorial board to claim that the board maintained its objectivity and was open to different ideas. On any important issue, the allegedly conservative writer for the *Daily Ledger* was bound to criticize the Republicans for being too reactionary, too conservative, for going too far too fast. In fact, the current faux conservative on the editorial board often abandoned the conservative argument completely and sided smugly with the liberals.

Austin Brant had wanted none of that amateurish, middle-school-ish drama. He wasn't willing to compromise his beliefs in print, even for the *New York Daily Ledger*. And the paper wanted none of his pure conservatism, or so he had always assumed. However, the ownership group at the *Daily Ledger* had been persistent in their efforts to hire him, and Brant was flattered by the attention. During several phone calls, office interviews, and discrete lunches, he and the *Daily Ledger's* management had danced a delicate dance. They never actually said that he would be expected to take certain liberal views in order to write for the *Daily Ledger*, and he never actually agreed to do so.

Brant eventually realized that he had a rare opportunity. The moderate, Republican-in-name-only Olivia Hollister was the presumptive Republican nominee for the 2016 presidential election. He could, he told his doubtful conscience, endorse Upton Landers, the Democrat, over Olivia Hollister, the moderate-to-liberal Republican, without compromising his principles. After all, Hollister was almost a Democrat herself, and if the American people wanted liberal Democratic policies, they might as well go for the real thing in Upton Landers.

Without actually saying the words, and certainly without putting anything to this effect in writing, Brant and the *Daily Ledger* reached an understanding. Brant would become their conservative political columnist, and he would have free rein to express his conservative views on the editorial page, with one exception: he would endorse Landers over Hollister in the 2016 election. At least, that was Brant's interpretation of the numerous vague, nod-nod-wink-wink conversations he'd had with the folks who now paid his lucrative salary.

Austin Brant consoled himself for this small compromise by taking a deep breath and enjoying the view of the New York skyline from his office on the forty-eighth floor. He knew he'd take some heat from his Republican friends and sources over the next few months, but Republicans were much better than Democrats at forgiving betrayals like the one that he had bound himself to deliver.

He also knew that he had work to do and that standing here staring out his window wouldn't help him complete the task. He sat down in front of his computer and began outlining the column in which he'd stab the Republicans in the back. It wouldn't run for several more months, after the two major parties held their conventions, but he wanted to put the distasteful task of writing away a part of his soul behind him sooner rather than later.

Chapter 12

Ackerman Campaign Strategy Memorandum

May 2015

STRICTLY CONFIDENTIAL;
ALL LEAKERS WILL BE SHOT

To: All Campaign Staff

From: Art Morgan

Date: May 15, 2015

RE: Campaign Strategy Memo Number 5
        (supersedes Memos 1–4)

Status of the Race: There's not a race at this point. We're getting our asses kicked all over Iowa by Senator Olivia Hollister, the most boring senator in the history of anyone's memory. She's only been to Iowa once since Jeff announced his candidacy. But neither Hollister nor any other intelligent observer can see any reason why she should trouble herself to come here to campaign against us. We're barely registering in the public polls. Voters have no idea who our guy is or why he should be president. To the extent anyone is talking about our campaign, they're asking why we're even bothering to spend time, money, and effort on a doomed campaign that barely even qualifies as a campaign.

Internal Polling Data: None. We can't afford it. We'll continue to rely on publicly available polling data for now. If we ever get to the point where we're close enough to Hollister to need a poll to evaluate our options, we'll consider hiring a pollster. Chances of this happening are agonizingly close to zero.

Financial Update: We're nearly broke. Donations started slowly and only got worse from there. Governor Ackerman's personal contribution of $200,000 to the campaign has kept us going to this point, but those funds will be exhausted in the next few weeks, even if we continue to run a bare-bones operation. [Hey, Jeff, if you're still reading this, can you throw us a little more cash? Or find a rich uncle who can?]

Media Strategy: We initially thought we'd struggle to respond to media requests due to slim staffing on the campaign. Unfortunately, that hasn't been a problem, because the media is completely ignoring us. No national paper has assigned a reporter to our campaign. We've been mentioned on the top cable news channel a grand total of twice. We've offered no-holds-barred interviews to every network and major newspaper, but they won't even return our calls. We get the occasional local/statewide reporter at our events, but only if it's a very slow news day (i.e., no cats getting stuck in trees). Maybe we could get one of those blogger guys to give us a boost? If any of you have any relationships with a new-media type or can call in any favors, now is the time to do so.

Operational Plan: We'll stick with the bus tour of Iowa for now, mainly because it's all we can afford. No private jets for us. Ackerman will deliver his stump speech at state fairs, festivals, church revivals, Rotary Club meetings, anywhere there's a ready-made crowd because God knows we can't generate a crowd on our own.

We'd like to make better use of campaign surrogates on the trail, but we don't have any. Iowa's governor and Republican Congress critters all endorsed Hollister before we announced. Ackerman's friends and political allies from Mississippi are too busy rearranging their sock drawers to come help us in Iowa. Perhaps we can improve this situation if we can somehow get a little momentum.

The original plan to travel back and forth between Iowa and New Hampshire is on hold for now. We'll stick with Iowa. Unless the numbers and contributions improve significantly, we'll be out of the race before the New Hampshire primary anyway. If we can somehow hang on through Iowa and New Hampshire, we'll get to more favorable ground when conservative states like South Carolina start to hold primaries.

Messaging and Themes: We've got to get voters to understand that nominating Olivia Hollister to run against Upton Landers is a complete waste of time. No matter who wins such a matchup, we'll be stuck with a squishy, weak-kneed, limp-wristed liberal in the White House for the next four years. On the other hand, Jeff Ackerman represents the Republican wing of the Republican Party and offers a real contrast to Landers. I can't for the life of me figure out how we haven't been able to get this idea to sink in with the voters. It's not complicated and has the unique advantage of being true. Do your jobs and sell it!

Examples:

Hollister has paid lip service to cutting back the role of government, but Ackerman has actually accomplished it. He led the charge to reduce the number of counties in Mississippi from eighty-two to seven, eliminating over one thousand duplicative government jobs in the process. This saved taxpayers over $50 million per year.

Hollister frequently talks about "the children," mainly when giving an excuse for torpedoing one piece of Republican legislation or another. Ackerman has actually improved children's lives by improving public education in Mississippi. He implemented school choice, cut bureaucracy, and instituted merit pay for teachers. The average teacher salary increased by $15,000 per year and the state still saved money overall. Reading and math scores are up and drop-out rates are down.

Ackerman is pro-life, period, full stop. Hollister is pro-life only on even-numbered dates in odd-numbered months while there's a full moon.

Ackerman has cut taxes. He cut Mississippi's personal and corporate income tax rates, along with real estate and sales tax rates. This helped encourage business and economic development in Mississippi, and overall state revenues increased after the tax cuts. Hollister cast the deciding vote against the last Republican tax cut plan.

We've got to sell voters on our guy's achievements and ideas. We don't have movie-star good looks going for us here; Jeff is average height with an average build and an average (but rapidly receding) hairline. In short, he's not an ugly guy but he's not winning the White House based on his commanding physical presence. But he wouldn't be the first president who looks like a typical suburban dad that you see at the youth soccer or softball fields. Accordingly, we're selling his resume and his policies to the voters.

Michelle Ackerman: From what we can tell, Michelle is the lone bright spot in this little venture. Iowans genuinely like her. After events, more folks line up to shake her hand than the candidate's. Some of them skip the speech and walk up afterward just to meet Michelle. Maybe we should fire Jeff and have Michelle run in his place? [Just kidding, Jeff. But your wife does have much better legs than you.] We'll consider having her give a speech or two in the near future (although she has flatly refused to do so to this point, citing stage fright). If we ever get a little extra cash, we can send her and the candidate to different locations in order to increase the campaign's overall exposure.

Conclusion: Yes, things are bad. Yes, they'll likely soon get worse. But we have a qualified candidate to sell to the voters. He has no skeletons in his closet that we have to defend against. Conservative Republicans will eventually wake up and hopefully bring some moderates along with them. Even as bleak as things are now, it won't take much to cause a momentum shift. We've got to work to make that happen and be ready to take advantage of our momentum when we get it. Press on!

Chapter 13

On a Bus Somewhere in Iowa
August 2015

What happens if a guy runs for president and no one notices? Jeff Ackerman asked himself for about the three-hundredth time as he sweated and slogged his way through Iowa. The weather was stifling, the crowds were small, the campaign fund was nearly empty, and the polls were discouraging.

Art Morgan was grumpy, but he was always grumpy and therefore not a useful barometer of the overall mood of the small campaign staff. Scott Williamson was a better gauge. He had an almost constant smile and seemingly boundless energy, but even Williamson had been subdued for the past several days. Conclusion: the staff was just as depressed as the candidate, perhaps more so.

Ackerman had always had a healthy skepticism about his chances in the race. He would fight the good fight in what was probably a losing cause, but maybe lightning would strike for him. Seeing Williamson sink toward depression, however, caused Ackerman's already low level of optimism to fall to the point of being immeasurable. They needed some good news from somewhere, and they needed it right now. He couldn't ask these folks to continue to slave away for him in a hopeless cause, especially if they got to the point where he couldn't pay them. It was bad enough that they'd have a losing campaign cluttering up their resumes; going broke in the process just added insult to injury.

The physical environment of the campaign didn't improve anyone's mood. The leased Greyhound bus that the Ackerman campaign dubbed the *Extremely Low-Flying Campaign Jet* was cramped and seemed to be shrinking as the days dragged on. The greasy smell of fast-food burgers and french fries lingered in the threadbare seat cushions. The wi-fi was spotty at best, and the video screens hanging from the ceiling didn't work. The temperature alternated between sweltering and frigid, with nothing in between. The miniature bathroom at the back of the bus always smelled like, well, a bathroom, and this odor seemed to be drifting slowly yet inexorably toward the front of the bus, gradually overwhelming the scent of three-day-old McDonald's fries.

Ackerman sat in a window seat, pondering his next steps. He tried without success to ignore the paper airplanes that periodically sailed toward his seat near the front. The young interns on the campaign, not surprisingly, gravitated toward the back of the bus. Paper-airplane-throwing contests were one of the more family-friendly ways that the youngsters passed the time as the bus lumbered along dusty Iowa state highways. Ackerman allowed himself a rare smile as a paper airplane drifted down onto the face of a slumbering, snoring Art Morgan.

The interns came and went so quickly that Ackerman had given up even trying to learn their names. He felt a twinge of guilt for this, and also for not providing better adult supervision for these twenty-somethings who were foolish enough to tag along with him through the Iowa cornfields. But they weren't completely out of control just yet. Besides, it wasn't like there were any reporters

around to notice their questionable behavior and write an embarrassing story about the campaign. In any event, the campaign was
doing an excellent job of embarrassing itself on its own, thank you
very much.

Ackerman hadn't found a way to connect with the voters, and his
frustration was mounting. Iowa Republicans were reliably conservative. Ackerman was a conservative Republican. His only opponent was a moderate-to-liberal Republican who was almost utterly
devoid of personality. And yet all indications were that voters were
completely indifferent regarding the race, and the few who had
a preference preferred Senator Hollister to the unknown former
governor from Mississippi.

Ackerman pictured Olivia Hollister jetting into Iowa, collecting
a few hundred thousand dollars in campaign donations, getting a
boost in the polls, and then jetting back to D.C. a day or two later.
He imagined—correctly—that his pathetic little campaign bus full
of has-beens and never-will-bes was a source of many jokes on the
Hollister campaign aircraft. Surely Hollister and her staff sat in their
comfortable leather seats, drinking good wine and availing themselves of a reliable internet connection, mocking the Mississippians
all the while.

Maybe they were right. Maybe he had leaped into this without
enough thought, without enough prayer, without laying enough of
a foundation for a candidacy. The unlikely candidate wondered if
running for president was his version of a midlife crisis. *Some guys
have affairs, others buy convertibles, motorcycles, or sailboats. Not me. I trudge
through God-forsaken Iowa on the most ramshackle bus this side of Central
America. Who am I to think I could be president? I guess Michelle was right
all along.*

His gaze drifted to his wife, who was sleeping in the seat next to
him. She had been amazing on the campaign trail. The person who

wanted to be here the least was doing a better job than any of the so-called political professionals. And she hadn't complained once. She had every right to whine, to complain, to roll her eyes, to say "I told you so" and then storm out of the room and slam the door, but she hadn't even come close to any of that, in word or in attitude.

A couple of weeks ago, Ackerman had argued to Morgan and Williamson that Iowa was a lost cause. The candidate favored abandoning Iowa, skipping New Hampshire, and focusing his efforts on South Carolina, which held the nation's third presidential primary. Morgan and Williamson each disagreed, but for different reasons.

Morgan pointed out that leaving Iowa so soon signaled weakness and a lack of perseverance. Campaigns were supposed to be long, difficult, and disheartening, he'd lectured. That was one way of separating the wheat from the chaff. Williamson, on the other hand, pointed out that Ackerman would need Iowa's electoral votes in the general election. It was one of the few remaining swing states and was very winnable against Landers in November 2016. Abandoning Iowa before establishing a solid foundation in the state would hurt Ackerman's chances of upsetting the sitting president if he somehow managed to overcome Senator Hollister's lead in the primary.

Ackerman had seen the wisdom in these views and continued to soldier on. But he had nothing to show for it except a few extra pounds from eating fried food at state fairs and a significantly depleted campaign war chest, despite the frugality of the campaign. Maybe it was time to take a few weeks off, go home, and recharge his batteries. Iowa would still be here in a month or two. Perhaps his absence would somehow make the voters' hearts grow fonder of the scrappy upstart from Mississippi.

As he drifted off to sleep, he said a quick prayer. *Lord, I really don't know what I'm doing here. Perhaps pride or selfish ambition led me on a fool's errand. I had the sense that running for president was Your will for me, but I've certainly been wrong on that score in the past and may be wrong now. Please guide and direct me on what to do now.*

If it's time to quit, please grant me the humility to do so. Dropping out now would be less embarrassing than sticking it out until I'm bankrupt and still getting crushed in the polls. Please show me Your will and provide me with the courage to follow it.

And thank You for providing me with such an amazing wife. Help me to be worthy of her. Amen.

Chapter 14

Brandon, Mississippi
September 2015

September meant crisp, cool fall weather for most of the country, but it was just another hot, humid summer month in central Mississippi. Jeff Ackerman and his campaign team were taking a few weeks off to rest, recuperate, and re-evaluate their little venture. The candidate alternated between feeling exhausted, embarrassed, and energized by the downtime.

But this afternoon he tended to much more mundane tasks. The Ackermans were hosting their friends Carl and Laura Irvin for dinner this evening. Actually, Laura and Michelle Ackerman were friends. Jeff got along okay with Carl, but he could barely tolerate Laura, who wore her left-wing politics on her sleeve. And her T-shirts. And the bumper of her car, which proudly displayed about eighteen stickers mocking conservatives, Republicans, Christians, and Southerners.

Jeff was pretty sure the feeling was mutual. Laura made it clear that she wasn't a member of the Jeff Ackerman Fan Club. The fact that this was a small, sad little club these days didn't improve Jeff's mood, nor did the list of chores Michelle had "suggested" he accomplish today. Having yard duty in the 95-degree heat, with a heat index of 103 degrees, made him even less enthusiastic about this dinner party of Michelle's.

Jeff walked into the kitchen, wiping sweat from his eyes after mowing and edging the Ackerman's modest yard. He wasn't much of a gardener, but he judged that his efforts today had moved the Ackerman residence from the bottom third on his mental list of the neighborhood's curb appeal rankings into somewhere around the middle of the pack. That was good enough for him. He had neither the energy nor the motivation to elevate the Ackerman's lawn and somewhat uninspiring flower beds into the subdivision's upper crust of lawns, the folks who had *Yard of the Month* signs near their mailboxes.

Jeff was sipping from his second glass of ice water when Michelle's cell phone rang on the kitchen counter nearby. He could hear her vacuuming upstairs and was too tired to sprint up there with her phone, but he checked the screen. Laura Irvin. *Maybe she's canceling for dinner tonight*, he thought hopefully as he answered the phone in a playful tone, "Ackerman Family Diner. We're open twenty-four hours, just not in a row. Press one if you'd like to speak to Lumpy the Cook, two for Imelda the Waitress . . ."

Laura was not amused, but she made a small little grunting sound to simulate a chuckle in a half-hearted effort to be polite. But her manners weren't sufficient to let Jeff complete his ridiculous routine. Besides, if she'd wanted to talk to that buffoon, she would have called his phone instead of Michelle's, so she had no problem interrupting him. "Jeff, it's Laura Irvin. Is Michelle available?"

"Not right now. We're having some Communist hippy-type couple over for dinner tonight, and she's busy removing all signs of capitalism and Christianity from the house." Jeff had promised Michelle that he'd be polite and avoid politics at dinner tonight, but dinner hadn't started yet, had it?

Laura mostly ignored Jeff's barb. "Unfortunately, our sitter canceled for tonight, so we're bringing Willow with us."

Who names their kid Willow? Poor child has no chance in life. Jeff was pondering whether it was too impolite to invite Laura to bring along as many trees and shrubs as she wanted when she continued. This time, she got in a jab of her own.

"As I'm sure you know, all of the modern parenting books written by respected experts say that you should never take your child to the home of a right-wing, conservative Christian fascist. But if it can't be avoided, you have to at least ask a few questions to make sure it's safe. So, do you have any guns in your house?"

"Yes, we do have guns in the house," he answered, "but we only have four. Of course, we're happy to share our firearms with you, Carl, and Willow. Or you could bring some of your own. Either way is fine with us. Maybe we could do some shooting after we eat? It's been months since I shot anyone, and I'm getting a bit antsy."

Long, uncomfortable silence on the call, followed by a deep breath. Finally, the flag of surrender from Laura Irvin: "Could you put Michelle on the phone, please?"

Michelle walked into the kitchen just then, so Jeff thrust the phone in her direction. "It's Laura." He then added, loud enough for the caller to overhear, "Tell her to calm down and relax, 'cause it's been weeks since I shot anybody."

Michelle sent an accusatory what-have-you-done-now glare his way, but all she saw was her husband's back as he conducted a strategic retreat toward the back door.

Jeff decided he needed to do some more yard work. He may have been dumb enough to start the verbal jousting match with Laura Irvin, but he wasn't a complete idiot. He knew full well that, as long as he was outside, the duration of whatever scolding Michelle had in store for him would be limited by the unbearable heat and humidity.

Laura and Michelle were childhood friends but rarely saw each other these days. They tried to get together on Laura's rare trips back home to visit family. Always a bit of an eccentric, Laura had vowed as a teenager that she was leaving the South and would never live there again. She'd made good on this promise, moving to Rhode Island after college and drifting around the Northeast ever since. She took a job with the United Way as a fundraiser and was rather quick to let new acquaintances know that she worked for a non-profit charity, as if she was some sort of martyr who piously rejected the riches of the corporate world.

Laura had also sworn that she'd never get married, as marriage was sexist or patriarchal or something like that. She gave every indication of fulfilling that promise as well, but then she'd met Carl when she was pushing forty, and was quite smitten. Laura broke another vow a year later when Willow was born. She'd always said she would never bring a child into the world to contribute to the overpopulation problem, the world's food shortage, global warming, or whatever was the most popular crisis du jour on the left.

Carl and Laura proved the adage that opposites attract. Carl was quiet, no-nonsense, and apolitical. He worked as a carpenter and was quite content to move around with Laura wherever the United Way sent her. They had been in Vermont for the past two years. Born in rural western Pennsylvania, Carl had more in common culturally with the smiling, laughing, backslapping Southerners from Laura's childhood than the standoffish New Englanders she preferred as an adult.

Notwithstanding the barbs traded by Jeff and Laura earlier in the day, dinner was a relatively smooth affair. Jeff grilled rib-eyes and Michelle added a spinach salad, together with a corn casserole that was sweet and tasty enough to be a dessert. Jeff blessed the food, which simultaneously confused, embarrassed, and amused the Irvins.

The Ackermans ignored this, and they all dug into the meal. They were pleased to see their guests enjoying the food, even though Jeff was secretly disappointed to see that the Irvins weren't vegans. He was hoping to have some steak left over for tomorrow.

Although it was probably too late to avoid a "discussion" with Michelle later that night about his phone conversation with Laura, he was on his best behavior during dinner. He avoided discussing politics and, given his embarrassment over his failing presidential campaign, was quite content to do so. Jeff and Carl talked football instead. Being a Yankee, Carl lacked the religious fervor for college football that gripped every red-blooded Southern male—and many females—so Jeff indulged Carl with talk about Carl's beloved Pittsburgh Steelers.

After dinner, Michelle cleared the dinner plates from the table, politely rejecting Laura's half-hearted offer to help. Willow and the Ackerman daughters found an excuse to get away from the adults and went upstairs to discuss whatever teenage girls talked about. Carl was wrapping up a passionate lecture about how John Stallworth, not Lynn Swann, was the key to the Steeler passing game in the late-'70s, and Jeff was trying his best to look interested. Then the trouble began.

"So, Jeff," Laura began, interrupting Carl as he was about to launch into a detailed analysis of why former Steelers head coach Chuck Noll was far superior to the more famous Tom Landry of the Dallas Cowboys, "I caught part of one of your speeches a few weeks ago."

Uh-oh. Here comes the political discussion I promised Michelle I wouldn't have. How do I get out of this? On the other hand, he was encouraged that Laura Irvin had somehow managed to hear one of his speeches. God knows the rest of the country had been doing an excellent job of pretending his campaign didn't exist. Maybe the media hadn't been completely ignoring him after all.

"You were saying something about building a wall on our border with Mexico. Isn't that a bit divisive?"

"It's extremely divisive," Jeff agreed with an emphatic nod, straining to remain civil and avoid rolling his eyes. "In fact, that's the primary purpose of a wall: to divide one plot of land from another. Any wall that isn't divisive has failed to accomplish its main objective. But enough about my proposals. I promised Michelle that I wouldn't ruin the evening by diving into politics." Michelle was in the kitchen, but Jeff knew she could hear every word spoken in the adjacent dining room. "Can I get you some more coffee?"

"No. And stop trying to avoid the topic. Back to this silly wall idea of yours. Can't you see how offensive it is, how racist it is, and how unwelcoming a wall would be to our neighbors?"

"Wow. Let's see if I can ease your worries about this issue and address those objections in the order you raised them," Jeff replied, trying to remain calm. He couldn't recall being called a racist at his own dinner table before. "As to being offensive, I really don't understand the problem. No rational person disputes the fact that thousands of people a year walk into our country illegally from Mexico. There's no real physical barrier other than the Rio Grande, and it's not enough of a deterrent. If we want to improve our border security, we need a wall. The only people who might be 'offended' are the ones who want to break our laws and come into our country illegally, and, honestly, I'm not particularly concerned about their feelings.

"As to the racism charge, I don't get that one either. Yes, the people breaking our immigration laws tend to be brown-skinned folks from Mexico or Central America. But we're not discussing a wall because of the color of their skin; we're discussing a wall because they're sneaking into our country illegally. If white-skinned folks from Canada started pouring over our border illegally into

Montana or North Dakota, then a wall along the northern border would be just as appropriate.

"That leaves 'unwelcoming.' I plead guilty as charged on that one. Just like being divisive, one of the purposes of the wall is to demonstrate to those who want to break our laws that they are not welcome to do so. So, yes, I agree with you there: a wall along our southern border would, in fact, be unwelcoming. In case you haven't figured it out yet, being unwelcoming is pretty much the point."

Laura Irvin wasn't ready to concede anything. "But there are millions of undocumented refugees already here, and we have to do something to resolve their status so that they can come out of the shadows. A wall won't do anything to fix that problem." She was getting a little heated now. Her voice was louder, her words came out faster, and her knuckles turned white as she tightened the grip on her dessert fork.

Jeff tried to defuse the tension by keeping a calm, reasonable tone. "You're absolutely right about the millions of illegals who are already here. A wall won't help that situation. But look at it this way. Let's say that Michelle gets so mad at me for ruining dinner by discussing politics that she plunges a steak knife in my back as soon as y'all leave this evening.

"I manage to stagger into the emergency room, and when the nurses cut off my shirt to treat the knife wound, the ER doctor notices that I have skin cancer all over my back. He knows that the skin cancer will need to be removed eventually, but he also knows that I won't live long enough for the skin cancer to matter if he doesn't stop the heavy bleeding from the knife wound first.

"Thus, the wall is designed to stop the bleeding and stabilize the problem. What did you call them? 'Undocumented refugees'? Whatever term you want to use: undocumented refugees, illegal immigrants, displaced migrants, illegal aliens, or Mexican Swim

Team members, there are millions of them in our country right now. Before we can address the problem of illegals in our country, we need to keep the problem from getting worse. The wall will do that."

"But they'll just get over the wall or dig tunnels under it!" Laura snapped back.

"Yes, a few of them will." Jeff took a deep breath and glanced at Carl.

Carl just gave a little shrug, as if to say there was nothing he could do once Laura started down a path like this.

Maybe a little humor would help lighten things up. "But most will be deterred by the wall. And the ones who show enough brains and ingenuity and persistence to overcome the wall might just have what it takes to become great Americans one day."

"Why do you care so much about people coming across the border? They just want a better life for themselves and their families!" Laura's voice bordered on shrill now.

"One of the most basic elements of a nation is to have a border and to decide who may and who may not cross it. Yes, some of the people who illegally cross our border are basically good, hardworking people who are just trying to better themselves. But some of them are gang members, murderers, rapists, kidnappers, drug pushers, and terrorists. If we don't enforce the border, we don't get the chance to try to keep out the bad while letting in the good."

Jeff glanced at the doorway into the kitchen, wondering what Michelle was thinking. "We can use our system of *legal* immigration to allow the good folks in and weed out the bad. We don't need to ignore the border in order to accomplish that sorting process. In fact, we can accomplish all of the stated goals of the anti-border-enforcement crowd by simply adjusting our policies of *legal* immigration. For example, do businesses need more cheap labor to do the jobs Americans won't do? I don't think so, because

I think most Americans are willing to work at even the most physically demanding jobs in exchange for a decent wage. But if the voters decide that we need to import more cheap laborers, then we can increase the number of unskilled immigrants to whom we grant green cards."

"And I guess you'd just round up all fifteen million undocumented workers and deport them, huh?" Laura said sarcastically. "There's no way you could do that."

"Again, you're absolutely right. There's no practical way to deport everyone who is in our country illegally. But that doesn't mean that we should simply ignore the problem. My proposal is to be as aggressive as we can on deportations. If we deport five hundred thousand or so, another million or two million illegals will take note of this and voluntarily leave the country lest they too be deported.

"But the most effective way to deal with the issue," Jeff continued, hoping his words didn't sound too much like a lecture, "is to make it unprofitable for illegal immigrants to be in our country at all. No jobs for them. Let's actually enforce the existing laws against hiring illegals. Let's restrict them from buying houses or renting apartments. No welfare or food stamps. No Medicaid, Medicare, or Social Security. No public schools for their kids. No bank accounts, no wiring money, no credit cards, no use of the U.S. mail. And, of course, no voting in our elections."

Jeff added that last sentence to show what he thought was the real reason that Democrats were so hell-bent on allowing illegal immigrants into the country: they needed to create more Democratic voters and were willing to have non-citizens cast fraudulent ballots in order to win elections. He then summarized his point: "Once an illegal immigrant sees that he just can't function in our society, he'll leave on his own."

"You can't possibly be serious about this!" Laura shrieked. "You'd be harming the children who were brought here by their parents. The kids had no say in what their parents did."

"Once again, you're correct," he agreed. "There would be negative consequences for some children who are here illegally. But let's say I rob a bank and give the money to my kids. They were completely innocent of my crime. But should the kids get to keep the money I stole? I don't think so. They shouldn't be allowed to benefit from my criminal behavior. It's the same thing with illegal immigration. We shouldn't reward the bad behavior of the parents by letting them or their children get the benefits of our society.

"Look, illegal aliens sneak into our country with their kids, knowing full well that they are breaking our laws and that they might one day be sent back. They are taking that risk, hoping that we're too weak or too nice as a society to bother enforcing our laws. And I know that it makes you and a lot of other liberals *feeeeeel* good"—he dragged out the word for emphasis—"to allow illegal immigrants to break our laws and not pay the price for doing so. It's a sort of no-cost charity for you. You get to feel virtuous for helping others without paying any money or giving up anything of value in exchange.

"You see, liberalism in America today is mostly about virtue signaling and *feeeelings*. It's not about logic or thought or reason. Lefties see something they think is bad, then they form a mob and hold a march somewhere, even though the so-called march is usually just a group of middle-aged, upper-class white folks strolling down a city street or two wearing fun T-shirts that they had made for the occasion, before grabbing brunch. They sing some songs, chant some chants, wave some almost-clever signs.

"Then, and here's the really fun part, they post pictures of themselves at their cute little march on Facebook and Instagram so they can let all their friends know how good and moral and decent they are. The not-so-subtle message is, 'I went to the anti-racism or pro-illegal immigration or pro-abortion march today and you didn't. Therefore, I'm a better person than you.' What have they actually accomplished? Nothing.

"On the other hand, liberals who claim to be so deeply concerned about the plight of Mexicans could help in ways that don't involve ignoring our immigration laws. You could send money to the poor in Mexico. Or you could sponsor a poor Mexican family to come to the U.S. to live with you and pay all of their expenses until they assimilate and become independent. But that involves actually giving money and putting forth real effort, and it isn't as easy or as fun as marching in a parade sponsored by the Democrats and then posting pics on Facebook. The open-borders crowd is essentially asking the U.S. taxpayer to support whoever shows up in our country in order to make the left *feeeeel* good about itself, all at no cost to the ignorant leftists who don't think too much about the real-world consequences of their policy preferences."

Jeff knew he was pushing Laura over the edge. But she had initiated this argument, and he didn't want to stop making his points just to spare her feelings. Michelle was going to be angry with him anyway, so he might as well win the argument by a knockout. So he continued, "You might think, so what? Let some immigrants sneak across the border so I can feel good about myself. No harm done. But illegal immigration has a real cost to our taxpayers and to our society. Again, the open-borders crowd uses illegal immigration in order to *feeeeeel* good about themselves and show how *tolerant* and *diverse* and *inclusive* they are. But these liberals are using this policy to boost their own feelings and egos at the expense of American taxpayers and even more so at the expense of lower-wage workers."

Jeff noticed Carl perk up a bit at this point. Jeff wasn't sure if Carl was about to agree with him or lunge across the table and stab him with a fork for lecturing Laura, but he continued anyway.

"Leftists frequently whine about increased income inequality and stagnation of wages. But they don't seem to understand that illegal immigrants are one of the main causes of wage stagnation. American construction workers, factory workers, and other manual laborers can't get work at decent wages—or can't get work at all—in large part because illegal aliens will work for less than minimum wage and get paid off the books, meaning there's no Medicare or Social Security tax withheld from their wages. And the employers don't pay the other half of those taxes that they're supposed to pay in addition to withholding amounts. Liberals claim to care about the poor and lower-middle class, but their open-borders policy really hurts these folks by keeping their wages low and their job opportunities limited."

Carl was nodding vigorously now, much to Jeff's relief, and he spoke up for the first time in what seemed like an hour. "He's right, Laura. I see this in the carpentry and homebuilding industry every day, even though we're not exactly flooded with illegals in Vermont. I lose bids on jobs to people who hire illegals as cheap labor. They pay them five or six dollars an hour in cash, underbid me for the jobs, and still make a nice little profit for themselves even with the low bids."

Laura wasn't yet ready to acknowledge anything, even if her dullard husband was siding with this knuckle-dragging Southerner. She tried one more leftist talking point: "But we're a nation of immigrants! Immigrants helped build this country!"

"Yes," Jeff responded, as gently as possible, "but mostly legal immigrants, like at Ellis Island. Legal immigration is like learning a little about someone before inviting them into your home—like whether or not they, *ahem*, have any guns in the house. Everyone understands the rules, and there's some give-and-take involved. Certain

114

expectations are made clear: we'll let you into our country and give you the benefits of legal residence or citizenship if you meet certain qualifications and do certain things, like learn English, for example.

"On the other hand, illegal immigration is like someone breaking into your house and setting up secret residence in your attic. They steal food and loose change and your prescription drugs when you're not at home. I'll concede that some illegal aliens turn out to be valedictorians or engineers or CEOs. But at least as many turn out to be gang members or murderers or drug dealers.

"Many more of them just suck up welfare benefits and free public services without paying taxes or adding any benefits to American society. Note carefully: a nation can have a comprehensive welfare system like ours, or it can have a relatively open border, but you can't have both at the same time. The open border will soon attract the very type of people who simply want to leech off our generous welfare benefits and public services without ever assimilating into our society, learning English, paying taxes, etc. That's what Europe is learning the hard way right now with their vast numbers of unassimilated immigrants from the Middle East and North Africa. We've got to change course ourselves before our problems reach that stage.

"Again," Jeff said as a way of hopefully concluding this topic, "organized, systematic, legal immigration has a better chance of allowing in the type of hardworking, America-loving immigrants that we want, while keeping out the criminals and the welfare queens. No screening system is perfect, but an open border gives you no chance to even try."

"I'm not saying we should have an open border," Laura responded, really on the defensive now. "I just feel sorry for these folks, and I don't feel that we should demonize them."

"Laura, you've just made my point for me," he said. "You're trying to base public policy on your feelings. What does this mean in practice? What do we tell our border-patrol agents who put their lives on the line to guard our borders? Because Laura Irvin *feeeeels* sorry for the people sneaking across our border at night, carrying guns and drugs and who knows what else, we should kinda sorta enforce our border, but not try too hard? Perhaps we turn the first guy back at the border, let the second one go free, and give the third one cookies and milk and point him to the nearest welfare office and Democratic Party voter registration station?"

"Well," Laura huffed, tossing her napkin on the table as Michelle walked back into the dining room, "I guess we'll just have to agree to disagree." She then turned to the hostess and stood. "Michelle, thank you so much for a very, uh, interesting evening."

Carl was still chewing his last bite of strawberry pie, but he reluctantly rose to his feet when Laura cleared her throat to get his attention and then tugged urgently at his elbow. Jeff was excluded from Laura's minimally polite expression of gratitude, but that became the least of his worries when Michelle shot him an icy, what-have-you-done-now-to-offend-my-friends look across the table.

Jeff closed the front door as the Irvins drove away in their Toyota Prius. He was disappointed that it was too dark for him to count the number of bumper stickers on the car as it pulled away. He really dreaded facing his wife, who stood behind him in the foyer. Maybe turning on the charm would work as a defense mechanism. "Wow, honey, that was a blast!" he exclaimed with false enthusiasm and a fake smile.

Hands on hips, head cocked to one side, Michelle was trying to glare at him, but she couldn't help but smile as he walked over to hug her.

Jeff breathed a sigh of relief when he felt the tension go out of Michelle's body as she belatedly returned his hug. "So you're not mad at me?" he asked hopefully, still embracing her. "If you plan to kill me, you better do it before I get elected president and get Secret Service protection. Those cats don't play around."

"Not tonight. But I haven't decided to let you live past tomorrow yet, so don't push your luck."

They walked into the dining room together to start cleaning up the dessert dishes. Just when Jeff was feeling jubilant about not only winning the argument with Laura but also diffusing his wife's anger, Michelle spoke up. "I do have one suggestion for you, however."

Uh-oh. I knew I wasn't going to get off that easy. Quick, try to make her laugh again. "Don't invite Communist hipster libtards over for dinner when I'm in the midst of a campaign?" he guessed.

"No, I'm being serious. I listened to your discussion with Laura while I was in the kitchen. And, yes, I heard you try to change the subject, and that's why I'm not mad at you, even though I'm disappointed that Laura left here all riled up. But here's the thing: you did a great job of explaining your positions to her. You were calm and reasonable and thoughtful. Perhaps you should incorporate explanations like that into your speeches?"

Michelle knew he took great pride in his speeches, most of which he wrote himself, and so she almost never offered advice or criticism in that area. Fearing that she might have overstepped her bounds and wounded his pride, she rushed to provide her rationale. "You do a great job of stating your positions when you give a speech, but you don't really explain the why, the background, or the reasoning. You just move on to the next item that you support or oppose. For example, I knew all along that you supported a wall on the border, but until I heard your explanation to Laura, I didn't know why. It seemed a little over the top even to me, your biggest fan, until I heard your reasons. Don't you think the voters might feel the same way?"

Jeff's first inclination was to defend himself and his standard stump speech, which he had written and revised several times over the course of the campaign. He was proud of both the content and how well he delivered it. But he quickly realized that Michelle was right. Way back in the first campaign meeting with Williamson and Morgan, he'd pledged to be the reasonable conservative. He had promised to be the conservative who would communicate to the voters the rationale for his various positions. Perhaps out of a need to cram as many different policy positions as possible into a speech that had to be relatively brief, he had stripped out much of the underlying background for his views.

Now it was his turn to get over his initial feeling of anger and agree with his wife. "Honey, you're exactly right. I need to fix my stump speech. And I'm going to do so right now."

She beamed with pleasure as he headed for his office.

He pulled up the current version of his stump speech on the computer and started making revisions. It was a win-win. Michelle got the pleasure of helping out her husband's struggling campaign, and Jeff got an excuse to avoid doing the dishes.

Chapter 15

Powerlineblog.com Blog Post

December 2015

J eff Ackerman and his band of misfits resumed their seemingly hopeless campaign, returning to Iowa in early December.
Their batteries were recharged a bit after some time at home and
off the road. The short-term rental on the Extremely Low-Flying
Campaign Jet was renewed, but only for two months. Ackerman
couldn't afford to sustain his campaign any longer than that unless
a significant uptick in contributions happened. This would be the
last-ditch effort to move the polls enough in his direction to attract
some positive media buzz and national attention.

The candidate had taken to heart his wife's suggestion about his
stump speech. He'd discarded the old version that was crammed
full of positions on everything from tax policy to foreign affairs to
border control. His revised approach was to focus on no more than
three issues per appearance and to flesh out the ideas and rationale behind the positions. Rather than one canned standard stump
speech, which was the method employed by every other presidential candidate in recent history, he now had five-to-seven-minute
snippets on about a dozen different issues. He was comfortable

delivering each of these on demand and from memory. He would pull two or three of these arrows out of his quiver per appearance, selecting among them based on the type of audience or the headlines of the day.

Ackerman tended to follow the same pattern for each of these issues: "We've done this or that in the past. It hasn't worked because of reasons A, B, and C. When I'm elected, the Jeff Ackerman administration will do X, Y, and Z instead. X, Y, and Z are better because of these three attributes. Critics will say we shouldn't do X, Y, and Z because of this reason, but they are wrong because they refuse to acknowledge this fact. The result of actions like X, Y, and Z will be to improve the lives of Americans in this way, and our country will be better because of it."

The refined approach on the campaign trail seemed to be working, but only to a limited extent. Crowds at Ackerman's events were slightly bigger, but still not large enough or enthusiastic enough to be accurately labeled rallies. Those in attendance seemed more engaged, and heads nodded in agreement throughout the audience as Ackerman spoke about cutting taxes or reducing federal spending or rebuilding America's military. But he still received only polite applause, rather than enthusiastic cheers or chants.

The candidate was a good public speaker but not a great one. He tended to be calm, rational, and reasonable at the podium, like one parent talking to another just before the PTA meeting got started. Ackerman was the type of person who had people saying to their spouses in passing, "I talked to Jeff for a few minutes before the meeting tonight. He's a pretty sharp guy." But he wasn't dynamic, he wasn't physically imposing, he wasn't bombastic, and he wasn't particularly inspiring. In short, Jeff Ackerman wasn't the type of politician who could deliver a speech and move the emotional needle of his audience. He was getting better, and things were improving a little.

However, at this pace he would be out of money and, consequently, out of the race before the first votes were cast in the primaries.

The worn-out Greyhound bus hadn't improved during Ackerman's break from the campaign trail. In fact, the bus somehow managed to retain the odors of stale pizza and french fries that the campaign staff had worked hard to forget during their time away from campaigning. The drab physical conditions and the brutal Iowa winter quickly wiped out the fresh optimism of the campaign. The below-freezing temperatures and frequent snowstorms had them all wishing that global warming was a real phenomenon rather than pseudoscientific propaganda and a leftist power-grab.

As the bus wheezed down the interstate toward Des Moines, the always-spotty wi-fi connection strengthened a bit. Ackerman fiddled with his laptop, careful not to elbow his sleeping wife in the seat next to him. He clicked through his daily dose of conservative-leaning websites, seeing nothing particularly new or encouraging for his campaign. But then he visited the Powerline Blog, scanned the headlines, and saw the following:

THERE'S A CANDIDATE WITH REAL CONSERVATIVE ACCOMPLISHMENTS RUNNING FOR PRESIDENT, AND NO ONE SEEMS TO HAVE NOTICED

Ackerman held his breath as he read the post once quickly, and then again twice more after getting his breathing under control. He couldn't suppress a satisfied smile as he read it once more:

For some strange reason, the Republican Party has all but conceded the 2016 presidential election to Upton Landers. Landers is somewhat likeable but certainly not beloved. He's delivered the bare minimum in economic growth, and his recent tax increases are likely to trigger a recession. I recognize that it is never easy to defeat an incumbent president who has been relatively free of major scandals, but the Republicans don't seem inclined to even give it the old college try.

Senator Olivia Hollister is the overwhelming frontrunner for the Republican nomination, but only because no other nationally known Republican has found the courage to throw his hat into the ring. The Republican establishment has evidently decided to keep its powder dry until the 2020 election and let Hollister take a bullet for the team. Hollister is a Republican that only a Democrat could love, and many Democrats do (at least until she runs against an actual Democrat, at which point she'll be painted as a Hitler-like monster who hates children, immigrants, and family pets).

But there's a real conservative alternative to Senator Hollister who has the backbone and intestinal fortitude to take on the centrist Hollister and, if he can prevail over her, the left-of-center President Landers. His name is Jeff Ackerman, and he's a former two-term governor of Mississippi. He's been touring Iowa on a run-down Greyhound bus that his staff has nicknamed the "Extremely Low-Flying Campaign Jet."

To call his campaign "bare bones" is an understatement, as he appears to have very little in the way of financial backing. His staff is very small. He has no campaign infrastructure to speak of in Iowa or New Hampshire. He's drawing small crowds at his events and hasn't been able to make a dent in the polls against Hollister. Ackerman is an average-looking guy and an average or slightly above-average speaker. So why should we pay attention? Because this unlikely candidate has delivered real results by implementing policies that Republicans have been touting for years.

Republicans love to talk about reducing the size of government, at least until they get elected and actually have the chance to do so. Once in office, however, they never seem to get around to scaling back government jobs or spending. But Jeff Ackerman has delivered. Mississippi had 82 counties when he took office, each with a full complement of county politicians, bureaucrats, and related support staff. Eighty-two school boards, sheriffs, coroners, and boards of supervisors is a lot of government for a state with a population of less than three million. Ackerman spearheaded a consolidation of the 82 counties in his state into seven. This eliminated over 1,000 *duplicative government jobs and saved Mississippi taxpayers over $50 million per year.*

Ackerman has also cut taxes and implemented a school-choice program. He's strongly pro-life. He has a solid, workable plan to deal with our illegal immigration problems. In short, this guy checks all of the conservative boxes and should, by all rights, be a superstar on the national stage. But the Republican establishment is asleep in a leather chair at the country club and can't be bothered to support a somewhat boring, strongly Christian white guy from a small state with a brutal racial history. However, if enough rank-and-file Republicans decide right now to support Jeff Ackerman with their money, time, and energy, his is the type of unlikely candidacy that can ride a new wave of conservative enthusiasm into the White House.

Wow. This was exactly what they needed to jump-start their campaign. Now, if only the rest of the conservative blogosphere would join in. Hoping against hope, he maneuvered his mouse to his *Favorites* tab and clicked on the link for the PunditryNow page. This site was mainly a collection of brief quotes from, and links to, longer stories published elsewhere on the internet. He scanned quickly down the page, and there it was: a PunditryNow link to the Powerline post about his candidacy. This link would draw the attention of hundreds of thousands of PunditryNow readers across the country, in addition to those who saw it on Powerline initially.

Ackerman knew he still wasn't on the radar of the national media, but at least his fellow conservative geeks on the internet had taken notice of him. He said a quick prayer of thanks, and then he reached across the aisle of the bus to wake up Art Morgan. The nearly computer-illiterate candidate and the completely computer-illiterate campaign manager needed to plot a strategy to take advantage of this new event in the blogosphere. They didn't have time to ponder the irony as they set aside their laptops, pulled out legal pads, and began to scribble out ideas.

Chapter 16

Corporate Headquarters of Harrington Farming Enterprises, Ltd. Des Moines, Iowa December 2015

The not-quite-gleaming, not-quite-plush headquarters of Harrington Farming Enterprises, Ltd. didn't quite blend into the surrounding landscape of cornfields and farmhouses on the outskirts of Des Moines, Iowa. But the office building didn't stand out as starkly as a casual observer would otherwise expect of the headquarters for one of the largest agricultural conglomerates in the world. Instead, it appeared as though the main office of a medium-sized insurance company or regional bank had parachuted into Iowa farm country.

The location, design, and style of the building served as a visual reminder of the delicate balance that Harold Hanson Harrington III attempted to maintain for the company he led. Harold was known as Hal to pretty much everyone. His grandfather founded the company, originally known as Harrington Farms, just after World War II by acquiring a large block of family farms. The company then followed the all-too-familiar arc of family businesses in America: the first generation founded the company, the second generation—Hal's father—nurtured and grew it, and the third generation—Hal himself—blew it up and sent it into bankruptcy.

Hal Harrington, like so many trust-fund kids, felt that he had to prove to the world that he knew better than his forbears how to run and grow a company. Not surprisingly, he ruined every aspect of the business he touched, leading to a disastrous bankruptcy during the U.S. farm crisis of the 1980s. But Hal then went off script. Rather than slinking off to Aspen or the South of France to live a life of leisure with his still-considerable millions of dollars that hadn't been lost with the company, Hal threw himself into rebuilding the family business.

His theory was simple: do the opposite of everything he had done previously that eventually bankrupted the company. His initial and largest mistake had been to erase the farming-related image of Harrington Farms. The old Hal wanted gold, glitz, and glamour in lieu of pastures, pigs, and pork bellies, so he'd changed the name from Harrington Farms to Harrington Enterprises and moved the headquarters from Iowa to New York. This new-but-not-really-improved Harrington Enterprises emphasized new lines of business that it entered into via a series of acquisitions: insurance, investment banking, and corporate consulting. Harrington Enterprises simultaneously de-emphasized all things farm-related.

After the crash, Hal pleaded with the board of directors for the chance to lead the company out of bankruptcy and rebuild it. The board reluctantly agreed, partly because Hal convinced them that he had learned his lesson but mainly because no one else seemed to want the job. So Hal again changed the company name, this time to Harrington Farming Enterprises, Ltd., and he sold the New York headquarters building for a nice profit.

He built the new, much more modest campus in Des Moines with half of the sale proceeds and used the other half to recapitalize the company. The idea was to proclaim to the business world that Harrington Farming was going back to its roots: Iowa, farming, modesty, simplicity, hard work. The relatively small size and modest décor of the headquarters building was intentional. Hal knew that anything lavish or over the top just wouldn't do here in Iowa.

To the surprise of all involved, including Hal himself, Harrington Farming was now a multibillion-dollar business with solid cash flow. Hal had reached the top due mainly to the accident of being born there, but he had real talent as well and had now earned the respect of both Wall Street and rural Iowa. Most people had forgotten—or at least forgiven—his initial failure with the company.

Although other lines of business—especially private equity and investment banking—accounted for the bulk of the profits, the company clung tightly to its farming image. The older, wiser Hal recognized that his firm's agricultural roots were much more of an asset with his farm-related customers than they were a liability with the financial community, who valued only financial results and didn't know or care about irrelevancies like corporate image.

Now that he had lost and regained his fortune and his business reputation, Hal Harrington sought to make his mark on the world at large. Harrington Farming Enterprises wasn't quite on autopilot, but it demanded less than half of his available time and energy. Hal began to cast about for his next challenge. He'd already donated hundreds of millions to charity, traveled to all of the sites he wanted to see, skied all the slopes that he wanted to ski, and played enough golf for several lifetimes.

Just as Hal was unique in his ability to rectify his early failures in business, he was also unique among the mega-rich in that he didn't crave any sort of fame, publicity, or other media recognition. He enjoyed wearing jeans and sweatshirts and eating breakfast at local cafés with real people. For this reason, he had long ago sworn that he wouldn't get involved in politics.

But then he'd caught a portion of a Jeff Ackerman speech while scouting a potential acquisition target in Ames. It struck Hal that he and Ackerman were similar in age, temperament, and political outlook, and Hal was impressed with the candidate but not his operation. This poor guy obviously had no financial backing whatsoever.

Wondering if he might be able to help his country by funding the Ackerman campaign, Hal had one of his many minions reach out to the Ackerman campaign staff, such as it was, to arrange today's meeting with the unlikely candidate at the Harrington corporate headquarters building. Knowing all too well that bored billionaire CEOs could be dangerous to themselves, their employees, and their shareholders, Hal promised himself that he wouldn't let his quest for personal fulfillment negatively impact the company. Mainly, he wanted to take the measure of Jeff Ackerman in person and decide whether this seemingly naïve Mississippian was worthy of Hal's backing.

Jeff Ackerman had agreed to meet with Hal Harrington in part because he was curious, but mostly because he didn't have anything else to do that morning. Ackerman knew enough about Harrington to know that the profitability of its agriculture division was contingent upon the continuation of the federal ethanol mandate. This program required that ethanol be included in gasoline with the goal of reducing pollution and boosting U.S. energy production. Corn was one of the main ingredients of ethanol, and Iowa farms produced massive amounts of corn, so Iowans were fully invested in maintaining the ethanol mandate. Presidential candidates who hoped to win the Iowa caucus—the first state primary of each presidential election cycle—had little choice but to support this program.

Promises made on the campaign trail for the Iowa caucuses were the main reason the unsuccessful program continued to exist.

But Jeff Ackerman was not the traditional presidential candidate, and he had bluntly opposed the ethanol mandate in several Iowa public forums. If there had been any serious media coverage of his campaign, the reporters would have declared that he had no chance in Iowa as a result of this stance. In any event, Ackerman expected this meeting to be a lobbying session in which Harrington attempted to change Ackerman's stance on the subject.

Art Morgan drove Ackerman to the Harrington Enterprises headquarters for the meeting. Morgan was a terrible driver, but it didn't seem proper for the candidate to drive himself, and Ackerman didn't want to bring along any other members of his staff. Morgan and Ackerman were ushered into the main conference room by a middle-aged staffer wearing blue jeans and a plain white dress shirt. No coat, no tie, and no word on what Mr. Harrington was doing or when he might arrive to begin the meeting.

Morgan was disappointed. He had expected to be greeted by the typical twenty-something-year-old female in high heels and a skirt that was about an inch short of appropriate. No such luck today. Just one more reason to hate Iowa.

The staffer took their coats and served them coffee in cheap-looking mugs while they awaited the arrival of Hal Harrington. But then the staff guy surprised them by pouring a cup of coffee for himself and taking a seat at the head of the extremely ordinary conference table. Only then did Ackerman and Morgan realize that this staffer wasn't a staffer at all. It was Hal Harrington himself.

Ackerman and Morgan each fought to hide their surprise while simultaneously wondering if Harrington had recognized their mistake. They had expected—and received—a polite, courteous welcome, but they also expected to be greeted by an underling and then forced to wait patiently for the arrival of a billionaire in a five-thousand-dollar bespoke suit. Instead, the billionaire was wearing thirty-dollar Levi's jeans and sipping bland coffee from a mug that probably came from the local Wal-Mart.

This meeting might be rather interesting after all, Ackerman thought once he convinced himself that Hal was unaware of his failure to recognize him.

However, Hal Harrington knew exactly what had just transpired. He'd used this maneuver several times before in order to put investment bankers, nosy reporters, and business adversaries off their game at the outset of a meeting. He maintained his poker face while mentally complementing the poker faces of Morgan and Ackerman. Each of them had been able to avoid glancing at the other when they simultaneously realized that they had mistaken one of the richest men in America for an administrative assistant or gofer. But Ackerman's eyes had widened noticeably and Morgan gave an involuntary twitch when Harrington took his seat at the head of the table, so Hal knew his ploy had worked.

After a few minutes of polite small talk, Hal initiated the substantive aspect of the meeting. "So, Governor Ackerman, can you tell me your position on the federal ethanol mandate?"

Well, this meeting might be a short one, Ackerman thought. "Certainly, but I'm afraid you won't like my views very much. I'm opposed to the ethanol mandate and think it should be abolished. The reason is simple: like so many other government programs, it doesn't work. Not only does it fail to accomplish its objective, it actually makes the problems it was designed to solve worse rather than better."

Ackerman paused at this point to give Harrington a chance to kick him out of his building.

Instead, with an earnest expression and polite tone, Hal said, "Very interesting. Can you expound on that for me?"

"Sure. As you know, Mr. Harrington, the ethanol mandate was designed to do two things: one, decrease carbon emissions from vehicle engines, and two, decrease the cost of gasoline. Ethanol fails on the first count even though gasoline with ethanol added does in fact reduce carbon emissions. But this ignores the carbon emissions that are produced by growing the corn needed for the ethanol and then manufacturing the ethanol. Once those factors are considered, the ethanol mandate increases, rather than decreases, carbon emissions. Thus, ethanol makes the first problem it was designed to solve worse, rather than better.

"The ethanol mandate has also failed to make gasoline more affordable. At the time it was enacted, the price of corn was historically low and the price of oil, and therefore gasoline, was historically high. But those conditions have reversed themselves, with corn costing more and oil and gas costing less. Rather than watering down expensive gasoline with cheap corn-based ethanol, we now water down cheap gasoline with expensive corn-based ethanol and accomplish nothing other than adding about fifteen cents per gallon to the cost of gasoline at the pump. Thus, the environment is harmed, and the American consumer is harmed, by the ethanol mandate. The only winners are corn producers, because the ethanol mandate inflates the price of corn significantly above what it would be otherwise."

"So," Hal interjected, "the only winners are people like me who profit from high corn prices. Don't you care about hardworking Iowa corn farmers?"

Ackerman waited for Hal to smile or otherwise show that he wasn't as dissatisfied with Jeff's answer as his words indicated. But no such softener was in the offing.

Ackerman sat a little straighter in his flimsy office chair. "Of course I care about hardworking Iowa corn farmers. But I also care about hardworking cotton farmers in Mississippi and hardworking orange growers in California and hardworking dairy farmers in Pennsylvania, all of whom have to pay more money for the fuel they need as a result of the ethanol mandate.

"I also care about truckers and commercial fishermen and barge operators and pilots and moms who drive their kids to school. They all pay more than they should for fuel because the federal government, while trying to accomplish a worthy objective, failed to do so. It's time to admit that failure and eliminate the ethanol mandate."

Art Morgan had wanted to weigh in on this key issue and finesse the answer before his client bluntly slammed the door in the face of their host. But he knew it was too late now. Morgan hadn't expected much benefit from this meeting but had held out a slim hope that Harrington might toss at least a few coins into Jeff Ackerman's ever-dwindling campaign coffers. The chance of that happening was now approximately zero, as Ackerman and Harrington engaged in a silent staring contest with each other across the table. Morgan reached down to pick up his ancient and long-out-of-style briefcase, certain that he and Jeff were about to be politely invited to leave the premises.

After what seemed like a very long time but what was in actuality about ten seconds, Hal Harrington broke into a grin for the first time since the meeting began. "Congratulations, gentlemen. You passed the test. Most candidates and campaign managers in your seats would tell me whatever it is they thought I wanted to hear in order to induce me to open up my wallet for them."

"Uh, well, you see, Mr. Harrington," Art Morgan said, speaking up for the first time in his best aw-shucks Mississippi drawl that he could turn on or off at will, "we can do unique things like tell the truth because our sad little operation barely qualifies as a political campaign. We've got no money, no media coverage, and precious few voters on our side. Hell, at this point we're more like a bunch of carnies with a third-rate traveling state fair than we are a presidential campaign. Why not be blunt and plain spoken? No one's really listening anyway."

Harrington grinned again, warming up to his guests. "Ahh, I'm not sure that that's true. And call me Hal, by the way. We're all friends here. Now, tell me what your internal polling is showing about the primary race here in Iowa."

"We don't have any internal polling," Ackerman said frankly. "We can't afford it, and to be honest, I don't see the value in it unless and until we get to the point where the race is really close. We don't need a pollster to tell us that we're running well behind Senator Hollister.

"If the race ever tightens, and if we get the cash we need, we can use polling to fine-tune our message as appropriate. But we decided at the outset of this little venture"—Ackerman winced internally at the memory of his wife's use of this same phrase several long months ago—"that our basic platform wouldn't change based on polling. And we definitely don't want to take any positions in the primaries that will hurt us in the general election. The goal is to win the presidency with a mandate for conservative principles."

Harrington nodded. "Gentlemen, it might surprise you to know that I commissioned my own private tracking poll here in Iowa."

The Mississippians were, in fact, surprised. They both knew that rich people spent money on unusual things, but neither had ever heard of a wealthy businessman, with seemingly no interest in politics, hiring a polling outfit for political information that was readily available for free in the press. Morgan and Ackerman each wanted the details on this tracking poll but were too polite to ask. They simply waited to see if Harrington would elaborate, which he did.

"As you can probably guess, Governor, you started out way behind

Senator Hollister at the outset of your campaign. No one here in Iowa had ever heard of you. The fact that you're from Mississippi didn't help. And, frankly, the announcement of your candidacy was pretty much a disaster."

Ackerman nodded, trying not to let his face show his embarrassment. He waited for Harrington to continue, hoping the news would improve.

"But your numbers have spiked up recently, and you're now running only slightly behind Senator Hollister. You're definitely within striking distance, something like five percentage points behind and closing fast. That Powerline Blog post was a big topic of conversation on Facebook and on email distribution lists throughout the state, and that clearly gave you a boost."

He looked from Morgan to Ackerman. "And something else is helping you. Folks here have noticed a different approach in your speeches: fewer issues being addressed per speech but more explanations for the positions you take on the issues that you do raise. Iowans are mostly conservative, and they already agreed with your positions for the most part. But your change in approach seems to have helped them connect with you on a personal level. They feel like they're getting to know you as a person, and they like what they see. My guess is that Senator Hollister is also drawing these same conclusions, and I think she'll be spending more time in the state in order to blunt your surge.

"I figured your campaign could use a dose of good news, so I thought I'd pass that along to you. But that's not why I invited you here today. I follow politics but don't consider myself political. To be honest, I don't put much hope or faith in politicians to do anything beneficial for the country. I mainly just hope and pray that the damage they do will be minimal. But when a man of a certain character type reaches my stage in life, he starts thinking about his legacy, hoping to make a positive impact on the world around him. Not for any type of personal glory or fame. We just want to do the right thing.

"Governor, you strike me as the same sort of man. And you seem like a different sort of candidate—blunt but not rude, willing to set big goals without being pretentious or unrealistic. I wanted to meet with you to see if my initial read on you was correct. Your campaign literature says that, as governor, you accomplished education reform in Mississippi. If you don't mind, tell me more about those reforms that you pushed through."

"I'd be happy to, Hal," Ackerman replied, flattered that this billionaire thought well of him and excited about the news of his improved standing in the polls. "And you can call me Jeff, by the way. Education reform in Mississippi is one of my proudest accomplishments. As you and way too many other people know, Mississippi ranks last or next-to-last in a lot of important categories, especially in the education arena. When my team and I came into office, we did a thorough but quiet study in an effort to figure out why. We determined that our public schools, from kindergarten through high school, said all of the right things but then did mostly the wrong things.

"It soon became apparent to us that public schools in Mississippi weren't run for the benefit of the students. They weren't even run for the benefit of the parents of the students or for the benefit of the taxpayers. And at this point, you might think they were run with the best interests of the teachers. But that wasn't the case either. Instead, almost every school district seemed to be run primarily for the benefit of the administrators and other non-teaching employees of the school district: the superintendents, principals and assistant principals, the counselors, the coaches, the school board members, and all of their various administrative assistants and other apparatchiks. In fact, we found that Mississippi public schools were employing about as many non-teachers as teachers, and most of these non-teachers have little or no impact on what happens in the classroom. But they have a big impact on the budget, and that impact gets larger every year.

"We knew that my administration had to do something to improve the schools and that nibbling around the edges wouldn't cut it. But we also knew that the state didn't have any extra money to throw at the problem. We'd already determined the source of the problems wasn't a lack of money, because per-pupil education spending in the state has been increasing—even on an inflation-adjusted basis—over the past twenty-five years. But even with that increased spending, test scores for reading, math, and science were flat at best and in some cases trending down. This caused us to look into *how* our government was spending taxpayer education dollars, as opposed to *how many* dollars we were spending. We quickly realized that we weren't spending more for teachers, because teacher salaries were flat over that time period.

"That's when we noticed a big increase in the number of administrators and other non-teaching positions throughout the school system. Our state had thousands of people working in public education, getting paid with taxpayer money, who had nothing to do with helping kids learn. It was a classic example of a bureaucracy taking over an institution and running it for the benefit of the bureaucracy: the bureaucrats got nice raises every year while teachers remained underpaid and school buildings crumbled. Teaching posts were being cut back, but additional secretaries were being hired for the superintendents.

"At this point, we knew we could eliminate thousands of non-teaching jobs and save millions of dollars. My team decided on a pretty radical approach: we fired everyone who couldn't clearly and convincingly demonstrate, in thirty seconds or less, that the work they were doing had a direct, positive impact on helping kids learn. But what would we do with that money? How could we use it in such a way that our students started learning more?

"That caused us to examine the types of incentives we had in place for teachers. We quickly found out that there were no such incentives. In Mississippi at that time, and I imagine in most other states to this day, teachers were on a lockstep compensation system in which salary and benefits were determined solely by the number of years of employment. Thus, an ineffective teacher with ten years of experience made much more money than a superstar teacher with three years of experience. The only monetary incentive was to do just enough work to keep your job; you certainly weren't going to get paid more money to put in the extra work necessary to be great at your career by helping kids learn more.

"We understood that there was a small core of teachers around the state who wanted to be great teachers regardless of pay, and that these teachers worked very hard to be the best they could be. But these kind souls were very much the exception to the rule. The rest of the teachers were simply collecting a paycheck and counting down the days until summer vacation. It didn't take us long to conclude that school systems are not immune to a very basic rule of our economy: the talent goes where the money is. The slacker teachers had no other job options, either because they weren't very bright or because they weren't willing to work hard. Or both.

"Therefore, my administration needed to find a way to bring smart, talented people into the teaching field, especially at the high school level. We wanted engineers and chemists teaching math and science. We wanted novelists and newspaper editors teaching writing and literature classes. We had to find a way to attract those folks to take teaching jobs in the public schools.

"My team took three steps to do this: first, we used the money that had been freed up by eliminating non-teaching positions to substantially increase the pool of funds available for teacher salaries. Second, we eliminated the lockstep compensation system for teachers and allowed school principals to decide, on a teacher-by-teacher basis, how much money each teacher would make. Third, we implemented a school-choice system in which any Mississippi resident could attend any public school in the state, and we tied school funding to student population.

"It was a massive set of changes, and numerous political oxen were gored. A lot of band directors, choir leaders, and defensive line coaches lost their jobs and weren't happy about it. Many said that such radical changes were too risky. But we responded that our state had little to lose: our kids were already behind the rest of the country, and we truly believed that we had nowhere to go but up.

"Fortunately, the changes are working well so far. We don't have enough data to make long-term measurements yet, but test scores are up in reading and math. Drop-out rates, discipline issues, and teen pregnancies are down. Although it's hard to measure accurately, parent involvement seems to be higher. We've got hundreds of professionals from other fields who are now teaching Mississippi's next generation of doctors, lawyers, and engineers, and these new teachers are getting rave reviews. The dead-weight teachers have been mostly weeded out. The star teachers who have been working for peanuts are now making a competitive salary, with the chance to make even more money going forward. In short, Mississippi is already climbing the charts of the state rankings in education, and we think the groundwork is in place for us to go all the way to the top.

"We also think that this educational leap forward will bring real improvement in the business climate, because, with better schools, firms are now more willing to locate new plants and offices in

Mississippi. More business and economic development will move us up the various state rankings even further and have additional positive ripple effects across the state."

Jeff Ackerman paused to take a sip of coffee and noticed that Hal Harrington was staring at him in amazement. He waited for Harrington to speak, and he finally did so while shaking his head.

"This is amazing. You're telling me that you cut bureaucracy, increased teacher pay, and provided kids and their parents with school choice, all without increasing government spending? And that these changes have produced good results thus far with the opportunity for great results down the road?"

"That's correct."

"Why am I just now hearing the details about this?" Harrington asked. "This should have been front-page news all over the country."

"Great question," Ackerman said, "and if you find the answer, please let me know. The Mississippi media is as left-wing as the national media as a whole, and they were very much against all of these initiatives, especially merit pay for teachers. So they ran a lot of editorials in opposition but then went radio silent when it became apparent that the changes were working. Then they cherry-picked a few negative examples of kids who didn't benefit from our changes and wrote about those without giving any sense of the overall improvement.

"As far as the national media goes, I have two alternative theories. One, they didn't notice because it's just a bunch of hicks down in Mississippi and no one cares about them anyway. Or, two, they didn't want to write about it because they didn't want to give other states any ideas about what's possible when it comes to conservative education reform."

Hal leaned forward in his seat and looked at his guests. "Gentlemen, this is very impressive. I don't usually get involved in politics because I don't trust many politicians to do the right thing for the country. But I think we're drifting aimlessly as a nation these days, and I think a Jeff Ackerman presidency is what we need. Therefore, I'm willing to fund your campaign."

"Well, we certainly thank you for that, Hal," Art Morgan replied on behalf of his client. "You can make a donation via our website at www.ackermanforpresident.com. The individual limit is two thousand dollars, as you probably know, and we'd love to have your full support."

Hal eyed him. "Sorry, Art, but I don't think I made myself clear."

"Oh, you're definitely not obligated to give the full two thousand at once," Morgan said quickly. "If you want to start smaller and work your way up to the two-thousand-dollar limit, that's fine with us. We'll take whatever we can get."

"No, no," Hal replied with a smile. "I said that I'll fund your campaign. And I don't think two thousand dollars is going to get it done. I was thinking more along the lines of two hundred and fifty million dollars. Fifty million for the primaries now, and another two hundred million for the general election later."

Morgan was stunned, and Ackerman nearly choked on a mouthful of bad coffee. This was easily enough money to fully fund the primary contest against Hollister and then the general election against Landers.

The candidate was the first to recover from the shock. "Uh, Hal, I don't really know what to say," Jeff Ackerman said to his new best friend. "Obviously, that's incredibly generous. I'm both flattered and honored. Please don't take this the wrong way, and I don't mean to sound ungrateful or naïve, but would such a big donation be legal?"

"Oh, no worries on that front." Harrington gave a dismissive wave. "We'll do it through political-action committees, bundling, and the like. I've got a team of lawyers that's always looking for new and creative ways to charge me exorbitant legal fees. I'll have them make sure all of this is fully above-board, with all I's dotted, all T's crossed, and all smell tests passed with flying colors.

"I know it may make you a little nervous, but keep in mind that the left has George Soros and several others like him funneling hundreds of millions of dollars to their candidates. There's no reason why I can't do the same for you. Of course, you'll want to have your campaign finance director and your own legal team look over the arrangements to be sure that you're comfortable with everything."

The Ackerman campaign had neither a finance director nor a legal team, but with two hundred and fifty million dollars at stake, they could certainly obtain both in very short order. Morgan was ready to take *yes* for an answer immediately. He wanted to grab his client and get out of the building before Ackerman screwed things up by asking too many questions or saying the wrong thing, thereby causing Harrington to come to his senses and pull his gift off the table.

But Jeff Ackerman was determined to nail down a few other details. "That sounds great, Hal. Please send us the details and we'll get our finance people to take a look at what you propose." He kicked Morgan under the table to keep him from muttering *What finance people?* "Just one more thing, and I hope this doesn't offend you. But we have to be very clear on this: even for a donation of this magnitude, there can be no quid pro quo. For that matter, *because* of the size of this gift, we have to be even more sure than normal that there's not even a hint of a kickback or policy change in your favor or at your behest. I know you're not expecting to be my vice president." He hoped he was correct on this assumption. Who knows. Maybe this guy thought he could buy his way onto the ticket. "Just keep in mind that I won't even be able to appoint you as the ambassador to Burma without the press going nuts. And, as I'm sure you appreciate, I can't change my view on the ethanol subsidy."

There goes the two hundred and fifty million, Morgan thought. *Oh*

141

well. It was fun while it lasted.

But Harrington was nodding along. "I understand completely. In fact, if I thought you'd change your position, on ethanol or anything else, I wouldn't be offering you the money. Believe it or not, even though it will cost me money in the short term, I agree with you in principle on the ethanol thing. It's a bad policy for everyone except a few hundred corn farmers. It'll hurt those farmers some. But it's time to rip that Band-Aid off and move on before we get even more addicted to the subsidy. Besides, agricultural policy is just a small part of a much bigger picture. I think you're the type of candidate that Iowans and the rest of the country can rally around from a cultural perspective.

"And don't worry. I won't call you up in the middle of the night and ask you to have the IRS audit a business rival or demand that you nuke Argentina in order to boost commodity prices. As you can probably tell from the way I'm dressed, not to mention my crazy offer to give two hundred and fifty million dollars to a huge political underdog from Mississippi, I'm a bit of an oddball. I really don't want anything other than what's good for the country. And it just so happens that I think you'll be good for the country." He stood up to indicate that the meeting was over.

Morgan and Ackerman eagerly got up and shook hands with their new benefactor before moving toward the door. Morgan couldn't resist a parting quip. "Don't listen to this guy fretting about the details, Hal. He's always been a worrier. Hell, for an extra one hundred million dollars, we'll put your corporate logo on *Air Force One* and re-name the Lincoln Bedroom in your honor."

Jeff Ackerman barely heard his campaign manager's remark. He was already thinking about what fifty million dollars could do for his primary race against Olivia Hollister. And he was smiling. The unlikely candidate had just become a bit more likely.

Chapter 17

Media Conference Call

December 2015

R ichard Jordan dialed into the conference call seven minutes late—as usual. His outsized ego insisted that he force the media members to wait for him, even though he had already scheduled the call at ten p.m. Eastern time, well outside of the normal working day for all of the participants. It was a silly stunt on his part, and he guessed—correctly—that the reporters groused about it behind his back. But Jordan didn't care as long as they continued to dial in to these extremely confidential calls in order to receive their marching orders.

Marching orders might be a bit of an exaggeration, as Jordan knew that he couldn't dictate exactly what they wrote or what they said on their broadcasts. Even though they were all on the same team, this environment included unspoken rules. Jordan had to pretend that the reporters, columnists, and TV personalities who joined these invitation-only calls remained at least arguably independent, free to write or say whatever they wanted. The media members, in turn, pretended to be at least a bit skeptical of whatever party line Jordan trotted out that day and acted as if they would conduct their own independent inquiry into whatever assertions Jordan threw against the wall.

But all involved knew the media was far too lazy, and far too loyal to their liberal tribe, to do anything other than blast out Jordan's talking points as verified, factual news on the front page and as their own well-thought-out opinions on the editorial page. In fact, Jordan's spin was usually presented as more than mere news: it was the only acceptable view that fair-minded, enlightened people could reasonably hold. Any deviation was beyond the pale and not worthy of consideration. And probably racist and sexist to boot.

The reporters knew that failure to follow the implicit orders from the White House would result in loss of access to valuable sources of information. More importantly, Pulitzer Prizes, Emmy Awards, and invitations to the elite cocktail parties in Georgetown and Manhattan would stop flowing to any media member who strayed from the leftist plantation. Power and access to power were the coin of the realm, and cozying up to the likes of Upton Landers and his toady, Richard Jordan, was a price that the members of the nation's top media organizations were all too willing to pay.

Jordan immediately took control of the call. "Who's on the line?" he asked brusquely, not bothering to introduce himself, say hello, or even apologize for being late.

"Ken Stiedman here," announced an opinion columnist from the *New York Daily Ledger*.

"Dan Milton is on," chimed in the *Washington Chronicle* opinion writer, silently chagrined that the *Daily Ledger* had checked in before he did.

"Randy Graham is here. Good evening, everyone!" This news analyst and former staffer for a Democratic president couldn't conceal his glee at being near the center of power, even if it was over a phone line. He had never succeeded in shedding the image of being a happy, loyal puppy dog, eager to do the bidding of any Democratic politician who reached down to scratch him behind the ears, mainly because he didn't try all that hard to hide said eagerness.

Representatives from *Broadcast News International*, the *Los Angeles Tribune*, and a leading liberal blog followed suit in announcing their presence.

Austin Brant, the token conservative columnist at the *New York Daily Ledger*, had been puzzled when he received an email from a White House email address inviting him to join the call. The email obviously went to some sort of distribution list in the blind-copy field, thereby preventing the recipients from determining who else had received the email with the dial-in number and passcode for the call.

Brant hadn't planned on joining the conference call—he was an opinion columnist, not a straight news guy—and it wasn't his job to listen to the daily spin from either side of the political spectrum. But he was in the office working late anyway, trying to overcome a mild case of writer's block, when a calendar reminder for the call popped up on his computer screen. He decided that this call wasn't just some run-of-the-mill periodic update, as those took place during normal business hours. Even the folks in the Pacific time zone would have ended their normal working days an hour or two ago. Perhaps the email invitation had come to him automatically, like several other emails intended for his predecessor at the *Daily Ledger*.

In any event, he was bored and a bit intrigued, so he dialed in to the call, put his phone on the speaker setting, and muted his end so that other participants wouldn't be disturbed by the sound of him pecking away at his keyboard in a futile effort to get his next column done. He announced himself—or tried to—just as Richard Jordan began to speak.

"Okay, that's everyone," Jordan said. "As you all know, this conversation is off the record and not for attribution." He didn't wait for his guests to acknowledge this understanding before moving on to the substantive aspects of the call.

Austin Brant realized his phone had been on mute, preventing the other participants from hearing him introduce himself. At the last second, he decided to simply stay quiet rather than interrupt the chief of staff, who had by now launched into the substance of the call.

"I want to update you on the president's view of the disturbing developments in the Republican primary race. Public polling, as well as our internal polls, show that Jeff Ackerman is surging against Senator Olivia Hollister in both Iowa and New Hampshire. He hasn't overtaken her lead yet, but he'll likely do so soon. This concerns us. Please note carefully that we are very confident that President Landers would easily defeat Ackerman in the general election. But we're concerned about his recent jump in the polls because we think it signals something deeply wrong with the country as a whole if a right-wing religious extremist like Ackerman can get this far in a national political campaign. In short, Jeff Ackerman represents all that is dark about America. He and his ilk are best left in the past where they belong.

"Let me elaborate. Jeff Ackerman is a former governor of a small, backward, racist Southern state. While we have no evidence that Ackerman himself is racist, the mere fact that he was elected governor of Mississippi is reason enough to doubt that he holds acceptable, enlightened views on issues related to race and sex. We doubt that Ackerman has been properly vetted in this area by the national press, as no one pays attention to gubernatorial races in backwater states. Ackerman has, to say the least, been under the radar until now.

"Moreover, it appears that he's recently received massive amounts of money from shadowy right-wing donors and political-action committees. Like Ackerman, these funding sources have not been examined by the media. We fully expect the national press to promptly rectify this lack of information about the background of the potential Republican nominee. I won't pretend to tell you how to do your jobs, but let me suggest that you start with an analysis of Ackerman's top campaign staff, which is exclusively male and includes only one token African American."

No one had the guts to point out that each person on this conference call was a white male, and this irony was lost on Richard Jordan.

Greg Peterson of *Broadcast News International* couldn't wait to pose the first question. Peterson was tall with a full head of prematurely gray hair, which gave him an air of wisdom that belied the fact that he was only slightly smarter than an earthworm. "Does the White House have a preferred candidate in the Republican primary?"

Dear God, what a fool, thought Richard Jordan. Had they taken a poll, the other participants in the call would have provided a similar assessment of Peters' intelligence. "Of course not," the chief of staff responded rather rudely, not bothering to hide his disdain for the question or his irritation at being interrupted. "But the two leading candidates for the Republican nomination offer a rather stark contrast, both between themselves and certainly with President Landers.

"Senator Hollister, of course, is far too extreme to serve as president. She favors draconian cuts to important entitlement programs like Medicare. She apparently prefers to let senior citizens go without crucial healthcare services in order to save a few dollars."

With these words, Jordan confirmed the elite media expectation that the Democrats would give Olivia Hollister the "McCain treatment"[2] if she became the Republican nominee. Senator Hollister,

---

2   Senator John McCain was lionized by the mainstream media while seeking the Republican nomination for the 2008 presidential election. But the media and the rest of the Democrats had turned viciously on McCain when he actually became the Republican nominee. Once he had the temerity to oppose a Democrat in a national election, the media immediately began

like Senator John McCain before her, was every Democrat's favorite Republican. She and McCain were both "moderate" and "reasonable" and "responsible," at least until the general election rolled around. Clearly, Richard Jordan was urging the media to turn on Senator Hollister just as they had McCain in the event she held off Ackerman's challenge and won the Republican nomination.

"But as extremist and unqualified as Hollister is, she pales in comparison to this nut-job Jeff Ackerman," Jordan continued. "I've already pointed out his racist tendencies."

No one seemed to notice the subtle shift in Jordan's description of Ackerman, from possibly racist to his having "racist tendencies," whatever that meant.

"But it goes beyond his unenlightened views on race." Just like that, "racist tendencies" morphed into "unenlightened views." "This Ackerman guy is seeking to roll back progress on other fronts as well."

Again, Jordan employed familiar Democrat rhetoric. Any law or policy implemented by a Democratic administration was automatically deemed to be not only good and right and true and just, but also forward-thinking. It was inevitably portrayed as *progress* toward some vague, unstated goal. Any Republican attempt to restore the status quo was, therefore, "rolling back progress" or "turning back the clock" on some newly acquired entitlement of the American people.

"Ackerman opposes reproductive healthcare for women and has promised to appoint reactionary judges who would reduce women's control over their bodies. He advocates trickle-down economics

---

portraying McCain as an extremist—a conservative beast who must be slain in order to preserve the republic. The media was shameless with the speed and logical incoherence with which they flip-flopped on McCain, but, because they all did so, there were no dissenting voices in the national media to point out their hypocrisy.

and wants to give tax cuts to the rich, who are only now starting to pay their fair share under President Landers' enlightened economic program. I wouldn't be surprised if he's even more extreme than Hollister on cutting Medicare and Social Security benefits for seniors, as he likely shares the general Republican view that our entitlement problems can be solved if seniors would just hurry up and die."

Ackerman had not yet publicly addressed Medicare or Social Security, but this didn't prevent Jordan from slandering him with speculation about his policy positions or his motives.

"But the worst aspect of Jeff Ackerman is that all of these extreme views and positions appear to be driven by the fact that he's a fundamentalist Christian. He's an active member of an all-white, right-wing Southern Baptist church. Of course, he's free to worship as he chooses, but he should not be allowed to impose his religion on the country. America is not ready to become a theocracy."

Jordan couldn't see his audience, but he had a clear mental image of brows furrowing and frowns forming as he delivered his diatribe on Jeff Ackerman's Christian faith. The American media held Christianity in low esteem, and they held an even deeper contempt for Southern Baptists in particular than for Christians generally. As a bigoted, backward Baptist from a racist Southern state, Ackerman couldn't have been a more ideal opponent. Jordan had already fantasized about the coming landslide for Upton Landers against this halfwit. Landers might win forty-seven states.

Jordan sensed that his message had been received, but he wanted to be careful. He fully expected his media allies to kill off any chance of Jeff Ackerman winning the White House, but he didn't want this to happen just yet. His purpose would be better served if Ackerman and Hollister battered each other for a few more months, causing each one to bleed money and favorability ratings in the process. So he closed on a more conciliatory note. "With all of that being said, we live in a democracy, and Republicans must be left to choose their candidate without interference. The White House, of course, will not weigh in on the relative merits, if any, of one Republican candidate over another. All Americans, even those in the opposing political party, deserve a full, complete, and thorough process in which each candidate can be tested and vetted over a period of several months. The country deserves no less."

That should be a clear-enough signal to these serfs to hold their fire for now but to be ready with the heavy artillery if and when Ackerman wins the nomination, Jordan thought. He now sought to plant one final seed in the minds of the media. "It will be very interesting to see the extent to which Hollister and Ackerman push each other further and further to the right in an effort to win the nomination. We'll then all have some fun watching the eventual winner try to sneak back toward the center for the general election."

The call continued for another half hour, but the columnists and TV personalities already had their marching orders/story lines from Richard Jordan: raise some red flags about Ackerman and prepare the battlefield against him for the general election. Be ready to attack Ackerman as a racist, an extremist, and a fundamentalist Christian who is not ready for prime time. But don't administer the killing blow yet. Let him bleed for now with pin pricks on the left from the media and attacks from Hollister from the center. Finally, pounce on any arguably inconsistent position that the eventual Republican nominee took in the general election compared to what was said in the primaries, in order to smear him or her as a hypocrite.

Richard Jordan ended the call as curtly as he had begun it. The chief of staff was satisfied with a job well done, regretting only that he couldn't manipulate attractive women as easily as he could pull the strings of the national press.

What just happened here? wondered a slightly confused Austin Brant as he dropped off the conference call. He hadn't paid particularly close attention during the call, as he'd finally broken through his writer's block and made some progress on his column that was due to run in two days. But he had heard enough to realize that this wasn't a normal press briefing.

Jordan hadn't been conveying the types of facts and figures that were the subject of more-standard interactions between political staffers and the press. Also, the people on the line—those who had managed to successfully announce themselves, anyway—weren't the run-of-the-mill reporters who handled hard news. Instead, these folks were the opinion writers and broadcasters, those who took facts reported by others and then formed opinions based on them in an effort to have their readers, viewers, and listeners adopt said opinions as their own.

Brant had never heard of a conference call or group meeting among such a group before, and it dawned on him that he was the only conservative on the call. The other opinion-shapers on the line were unanimously left of center, some decidedly so. He resolved to pay much closer attention during any similar event in the future, and to refrain from announcing his presence on any such call.

Maybe I should figure out how to record a phone call, he thought as he put the finishing touches on his column.

Chapter 18

Ames, Iowa

January 2016

Jeff Ackerman took his customary seat near the front of the Extremely Low-Flying Campaign Jet. He closed his eyes, took a deep breath, and exhaled slowly. Not even the ever-present odor of stale fast food could dampen his spirits today.

He had just delivered an outstanding speech to his largest, most enthusiastic crowd to date. He was in Ames, Iowa, the home of the Iowa State University Cyclones, and his campaign rally had taken on the air of a Big 12 football game. The raucous applause, the home-made signs waved by the crowd, and the enthusiastic handshakes and hugs along the rope line after the speech sent what seemed like gallons of adrenaline surging through his body. Soon fatigue would hit him hard as the adrenaline rush subsided, leaving him feeling like a wrung-out dish rag. He waved Morgan and Williamson over to his seat, hoping to get in a quick strategy session while his energy level was still high.

"Great job, boss!" the ever-upbeat Scott Williamson exclaimed.

"Coulda been better," grumbled Art Morgan.

Ackerman grinned at both of them, knowing that Williamson's

assessment would have been positive and that Morgan's would have been negative no matter how well or how poorly the speech had gone. But this had been an excellent performance.

Hal Harrington had come through with his initial fifty-million-dollar contribution. The press had made a minor stir over the sudden influx of cash, but Harrington's attorneys had made sure that the donation fully complied with the vast labyrinth of campaign finance laws and regulations, and the issue had petered out after a few days. Ackerman resisted the urge to use his newfound campaign wealth to replace the ancient campaign bus with a leased jet, but he had hired some additional campaign staff and engaged some private pollsters. The latest polling data had just arrived by email, and he wanted to discuss it with Morgan and Williamson before taking a well-deserved nap as the bus chugged along toward Cedar Rapids.

Morgan took the window seat next to Ackerman, leaving the younger Williamson to kneel on one knee in the aisle so that each could look at the polling data on Ackerman's laptop screen. None of them thought of Ackerman simply forwarding it to the others so each could review it on his own laptop, as lack of sleep was having a negative impact throughout the campaign.

After making sure that his top two aides could see his screen, the candidate started scrolling through the report. All three of them honed in on the executive summary and then stopped to grin at each other. Without resorting to the usual qualifiers and other weasel words that usually permeated such documents, the summary stated clearly and concisely that Jeff Ackerman had taken a statistically significant lead over Olivia Hollister. This was true not only in Iowa, but also in New Hampshire as well as nationwide.

Conservatives had rallied behind Ackerman, which wasn't a huge surprise. But Republican moderates were now flocking to Ackerman as well. This data flew in the face of the received political wisdom that Hollister, who never saw an issue that couldn't be settled with a compromise, would easily capture the center of the Republican electorate. Ackerman led the senator 48 percent to 40 percent in Iowa, and he had pulled ahead 44 percent to 39 percent in New Hampshire, despite not having set foot in the Granite State. Nationally, likely Republican primary voters favored Ackerman over Hollister by a five-point margin, 45 percent to 40 percent. Each of these leads was in excess of the margin of error for the underlying poll.

Scott Williamson was about to suggest that they find some champagne somewhere along the route in order to celebrate, but Art Morgan spoke first. "Don't get cocky, Jeff," the veteran politico growled. "The media has held their fire on you thus far, hoping to let you and Senator Let's-Meet-Each-Other-Halfway beat each other up for a few months during the primaries. The media has pollsters just like we do, and they're seeing similar data. Now that it looks like you're pulling away in the race, you'll start to see some negative press. Nothing major just yet, but the media will do what they need to do in order to keep you and the wishy-washy woman neck and neck in the polls. We need to be on our toes now more than ever, ready to respond quickly to whatever hit pieces get thrown out there."

Williamson had never won an argument with Morgan, and he didn't want to start one now. He agreed with Morgan's assessment, but also felt that the candidate and the staff alike needed a brief bout of positive reinforcement in order to keep charging toward the finish line. Williamson was trying to formulate this in his mind when his phone began to blow up with both incoming calls and text messages. As he reached into his coat pocket for his phone, a murmur, then a buzz, then a roar erupted from the staffers seated in the rows behind him.

"Oh my God!"

"Get online and check the Hurst Record!"

"Are they all dead?"

"We've got to get a statement out!"

Even the slightly deaf Art Morgan noticed the commotion spreading through the bus. He caught the eye of Ackerman, in the seat next to him, and the two men simply shrugged at each other. Ackerman's phone was erupting now as he moved his mouse to the *Favorites* bar on his web browser and clicked the link for The Hurst Record.

The familiar red light was blinking at the top of the popular website, indicating an urgent, major news story. The headline blared out Hollister Campaign Jet Crashes; Candidate And All Aboard Feared Dead.

Jeff Ackerman sat in stunned silence for a few seconds, trying desperately to organize his thoughts and control his emotions. Ackerman was simultaneously saddened by the loss of life, elated at being the likely presidential nominee of the Republican Party, ashamed at such elation in light of the tragedy, and burdened with a great responsibility for his party and his country. He had to address his campaign staff quickly, as media outlets were already seeking comment on the tragedy from the Ackerman campaign. He needed to provide them with guidance and set the tone for how the campaign would respond.

Everyone seemed to be talking at once. The volume rose to a crescendo as the candidate stood slowly and took the microphone for the public address system on the rusting Greyhound. "Ladies and gentlemen, could I have your attention, please?"

The staff quickly fell silent, many of them trying to recall if the candidate had ever addressed them as a group on the bus in this manner.

Jeff Ackerman looked down the aisle at his wife and campaign staff as he began his talk. He spoke in a calm, measured voice in an effort to keep control of his emotions, consciously loosening his grip on the microphone in yet another effort to appear calmer than he actually felt. "We've all just received news of a terrible tragedy involving a worthy opponent and her campaign staff. Like you, I haven't had a chance to really process this event and sort out all of my thoughts and feelings. One of the platitudes we often hear in times like this is something like 'Our thoughts and prayers are with the families of the victims.'

"Folks, I don't want that to be just a platitude for us. I want us to actually pause for a moment and think about those who were killed. I want us all to pray for the spouses, children, parents, and friends who have just had a loved one torn out of their lives. I also want to *actually* pray for them, rather than just say that they are in our prayers. I'll do that right now. I'll pray aloud, and I invite you to join me in silent prayer if you'd like to do so."

Still standing in front of his staff, with the microphone raised to his lips, Jeff Ackerman bowed his head and closed his eyes. "Father, I acknowledge you as the King of the universe and the one true God. In this time of sadness and horror, I want to simply pause for a moment, to be still and know that You are God, that you created all things and that you control all things.

"First of all, God, we pray for everyone who was on that plane and ask that perhaps some survived the crash. We ask that you'll be with the firemen and ambulance crews and medical personnel involved, and that you give them skill and wisdom in how best to respond to this event and how best to help any of those who may have survived. We also pray for those who did not survive, and we urgently hope that they are in heaven with you now even as I speak.

"Lord, we certainly don't claim to understand why bad things happen, and we know that there are many loved ones left behind who are hurting and grieving and in shock right now. I ask that You'll provide them with a sense of peace that surpasses all understanding and that You'll blanket them with Your love, even though they are probably feeling very unloved right now.

"Father, I ask that You'll bless me and everyone on this bus as we respond to this tragedy and determine how to conduct ourselves going forward. Help us to convey our sorrow and respect in a sincere manner. Please give us wisdom and patience in our dealings with the media. Please let us be a source of comfort to the families who have lost loved ones.

"Lord, You know that I want to serve this great nation as president. But You also know that neither I nor anyone on this bus wanted to obtain the nomination like this. Father, I'm struggling to think of an historical precedent to follow or to draw on, but I've got nothing. My first reaction is that life goes on and that we need to continue with our efforts to win the presidency, but that feels small-minded and selfish in light of this horrific event. Whatever we do, Lord, help us to act in a way that is pleasing to You and that brings You praise, honor, and glory. All these things I ask and pray in the matchless name of Your Son, Jesus. Amen."

Ackerman sat down and motioned for Williamson and Morgan to stay near him at the front of the bus. Each of them was eager to weigh in with advice, but Ackerman began issuing instructions that quickly showed them that his thought process was far ahead of theirs at this point.

"First item: let's get a statement out to the press. Be respectful and sincere. Try to avoid clichés to the extent possible. Convey the message that Senator Hollister and the others involved in the crash, as well as their families and friends, are in our thoughts and prayers, but find a better way to phrase it. She was a worthy opponent and a great public servant. We were looking forward to a contest of ideas and to debating her on policy, not personal, grounds. Let the country know that, while our campaign might benefit from this horrible event, we certainly didn't want to win the nomination this way. Second, we're going to suspend our campaign for a couple of days."

"How will anyone be able to tell?" grumbled Art Morgan, who had unsuccessfully advocated a massive increase in the number of campaign events since Hal Harrington's donation had arrived.

"Here's where we need to be careful," Ackerman continued, ignoring the comment. "A Democrat in our position would jump on an opportunity like this and not waste a day that could otherwise be spent chasing votes. The typical limp-wristed Republican, on the other hand, would go too far in the opposite direction out of fear of criticism from the press. McCain, for example, suspended his campaign for no good reason when the financial crash hit in 2008. He was leading at the time but promptly lost his lead and never recovered. So, we'll stand down for two or three days, tops. We need some time to regroup and recharge anyway. After that, we come out with guns blazing on Landers.

"Third, we all know that the Republican establishment isn't exactly on board with my candidacy. They'd rather run a squishy moderate and lose than run a true conservative like me and win. They have no appetite for defending someone like me, who they view as a loose cannon at best, against major left-leaning news outlets like the *New York Daily Ledger*, the *Washington Chronicle*, and the *International News Network* for the next four to eight years. Therefore, they'll encourage some dried-up old war horse to pick up the moderate mantle and run in Hollister's place. We'll start to hear rumblings about some Bob Dole clone throwing his hat in the ring sooner rather than later, and we need to be ready for it. It shouldn't matter too much in the long run, because we can just run the same race against the new guy that we were using to defeat Hollister.

"Fourth, the media onslaught against us will begin today. Art, you were right earlier when you said that they'd been holding their fire thus far. They have no reason to do so now that I'm essentially the only Republican candidate in the race. They'll use Hollister's death, and our response to it, as their initial hammer. No matter what we do or say, it will be portrayed as insufficiently respectful to Hollister and her family. Editorials will lament the fact that fate has handed the Republican nomination to a racist, extremist conservative from a poor Southern state.

"This is where we'll really differentiate ourselves from other Republican campaigns. We'll go on offense, not play defense. We're not wasting time whining about a biased media. Everyone knows it to be true by now. Instead, we point and laugh at the press while we take our message directly to the people. Landers is Opponent Number 1, but the media is Opponent Number 1A. We'll ridicule them for their leftist leanings, question the premise of every leading question, and mock them at campaign rallies.

"On a related note, the press will search diligently for a way to portray our campaign as an unworthy beneficiary of a tragedy. They'll jump on anything that even remotely looks like we're happy about the plane crash. I want the two of you to make it crystal clear to the entire staff, especially the youngsters, that nothing like that will be tolerated or forgiven. This applies not just to dealings with the press. Let them know that social media, phone calls, texts with friends and family, personal emails, and any other form of communication will be nothing short of respectful and sincere, unless they want to get fired right away.

"Fifth, never underestimate the ability of Republicans to form a circular firing squad. Everyone will be greatly saddened by Senator

Hollister's death, and they'll want to show their remorse in a tangible way. I wouldn't be surprised if some sort of 'Vote for Hollister Anyway' movement springs up among her loyalists, and the press will definitely encourage this. While I was willing to risk losing to Hollister in the primaries before today, I definitely don't want to be the guy who loses an election to a deceased candidate. Start thinking about how to gently nip something like this in the bud before it kicks us in the teeth.

"Finally, we need to reach out to Senator Hollister's family. I want to call them personally and convey my condolences, and then we'll need to follow up with handwritten notes and flowers from me and Michelle. Attending her funeral—or not—is a no-win situation. If I go, then I get criticized by the press for political grandstanding. If I don't go, then I'm criticized for being disrespectful and heartless. I want to let the Hollister family know that I'll follow their wishes on this point. I'll attend the funeral or stay away, whatever they want. We'll leak to the media what the family wants so that we can, hopefully, avoid a round of negative editorials hitting me on this issue. Anything else, gentlemen?"

Morgan and Williamson shook their heads, each somewhat in awe of their boss's ability to absorb such a surprising event and formulate a political strategy in light of it with such quickness and clarity. They each respected Ackerman a great deal for his personal integrity and policy positions, but neither Morgan nor Williamson viewed Ackerman as much of a political strategist. Until now, anyway.

The two senior staffers stood up to end the meeting and get started on Ackerman's directives. The candidate, meanwhile, reclined his seat, closed his eyes, and said a silent prayer.

Lord, I won't pretend that I understand this event or why it happened, but it looks like I'll be the Republican nominee for president of the United States. I wanted to win the primaries, and I want to win the general election, but I feel so unworthy. Please help me to earn the trust of the American people, and please let me avoid saying or doing anything that makes people think less of You or less of Christians in general. My family and I are about to be subjected to severe and unfair criticism, in part because I believe You exist and that You created the universe. I pray for strength, wisdom, patience, grace, and endurance. And I pray that no matter what else happens, You'll be glorified as a result. Amen.

Chapter 19

The White House
January 2016

G retchen Lewis was the last to arrive for the campaign strategy meeting in the Oval Office. Although she was technically only about a minute late, it was bad form to keep the president waiting for even a second. Unfortunately for her, President Upton Landers was uncharacteristically prompt for this meeting. Her tardiness would have been easily overlooked a year ago, when she was still sleeping with the president, but not so much today now that she had been—she assumed—traded in for a newer model.

Lewis was more than the president's former mistress. She was his campaign manager for the 2016 election, and this should have been her meeting to run, not Richard Jordan's. Jordan was clearly infringing on her turf, but he had the president's ear these days. Because Gretchen Lewis had neither the president's ear nor any other part of his anatomy any longer, she'd meekly agreed to come to the White House when Jordan summoned her.

As she rushed into the Oval Office, she was flustered to see President Landers already seated behind his desk, with Chief of Staff Richard Jordan and Political Director Chloe MacKenzie occupying the only two guest chairs opposite the boss. Neither Jordan nor Landers bothered to so much as look up when she arrived, much less offer her a chair, so Gretchen was forced to set her briefcase on a wing-back chair across the room and awkwardly drag the chair toward the desk—not the easiest task for one wearing high heels and a short skirt that barely fit her seven pounds ago and was now stretched to the limit.

Landers wondered if Lewis and MacKenzie knew about his dalliances with the other. He got a partial confirmation when a smirk briefly appear on the youthful, wrinkle-free face of Chloe MacKenzie. She was enjoying her predecessor's discomfort way too much, as the forty-eight-year-old Gretchen Lewis huffed and puffed her way across the room, struggling to get the chair into a position from which she could feel a part of the gathering.

Landers derived a strange sense of excitement from having his former mistress sitting three feet away from his current mistress, with both of them in a clearly subordinate position across the big oaken desk from him. Most men would be at least somewhat uncomfortable in such a situation, but then most men had at least some sense of honor and decency. Landers had abandoned quaint notions like those long ago in his quest for power, and he'd found that he didn't miss them all that much now that he'd obtained the presidency. He had once worried—briefly—that unburdening himself of his sense of shame might have negative long-term consequences. Now he smiled a sardonic smile as he realized that doing so had actually helped him achieve his goal of winning the White House, and would help him even more in winning a second term.

Landers glanced up from the papers on his desk, curious to see if his prior evaluation of Lewis's appearance was still valid. This provided sufficient confirmation that Gretchen Lewis was, in fact, well past her prime. Her face should have retained at least some traces of her former beauty but did not, as if she had waited a year too late to quit drinking, or two years too late to quit smoking.

Richard Jordan now made a big show of checking his watch, with the dual purpose of showing off his twenty-thousand-dollar Rolex and hammering home the fact that it was past time to begin the meeting. "Well, I guess we can finally get started," he announced, not bothering to hide his exasperation with the delay.

Chloe MacKenzie smirked again.

Gretchen Lewis mumbled an apology for being late.

President Landers just gave a quick flick of his wrist, as if to say *Let's get on with it.*

"As you know, we're here today to discuss the seismic shift in the Republican electoral landscape following the death of Senator Hollister," Jordan began. "First off, we need to issue a statement about the event. 'Our thoughts and prayers are with the senator's family and the families of the other victims, blah blah blah.' Then—"

"Do we have to include a reference to *prayers?*" To Jordan's surprise, the president interrupted him. "No one's actually going to stop and pray to the so-called God who just let the airplane fall out of the sky and ask that same God to comfort the families of the people that He just sent to their deaths."

The three staffers exchanged a quick look among themselves. Each of them disagreed with the boss here, if only for political, rather than theological, reasons. But no one was eager to contradict the president, who seemed more irritable than usual today.

Finally, Jordan gave Chloe a direct stare with both eyebrows raised, imploring her to respond. The nonverbal message was clear: "You're sleeping with him, so he won't bite your head off when you tell him he's wrong."

"Um, Mr. President, you're correct that most people won't actually pray about this event," the political director said. She didn't really believe this, although the statement would have been true if she had instead referred to "most people in the Landers administration" or "most Democrat voters." "However, a significant number of Americans remain religious, even here in the twenty-first century. Those religious Americans vote. And they'll notice if we exclude the customary reference to *prayers* from our statement.

"On the other hand, the phrase *thoughts and prayers* is pretty much a cliché at this point, and you're not risking offending more-enlightened, less-religious Americans if you refer to *prayers*. Therefore, I recommend that we stick to convention here."

Upton Landers had stopped listening almost as soon as Chloe began speaking, having noticed that her skirt had slid up her leg a bit when she shifted in the chair. He was trying to find a way to remain discreet yet continue staring at her legs, when he suddenly realized she had stopped speaking. "Yeah, well, okay, that's fine," the president stammered. "Let's move on."

"Excellent." Extreme sarcasm colored Jordan's voice. "The next order of business is to plot a big-picture strategy for the upcoming general election. Jeff Ackerman isn't officially the Republican nominee yet, but that's really just a formality at this point.

"We have two options. One, we could run essentially the same campaign we planned to run against Hollister: centrist in tone, we're experiencing peace and prosperity, the president's policies are starting to have a positive effect, and he deserves a second term to cement them, et cetera, et cetera. We'll call this the *safe approach*.

"The reason I use this term," Jordan continued, "is that President Landers could defeat Jeff Ackerman simply by pointing out that the president, unlike his opponent, is not an extremist, racist, ignorant former governor of a backwater state which, by the way, ranks last in most categories. We wouldn't have to talk much at all about the president or his policies or beliefs. We just show the voters a relatively scandal-free administration going about the business of governing a country that's not at war and not experiencing an economic crisis.

"This is the safe approach because it pretty much guarantees a win in the general election. But the margin wouldn't be all that impressive, something like fifty-one to forty-six, and there wouldn't be much of a mandate for anything exciting or transformational in the second term. Congress would be almost evenly divided, thereby eliminating any chance of major liberal legislation.

"This brings me to the second option, which I'll call the *aggressive approach*. Under both plans, both the gloves come off, and we attack Ackerman—and Republicans in general—as racist, religious rednecks who want to establish a theocracy in America and take us back to the Dark Ages. But under the aggressive approach, not only do the gloves come off, but the masks come off as well."

Jordan paused for a moment to look at each one. "As you know, ever since the Reagan landslide in 1984, Democrats have been forced to tack toward the center in order to win presidential elections. We disguise ourselves as centrists, even though we actually want progressive policies. But Jeff Ackerman is so conservative, so extreme, that he gives us an opportunity to run as unapologetic liberals, pitting the forces of progress and enlightenment against the darkness of a Republican Party that yearns for the days in which women couldn't vote and blacks were in chains."

Although neither MacKenzie nor Lewis had spoken up during the meeting, each of them recoiled in horror as Richard Jordan outlined this so-called "strategy." First of all, he was way outside his lane here. His job was to make the White House run smoothly, and their job was to get the president re-elected. This meeting should have been run by Lewis or MacKenzie, with Jordan taking notes and nodding along. But Jordan was a powerful figure in Washington and in Democratic political circles, and the president clearly valued his advice more than anyone else's, so the two women held their tongues.

"The advantage to the aggressive approach is clear: we'd win in a landslide—in the range of fifty-five percent to forty-two percent—and obtain a clear, inarguable mandate for liberal policies. We might even get enough Democrats elected to Congress to put our policies in place via legislation so we don't have to resort to the courts and 'legislate' through the judiciary. We'd also have the chance to establish an enduring liberal majority on the Supreme Court. Finally, we'd bury conservatism and Christianity for a generation or two, cementing the president's legacy in the process.

"Now, admittedly, there is some risk involved in this aggressive approach. While I estimate that we have about a ninety-nine percent chance of winning the election under the safe approach, I'd say our chances go down to something like eighty percent under the aggressive approach. The reason for this is that it's possible, albeit highly unlikely, that we alienate centrist voters so much that we lose the election."

Richard Jordan had never managed a political campaign and never run for office himself. Both Lewis and MacKenzie were way too professional to pretend to be able to assign percentage chances of victory with anything like the certainty that Jordan projected here. The women were each trying to formulate a way to tamp down Jordan's optimistic projections without offending either Jordan or the president, when the chief of staff put them on the spot: "So, Gretchen and Chloe, I've talked enough at this point. Which approach do you suggest we go with?"

Thanks for putting us on the spot to try to bring some sanity to this process, thought the political director. *Oh,* now *he wants our opinions!* raged the campaign manager. The two women were truly in a no-win situation here. Each of them could tell from Jordan's tone and from the president's body language that the two men preferred the aggressive, liberal-purist approach, and they had little doubt that Jordan had planted that seed in the president's mind months ago.

But their job was to get the president re-elected. Period. Full stop. They weren't concerned, professionally anyway, about how he would govern in his second term or what his legacy might be. Their jobs, reputations, and futures hinged on winning this election. Thus, from their perspective, any strategy that decreased the president's chances of winning was by definition a bad idea.

Although tempted to say just that to Jordan and Landers, each one knew she had to walk a fine line. The president had the final say, and he would almost definitely choose the aggressive option. If the women pushed too hard for the safe approach, Jordan might decide they weren't fully invested in the aggressive strategy, and he'd convince the president to replace them with leftist cheerleaders.

Neither Lewis nor MacKenzie had any doubt that Jordan could find such replacements immediately. The meticulous Jordan probably already had a list of possible replacements in hand. The president wouldn't even care too much about having his mistresses leave the administration. After all, there were plenty of potential substitutes out there who would jump at the chance to get a very special, intimate tour of the White House residence.

In order to buy some time, Gretchen Lewis asked an intelligent question. "Richard, can you give us some specific examples of what policies we'd be selling under this aggressive approach you've outlined?"

Jordan eyed her with a condescending expression. "Please keep in mind, Gretchen, that you're selling Upton Landers first and foremost, not any particular policy."

Lewis gripped the arms of her chair, resisting the urge to claw Jordan's eyes out. What made this glorified errand boy think he was qualified to tell her how to do her job?

"But, to answer your question, we'd push for a doubling of the minimum wage, single-payer healthcare, and a big cut in the military budget," Jordan continued. "We want to unwind work requirements as a condition to welfare payments. We'll increase food stamps and federal housing allowances. We want a comprehensive gun-control law that drastically reduces the number of privately owned firearms and that bankrupts the gun manufacturers.

"We'll create a massive infrastructure project that we can use to funnel taxpayer money to union bosses. Who knows, we might just get a few new roads and bridges out of it as a side benefit. We'll need plenty of cheap labor for this, and we'll get it by opening up our Southern border to thousands of cheap workers who, not coincidentally, will soon become faithful Democrat voters.

"We want to eliminate coal as an energy source and use renewable energy sources to take up the slack. I don't think we can get away with outlawing fracking outright, but we'll promise a fulsome EPA review of the practice and then have them regulate the industry into submission.

"We want Supreme Court justices who are committed to protecting abortion rights. We'll push to eliminate the tax exemptions for churches and keep working to remove all references to God or the Bible from public schools. We'll work hard to keep the religious right from forcing their wacko views on the rest of us. The goal is to drive Christianity completely out of public life and into the dark corners of society where it belongs.

"That's just the start, but hopefully it gives you a flavor of where we're headed. None of these ideas are really new. What's different about this approach is that we won't apologize for these positions any longer or try to hide our intentions. We'll let the voters choose between Jeff Ackerman's racist, sexist theocracy and Upton Landers' vision for a safer, fairer, more equitable America in which the poor and middle class have better lives, the rich finally pay their fair share, and religious bigots are forced to shut up and leave the thinking people alone."

"That's quite an ambitious agenda," Chloe MacKenzie said in the understatement of the century. She had no objections to any of this on policy grounds. She was a committed leftist, just like the other three participants in the meeting, and just like all of her professors from her undergraduate days at Brown University. But she knew that only a very small portion of the electorate was as enlightened as she was, and all those little people in flyover country might not appreciate these new policies. Rather than be seen as siding with one of those uneducated hicks on policy matters, she raised what she hoped would be viewed by Landers and Jordan as a practical objection: "The voters will want to know how we're going to pay for it all."

So would I, President Landers and Gretchen Lewis thought simultaneously.

"Simple," Jordan replied. "We'll just raise taxes on the rich again."

"That'll be a tough sell after the 2013 tax increase on the rich," Gretchen Lewis countered doubtfully. "Republicans drilled us for enacting the biggest tax increase in history, and they're still wailing about it. Keep in mind that the rich now support Democrats more so than Republicans. Sure, from a political standpoint, we still play the game of the Rich Republican Country Club White Guy versus the Hardworking Democrat Black Single Mom, but we'll kill the goose that lays the golden eggs if we keep increasing taxes on the rich. At some point, the wealthy will turn on us and go back to the Republicans."

Richard Jordan gave an I-know-something-you-don't-know grin, then shook his head slowly, as if the burden of educating this simpleton was almost too much for him to bear. "Yes, the Democrats are now the party of the rich, and, yes, we have to keep that information out of the public narrative. But it's not that simple. You see, your normal, run-of-the mill rich guy with 'only' two or three million dollars to his name"—Jordan used his hands to air-quote the word *only*—"is still solidly Republican. He's worked his way up from middle management, saved and invested, played by the rules, and believes in all that free market and personal responsibility claptrap that Republicans are always rambling on about.

"But what most people don't realize is that the Democrats are now the party of the super-rich, the people that think two or three million dollars is just a rounding error on a financial statement. Think billionaire hedge-fund managers in New York, tech company CEOs in Silicon Valley, and trust-fund babies in Connecticut. These folks have billions of dollars; they're repulsed by flag-waving, Bible-quoting conservative Republicans; and they vote Democrat almost exclusively. And here's a dirty little secret: they don't care about an increase in marginal income tax rates, and they won't punish Democrats for enacting them. There are two reasons for this.

"The first reason is that most of these people don't pay ordinary income taxes anyway. The hedge-fund guys and private-equity people get the carried interest exception, so their tax rate is something like twenty percent. The tech titans use stock options and other loopholes to get out of paying taxes at the top marginal rate for individuals. And the trust-fund babies are just making withdrawals from investment accounts, so capital gains are all that they are taxed on.

"In other words, an increase in the top marginal individual tax rate on wages puts a big dent in the wallet of the 'merely rich' middle manager of the manufacturing company in Nebraska or the 'merely rich' bank vice president in Kentucky. But both of these guys are Republicans anyway and deserve to be forced to pay more.

That same increase in tax rates has very little impact on the hedge-fund master of the universe, the tech titan, or the trust-fund kid, who will all continue to vote Democrat."

Jordan took a moment to catch his breath. "The second reason why jacking up individual tax rates doesn't hurt Democrats with the rich is because wealth is all relative. Most really wealthy folks don't care very much about having a certain amount of money. What they want is to have more money than their friends and neighbors. And tax increases have the effect of pulling up the ladder that the middle class might otherwise use to become upper class, and those currently in the upper class are just fine with that.

"Besides," Jordan added as a cynical aside, "we don't actually have to raise enough revenue to cover the cost of what we want to do. We just have to convince the undecided voter that we'll be able to pay for our programs with tax increases—all of which will be paid by someone else. Whether those additional revenues actually material-ize is irrelevant. And we can always find plenty of economists dumb enough or loyal enough to say on TV and in the newspapers that our numbers add up just fine, thank you very much."

Upton Landers spoke up for the first time in what seemed like an hour but was actually only about ten minutes. "Thanks, Richard. You sold me. We're gonna go with the aggressive approach: all-out liberalism, with no holds barred, no shame, and no apologies."

"Mr. President," Gretchen Lewis said, "with all due respect, I suggest that you consider this a bit more fully. I know your goal is to be able to govern from the liberal end of the spectrum, but you can't govern at all if you don't win the election. Frankly, I think you're taking a bigger risk than Richard appreciates if you go full-scale liberal in the campaign. Democrats have successfully run as centrists and governed as liberals ever since Bill Clinton, and you could certainly find a way to pull that off."

Landers glanced at Chloe MacKenzie, who had been nodding along with Lewis. He was irritated at being second-guessed, and even more irritated to have Chloe side with the second-guesser, but he understood how the Washington political game was played. His response was more benign than anyone across the desk expected.

"Look," the president said gently, "I get it. Your only job is to get me elected, and you want to make that happen via the most certain route. And your objection to my decision is noted. That goes for both of you,"—he nodded toward Chloe to indicate that she was absolved along with Gretchen—"but it is my decision, and the decision has been made. I'm sure you'll each want to follow up with an email or a memo to me and Richard in which you renew your concerns."

Damn right we will, read the facial expression of each of the women in the room. *We're not interested in taking the fall for this upcoming electoral disaster.* Rule number one in Washington politics had been pounded into both of their heads over the years: *Whatever you do, cover your ass.* It even had its own acronym in a city full of them—CYA. Whatever the policy initiative, whatever the strategy, something would inevitably go wrong, and any staffer who wanted to survive knew that he or she had to be able to prove that the catastrophe was someone else's fault.

Chloe and Gretchen were already mentally composing their CYA memos when the president concluded the meeting by saying, "We'll give those memos the attention they deserve."

He had meant this last sentence as a friendly, peacemaking gesture, but his tone betrayed him, and he failed to conceal the real meaning behind his words: *Write your little memos if you must, but no one will ever read them, and, on the off chance that I ever want your opinion, I'll ask for it. Until then, shut up and do what I say.*

Chapter 20

On the Campaign Trail
in the Upper Midwest

March 2016

The Extremely Lowz-Flying Campaign Jet sped down an interstate highway that had only recently thawed following a snowstorm that everyone hoped was winter's last hurrah. Hal Harrington's money enabled the Ackerman campaign to use chartered jets now, but some bizarre sense of sentimentality caused them to keep the ancient Greyhound in service for jaunts around the Upper Midwest. This seemed like a good idea until the team actually boarded the bus, at which point they started arguing about who had the terrible idea to lease the bus for another few months.

The candidate and now presumptive Republican nominee woke up from a nap in his seat in the front row. He felt refreshed for the first time in weeks. Spring was on the way, the nomination was in hand, and his campaign seemed to have found a bit of rhythm after its horrendous start.

Ackerman tried to determine where they were. He guessed Minnesota, but they were actually in Wisconsin. The South would have been preferable just now, where spring was a reality and not simply a desperate hope. The political climate was definitely warmer and friendlier to him there too. But practical realities dictated that he slog across Pennsylvania, Wisconsin, Minnesota, Michigan, Ohio, Iowa, and Missouri, seeking to shore up support in marginally Republican states and work to flip one or more traditionally Democratic states into the Republican column.

Ackerman's optimism ebbed as Art Morgan plopped into the seat beside him. No one could kill a good mood like his cantankerous campaign manager. Not willing to surrender his optimism just yet, Ackerman greeted him cheerfully.

Morgan grunted. "Michelle's in the back, chatting up the youngsters. I wanted to give you a heads up on something while we have a minute without your wife nearby."

Intrigued, Ackerman nodded for Morgan to continue.

"Look, I know you're a good guy and good husband and all, but I need to warn you about the women." Art seemed uncomfortable.

Ackerman's brain was programmed to run everything he heard through a political matrix, which he did as he tried to understand where this was going. *Warn me about women? Women voters? Independent women? Republican soccer moms? Who are we talking about here?*

"There's no easy way to say this, so I'll just spit it out. Now that you're the presumptive nominee, you'll have women throwing themselves at you. You need to be ready for that."

Ackerman smiled. "Art, I'm fifty years old. I have a receding hair line, a flabby body, and a nearly overdrawn checking account. I also have a wife. I've never had random women throw themselves at me, and I really don't expect it to start happening now."

"Don't be a moron," Morgan growled back. "The women will be coming at you in droves. And I don't want to trample on the ego of the almost-Republican-nominee-even-if-by-accident, but they won't be throwing themselves at you because of your rugged good looks or irresistible charm. Not even because of your huuuuge—"

"Don't say it!"

"I was going to say *net worth*, Mr. Pervert." Morgan gave a rare chuckle. "Seriously, get ready to deal with this. Some of them will want to brag to their friends about sleeping with someone famous. Others might have the crazy idea that you'll actually win this election and become president, and they want a job from you. And it wouldn't shock me if some Democratic operative decided to see if he could get a woman to pick up the Republican nominee in a random hotel lobby in Michigan or Ohio or Wisconsin and then leak the whole thing to the press.

"Just remember: all that you'll get out of any sort of fling will be a disease, a dependent, or a divorce. Or some combination thereof. So gird up your loins and be prepared, Mr. Clean-Cut Christian Conservative." The lesson over, Morgan pushed himself to his feet using the armrest. He let out a depressing groan as he did so, indicating pain and fatigue, and then shuffled his way to the rear of the bus to yell at the twenty-somethings to keep the noise down.

The candidate was once again alone in the front row with his thoughts. Surely not even the Democrats would try something like that, would they? It didn't take Ackerman long to conclude that yes, they probably would.

Chapter 21

Republican Party Convention, Atlanta, Georgia

July 2016

T he Jeff Ackerman for President Campaign didn't exactly limp into Atlanta for the Republican Convention that would officially nominate Ackerman as the Republican presidential candidate, but neither did it roll triumphantly into town to seize the Republican mantle. The sudden death of Senator Olivia Hollister, Ackerman's closest competitor, cast a heavy pall over the primary process. The heat, haze, and humidity, with its remorseless grip on the asphalt island of downtown Atlanta, seemed to embody the Hollister tragedy. Both the unpleasant weather and the fate of Senator Hollister enveloped the campaign staff and convention goers alike, adding a dark layer of sadness and dread to what should have been an upbeat occasion.

Ackerman had played the best hand possible with a terrible set of cards. He easily fended off a couple of octogenarians that the GOP establishment half-heartedly pushed into the primary process. And he managed to avoid embarrassment in the New Hampshire primary despite a tepid "Vote For Olivia Anyway" movement among her supporters. It turned out that most of Hollister's most die-hard fans were either registered Democrats, media members who lived outside of New Hampshire, or both, so there weren't too many hardcore Hollister supporters who were actually eligible to cast a vote in the Granite State. Ackerman ended up with 83 percent of the vote in New Hampshire, whose primary was ultimately meaningless but for the risk of losing to a corpse.

Yet even though he had surged past Hollister in the polls and would likely have defeated her easily, the media consistently painted Ackerman as the unwarranted beneficiary of the senator's untimely death. He was the unlikely candidate—the unworthy successor to a crown that should have been hers—and the media clearly resented him for it. The reporters' and columnists' viewpoint was as simple as it was childish: We liked her because she was a Northeastern liberal, we don't like him because he's a Southern conservative and one of those icky Christians, and he needs to suffer for her untimely death.

Ackerman and his staff pointed out that he was already the front-runner for the Republican nomination at the time of the senator's demise, but these efforts backfired when the media portrayed the statement as immodesty and as speaking ill of the dead. The tone of their articles was clear: *Can't you just hold off on bragging about yourself for a few minutes while we mourn the death of this great woman?*

The Democrats played the issue brilliantly. Through innuendo and inflection, they established the questionable, accidental, unlikely nature of the Ackerman campaign without going too far in that direction. After all, they didn't want to tarnish their inevitable victory in the November general election. Instead, they ensured that the Ackerman campaign suffered several body blows but not quite a knockout punch.

Conspiracy theories inevitably emerged, claiming that the same dark forces that bankrolled Ackerman's campaign had murdered Hollister and her staff by sabotaging their campaign jet. The establishment media couldn't make these outlandish claims itself, as they clearly weren't true and had no evidence to support them, so the media did the next best thing: reported that *others* and *some* were making these claims against Ackerman. These "news" stories inevitably noted that the Ackerman campaign had offered no evidence to refute the allegations, as if it were possible to prove a negative, thereby leaving viewers and readers with the impression that the conspiracy theories had some validity.

Additionally, as Ackerman had feared, he was heavily criticized for not attending Senator Hollister's funeral. Ackerman's camp had reached out to the Hollister family representatives and gave them the choice of whether he would attend her memorial service. He received a very frosty *no* in response and complied with the family's wishes.

Ackerman's staff dutifully informed their media contacts that the family had made the decision for Ackerman to stay away, and the media dutifully ignored this information and presented Ackerman's absence as a slight to the grieving Hollister family. The campaign noticed with frustration that no one ever asked them a question about this, so they had no chance to inform the public directly about the family's choice. It seemed petty and small to issue a press release on this or to have the candidate mention it in a speech, so the campaign simply absorbed the negative impact and tried to move beyond it.

The campaign fervently hoped that the Republican convention would cause the media to shift away from the Ackerman–Hollister race and the "accidental candidate" narrative and toward the looming contest in November between Jeff Ackerman and President Upton Landers. While the Hollister talk did abate somewhat, there was precious little substantive coverage of Ackerman's policy proposals, and even less analysis of how they differed from those of the current administration. Instead, the networks and major newspapers covering the event engaged in a contest among themselves to determine who could offer the most stinging rebuke to the Republicans over the most trivial of issues.

On the opening day of the convention, the media narrative was the lack of diversity on the convention floor. *The Republican Party still struggles to attract minority supporters*, they said and wrote. *Way too many white faces.* An abundance of what the reporters liked to call "angry white men."

Of course, these were gentlemen known to their families as "Grandpa Joe who takes me fishing and to baseball games" and to their communities as "Fred, the friendly retired guy who waves at me from his porch." Even though the video showed them on the convention floor, relaxed, smiling, and waving, the "angry" subplot continued unabated: *They're old, they're white, they're male, and they disagree with the Democrats, so they must be angry, dammit! Some of them probably even own guns and go to church!*

The Republican spin operatives countered the "too white" claims by pointing out a rather significant number of African Americans and Hispanics in the audience. The media responded by sneering at the "token minorities" who were being "used" by cynical Republicans to distract viewers from an audience that otherwise consisted of the aforementioned "angry white men." The media also painted the "strategic placement" of these "token minorities" in "prominent places" in the convention hall as a response by Republicans desperate to mitigate criticism for having a "nearly all-white contingent" on the convention floor, as if they had been bussed in on the second day of the convention and given front-row seats so the cameras would find them. When Republicans calmly provided video evidence demonstrating that the same minorities were sitting in the same area on both the first and the second day of the convention, the media ignored it as "old news" and portrayed thin-skinned Republicans as whining like children with "unfounded claims of media bias."

By that time, the media covering the convention had moved on to their next line of attack: protesters outside the convention hall. To the unbiased observer, these fine folks snarling into bullhorns and chanting violent slogans seemed much angrier than the "angry white males" on the convention floor. But the media didn't point this out because . . . well, just because.

To the extent the emotions of the protesters were mentioned, such emotions were consistently portrayed as righteous anger in the face of oppression. And even though the protesters wore matching T-shirts and carried the same pre-printed signs, the reporters described the protests as "spontaneous" and "grassroots." No one bothered to ask who paid for the signs or the T-shirts, or who paid for the busses that brought them to the convention center, often traveling from hundreds of miles away.

In fact, the marchers were the same tired old gaggle of rent-a-protester that the Democrats rolled out whenever it was convenient to do so. They were mostly union employees of the federal government, happily taking a day off from their boring jobs pushing paper on behalf of Uncle Sam. And they got overtime pay for being there! Mixed in with the union goons were a few recent college grads with degrees in challenging fields such as Women's Studies. These poor lost souls were mainly seeking some free marijuana and looking to have a little fun on someone else's nickel before taking up permanent residence in their parents' basements.

Nevertheless, the media portrayed these paid protesters as representative of the country at large. The scraggly band of marchers was, somehow, both the calm, rational voice of reason and the righteously angry underdogs who were bravely standing up to the forces of evil who were safely ensconced in the convention hall. These marchers were speaking truth to power!

But perhaps the most ridiculous line of criticism aimed at Jeff Ackerman was the location of the convention itself. Why were the Republicans nominating Jeff Ackerman, who hailed from the deeply troubled Southern state of Mississippi, at a convention in the Southern city of Atlanta? With furrowed brows and doubtful tones, the broadcasters expressed deep concern that perhaps Ackerman was "not comfortable" outside his home region, or maybe he lacked the "cultural empathy" to "reach across regional and racial lines." Of even deeper purported concern was the fear that holding the convention in Atlanta "carried hidden racial undertones" and "might be a dog whistle" for his supporters, many of whom were Southerners and, therefore, inveterate racists.

Lost in all of this insincere and unjustified concern was the fact that the convention site had been selected two years ago. Thus, the selection was made and plans to address the vast logistical complexity of the convention commenced long before Jeff Ackerman even thought about running for the presidency. But the media couldn't let mere facts stand in the way of speculating about whether Jeff Ackerman had "racist tendencies." Richard Jordan frequently congratulated himself for planting that phrase in the minds of the media on the first of his secret conference calls.

Even the concerns of Atlanta's mayor and city council, who were all Democrats and almost all African Americans, were cavalierly brushed aside. They didn't appreciate having their city portrayed as racist. They especially resented the frequent media comparison of Atlanta, which billed itself as "The City Too Busy to Hate," to the likes of Mississippi, as Atlanta and Mississippi alike were noted in the convention news coverage for "maintaining some of the vestiges of slavery." But the city leadership failed to have enough foresight to refuse to take the Republicans' money. Accordingly, at least in the eyes of the national media, they would have to pay a reputational price as punishment for hosting such a gathering of undesirables.

Despite these negative portrayals in the national press, the convention ran smoothly. Anyone who actually watched for himself, rather than relying on the leftward-slanted analysis, would have seen speakers from a cross-section of America advocating for traditional, conservative American values and policies. The speakers were polished without appearing overly rehearsed or mechanical. Technical glitches with the sound system and giant video screens were minimal. On the rare occasions when they occurred, convention staff quickly remedied them. Security staff succeeded in keeping the protesters in a designated area outside of the convention hall, thereby avoiding embarrassing incidents on the convention floor during the prime-time television broadcasts.

Political precedent mandated that the candidate's wife give a major speech, usually on the first evening of the convention. The idea behind this speech was almost universally described as her chance to "introduce her husband to the country." Michelle Ackerman was terrified at the thought of speaking live to five thousand people in the arena, with ten million more watching on television. She didn't want or need any attention at all from anyone outside her family and small circle of close friends, but now everything from her hairstyle, to her dress, to her Southern accent would be coldly dissected—and likely criticized—by people she'd never met.

However, appearing calm and confident despite her inward fears, she hit it out of the park. Her theme was "Jeff Ackerman: A Good Man for a Great Nation," and she delivered the speech perfectly. She noted Jeff's characteristics as a loyal husband and loving father, as a Sunday-school teacher and youth soccer coach. She painted him as the neighbor you trust to get your mail and feed your dog when you travel, the worker you could always count on to show up early and stay late whenever it was necessary. And she focused on examples of when Jeff had done good, kind, and decent deeds outside the spotlight, when he would score no political points for doing so.

Other speakers at the convention would elaborate on Jeff's keen intelligence and powerful policy insights, but Michelle's job was to humanize her husband for the nation. Rightly or wrongly, many voters chose their candidate based on qualities such as "Does he care about people like me?" or "Would I enjoy having a beer with this guy?" Through humorous anecdotes and kind words about her husband of nearly thirty years, Michelle Ackerman made the sale.

In fact, she performed so well that the major TV networks covering the event weren't able to credibly attack her delivery, but certainly not for lack of trying. One analyst speculated on the air that Michelle had used some sort of illicit drug to enhance her performance. While his producers and upper management were not inclined to question this line of thinking, a flood of critical calls, emails, texts, and Twitter messages to the network caused this speculation to die a quick death. Of course, no apology or retraction was forthcoming.

Instead, the commentariat parsed Michelle's words in an effort to undermine her salesmanship on behalf of her husband. They couldn't find any overtly racist references. A political analyst on the notoriously left-wing cable channel HBT even complimented Michelle and her speechwriters for cleverly hiding their racism—which was simply assumed to exist; after all, she was a Southerner, a Republican, and a Christian—beneath a layer of false kindness: *She did so well that you couldn't even tell she's a racist!* If there were an Emmy Award for Backhanded Compliment of the Year, this would be the leader in the clubhouse.

That left them with only the phrase *great nation* to quibble about. Michelle had simply used it several times in her speech without expounding on the greatness of America. Her emphasis had instead been on the "good man" portion of the theme. Michelle and all of the sane, rational people who listened to the speech were perfectly willing to acknowledge the heretofore unquestioned greatness of the United States. But with an obtuseness unique to leftist intellectuals, the media cast doubt on the premise.

They grumbled that she had provided no evidence to support her claim that America is, in fact, a great nation. She hadn't apologized for slavery or the oppression of women. If America was so great, why were there poor people struggling to get by? Why didn't everyone have health insurance?

In a failed attempt to avoid being seen as petty, the media resorted to condescension. They noted that Michelle was simply an undereducated housewife, so she couldn't be expected to understand the baseness of America: *Let's cut her a little slack, because she's too stupid and too unsophisticated to realize how terrible this country really is.*

The pattern established with Michelle's headliner speech on the first night of the convention continued for the next two days: good-to-great speeches containing innovative policy ideas, followed immediately by negative commentary from the press. Perhaps the worst offender was Broadcast News International. The cable channel hired Hillson Hollister, the nephew of the deceased senator, as a political analyst to provide commentary on the Republican convention. While BNI never actually identified Hollister as a Republican, the network gave the impression that he was there to provide balance against the liberal opinions of other commentators, along with behind-the-scenes information about the inner workings of the Republican Party. After all, he had once had Thanksgiving dinner with the woman who almost became the Republican nominee, so he was clearly qualified to provide a breakdown of the economic impact of the flat tax and to analyze Iran's most recent provocation in Syria.

Young Mr. Hollister did more damage to the Republican image than the other talking heads because of the assumption that he was one of them, and that he was providing constructive criticism regarding his fellow conservative Republicans. His themes alternated between "Olivia Hollister would have been a better candidate" and "the Republicans have become too extremist." His commentary was hurting the GOP with the centrist voters that they needed most in order to pull off the upset against President Landers in the November election.

But neither BNI nor Hillson Hollister revealed that Hillson was actually a Democrat, that he'd donated heavily to Democratic candidates and liberal causes, and that he had even been employed as a staffer on several Democratic congressional campaigns. Instead of being up-front with their viewers, BNI planted the seed of "Look, even fellow Republicans don't like the Republicans at this disaster of a convention. Nobody's gonna vote for this guy Ackerman." Perhaps due to inexperience, or perhaps because they were fighting negative media coverage on too many fronts, the Ackerman campaign didn't discover the truth behind Hollister's background on their own.

But Hal Harrington, the Iowa billionaire whose money had helped Jeff Ackerman get this far, was not one to make an investment and then ignore it. Harrington and his people noticed the damage that Hillson Hollister was inflicting on the Ackerman poll numbers, and they quickly conducted a quick review of the publicly available information about him. Hal himself made the call to Art Morgan to convey the truth about BNI's newest political analyst, and Hal made no attempt to hide his disgust with Morgan and the rest of the Ackerman staff over their amateurish failure to counter BNI's maneuver.

His pride still stinging from having an Iowa farming magnate provide better political information than what he—the would-be political professional—had provided to his client, Art Morgan grabbed Scott Williamson and went to see Jeff Ackerman in his hotel suite.

It was midafternoon on the last day of the Republican convention, and Ackerman would give his major speech to formally accept the Republican nomination that evening. The speech had been written, revised, and rewritten several times, and Ackerman had just given final approval to version twenty-three of the biggest political speech of his life. The candidate was beyond frustrated with the nearly endless process but was relieved to have the writing and revision process finished.

He was not happy when his two primary staffers shared the latest intelligence about Hillson Hollister and BNI's duplicity. But the candidate was not one to dwell on mistakes, especially now that he saw an opportunity to go on offense against his critics. He asked an aide for three copies of his speech, which had just been distributed to the networks under embargo so that their talking heads would be prepared to discuss it after Ackerman completed his delivery. But they wouldn't be completely prepared, because Jeff Ackerman had an idea for some last-minute changes. Due to a "clerical error," these final revisions would not find their way into the advance copies of the speech distributed to the media.

Chapter 22

Republican Party Convention – Atlanta, Georgia

July 2016

Jeff Ackerman strode to the podium to thunderous applause. As he waved at the crowd and waited for them to settle down, he realized he should be nervous but wasn't. Perhaps he was so exhausted from the campaign trail that the prospect of giving the most important address of his life didn't raise his pulse. Or maybe his prayers for peace of mind and clarity of thought had been answered. The spotlights nearly blinded him, but he resisted the urge to squint. The same lights threw off intense heat that nearly took his breath away, but he willed himself not to sweat.

He had worked hard with his staff to make the speech clear, punchy, and bold. They stripped out as many unnecessary clichés and transitional phrases as possible, and now it was up to the candidate to deliver it well. The crowd finally quieted down enough for him to begin.

It's time to roll. Let's do this.

"I'm Governor Jeffrey Ackerman, and I'm running for president of the United States of America!" No soft introduction, no thanking the person who had introduced him, no wasted words. Just the exact same line he used in that disastrous speech at the Mississippi Governor's Mansion over a year ago when he first announced his candidacy. Back then, the line had generated a terribly awkward silence and made him a laughing stock. But now the same phrase, delivered in the same tone and with the same cadence, generated an enthusiastic roar from the crowd on the convention floor.

With perfect timing, he then delivered a bit of self-deprecation: "I'm glad to see that phrase work a little better this time than it did when I first used it back in April of last year." Already, a clear distinction between Jeff Ackerman and Upton Landers: Ackerman could laugh at himself. No one could imagine such an approach from the haughty, arrogant occupant of the Oval Office.

The candidate then transitioned into the policy portion of his speech. He incorporated and expanded on the common themes he had been addressing on the campaign trail, which he summarized in twelve words: *Cut taxes. Cut spending. Reform entitlements. Protect our borders. Appoint conservative judges.*

Ackerman used plain language and common-sense arguments to make his case. He noted that if you want more of something, you should tax it less. Do you want more jobs, more employment, more income? Then cut income taxes.

"President Landers and the Democrats did the opposite by raising income taxes," Ackerman told his audience. "The Democrats claimed that the government needed additional revenue. However, a tax on income is a tax on work, on investment, on effort. If you tax work, investment, and effort more, then you get less of it.

"Yes, there was a temporary increase in government revenue as a result of the tax increase. But now that Americans have had a chance to adjust their behavior in response to the tax increase, revenues are going down, unemployment is going up, and incomes are going down. Additionally, lower tax rates do not necessarily mean lower government revenues. President Kennedy and President Reagan pushed through significant cuts in marginal income tax rates, and government revenues surged in response to the economic growth that resulted from those tax cuts.

"In any event, a lack of revenue for the federal government isn't the main source of the country's fiscal problems. Government revenues have steadily increased over time at a healthy rate. But government spending has grown much faster than revenues, and both political parties have contributed to this excessive spending."

Ackerman noted that the United States spent approximately three trillion dollars per year, while taking in approximately two trillion dollars per year in taxes, fees, and other revenue. This one-trillion-dollar annual deficit couldn't continue. Common-sense spending cuts, which most Americans wouldn't even notice, would eliminate a significant portion of this annual deficit. Increased economic growth, fostered by tax cuts, would eliminate the remainder of the deficit, at least with respect to discretionary spending.

"Thus," he said, "we can solve some of our problems via a combination of spending cuts and tax cuts, and thereby grow our way out of the portion of the deficit that relates to discretionary spending—such as the military, foreign aid, education, and the like.

"Unfortunately, our unfunded liabilities with respect to welfare, Social Security, Medicare, and Medicaid—commonly referred to as entitlement programs—are so vast as to be almost beyond comprehension. We can't make these entitlement programs solvent by raising taxes. And, even worse, we probably can't grow our way out of the entitlement mess. Not even massive economic growth triggered by cutting taxes and regulations will be able to overcome the shortfall on entitlements."

Ackerman noted that economists had calculated the difference in value between the country's stream of revenues and the country's liabilities. The result was terrifying: the present value of future liabilities exceeded the present value of revenues by more than two hundred trillion dollars. This figure was more than the value of all the assets, including money, stocks, bonds, houses, commercial real estate, et cetera, in the entire world.

Accordingly, even if the United States were to seize all the wealth of every human being on the planet, it would still not be able to pay its bills. Therefore, there was no doubt that America would not fulfill the promises it had made to its citizens in their current form. The question was not whether or how the country was going to pay its bills; instead, the question was how it was going to manage the process of not paying its bills.[3]

"Presidents and congressional majorities of both parties have ignored this problem for far too long," Ackerman continued. "It is the nature of politics to focus on the immediate issues at the expense of addressing problems, even fiscal emergencies, that will only manifest themselves in future years. After all, the insolvency of our entitlement programs won't hurt anyone today. And it won't hurt anyone tomorrow. Or next week. However, this ever-worsening state of insolvency, if unaddressed, will be a tremendous problem for our children and grandchildren. But they don't vote yet, and thus the problem goes unaddressed and gets worse every day."

Ackerman went on to outline the broad strokes of entitlement reform. He advocated market-based reforms that increase individual incentives to work, save, and invest. He pushed for decreases in government subsidies, which, while intended to alleviate the pain

---

3   Please see *The End is Near and It's Going to Be Awesome* by Kevin D. Williamson, which is this author's original source for this information on the size and scope of America's unfunded liabilities with respect to entitlement programs.

of higher prices, only caused those same prices to increase by the amount of the subsidy and then some.

He stated that the best way to improve the financial condition of the medical-related entitlement programs such as Medicare and Medicaid was to reduce the cost of healthcare for everyone. The candidate pointed out that the United States has the best doctors, nurses, and medical technology in the world. On the other hand, it also has one of the worst mechanisms for paying for healthcare in the world.

"The main problem," Ackerman said, "is that our current system offers patients no incentive to shop for healthcare based on price. Even if a person was willing to seek out the lowest price—instead of simply relying on the insurance company to pay—doctors don't publish their prices for medical procedures, so patients can't easily go to the doctor down the street in order to get a better deal."

The candidate pledged to work with Congress to enable patients to find and compare prices among doctors. Simply introducing the market forces of price competition into the medical arena would serve to slow, and possibly even reverse, the recent massive increases in American healthcare costs.

As with medical entitlements, the Social Security program's financial condition could be repaired with a fairly simple fix: allow everyone to elect whether or not to participate in the program. Those who elected to participate would continue to pay Social Security taxes and, when they retire, receive the promised benefits. Ackerman explained that people who opted out of Social Security would neither pay Social Security taxes nor receive benefits. Instead, they could keep their money that would otherwise have gone to the government and invest it for their own retirement. The government's financial condition would improve from this because its promised benefit payments for each participant almost always exceeded the amount of taxes paid by that particular person. Thus,

Social Security's income would decrease, but its liabilities would decrease much more.

"Yes, the Democrats will attack these ideas," Ackerman conceded. "They'll claim that we're trying to kill Grandma and Grandpa just to save a buck. But we have to trust the American people enough to have an adult conversation about our entitlement problems, because they must be solved before it is too late."

He went on to expound on his proposed immigration policy—which was very similar to his dinner-table debate with Laura Irvin ten months earlier—and his commitment to appoint federal judges who would be faithful to the text of the Constitution rather than their own policy views. Then, the candidate transitioned into the portion of the speech he'd inserted at the last minute after learning of BNI's cute little stunt with Hillson Hollister. He tried not to laugh as he thought of the media members flipping furiously through their copies of his speech, looking for the text of the passage he was about to deliver. They wouldn't find it.

Instead, the talking heads on the networks would actually be forced to listen to his speech and think for themselves for their reaction, rather than relying on much smarter folks behind the scenes to script their reactions for them in advance. *Sorry, y'all. Don't know why you didn't get the updated, final version of the speech. Must have been some sort of technical glitch.* He was relieved, however, to see that the newly inserted text appeared just fine on the teleprompter in front of him.

"My friends, you have all seen the intensely negative coverage of this convention by the mainstream media. My staff and I have done our best to work with the media in order to give them full access and to help them report fairly on the convention. Unfortunately, we haven't had any more success in achieving fair media coverage of this convention than our Republican predecessors had over the past twenty or thirty years.

"For those of you who are veterans of conservative politics, this is certainly nothing new. You've seen the media do all that it can to boost the Democrat Party at the expense of Republicans, and to the detriment of the country as a whole. You've come to expect nothing less. But we need to educate those who are new to the Republican Party, and those who don't pay much attention to politics or the political media except during the party conventions and the presidential election that follows them a few months later.

"During the days of the state-controlled media in the Soviet Union, Russians learned to read between the lines of *Pravda* and other newspapers in order to glean the hidden messages that the writers wanted to convey but couldn't get past the government censors. Unfortunately, we here in America today must undertake a similar task when reading the *New York Daily Ledger* or the *Washington Chronicle*, or when watching a news show or political show on a major network or cable channel. If you want to fully understand what's going on in the world, you must understand the tricks and tactics that these media outlets use in their news stories and broadcasts. It's very sad that we've reached the point in the U.S. where once-great media outlets have come to resemble *Pravda*, but that's where we are."

Ackerman had no way of knowing it at the time, but this line of thought immediately grabbed the attention of the audience, both those in the arena and those watching on television around the world. Facebook flooded with reactions to the candidate's media criticism. #*Pravda* immediately began trending on Twitter.

The candidate continued, "So what specifically do these leftist media outlets do, other than report generally negative things about Republicans and generally positive things about Democrats? Let me give you five tactics that the media uses.

"First of all, the media does all it can to prevent news that could hurt Democrats from being published or broadcast in the first place.

We don't think about it much, but upper management at leading newspapers and TV networks are the people who decide what stories show up in print or get discussed on the news broadcast. And the media is very good at suppressing stories that help Republicans or hurt Democrats.

"As commentator Jim Treacher stated so poignantly on Twitter, 'Modern journalism is all about deciding which facts the public shouldn't know because they might reflect badly on Democrats.' David Burge, often better known via his internet handle, Iowa-Hawk, noted that 'Journalism is about covering important stories. With a pillow, until they stop moving.' The point that both of these insightful gentlemen are making is that the media will do all it can to suppress news that casts leftists in a bad light.

"But sometimes," Ackerman continued, "the story is already out there, and the media can no longer suppress it. That brings us to the second cute little trick the media uses to assist the Democrats: they omit the party affiliation of Democrats who have behaved badly. Think about the most recent news articles you've seen about politicians who have gotten DUIs or been indicted for embezzlement. If the politician is a Republican, that fact will be noted in both the headline and the first paragraph of the story. But if the misbehaving politician is a Democrat, that fact is omitted from the story altogether. There will be no mention of the bad actor's party affiliation."

Even though he was nearly blinded by the stage lights and TV lighting that blared directly into his eyes, Ackerman could tell that his audience was tracking with him. They were laughing and cheering, urging him on as he continued to skewer the press.

"The third tactic is a bit more subtle. In this one, the media doesn't report about the bad deeds of the Democrat in question, at least not directly. Instead, the news story is about how those big, mean Republicans will 'pounce' or 'seize on' the story for political gain. Thus, rather than focusing on the Democrat's sex scandal or crime or broken promise or whatever it is, the story is instead used to show that Republicans will make use of the news. This is always done with a sort of head-shaking, tsk-tsk tone, as if the Republicans are just too eager to take unfair advantage of the misdeeds of their political opponents.

"The fourth trick used by the left-wing media involves labels. The *New York Daily Ledger, Washington Chronicle*, BNI, and the major networks often label conservatives and conservative positions as 'far-right,' 'extremist,' or 'extreme right-wing.' For good measure, they throw in adjectives like 'angry' and 'bitter.' But you almost never see similar labels applied to liberals or liberal positions, no matter how extreme. When was the last time the mainstream media described Nancy Pelosi as 'far-left' or Joseph Stalin as a 'left-wing extremist'? In short, the media likes to pretend that Democrats are the calm, reasonable voices of logic and moderation, while Republicans offer only violent extremism."

Jeff Ackerman paused for a moment to let the laughter die down, and then he began to wrap up the section of his speech dealing with the media. "Now, bear with me just a moment longer as I describe for you the fifth and final misleading tactic employed by the media in their service to their Democrat Party overlords. This is the one we've seen most often during our convention this week. Picture, if you will, the typical panel of political experts on a debate-style show on a major network. The idea here is to have a Democrat, a Republican, and a moderator discuss and debate a particular issue or two, or to have a Republican on the air to defend a particular conservative idea.

"Please understand that I have no problem with this concept in theory. The Democrat representative is always a loyal leftist, ready to spout party propaganda on demand. Again, there's nothing particularly wrong with this. But the so-called Republican in this scenario is almost never actually a Republican, and certainly not a conservative Republican with the intestinal fortitude to stand up for what we believe in. Instead, the person purporting to speak on our behalf is inevitably some spineless weasel who just can't wait to show how moderate and reasonable he is by disagreeing with the values and the policies that conservatives hold dear."

The audience roared in approval. Their nominee was perceptive enough to see through the duplicity of the supposedly neutral national press. Not only that, but he had the backbone to call them out on it! With the world watching, Jeff Ackerman was giving voice to what they'd been grumbling about among themselves for years.

"They'll have someone like Davis West or Drew Haughton on the air to stab their fellow Republicans in the back. The only 'debate' will be on just how terrible the Republican stance is on the particular issue being discussed. The Democrat or moderator will criticize the conservative viewpoint, and the fake Republican will bravely respond, 'Well, it certainly is mean-spirited and short-sighted and will probably hurt women and children the most, but it could be worse.' The idea behind this tactic is to make the audience think, *Wow, those Republicans sure are extremists. Not even the Republican guest on the TV show thinks this is a good idea.*"

The Republican crowd cheered mightily in response. Ackerman wasn't just criticizing the press generally. He was naming names! West had served as chief of staff for several Republican presidents, and now he served only Davis West. Similarly, Drew Haughton had been an economic advisor to Ronald Reagan and had helped implement Reagan's supply-side tax cuts that had launched the greatest economic boom in history. Sadly, Haughton was now all too willing to whore himself out to any media outlet that needed someone to criticize any Republican tax plan or economic policy.

"We've seen a particularly egregious example of this form of falsehood from BNI during our convention this week," Ackerman went on.

The crowd grew still, waiting anxiously for the candidate to roast their least-favorite cable network.

"BNI hired Hillson Hollister as an analyst to give his opinions about the various speeches and the Republican Party platform. Now, to be fair, BNI never actually said that Hillson is a Republican. They simply implied it by noting, with great frequency, that he is a political advisor and the nephew of Senator Olivia Hollister, my worthy opponent in the Republican primary before her tragic death seven months ago.

"BNI portrays Hillson as a former advisor to his late aunt, and Hillson follows suit by using terms like *we* and *our* when discussing the Hollister campaign. Thus, the viewer is led to believe that Hillson Hollister is a loyal Republican in good standing with our party. He then proceeds to brutally criticize every aspect of our party, this convention, our platform, and our core beliefs. Again, this gives the viewer the impression that 'Wow, here is a respected Republican who really hasn't bought into this Ackerman guy.'

"Well, my friends, it just so happens that Hillson Hollister is no Republican. He not only had no role in Senator Hollister's campaign, but he's been a frequent donor to Democrat candidates and liberal organizations. He *has* served as a political advisor, but for Democrats, not Republicans. Thus, BNI is defrauding its viewers through a highly misleading stunt, all in an effort to hurt Republicans and help Democrats.

"And, just in case you think I'm exaggerating, when Hillson's background as a Democrat advisor and liberal activist came to our attention, we had a staffer go back and review everything that Hillson has said on BNI during our convention. Yes, this was a very unpleasant task, and we paid our staffer a little extra for undertaking such depressing work."

Chuckles rippled through the audience.

"Our research confirmed that Hillson Hollister, during more than six hours of airtime, did not say a single positive thing about me, my wife, our party's platform, or Republicans in general. Not one!"

The crowd hissed, booed, and sneered.

"To the upper management at BNI, we say that we no longer expect you to be fair," Ackerman went on. "We certainly don't expect you to be honest or honorable. You've demonstrated on far too many occasions that your network is capable of neither honesty nor honor. But, come on, folks,"—he gave an incredulous smile—"couldn't you at least be a little more subtle? I was pretty sure Hillson wouldn't like my speech tonight, and that was before we revised it this afternoon to point out his fraud. My friends, I know he's not gonna like it now!"

Jeff Ackerman bathed in the loud applause and absolute approval of the crowd. He took a brief moment to enjoy a mental image of the BNI talking heads that were on the air right now, listening to him call out their network and challenge their honesty with millions of viewers watching in real time. "And so, ladies and gentlemen, I hope that these examples of the media's underhanded tactics will help you read and watch the news in a different light as our campaign unfolds. Just pretend that you're living in Moscow during the days of the Soviet Union, reading *Pravda* and trying to figure out the hidden messages between the lines on the printed page."

The candidate then prepared to transition into the next section of his speech. "I've learned a lot during my campaign. One of the things I've learned is that a presidential candidate receives a tremendous amount of advice from people who *seem* to be really smart. A lot of those kind people advised me, both in person and in various media outlets, to downplay the fact that I'm from Mississippi. These would-be advisors go on and on about how 'Mississippi has a horrible reputation,' or 'Mississippi is a backward state,' or 'Mississippi is at the bottom of a lot of statistical categories.' According to these self-anointed experts, I shouldn't even say the word *Mississippi*. Well . . . bless their hearts."

Another murmur of laughter from the convention floor.

"Let me translate that phrase for those of you who don't speak the Southern dialect of American English. You see, in the South, even in these modern, politically correct times, we're taught to have good manners. This includes the fact that you shouldn't say negative things about other people. But there's an unspoken exception to this rule: you can say anything you like about others, as long as you begin or end your criticism with the phrase 'bless their hearts.'"

More chuckling from the audience.

"Even though I'm now fully protected by the safe harbor of 'bless their hearts,' I don't intend to be too harsh on those who would have me disown my home state of Mississippi, because at least some of these folks offered this advice in good faith. They were genuinely trying to be helpful. Thus, I'll simply say this: Yes, Mississippi has its faults. Yes, Mississippi has its challenges. But so does every state in this great country. And I love the great State of Mississippi!"

Wild cheers came from the Mississippi delegation off to Ackerman's right, but only polite applause from the remainder of the large crowd. *Where's he going with this?* many of them wondered. *Shouldn't he be discussing national issues? He's running for president of the whole country, not for governor of a single state.*

"Mississippians give more of their income to charity than residents of any other state. The first heart transplant was performed in Mississippi. Mississippi facilities were instrumental in the development of the space shuttle. Mississippians build cutting-edge ships for our navy at Ingalls Shipyard in Pascagoula, on Mississippi's beautiful Gulf Coast.

"Legendary musicians Elvis Presley, B.B. King, and Jimmy Rogers are all from Mississippi. Think about that. These three men, known respectively as the King of Rock and Roll, the King of the Blues, and the Father of Country Music, all hail from the Magnolia State.

"Outstanding authors such as William Faulkner, Tennessee Williams, Eudora Welty, Richard Wright, Walker Percy, and John Grisham are all native Mississippians. The current chief executive officers of Federal Express and UPS, the two largest package delivery companies in the world, grew up about sixty miles away from each other in the Mississippi Delta.

"For all the faults and shortcomings of my home state, and I freely admit that those exist, Mississippi and Mississippians have achieved great things and will continue to do so. As governor of the Magnolia State for eight years, my administration and I worked very hard to improve the lives of Mississippians, and we made tremendous progress on multiple fronts. So, to all of the pundits and would-be political advisors out there, I will not disown my home state. I will not slink away from the public stage because some so-called journalist from New York ranks Mississippi as one of the worst states in the U.S.

"So, at this point, you may well be asking yourself, 'Why is he rambling on about Mississippi? Is this guy running for governor of Mississippi, or for president of the United States?' The point is this: there is a very significant overlap between those who want to disqualify me from the presidency because I'm from Mississippi and those who criticized my wife Michelle's references to America as a great nation in her speech a few nights ago."

Ahhh, we get it now, the audience seemed to think by nodding their heads and clapping.

The candidate continued, "Like you, I think the United States of America is the greatest nation in the history of the world."

Thunderous applause erupted throughout the arena.

"Our friends in the Democrat Party keep telling us that they want to transform America. Well, bless their hearts."

Raucous laughter spread through the audience.

"But I think you would agree with me that America is a great nation, and America doesn't need to be transformed!"

The volume of the cheering increased, with the entire audience on its feet now.

"America's critics, which mostly consist of Democrats and their servants in the media, seem to assume that slavery, racism, and the struggle for women's rights are somehow unique to America. This is not even close to being true. In fact, slavery still exists in some parts of the world today, while America freed its slaves over one hundred and fifty years ago.

"Yes, racism still exists in the United States, but it has been driven out of public view and now cowers in the dark corners of society, powerless and weak. Racism still thrives in the seats of power in other countries around the globe, but not here in America. And so, the disdain that Democrats have for our country is just as irrational as their economic policies, just as uninformed as their immigration ideas, and just as ridiculous as their foreign policy approach. The Democrats want us to think that because America has not always been perfect in the past, that America is not great today. Well, bless their hearts."

Laughter and rabid applause.

"The current president's wife said that she was proud of her country for the first time when her husband was elected president. Bless her heart."

Laugher again, mixed with boos and shouts of derision for the First Lady.

"But unlike her, and unlike the rest of the Democrats, I've always been proud of the United States of America, and I always will be!"

A nearly visible wall of sound rocketed outward from the cheering crowd as they enthusiastically waived American flags.

"Just like I'm proud to stand up for Mississippi in spite of its past shortcomings, I'm proud to stand up for the United States of America in spite of any problems in the past. And just like I worked to improve the situation in Mississippi, I'll work to help improve America. America *is* a great nation today, and, with your help and support, we can make it even greater!"

Ackerman didn't think the crowd could roar any louder, but it erupted in a sonic boom that echoed through the rafters when he delivered his closing line: "I'm Governor Jeffrey Ackerman, and I'm running for president of the United States of America!"

Chapter 23

Democratic Party Convention, Detroit, Michigan

July 2016

Two weeks after the Republican Party convention in Atlanta, the Democrats gathered for their own convention in Detroit. Although they would not say so publicly, top Democratic strategists conceded privately that the Republican convention had been a successful event. The Republicans introduced Jeff Ackerman to the nation on their own terms, and Republican voters bought what the party was selling. By skillfully attacking the media in his acceptance speech, Ackerman also managed to reverse the damage inflicted by the media earlier in the convention.

But, because Ackerman had been such an unknown figure prior to the Republican convention, the GOP candidate was still well short of where he would normally be at this point in the election cycle. Independent voters were still leery of the former governor of Mississippi, and Upton Landers enjoyed a solid-if-not-spectacular approval rating of 51 percent. The polls showed Landers with a 49 percent to 39 percent lead over Ackerman as the Democratic convention began. The election was four months away, and no Republican in modern history had overcome such a large deficit at this point in the calendar to win the general election. Even if Landers didn't get the normal post-convention bounce in his polling numbers, the incumbent president was very well positioned to cruise to re-election.

With these numbers in mind, Chief of Staff Richard Jordan began to second-guess himself. He wanted to help Upton Landers run an unapologetically leftist campaign, but the numbers showed that Landers didn't need to do so in order to win. He could simply "act presidential," do what he'd been doing for the past four years, not take any risks, and cruise to a relatively easy win in November. Yes, tacking hard to the left would be more fun, and it would carry more long-term benefits for the Democratic Party and for Upton Landers' legacy, but only if he won. And, yes, he'd probably win anyway, no matter what type of campaign he ran. But scaring the electorate by ripping off the moderate mask was about the only way that Landers could lose this election, and a loss would be the biggest political upset of the past two hundred years.

Landers had already signed off on a hard-left campaign approach. But Jordan knew he had to give Landers one more chance to change his mind before his speech on the last night of the convention. Landers' campaign manager/former mistress Gretchen Lewis and his political director/current mistress Chloe MacKenzie were both screaming behind the scenes for a moderate, centrist campaign. And all the polling data supported this careful approach. "Govern however you want once you get re-elected," Lewis and MacKenzie said to every Democratic strategist who would listen, "but for God's sake, make sure you get re-elected."

Thus, Richard Jordan approached President Landers in the office area of his Detroit hotel suite. Jordan was glad to see Chloe

MacKenzie with the president. The chief of staff wanted MacKenzie to witness the president making his final call about the campaign strategy so no one could argue later that Jordan hadn't given Landers a final chance to play it safe.

"Mr. President," Jordan began as he took a seat in a chair near the sofa where Landers was huddled close to Chloe, "you've seen the latest polling data. It's pretty clear that you'll win in November, barring a seismic shift in the polls. There's a lot to be said in favor of going the moderate route between now and then. In light of that, I thought we might want to discuss whether or not you still want to go full-on liberal with your general election campaign."

Landers was clearly irritated, although Jordan wasn't sure if it was because of what he'd said or because he preferred a private strategy session with Chloe, who was wearing the shortest skirt Jordan had ever seen. Maybe both reasons. Jordan struggled to avoid staring at her legs.

"What the hell are you talking about, Richard?" the president snarled, snapping Jordan back into the moment. "First of all, we had this conversation six months ago. We decided to take off both the gloves and the mask, to be unapologetically liberal and bury conservatism, especially Christian conservatism, for all time. Remember that little chat?"

The sarcasm was not lost on the chief of staff, who simply nodded meekly.

"Second, in case you haven't noticed, we're already in the midst of the most left-wing, tree-hugging, peacenik, granola, anti-Christian convention since George McGovern's disaster in 1972. We just adopted a platform provision calling for amending the Pledge of Allegiance to strike the phrase *under God*, and every speaker so far has called for higher taxes, open borders, and increased welfare spending. And my speech is already written, including bold and shameless endorsements of abortion on demand and decreased military spending. Don't you think it might be a tad bit too late to go back to pretending to be the party of moderation?

"And third, I told you back in January and I'll say it again now, I'm tired of running as a moderate and then trying to govern as a liberal. I'm ready to build a legacy, and it all starts with burying these fascist Bible-belt bigots with a landslide in November."

Well, Jordan thought as he mentally consoled himself, *at least the historians won't be able to say that the president was unclear about his instructions. No room for misinterpretation here.*

"Yes, sir," Jordan said quietly. "I understand all that. I just wanted to be sure we were still on the same page. And you're right, the convention has been clearly liberal thus far, although no one will really remember anything about the convention but your acceptance speech. If you want to tack back toward the center, you can do so when you speak tomorrow night. I'm sure the speechwriters still have six or seven prior drafts that are more moderate than the current version."

"He's right, Mr. President," Chloe MacKenzie added. She was pleasantly surprised that Jordan seemed be advocating her preferred approach, even if he was just covering his ass. "Your speech will set the tone for the final stretch of the campaign. It's not too late to give a politically safe yet still inspiring speech tomorrow night. You could then just keep doing what you've been doing: running the country and acting presidential. There's no way Ackerman can close such a big gap in less than four months unless we spook voters away from us and toward him."

President Landers was just as irritated with his political director as he was with his chief of staff, but his tone was kinder because the political director had such a great pair of legs. "Look, I understand where you're both coming from. And, yes, you could read the election polls and conclude that we should just run out the clock on this yahoo from Mississippi. But I've been looking at some other survey data as well. I trust that you two geniuses"—the sarcasm was back in full force now—"have seen all the recent articles about how people are deserting Christianity in droves. Secularism is winning, and the religious freaks are losing. As Democrats, we don't have to keep up the religious façade any longer. Let Ackerman have the fundamentalist vote. He was gonna get it anyway, and the Sunday-school crowd is way too small to elect a president in twenty-first-century America."

Both Richard Jordan and Chloe MacKenzie had grave doubts about the president's conclusions on this score. Yes, polls showed that fewer Americans claimed to be Christians. But this was because people who previously pretended to be Christians due to cultural peer pressure to conform to a religious stereotype now felt free to openly distance themselves from organized religion. In other words, there weren't really fewer Christians in America today, just fewer people pretending to be Christians. Also, there was no data to suggest that those who now admitted to being atheists or agnostics were likely to vote any differently than they had years ago while faking their faith. But the presidential mind was clearly made up and the matter was obviously closed, so neither staffer pushed back.

With that decision made—for the second time—the convention proceeded as initially planned. Speaker after speaker took to the podium to denounce America as racist, sexist, and hateful, both in the past and in the present. Various Democratic governors and members of Congress called on voters to continue the transformation of the United States bravely initiated by President Landers in his first term. These speeches were all heavy on rhetoric and light on details, which wasn't terribly unusual. The public wasn't paying particularly close attention to these warm-up acts in any event.

Voters who hadn't already made up their minds were waiting for Upton Landers' acceptance speech in order to choose a preferred candidate for the November election.

Meanwhile, as any experienced observer would have predicted, the media followed the marching orders issued by their Democratic overlords quite nicely. The national media ignored the fact that the Democrats abandoned the tradition of opening the convention with a prayer, as well as the addition of a new party platform provision that called for striking the phrase *under God* from the Pledge of Allegiance. News of these items was instead fed to sympathetic audiences on certain blogs and other liberal websites, where they were met with near-unanimous approval.

Reporters spent an inordinate amount of time covering the small crowd of protesters outside the convention hall and the even smaller number of Republican pundits who voiced criticism of the Democratic convention. The media seemed disappointed that the Ku Klux Klan was not there in full regalia, burning crosses in front of the arena. Instead, they were forced to resort to portraying Republicans as "closet racists" who didn't have the "courage" to be open about their feelings. Viewers and readers were treated to news segments and articles about conservatives who use "code words" to deviously communicate their messages of hate.

This year's winner of the formerly-acceptable-but-now-completely-racist-phrase-because-some-Republicans-say-it prize was "welfare reform." With no explanation as to why or how this phrase had morphed into an indicator of hatred for African Americans, the media mavens simply deemed it to be so. As the Democratic convention went on, the media gleefully portrayed any Republican who had ever supported welfare reform as a hateful bigot, again with no rationale for why such a policy position that was perfectly mainstream a week or two ago was now beyond the pale.

But the media sideshow and speeches by party elders faded into the background as President Upton Landers strode with purpose and confidence to the podium to deliver his acceptance speech, by far the most important aspect of the 2016 Democratic Party convention. Tall and patrician, with silver hair perfectly styled and sprayed into permanent perfection, he seemed born for this moment. With a baritone voice and an exceptional delivery, Landers was currently the best orator in American politics, perhaps the best since Ronald Reagan.

His speeches over the past four years were more memorable for his speaking skill than for their content. Landers and his speechwriters tended to play it safe, filling his speeches with flowery rhetoric and high-minded platitudes but little in the way of concrete policy proposals. Since clinching the Democratic nomination for his first term, Landers studiously avoided controversial topics and resisted the urge to throw red meat to his liberal base. But that would all change tonight.

Landers' elegant appearance and stylish delivery were still very much in evidence. But tonight he delivered the speech every liberal Democrat had yearned for since George McGovern defiantly consigned himself to the dustbin of history in his 1972 landslide defeat by Richard Nixon. No left-wing wish-list item was omitted by Upton Landers as he threw down the gauntlet, boldly contrasting himself and his party with Jeff Ackerman and the Republicans.

President Landers called for more generous welfare payments to the poor, the construction of new federal housing projects, and increased unemployment benefits with no time limits. He advocated a single-payer healthcare system that would eliminate private health insurance and subject all doctors to government price controls. Landers demanded that the federal government fully fund the public schools and crack down on the growing school-choice movement. All of this would be paid for, Landers claimed to full-throated cheers, by higher taxes on the wealthy. The rich would at long last be compelled to pay their fair share.

Landers bemoaned income inequality, excessive pay for corporate executives, and underrepresentation of women and African Americans on corporate boards. He promised a new round of legislation, regulation, and taxation on corporations. He proclaimed that, under his watch, boards of directors and executive office suites would be more diverse and "look like America." Companies that failed to comply would pay a steep price. Corporate America had sinned, and Landers promised vengeance.

While bold and fearless, the speech wasn't completely devoid of euphemisms and artful wordsmithing. For example, although Democrats were nearly unanimous in their support for abortion on demand, the word itself still had a negative connotation with the general public. Thus, Landers called for "unlimited and unfettered access to affordable reproductive healthcare in every community in America," subsidized by the federal government if necessary. He scolded Republicans for their willingness to subject women with unwanted pregnancies to "back-alley butchers."

Likewise, as the chief law enforcement officer in the country, the president couldn't quite express the liberal desire that the nation's immigration laws be ignored and that the borders be opened to all comers. Instead, he promised that in his second term he would promote "compassion and compromise" in all aspects of immigration policy. Landers denounced Jeff Ackerman's call for a wall along the Mexican border, and promised, in his second term, that America would at long last be a "good neighbor to the world."

President Landers aimed his harshest criticism at Christian conservatives. He sneered that Republicans used "that old-time religion" as cover for their efforts to "turn back the clock" on racial equality and social progress for women. "I have a message for the rabidly right-wing, fundamentalist mouth-breathers who descended on Atlanta recently for their little revival service disguised as a political convention," Landers roared. "America has never been, and never will be, a theocracy!"

Thunderous cheers nearly drowned out his next lines.

"We're tired of being lectured by so-called Christians, and we're tired of your attempts to legislate morality! We've chased the racists from the public square, and the sexists are on the run even now. Hear me clearly: the intolerant, moralizing, Bible-thumping fundamentalists are the next group that will be tossed on the ash heap of history!"

To any unbiased observer, and to more than a few undecided voters, Landers was a study in contrast and contradiction on this hot, humid Detroit evening. He pounded the podium with a scowl as he denounced the Republicans as being perpetually angry. He hatefully condemned the GOP as the party of hate. Although his personal net worth exceeded fifty million dollars, he proclaimed himself the champion of the poor while accusing the middle-class Jeff Ackerman of being a tool of the wealthy. Landers wore a five-thousand-dollar hand-tailored suit from London's Savile Row, a three-hundred-dollar Hermes tie, and eight-hundred-and-fifty-dollar Italian leather shoes as he chided the Republicans for their materialism and greed. Despite being white, male, and a graduate of Andover and Harvard who only interacted with African Americans when he summoned a household servant, Landers shamelessly portrayed Republicans as out-of-touch elitists who perpetuated America's sad history of racism, sexism, and classism. Yes, to a neutral observer, all of this would seem . . . unseemly.

But there were no neutral observers in the convention hall. The crowd of Democratic delegates was enraptured, erupting in thunderous applause at every opportunity. The reporters and broadcasters in the media section near the stage were only slightly less thrilled as they fought to maintain neutral expressions and body language. Print reporters pounded out positive—and nakedly partisan—news stories on their laptops, while the TV and radio talent mentally composed their next paean to President Upton Landers.

Landers closed his speech with one final not-so-subtle jab at Jeff Ackerman by tweaking Ackerman's signature line: "I'm *President* Upton Landers, and I'm running for *re-election* as president of the United States!"

The stage was now set for the most clearly partisan presidential election campaign in over a hundred years: an uncompromising conservative versus an unapologetic liberal.

Chapter 24

New York Daily Ledger
Headquarters Building – Manhattan

July 2016

Austin Brant submitted his latest editorial column to his editor at the *New York Daily Ledger*, Fred Sullivan. In it, Brant endorsed Jeff Ackerman for president over Upton Landers. In some ways, it was the easiest column he had ever written. Landers had clearly gone off the rails in his acceptance speech at the Democratic Party convention last week, tacking hard to the left. The sitting president had somehow managed to appear even less presidential than even the relatively inexperienced Ackerman.

It was only Tuesday. The column wasn't scheduled to run until Friday, but this one almost wrote itself. Brant barely had to pause as he hammered out the words on his laptop. *Might as well get one turned in well in advance of the deadline for once*, he decided. He could use this episode as a counter-example the next time Sullivan accused him of *always* waiting until the last minute to submit his column.

Although the endorsement column was extremely easy to write, Brant was somewhat uneasy as he emailed it to his boss. He was well aware of the unspoken bargain he'd made in order to get his dream job at the *Daily Ledger*. He'd very strongly implied, but not quite promised, that he would endorse Landers over Senator Olivia Hollister in the general election.

Yes, Brant felt guilty about making that implied promise. He worried that he had violated the conservative principles he'd long advocated in his writing, and that he'd done so purely for personal gain. He tried to ease his conscience by telling himself that Hollister was just as liberal as Landers. And so, if the country wanted a center-left president, they might as well go for the real thing in Upton Landers. Therefore, he tried to convince himself, endorsing Landers over Hollister wasn't a total betrayal of his ideals.

But this rationalization for making such a bargain and endorsing Landers no longer applied now that Hollister was dead and Ackerman, the unlikely candidate, was the nominee. Instead of center-left Hollister versus a slightly-left-of-center version of Landers, the country was now faced with clearly conservative Ackerman versus the now openly far-left-wing Landers. The endorsement was an easy call to make from Austin Brant's ideological perspective: it was Ackerman over Landers all day long and twice on Sunday.

However, Austin Brant now had a different dilemma. Could he endorse Ackerman over Landers without breaking his not-quite-a-promise to his new employer? And would there be any repercussions from left-leaning management for writing his conservative conscience? *I guess I'll know in a day or two*, Brant thought as he clicked *send* on his email to Sullivan with the column attached.

Brant then responded to a few emails, deleted the spam, and checked a few news-related websites. It was a quiet day on the news front, so he decided to reward himself for the early completion of his column with a stroll over to Central Park and a hot dog or three from Gray's Papaya. A scorching heat wave in the city had recently broken, and he looked forward to walking in weather that didn't quite resemble a sauna.

Brant had just closed his laptop and stood to leave his office when Fred Sullivan tapped on his office door.

"What's up, Fred?" the columnist asked the tall, thin, and perpetually gloomy-looking editor.

"We're not gonna run your column this week," Sullivan answered with characteristic bluntness.

"And why is that?" Brant dropped back into his chair as Sullivan folded his lanky frame into a guest chair on the opposite side of the cluttered desk.

"Management isn't happy about Ackerman's attacks on the press during the Republican convention. The paper is officially endorsing Landers on Friday in an unsigned editorial, and the powers that be want no dissenting voices on the editorial page that day. So we can't run your column endorsing Ackerman."

Brant decided not to quibble with Sullivan's characterization of Ackerman's speech as an "attack" on the press. The candidate had merely explained the reality of the situation and revealed some facts that the media found uncomfortable. But that wasn't his fight today. Instead, he decided to try to get to the heart of the matter, at least as far as it concerned himself and his future at the *New York Daily Ledger.* "Are you saying you can't run my endorsement column on Friday, or that you can't run it at all?"

Sullivan shrugged. "I honestly don't know. The folks upstairs just told me to be sure we spoke with a unanimous voice on Friday's editorial page. I asked them what I should do about your column, since it runs every Friday. It struck me as rather unlikely that you'd write something praising Landers or criticizing Ackerman, and we have to fill the space somehow."

As far as Brant knew, Fred Sullivan was unaware of his implied promise to endorse Landers over Hollister. "And?" he prodded.

Sullivan took a deep breath. "They told me to hold off on talking to you until you submitted your piece. They wanted to see what you wrote. If it was pro-Landers, then fine, run the piece as usual. But if not, then they told me to spike your piece and run a guest column in its place."

That explains the lightning-quick decision to spike my column, Brant thought. "A guest column by whom?"

"Grant Danielson."

"Who's that?"

"Some former ambassador to some little country no one has ever heard of. A seventy-something-year-old George H. W. Bush appointee. He's apparently the only Republican we could find who was willing to endorse Landers over Ackerman, especially in light of Ackerman's stunt where he claimed that the media orchestrates this stuff to make Republicans look bad."

Well, isn't that what the paper is doing right now? Brant wondered. But a conversation with a mostly non-political worker bee like Fred Sullivan was not a productive way to influence the hard-left political stance of the *New York Daily Ledger.* Accordingly, Brant tried to focus the conversation on his immediate future with the paper. "So, in summary, the instructions were to spike the column if I wrote something that reflects my genuine, long-held political beliefs and positions, but gleefully run the column if I kowtow to the political leanings of management."

Sullivan simply shrugged and gave a brief nod.

"What about other columns going forward related to the presidential election? Is this a one-time thing, or do I have to worry about continued censorship from above?"

"*Censorship* is kind of a strong word," Sullivan answered. "But to answer your question, I don't know how this effects future columns.

My job is to get the paper out tomorrow. I'll worry about the next day when it gets here."

A flurry of thoughts flashed through Austin Brant's mind as his boss got to his feet and left the office. He knew that he should resign in protest. No opinion columnist could tolerate having management dictate what he wrote. But he also knew that doing so wouldn't change anything in the long run. Even if he shouted "Censorship!" to the highest heavens, his resignation would be a one-day news item at best. The *Daily Ledger* would simply find another arguably conservative columnist to replace him, one who was more willing to bend his views to the bosses' will.

Instead, Brant tried to think of a way to address his problem in a way that might lead to some sort of media reform. He then remembered that he was still on an email distribution list that he shouldn't be on, inviting him to periodic conference calls that he wasn't meant to hear. He powered up his laptop, opened his email program, and began scribbling notes to himself.

Chapter 25

Ackerman Campaign Strategy Memorandum

July 2016

**STRICTLY CONFIDENTIAL;
ANYONE CAUGHT LEAKING WILL BE KICKED IN
THE FACE**

To: All Campaign Staff

From: Art Morgan

Date: July 20, 2016

RE: Campaign Strategy Memo Number 23

Status of the Race: Awful, but with just a little more effort we can improve to "Really Bad." Republicans have come home to us, but Democrats remain loyal to Landers. We've seen no evidence that independents are moving our way or even paying very much attention to what we have to say. If we don't start convincing some independents or flipping some Democrats to our side, we'll lose a race that will give new meaning to the word *landslide*.

Internal Polling Data: Landers is up 48%–39% nationally. State-level polling is similar, with no indication that we can pull off a win in purple states like Florida or Ohio, much less win a blue state like Michigan or Pennsylvania.

Financial Update: We're in good shape on the money front. Hal Harrington came through with the $200 million he promised for the general election, and other big-time Republican donors opened their wallets when Jeff kicked a little Democrat ass at our convention. We could always find ways to spend more money, but all indications are that we have enough cash on hand such that money won't be the reason we lose this thing.

Media Strategy: Many of you have wondered why Governor Ackerman went out of his way to attack the media in his acceptance speech. He even went so far as to insert the bulk of the attack lines at the last minute, after the copies of the speech had already been distributed to the media for review and analysis, thereby catching the talking heads off guard and making them look even more stupid than usual. Your humble campaign manager questioned the strategy as well, but the governor explained his thinking to me later when I asked him why he declared war on the press. He said that the media had been at war with Republicans for decades; we just hadn't bothered to fight back. Republican candidate after Republican candidate has tried to woo the media and convince them to at least be neutral even if they won't come over to our side. Clearly that hasn't worked, as the media has moved ever more leftward over the years, dragging a large part of the unsuspecting electorate along with them.

Governor Ackerman simply decided to face reality and treat the press for what it is: an extension of the Democrat Party. That doesn't mean that they are our enemies, but they are our opponents. No longer will they get the benefit of the doubt from our campaign. Unless and until a reporter proves otherwise, we will assume that his goal in life is to help Upton Landers get re-elected. We won't treat them with hatred or anger. Instead, we'll just point at them and laugh at their pathetic efforts to try to hide their biases. We'll chide them and tweak them, smiling all the while.

Strategic Plan: The Democrats really did us a favor by ripping off the moderate mask at their convention. Landers could have just mailed in a boring, middle-of-the-political-road acceptance speech. This would have virtually guaranteed him a four- to six-point win in November. All they had to do was be reasonably sane, but that was too much for them.

By revealing their true leftist roots, the Dems have opened a door for us. This is a center-right country, and we now have a shot at winning the votes of the moderates who would have otherwise voted for Landers. Thus, the strategic plan is to stay on the conservative message, but try to convince moderates to join us. We'll do this by continuing to explain the thought process behind our conservative positions. Moderates might not agree with our conclusions, but they'll at least see that we're sane and rational, unlike that Marxist clown show in Detroit last week.

Operational Plan: We've got a big hill to climb in the polls and a media environment that's even more hostile than usual. Traditional Republican methods are unlikely to help us close the gap fast enough, so we have to be unconventional. Governor Ackerman wants to make a concerted effort to win a bigger-than-usual slice of the minority and ethnic vote.

Hispanics, Asian Americans, and especially African Americans are all relatively conservative from a cultural point of view, but they vote overwhelmingly Democrat. We can win this election if we take just a few bites out of the normal Democratic share of these voters. We don't have to win a majority of these votes. But let's assume that we go from getting only 5% of the black vote to getting 15%. In this scenario, we win Florida and Ohio. Michigan, Pennsylvania, and Wisconsin would be in play, although we probably wouldn't be able to overcome the Dem's usual election fraud and dirty tricks unless we get the black total up to the 18%–20% range.

Republican candidates always pay lip service to these voters but then give up way too early and easily. We're going to push much harder for these votes. The governor will be speaking in black churches and spending a lot of time in Hispanic and Asian communities.

Messaging and Themes: Twelve words: Cut taxes. Cut spending. Reform entitlements. Protect our borders. Appoint conservative judges.

Conclusion: Yes, things are bad. You all knew that when you joined up for this little venture. But we have a real shot to win, thanks in no small part to the idiocy of the other side. Let's go win some votes. Press on!

Chapter 26

Franklin Avenue African Methodist Episcopal Church Lansing, Michigan

July 2016

Jeff Ackerman sat on the hard, uncushioned wooden pew near the front in the century-old sanctuary of one of the oldest and largest African-American congregations in Michigan. He had six or seven staffers with him, none of whom thought this visit was worth the candidate's valuable time. Surprisingly, Ackerman had asked Scott Williamson, his campaign's highest-ranking African American, not to attend the church service on this cloudy, muggy, steamy August Sunday morning. Heavy rain was imminent, and thunder rolled in the distance.

Rain would match the mood of the small, pale-complexioned group of staffers around Ackerman. They were surrounded by a sea of blacks in their Sunday finest, who cast cold, hostile glances toward the timid white contingent. None of these church members had ever voted for a Republican. All of them had been taught since birth that white Southern Republicans like Jeff Ackerman were racist crackers who lynched blacks for sport and worked hard to keep black people poor and subservient. And the very white Jeff Ackerman had decided to leave his best asset for this setting, the very black Scott Williamson, back at the hotel doing God knows what. So much for the purported wisdom and vision of their boss.

The candidate couldn't suppress a smile as he noticed his staffers fidgeting impatiently. He'd made them surrender their cell phones before entering the church, nearly inciting a riot among his entourage. But he knew he had to keep these youngsters from spending the entire service doing whatever it was that Millennials did with their phones, because texting during a church service was neither proper nor respectful. *And God help us if one of our phones were to ring during the sermon*, the candidate thought with a grin.

Ackerman knew that his staffers viewed this Sunday morning visit to a black church as a complete waste of time, given the nearly complete stranglehold that Democrats had on the black vote. "Why don't we spend time talking to people who might, you know, actually vote for us?" was the prevailing attitude among the staff. And why not take advantage of Scott Williamson's dark skin to at least show some solidarity with the audience? Having their cell phones taken away exacerbated their frustration. Now they couldn't salvage the wasted time by at least answering some emails and text messages.

Despite the unhappiness and discomfort of his staffers, Jeff Ackerman was at ease and at peace. To win the election against nearly impossible odds, he knew he had to make more than the traditional token effort by Republicans at winning the black vote. And his best chance for winning in the Electoral College was to flip a traditionally blue state into the red column. Here, with an audience of nearly a thousand African Americans in the blue state of Michigan, he hoped to take a big step toward accomplishing both goals. In fact, he'd instructed Art Morgan to get him at least one speaking opportunity—and hopefully two or three—in a black church in a swing state on every Sunday between now and Election Day.

Great leaders didn't explain themselves to underlings. At least, not at the time at which the big decision was made. Thus, Ackerman consciously decided not to explain his seemingly bizarre decision to exclude Scott Williamson from this campaign appearance.

Ackerman wanted his appearance and his speech today to be about substance, not symbolism. He knew that having Scott Williamson at his side would simply invite a few lazy stories from the press about how Williamson was one of only a handful of blacks among his campaign workers. Thus, they would write about the racial composition of his campaign staff, rather than the words he was about to say to this black congregation. Ackerman also knew that he would still be criticized by the media even if he paraded in with a staff of nothing but African Americans, in which case he'd be accused of "pandering" and "a cheap political stunt" for hiring nothing but "tokens who weren't authentically black." As it stood, he didn't expect the press to congratulate him in print for nobly leaving behind his high-ranking black staffer, but he hoped that they would at least ignore the issue and write about his speech instead.

Although Ackerman didn't have Williamson at his side this morning, he had picked the staffer's brain in an effort to determine why blacks are so hostile to Republicans. The response was depressing. Williamson told his boss that black hostility to Republicans is so ingrained that it is pretty much inherited at birth. Republican racism and other evils are simply assumed as facts, and precious few African Americans question that received wisdom or seek the truth for themselves. Williamson pointed out that no one has to work to convince you that Satan is evil; you just somehow know it because you've always known it and have never had to think about it.

Unfortunately, Williamson continued, the same is true for Republicans when it comes to blacks in the United States.

Ackerman was wishing he hadn't even asked his senior advisor the question when the news got even worse. Williamson mentioned that blacks who leave the liberal plantation are denounced as Uncle Toms, traitors to their race, or in some cases as not really black at all. He cited Supreme Court Justice Clarence Thomas, former Secretary of State Condoleezza Rice, and brilliant economists Thomas Sowell and Walter Williams as examples of this phenomenon.

Despite this depressing news, Ackerman knew he had to make a real effort to peel some black votes away from Landers. Prior Republican presidential candidates had made half-hearted efforts on this front and then retreated quickly after poor initial results. But Ackerman vowed to press on regardless, as this was not only the right thing to do, but also his only path to winning the election.

Now that he was in the habit of giving three or four speeches per day, he no longer got pre-speech butterflies. But the typical campaign address contained a positive message and was delivered to a friendly, appreciative crowd. This morning he would deliver an unvarnished, unpopular message to an unfriendly audience, and the jitters seized him with a vengeance. As the choir's beautiful rendition of "Amazing Grace" filled the sanctuary, Ackerman prayed silently. He asked for peace, for wisdom, and for an open-minded audience.

The prayer calmed him briefly, but his nerves flared up again as the senior pastor of the church introduced him from the pulpit. The introduction was short, cold, and just shy of disdainful. Ackerman was sure his campaign staff had been forced to make some promises in order to secure this speaking opportunity for him, but he hadn't asked the details, mainly because he didn't want to know. Evidently, those promises, donations, or gifts—Ackerman fought to keep the word *bribes* from entering his mind —had been sufficient to secure the chance to address the congregation but not enough to buy the candidate a warm, friendly introduction.

Ackerman strode toward the pulpit, buttoning his suit coat as he walked. He was in the process of lifting his right hand from his side to shake hands with the pastor as he reached the podium, but the elderly clergyman abruptly turned his back and returned to his seat. Hoping he looked less awkward than he felt, Ackerman simply kept his unshaken right hand moving upward and leftward, using it to reach into the breast pocket of his coat to retrieve his written notes.

After quickly arranging his text on the podium in front of him, Ackerman forced a broad smile onto his face and looked up to face his audience. No one smiled back. Lots of heads were down, staring at cell phone screens. Even more arms were crossed across chests, accompanied by facial expressions that radiated contempt. A few of the elderly matrons in the congregation looked up at him with a trace of sympathy, almost speaking with their eyes as if to say, "You poor, lost Republican white boy. You don't know what you've gotten yourself into, do you?"

Unfortunately, I do know what I've gotten myself into, Ackerman thought. *Now it's up to me to see if I can accomplish something with this crowd before they throw me out of here.* With the big smile still affixed to his face, he began to speak. "Thank you so much for having me here today." He glibly skipped over the language of his written text, which called for him to thank the pastor for such a kind introduction. "It's a pleasure to be here to worship with you in such a beautiful and historic sanctuary. I appreciate the chance to speak to you today. I know you often have political candidates come to visit you during election season, but I'm guessing that you don't often have *Republican* candidates here on Sunday mornings. It's probably even more unusual to have a *white* Republican candidate who wants to

231

talk to you, and I want you to know that I appreciate your willingness to hear what I have to say."

Ackerman sensed the slightest thaw in the congregation's attitude. This was probably not because they liked him, but because these were genuinely warm, nice people who had a hard time being unfriendly to anyone who was willing to treat them with kindness and respect. On the spur of the moment, he decided to take a detour from his prepared text. "Before I get into my remarks, I'd like to pray for our time here together. Please bow your heads and join me in prayer." Ackerman hoped the pastor wouldn't object. His staff had promised a quick, rather secular speech. The pastor didn't want Ackerman to mislead his flock with a pseudo-sermon that would no doubt be theologically incorrect. But surely a quick prayer would be all right, wouldn't it?

"Father, we come before Your throne this morning in awe of who You are. You are the God of the universe, the King of kings, and the Lord of lords. Thank You for this opportunity to speak directly to You. Lord, I just want to pause for a moment, to be still and know that You are God, to acknowledge that You are God and that we are not." The candidate did in fact pause here for a moment after quoting Psalm 46:10. Eyes tightly shut, he nevertheless noticed an absolute stillness in the sanctuary as he continued his prayer. "Lord, I thank You for the gift of Your Son, Jesus. Because You loved the world, You gave Him up into the hands of sinners like us, to pay the ultimate penalty for the sins of the world. John 3:16 tells us that You did this, Father, not because You love white people, or because You love black people, but because You love *all people*, because You love *the world*. Because You love the world, You *gave*, and we can never thank You enough for such a tremendous gift on our behalf."

A few approving murmurs rippled through the crowd, along with an "Amen!" or two. *This guy may not look like us,* many of them thought, *but he sure sounds like us.*

"Father, please bless this time that I have together with these good and decent and kind people who love You. Yes, Lord, I'm white and they are black. Yes, I'm a Republican and most of them are Democrats. We've had different lives and different experiences and have very different political views. But I ask that You'll allow all of us to set those differences aside this morning and truly seek to understand each other."

A few more indications of approval and affirmation now emanated from the worshipers.

"Help each one of us see everyone else here as You see them, Lord: as one of Your children that You loved enough to sacrifice Your Son on a Roman cross, in an agonizing and humiliating death, all for our sake. Thank You, Lord, for raising Jesus from the dead, thereby giving us the hope of joining in that resurrection one day. And it is in the matchless and holy and powerful name of Jesus that I pray. Amen."

"Amen!" echoed the congregation with much more enthusiasm than Ackerman could've dared hope for.

The candidate opened his eyes and found the audience transformed before him. Smiles replaced scowls. The cell phones were no longer in evidence. Arms were no longer crossed forebodingly across chests.

Ackerman grinned at his audience and joked, "A brilliant speechmaker would look out at this crowd, see the improvement in your body language and expressions, and end his speech right here. He'd skip his actual speech, take the small victory of improving your mood and your impression of him, and sit down and shut up before he blew it. But no one ever accused me of being a brilliant speechmaker, so I'm going to keep going for a few more minutes."

The crowd chuckled. A little self-deprecation went a long way.

"I need to warn you folks up-front that you're not going to like what I have to say today. At least, not at first. You might like it later, or at least agree with me a little, after you've had a chance to think about it for a few minutes.

"Because, you see, this is not going to be the type of speech you'd hear from a Democrat candidate. A Democrat would stand here in this pulpit and talk about how racist the Republicans are. He'd tell you that white people like me, and especially white Republicans like me, want to keep you down. That Democrat speaker would convince you that he was the only thing standing between you and a return to the chains of slavery.

"Once he had you appropriately riled up against white Republicans, he'd start making promises to you. He'd tell you that he would increase your welfare payments and make food stamps more readily available. He'd promise to boost your unemployment benefits. He'd promise to fill his staff and his administration with black people, folks who 'look like you.' He'd make some vague promise about 'fully funding' the public schools. Yes, a Democrat candidate, if he were here today, would promise all sorts of goodies for you. And he'd promise to increase taxes on racist wealthy white people and businesses in order to pay for it all."

The audience turned thoughtful, and Ackerman could tell that he was hitting the mark.

He went on, "Democrat candidates use that combination of stirring up resentment and then promising free stuff to you for one reason: it works. They come to churches like this one, and give speeches like the one I just described, and then you go and vote for them. Democrats own the black vote almost completely, routinely getting ninety to ninety-five percent of the black vote in presidential elections. And because of your vote, Democrats like Upton

Landers get elected. Ladies and gentlemen, I have to ask you a question: how's that working out for you?"

Murmurs in the crowd again. One person actually said, loud enough for all to hear, "Not so good!"

"In fact," Ackerman went on, "I think it's safe to say that you're not any better off now than you were four years ago when you voted for Upton Landers. It's also safe to say that the black community as a whole is much worse off today than it was when these government-sponsored giveaway programs began back in the 1960s."

Heads were really nodding now.

"So let's examine the two main messages that Democrats like Upton Landers tell audiences like you. Again, the first message is that Republicans are racist, and the second message is that welfare, food stamps, and the like will help lift you out of poverty and out of the lower class. Both of these are blatant lies.

"First things first. Are Republicans racist? President Abraham Lincoln, who led the fight to free the slaves, was a Republican. He was opposed by Democrats. Which party sounds more racist to you? General Ulysses S. Grant, later President Ulysses S. Grant, was the commander of the Northern army fighting to free the slaves. He was a Republican, and he was opposed by Democrats. Which party sounds more racist to you? Republican presidents and congressmen enacted the constitutional amendments that freed the slaves and made them full citizens. They were opposed by Democrats. Which party sounds more racist to you?

"Republicans worked for full civil rights for blacks in the years following the Civil War. Democrats countered by forming the Ku Klux Klan and implementing segregationist policies, poll taxes, and other Jim Crow measures, all in an effort to make sure blacks remained second-class citizens. Which party sounds more racist to you?

"Republican President Dwight Eisenhower and Republican congressmen and senators passed the Civil Rights Act of 1957. Democrats in Congress opposed them. And it wasn't just Southern Democrats that opposed the bill. For example, Democratic Senator—and later President—John F. Kennedy of Massachusetts voted against the bill, while Republican Vice President—and later President—Richard Nixon supported it. Which party sounds more racist to you?

"And the Republicans weren't interested in just civil rights legislation. They wanted to help black people by actually desegregating our society. For example, Republican President Eisenhower sent federal troops to places like Little Rock, Arkansas, in order to enforce civil rights for black Americans. Democratic governors like Orval Faubus in Arkansas, George Wallace in Alabama, and Ross Barnett in Mississippi all openly defied the law in order to keep black people down. Which party sounds more racist to you?"

Ackerman could almost hear the wheels turning in the minds of his audience members. This was certainly different from the anti-American version of American history they had learned in school. And this guy was speaking to them as peers, as adults capable of rational thought, not as if he were some sugar daddy coming to hand out goodies to helpless, unthinking serfs.

Ackerman seized on the momentum and continued his address. "In order to excuse all of this horrific and racist behavior, the Democrats would have you believe that the two parties just switched positions: they claim that all the racists in the Democrat Party became Republicans, while the non-racist Republicans simultaneously became Democrats. There's no evidence to support this bizarre theory, mainly because it isn't true. This would be the same as all Detroit Lions fans suddenly converting to Chicago Bears fans, while all the Bears fans became Lions fans at the same time. There's no reason for such a switch, and thus it would never happen."

236

The audience there in Lansing, consisting mostly of longtime Detroit Lions fans, nodded along in agreement. There was no way they would ever cheer for the hated Bears, and they'd never expect Bears fans to ditch the navy blue of Chicago for the silver and electric blue of Detroit.

Ackerman then offered a better, much more plausible explanation for the current political landscape. "What actually happened was this. Blacks were voting for Republicans in large numbers, mainly because of the historical examples of non-racist Republican politicians I mentioned earlier. Democrat Lyndon Johnson wanted to change that. His so-called 'Great Society' program was a cynical ploy designed to help Democrats win the black vote while simultaneously creating a permanent class of Americans that was dependent on federal government benefits to survive. Johnson famously said, 'I'll have them blacks voting Democratic for two hundred years.' Except Johnson didn't use the word *blacks* in that quote I just gave you. He used the n-word instead, and I think you can understand why I didn't quote him verbatim just now. In any event, again I ask you, which party sounds more racist to you?

"And so, ladies and gentlemen, the first message of Democrats like Upton Landers to black audiences like this one, that Republicans are racist and Democrats are not, is utterly false. Now, what about the second message—that welfare and other government programs like those enacted by racist Democrat Lyndon Johnson, which still continue to this day, are the best means of helping blacks overcome the vestiges of slavery and climb the economic ladder? Is this true? Unfortunately, one doesn't have to review the facts very long to determine that this is also a lie.

"Democrat President Lyndon Johnson launched the Great Society program in large part to entice black voters to switch to the Democrat Party. As part of the Great Society, Johnson declared 'war' on poverty. Unfortunately, poverty won. Poverty rates in the U.S. had fallen from 32.1% to 14.7% prior to Johnson's declaration of war on poverty. Fifty years later, after spending hundreds of billions of dollars, the poverty rate is essentially unchanged, hovering in the neighborhood of 13%.

"This was not a case of a well-intentioned plan going wrong, and the results are a lot worse than simply wasting massive amounts of taxpayer money. The Great Society and Johnson's War on Poverty programs destroyed incentives to work, save, and invest. This was a feature, not a bug. Now, in 2016, we have generations of families, one after the next after the next, who live in government housing projects and live off of welfare checks and food stamps.

"As you know all too well, generational poverty is a particular problem in the African-American community. Prior to the Great Society, black families were relatively stable. Rates of unemployment, incarceration, divorce, and births to unwed mothers among blacks were close to those of the rest of the country. The Great Society changed all of that. Now, after generations of so-called 'help' from the federal government in the form of welfare, food stamps, housing, and other programs that encourage dependency on government rather than self-reliance, blacks have fallen far behind whites and Asians in America today. In some current statistical categories, blacks are even trailing Hispanics, who have to fight through language barriers in addition to racial prejudice.

"You see problems in your communities every day, where teenage mothers struggle to raise children, often dropping out of school to do so. The father is long gone, often in prison. The teenage mother walks down the stairs of the crumbling apartment building in the projects to the mailbox to collect her welfare check each month. Perhaps she's accompanied by her thirty-something-year-old mother and forty-something-year-old grandmother, who are also on welfare. None of them have any concept of a career, or even working a steady job. Having a stable family life with a husband who works to provide for his wife and children is just a fairy tale to folks like this."

Ackerman could tell that his audience was tracking along with him. They wanted to believe him, even wanted to applaud him. He hoped he wouldn't lose this goodwill as he launched into the difficult concluding section of his address. "My friends, Democrats tell you that this is all a result of racist Republican policies. According to them, you're suffering due to some evil, sinister white Republican plot to harm black people. But, ladies and gentlemen, I'm here to tell you today that this is not the case. African Americans are suffering in poverty and in prison today not because of too little welfare spending, but because of too much!

"Whether it was well-intentioned or not, our system of welfare and food stamps and subsidized housing and free school lunches simply hasn't helped the recipients of this type of aid. In fact, if you sat down and designed a batch of government programs that seemed generous and helpful at first glance, but which were actually intended to harm its so-called beneficiaries, you couldn't do a better job!

"Our benefits system seems helpful, but it keeps you poor! It seems helpful, but it keeps you unemployed! It seems helpful, but it keeps you uneducated! It seems helpful, but it keeps you imprisoned! It seems helpful, but it destroys the family unit! It seems helpful, but it keeps you dependent on government handouts for generation after generation!

"You see, my friends, people respond to incentives. We all know that if you punish a child for bad behavior and reward him for good behavior, that child learns to act correctly. The same is true for adults: if you reward hard work and punish laziness and wrongdoing, adults are more likely to act in ways that benefit themselves, their families, and society as a whole.

"With that in mind, let's look at what type of behavior our welfare system encourages. For many years, a young black mother could receive more money from welfare if she was unmarried than if she was married. And she'd receive even more money if she had more children. Thus, the welfare system discouraged marriage and encouraged out-of-wedlock births. The same perverse incentives apply to public housing. If you give someone a place to live as a government entitlement, they have less incentive to move out of the projects and into a better neighborhood.

"This bizarre system utterly destroyed the black family. Again, this is so because people respond to incentives. Now, my friends, I'm about to lay out some facts for you, things that you know are true because you see examples every day. And yet a white guy like me will be called a racist for stating the truth. I'll just have to live with that, because as a Republican presidential candidate I'll be called a racist by the media no matter what I do or say. In any event, here are the cold, hard facts.

"A child born today to a black mother has less than a ten percent chance of being raised by a mother and father who are married to each other, stay married, and live in the same home together until that child is grown. A child born to a mother living in the projects today has very little chance of escaping the projects, and that child's own children will likely live in the projects as well. A black baby conceived today is more likely to be aborted than he is to graduate from college. Therefore, the second message that Democrat politicians preach to black audiences, that welfare is a means to boost its recipients upward in society, is just as much of a lie as the blatant falsehood that Republicans are racists.

"So we see that Lyndon Johnson succeeded in his goal to flip black voters from the Republican Party to the Democrats. Initially, it was because black voters were grateful for the welfare plans of the Great Society, but over time they've stayed with the Democrats because they are now dependent on federal government programs to survive. They crave the next government handout as much as any crack addict craves that next draw on the pipe.

"As an added bonus for Democrats, they can now challenge any Republican ideas to solve the problem as racist! Thus, Republicans have learned through painful experience not to even bother trying to solve these problems. Again, people respond to incentives. The political wisdom is that blacks won't vote for Republicans, so Republicans don't really try to win the black vote. And they know their careers will suffer if they propose welfare reform, so they don't do it. Democrat politicians also respond to incentives. Because they must have ninety percent or more of the black vote to win national elections, the Democrats' goal is to keep you poor enough to need welfare and scared enough of the Republicans to keep voting Democrat.

"In summary, the two primary messages that Democrats speak to black audiences like this one are lies. The truth is that Republicans are not racists, and that welfare ultimately harms, rather than helps, poor blacks. What does that mean for you and me here today?

"I said a few minutes ago that political wisdom dictates that Republican candidates ignore black voters and stay away from issues like welfare. If a Republican insists on reaching out to black voters, political pundits and advisors expect him to renounce conservatism, apologize for Republican racism, and then promise blacks even more handouts than Democrats. Well,"—Ackerman gave a rueful shake of the head—"no one ever accused me of having all that much political wisdom, because I'm here today talking to black voters about welfare. And I'm not here to grovel or apologize or promise any political goodies.

"I'm here today to ask for your vote in November. And I ask you to vote for me, not because I'm going to give you a bigger welfare check or a slightly newer government apartment in a housing project or more food stamps. Those are the types of goodies that Democrats promise in order to buy your votes. I'm asking for your vote today because if you help me, I'll get elected. And if I get elected, I'm going to work with my friends in the African-American community to break this cycle of welfare and dependency!"

The candidate feared an awkward, stony silence at this point in his speech. He was ready to plunge forward quickly with the next lines in order to avoid such an embarrassment. Instead, shouts of "Amen!" rippled through the congregation, and there was even some scattered applause.

Encouraged by the positive reaction, the candidate nodded along with his audience and went on, "Yes, in order to undo the damage that welfare has imposed on you, your friends, and your neighbors, we'll have to do some things that are painful in the short run. What are those things? My plan is to impose time limits on cash welfare benefits, food stamps, and government housing in order to nudge people toward independence and freedom. I also plan to slash the number of federal government jobs that measure their so-called 'success' by how much welfare money they hand out.

"I want to encourage local governments to increase the police presence in poor areas in order to protect law-abiding black citizens from all criminals, whether those criminals are black or white. I want to unchain your public schools from federal bureaucracy so that they can be free to find innovative ways to teach your children.

"Yes, it will be a difficult transition for some people. Yes, there will be some folks who simply can't make the transition away from government dependence. Yes, charitable groups like your church here will need to step up to help. Yes, the media will focus on the negative aspects exclusively and ignore everyone whose lives are improved as a result of our efforts. Yes, it will be a long and difficult transition with few immediately obvious benefits. And, yes, I'll be called a racist and a bigot and a Nazi and whatever other names the press can come up with in order to disparage me.

"But understand this, ladies and gentlemen: together, we can break this cycle of poverty and prison! Together, we can help rebuild the idea of a black family so that it once again includes a mother and a father, married to each other, and raising their children together in a house that they own, rather than a rusting, ramshackle apartment in the ghetto! Together, we can transform schools in poor black areas from war zones into true places of learning! And together, we can replace the welfare check with a paycheck!"

With the congregation now on its feet, clapping and whistling, the candidate closed with his standard line, altered a bit to fit the setting: "I'm Governor Jeff Ackerman, and I'm running for president of the United States! May God bless you and your families, and may He bless this church and its ministries! Thank you for having me today!"

As much as Ackerman wanted to stay and bask in the newfound approval from this audience, he and his staff hustled out of the sanctuary as the pastor walked to the pulpit to begin his sermon. The candidate was scheduled to speak to another black church in Lansing later that morning, followed by two more in Detroit that same Sunday evening. He said a quick silent prayer of thanks as he hustled onto the campaign bus, and then asked God for a similar result at his remaining three stops that day.

Chapter 27

Powerlineblog.com Blog Post

August 2016

Jeff Ackerman wasn't making much progress in the polls, but he was winning fans in the conservative blogosphere. Ackerman and his campaign were buoyed to see the following post on the Powerline Blog, and they quickly forwarded links to their email contact lists.

Ten Things to Like About Jeff Ackerman

We don't like to brag (okay, sometimes we do), but we'll pat ourselves on the back for identifying Jeff Ackerman as a rising conservative political star way back when he was a no-name nobody polling in the low single digits against the late Senator Olivia Hollister. Ackerman was gaining rapidly on her and likely would have eclipsed her in the primaries before her untimely death made Ackerman the nominee almost by default. The former governor of Mississippi continues to impress us, not only with his policy proposals, but also with his wisdom and cultural insight generally.

In addition to taking the right (in more ways than one) positions, Ackerman is an effective advocate for conservatism writ large. He's the first Republican presidential candidate since Ronald Reagan who combines true conservative beliefs with the verbal and oratorical ability to explain them and sell them to the masses. He's doing so on a daily basis in spite of a media environment that is even more overtly hostile to the Republican candidate than usual.

We've been particularly pleased with the candidate's stance on the issues. Here are our five favorites, in no particular order:

1.   The Supreme Court. *Ackerman favors originalists and textualists in the mode of Justices Scalia and Thomas. We particularly enjoyed his description of the current crop of intellectually incurious liberals on the Supreme Court: "They have the easiest job in Washington. I'm not saying they aren't smart; they appear to be so. But any halfwit could do their job. Just take the latest set of talking points from the Democratic National Committee about some new constitutional right that no one thought of until about twelve minutes ago. Then, claim that the Constitution does in fact confer said right in some hidden penumbra or emanation that's not actually in the document itself. Take phrases like* living Constitution, substantive due process, *and* equal protection of the laws; *throw them in a box; shake them up; and spit out an opinion. No thought, no intellectual heavy lifting, required." Ackerman has also pointed out that conservative justices sometimes differ on major cases, but he challenges anyone to name the last time any of the liberal justices veered rightward on a major case where their vote was needed. It just doesn't happen. This is because liberal justices are more beholden to their tribe (the Democratic Party) than they are to the Constitution and federal law. To leftists, this is a desirable attribute.*

2.   Abortion. *Ackerman has made the very important point that overruling Roe v. Wade doesn't automatically make abortion illegal or unavailable. It simply means that killing babies is no longer a constitutionally protected right, a right that was invented in the Roe decision via an exercise of raw judicial power and so-called legal reasoning that embarrasses even pro-abortion legal experts. In a post-Roe world, states would be free to regulate and/ or restrict abortions as their voters deem appropriate. Thus, abortion would* *be returned to the political process. Some states will ban abortion outright, while others will encourage it. This is the essence of our federalist system as envisioned by our Founders.*

*3.   **Education.** Governor Ackerman is the first presidential candidate with the wisdom and courage to clearly denounce federal education spending as a miserable failure. Ackerman notes that since 1970, spending per student has nearly tripled (in constant dollars), and the number of school employees has nearly doubled, and yet test scores are flat (and by some measures worse). During that period, the federal government has spent nearly $1.5 trillion on education, all with nothing to show for it. In light of this miserable failure and this massive waste of taxpayer funds, Ackerman's bold proposal to eliminate the U.S. Department of Education and federal funding for public schools is a step in the right direction and should be more popular than it is. On the other side, President Landers proposes to double down on past failures, claiming that he'll "fully fund" public schools. Ackerman responds, "What does that even mean? Does he have some specific dollar amount in mind? Does he have any convincing evidence that 'fully funding' our public schools will actually improve education for our kids?" Although these are rhetorical questions, we'd enjoy seeing someone actually pose them to President Landers.*

*4.   **Energy.** As in other policy areas, Jeff Ackerman's energy proposals would unleash American ingenuity and innovation and get government out of the way of the useful, productive elements of society. He proposes to ease restrictions on fracking, off-shore drilling, and exporting oil and natural gas. He also advocates the common-sense notion of increasing nuclear power, one of the safest and most environmentally friendly sources of energy. The Democrats and their media allies are howling about this, pining for more wind and solar power instead. Governor Ackerman accurately notes that wind and solar are fine as far as they go, but they are not yet reliable means of producing the volume of energy required to run our economy. And he succinctly describes the reason for the left's opposition to his energy proposals: "Democrats only* *like energy sources that don't work. The only way to rationally explain their energy policy is that they want the United States economy to shrink and the world to have less energy."*

5. **Military Spending.** *As advocated by many military experts but few politicians, Governor Ackerman would beef up our military. But he'd do so on a cost-neutral basis by cutting bureaucracy and the number of non-combat military personnel, consolidating bases, and modernizing the procurement system. Almost everyone agrees that it takes too long and involves too much red tape to get a new plane, ship, or weapons system in place. If our troops in the field need a gun, then let's by God get it to them right the hell now. Also, Ackerman rightly criticizes President Landers for using our military for "peacekeeping" missions, especially where there's no peace to keep in the first place and no American interest in the area anyway. Our troops, he notes with admirable bluntness, are trained to kill people and break things. If they're not going to be used for what they trained for, keep them at home and save American money and American lives. For God's sake, don't use them as a buffer (or target) by placing our troops in between two groups that want to kill each other.*

In addition to solid, proven conservative policy positions like the five described above, Governor Ackerman has demonstrated unique wisdom and insight on our culture and our political scene. Our five favorites thus far:

1. **Identity Politics.** *Ackerman rightly states that left-wing identity politics merely pit groups against each other in a constant battle for victim status, and will eventually conflict and implode. For example, Democrat opposition to enforcing our southern border helps illegal Latino immigrants and has the effect of depressing African-American wages. Likewise, in a purported effort to help blacks and Hispanics, left-wing-dominated institutions such as Ivy League universities are discriminating against Asians. At some point, even a leftist media outlet like the* New York Daily Ledger *will notice this shabby treatment of high-achieving Asian students, which strongly resembles the anti-Jewish stance of the Ivy League in the 1950s.*

2. **Racism.** *Jeff Ackerman has candidly noted the left's burning psychological need for conservatives to be racist. The only way for a leftist to feel good about himself is to demonstrate how tolerant and inclusive and non-racist he is, but that's no fun if there's no one on the other side to label as a racist and a bigot. In short, if Republicans aren't evil, then Democrats have no means of being good. And thus we have the ever-lengthening list of microaggressions, fake hate crimes, and "dog whistles" that purport to demonstrate Republican racism.*

3. **Gay Marriage.** *Ackerman is the first national politician to point out that the goal of gay marriage is to force Christians and religious Jews to celebrate something that is sinful according to both religions. Most folks (including conservative Christians) are willing to tolerate, and frankly don't really care about, what two consenting adults do with each other in private, but mere tolerance is not enough for gay rights advocates. They aren't content to simply be tolerated; they now insist on being CELEBRATED. They want society to look at them and call them not only acceptable but also good. And thus they insist that Christians be forced, at gunpoint, to bake cakes, provide flowers, etc. for their "weddings." Christians and others should have the right to politely decline to participate in such a celebration, just as a leftist can decline to bake a cake celebrating the election of a conservative president. When Governor Ackerman was derided for this "gunpoint" argument, he calmly stated that all laws ultimately give the government the power to put you in a cage if you violate them and to shoot you if you resist the cage.*

Ackerman also had a unique observation on how damaging and destructive so-called progressives have been when urging the rest of us along toward "progress" on matters of culture. He said:

We were told by the cultural elite that having mothers with young children enter the workforce was a good thing and that daycare or coming home to an empty house after school would have no negative impact on children. The cultural elite was wrong. We were told by the cultural elite that divorce was really okay, and that children were better off if their parents simply divorced instead of fighting all the time. The cultural elite was wrong. We were told by the cultural elite that abortion on demand and readily available birth control and removing the taboos on premarital sex and out-of-wedlock babies would empower women and give them more control over their lives. Instead, all of this simply gave young men a license to have sex without taking responsibility for marriage or for fatherhood, leaving young women with fewer good options, not more. And, so, again, the cultural elite was wrong. Now, the cultural elite is telling us that "marriage" between two men or between two women is a good thing and will have nothing but positive consequences. The cultural elite is telling us that gender is completely fluid and that there are actually hundreds of different genders, rather than two. It won't be long before we have clear evidence that the cultural elite is, once again, wrong.

*4. **Politics and Religion.** In the face of an unprecedented frontal assault on his Christian faith, Governor Ackerman has noted time and again that you don't have to be a Christian to be a conservative and that you don't have to be a conservative to be a Christian. But he's also demonstrated that there's nothing inconsistent with being both a Christian and a conservative. In fact, he's provided solid arguments and explanations in favor of both Christianity and conservatism. The left, of course, got the vapors when Ackerman implied that his religion is "better" than others. His response? "Of course I believe that. If I didn't, what would be the value in my belief system? I believe Jesus is who He says He is, and others believe that Jesus isn't who He claims to be. We can't both be right."*

*5. **On the Risk of Losing Touch with Real Americans.** Governor Ackerman has made one campaign promise that we hope will become a staple of both parties going forward: "I will have at least three trusted advisors who do not live in Washington and who are free to contact me at any time and speak bluntly and frankly. They will have full access to me at all times. Their main task will be to monitor my presidency and let me know if and when*

I'm losing sight of the needs and desires of real people outside Washington. They'll be an early warning system against being captured by the bureaucracy or overly focused on the views of the Washington establishment."

In addition to our ten favorite policy positions and bits of wisdom noted above, Jeff Ackerman has managed to make Republican politics fun again. Republican presidential rallies are not generally viewed as festive occasions, but, once again, Jeff Ackerman is having success by going against the grain. At a recent rally in Ohio, for example, the campaign played a video montage of liberals literally crying about one conservative policy or another. Ackerman then led the crowd in a cheering contest to describe what they like most about liberal tears, with one side of the room yelling "Less filling!" and the other side countering, "Taste great!" For readers who are younger than forty, this is a take-off on the famous Miller Lite beer commercials of the 1970s and '80s.

Another example with a similar theme: After a video montage of leftists complaining about one Ackerman proposal or another, the candidate took the stage to raucous cheers and announced, in his best impersonation of Robert Duval's character in Apocalypse Now, "I love the sound of leftists whining in the morning. It sounds like . . . victory!"

Unfortunately, while Governor Ackerman's polling numbers have improved slightly, it appears that he's not making enough progress in order to pull off an upset victory over President Landers. We take comfort from the fact that, even in the face of a likely loss on Election Day, Jeff Ackerman is growing the Republican Party and improving the public's views of conservatism. Bush I, Dole, Bush II, McCain, and Romney all failed to do that. To one extent or another, they acted as if conservatism was something to hide, something that had to be softened, something to be ashamed of, and they all suffered reputational damage despite their efforts to distance themselves from those icky conservatives. Our fervent hope is that even an Ackerman loss will advance the cause of conservativism and lay the groundwork for a Republican resurgence in 2020.

Chapter 28

Harrisburg, Pennsylvania

August 2016

Jeff Ackerman's bad mood was getting worse. Although he entered the race as one of the biggest underdogs in U.S. political history, he'd recently allowed himself to start thinking he could actually win the general election in November and become president of the United States. He and his staff had been working hard toward that end, crisscrossing the country and holding three or four rallies per day.

Audiences were receptive, even in traditionally Democratic areas. Ackerman yard signs, billboards, and bumper stickers were everywhere. Thanks largely to the generosity of Hal Harrington, Ackerman advertisements on television and radio were at least as prevalent as those from the better-funded Upton Landers. The strategy of trying to make at least a minor inroad into the Democratic dominance of the black and Hispanic vote still seemed sound.

But the polls weren't moving. Upton Landers still enjoyed a seemingly insurmountable lead, both in the national polls and in the polling in key swing states. Ackerman simply couldn't move the political needle, despite his hard work, the money he spent, and the sound strategy he employed. The unlikely candidate was exhausted, both physically and mentally.

Thus, the bad mood. And the reason that the bad mood was getting worse was that Ackerman was about to hold a press conference. The political press, not surprisingly, had been brutal. Intellectually, he knew it would be the case, but this head knowledge didn't come close to preparing him for the waves of snark and criticism that rained down on him, his family, and his political party on a daily basis. Of course, the candidate hadn't helped matters with his harsh words for the media in his acceptance speech. At the time, he'd calculated that his relationship with the press couldn't get any worse, so why not speak a little truth? He figured wrong.

Even traditionally right-leaning newspapers and cable channels had been lukewarm at best toward the Ackerman campaign. It seemed that these news outlets had determined that he had no chance to win, and so they were using this opportunity to create examples of how "fair and balanced" they were by dishing out unfavorable columns and news segments about Jeff Ackerman. The candidate had not expected to be used in this fashion by the few media outlets that he thought would be in his corner, and it hurt.

Ackerman had just finished addressing the Pennsylvania state legislature, followed by a brief rally near the steps of the state capitol building. Each of those events had gone rather well. But now he had to stand before a gaggle of hostile reporters and pretend that they were actually fair-minded, rational, intelligent, decent human beings. Yes, the bad mood was indeed getting worse.

Time to get this over with. After a brief greeting and cursory introductory remarks, Ackerman called on a BNI reporter to begin the press conference.

"Governor, you've held yourself out as a Christian conservative. And yet your proposal for building a wall on our southern border has been denounced not just by President Landers, but by the Pope as well. The Pope has been especially critical of the idea, calling a wall divisive and unwelcoming. He's even strongly hinted that the idea is anti-Christian. Doesn't this criticism undermine not just your policy proposal, but also the Christian underpinning of your campaign?"

With his head tilted slightly to one side, the candidate responded thoughtfully, "I've certainly held myself out as a conservative, and I'm definitely a Christian. I have not and will not deny my faith. But I've never identified myself as a 'Christian conservative.' That label comes from you fine folks in the media. I haven't used my Christian faith as a reason why I should be elected or to justify my policy proposals.

"But I'll address the substance of your question notwithstanding your misleading premise. There's nothing un-Christian about a wall. Biblical cities like Jerusalem and Jericho were surrounded by walls. Walls are sometimes necessary to protect the sovereignty of a nation-state or the seat of government of a country.

"As you know, the Pope is the head of government of the Vatican, which is a sovereign nation. And guess what surrounds the Vatican? A wall. I'd be curious to hear the Pope's view of why his wall is acceptable while my proposed wall is 'divisive and unwelcoming.' The same goes for President Landers, who lives in the White House. The White House is surrounded by a tall iron fence. I can't wait for you fine reporters to quiz both the Pope and the president on their hypocrisy here. People who live in walled houses and cities shouldn't be too quick to criticize walls."

A hard-left reporter from Seattle's *Daily Tribune* got the next question in ahead of her colleagues. "Governor Ackerman, you've been speaking in a lot of Christian church services. Are you concerned about alienating non-religious voters?"

"Not at all. I believe the only church services I've spoken in have been on Sundays. America is a largely Christian nation, and many voters attend church on Sunday. A political candidate needs to go where the voters are, and, on Sundays, many of the voters happen to be in church. I can't imagine that a non-Christian voter would have a problem with that."

The *Washington Chronicle* was next. "You've introduced a heavy dose of religion into your campaign. Is that a conscious decision on your part?"

"It must not be," Ackerman responded, "because I honestly can't think of anything we've done or said that constitutes a 'heavy dose of religion,' as you put it. I'm not citing Bible verses in support of my policy proposals, and I'm not criticizing my opponent on religious grounds. And it's been weeks since we baptized anyone at a political rally."

The half-humorous, half-sarcastic statement failed to relieve the tension or to change the subject.

The *Chicago Daily Times* now weighed in. "Governor, you seem to be spending an inordinate amount of time speaking in African-American and Hispanic churches. Critics have accused you of pandering to minorities and using the religious angle to win votes. What's your response to that criticism?"

Ackerman frowned. "Well, first of all, I'm not aware of any such criticism, so I can't address the details of any such statements. However, my guess is that anyone who would criticize a Republican like me for speaking to minority groups would also be very quick to criticize me if I *didn't* speak to minority groups. So I'll either be accused of pandering or racism, and this is just one more example of how the press treats Republican candidates unfairly."

A *San Francisco Record* reporter spoke up next. "Governor Ackerman, do you believe a fundamentalist Christian like yourself can actually be elected to the presidency?"

The candidate gave a forced chuckle that didn't come close to reflecting his actual emotions. "Wow, there's a loaded question. Let's see if we can unpack your question a bit." He struggled to reign in any outward sign of impatience. "It seems that you're calling me a fundamentalist Christian and implying that being a fundamentalist Christian is a hindrance in electoral politics. Now, obviously, I think I can win the presidency, or I wouldn't be spending an otherwise beautiful Thursday afternoon with you fine folks. With that out of the way, in order for me to give you a useful answer, we need to make sure we have the same understanding of what it means to be a 'fundamentalist Christian,' a phrase that often has a negative connotation. So before I admit to being one, can you give me your definition of that term and explain how, in your expert opinion, a fundamentalist Christian differs from a regular, plain old Christian?"

The reporter wasn't accustomed to being on the receiving end of questions, especially in the realm of theology. He knew about as much about Christian theology as he did quantum physics, and he struggled to respond. "Hmmm. I, uh, I guess a fundamentalist is someone who believes the Bible is true and, uh, well, maybe someone who goes to church a lot."

Ackerman smiled a smile that he hoped didn't convey as much contempt as he felt. "I don't know of anyone who calls themselves a Christian, fundamentalist or otherwise, who doesn't believe that the Bible is true. After all, the term *Christian* means a follower of Jesus Christ, and the Bible is our primary source of information about Jesus. If we didn't think the Bible was true, we wouldn't be Christians in the first place. And," he added, "I have no idea what you mean by 'goes to church a lot.' Does that mean every Sunday? Every other Sunday? Any Sunday other than Easter?"

The reporter looked embarrassed and uncomfortable and gave no indication that he had any idea how to respond to the religious freak standing behind the podium full of microphones. Hoping to avoid singling out this particular reporter any longer, Ackerman continued in a fashion that was directed to the press corps before him as a whole. "Look, folks, terms like *fundamentalist Christian* are loaded and vague. They mean different things to different people. But let me give you my thoughts on what I think most people, at least most non-Christians, mean by the phrase.

"My impression is that non-Christians, perhaps unconsciously, divide Christians into two groups. There are 'fundamentalist Christians' on one hand, and, on the other hand, for lack of a better term, there are 'regular Christians.'"

Surprisingly, the press seemed unusually interested in his answer.

"Regular Christians might better be described as 'cultural Christians.' They call themselves Christians because their parents or grandparents were Christians. They're not Jewish or Muslim, and they aren't quite willing to declare themselves to be agnostics or atheists. Thus, for lack of a better term, they identify as 'Christians.' They show up for church on Easter, and perhaps on Christmas Eve, but otherwise find something else to do on Sunday mornings. They pray only when faced with a life-threatening disease, job loss, or other life crisis. There's probably a Bible somewhere in their house, but it would take them quite a while to find it, and they can't tell you much about what the Bible actually says.

"Friends and neighbors of these 'regular Christians' would describe them as 'nice people.' But they don't live their lives any differently than the atheists that live next door to them. And they're somewhat embarrassed by the fundamentalist family across the street that hosts a weekly Bible study in their home for anyone in the neighborhood who wants to attend. That's the type of people I think most of you consider to be 'non-fundamentalist Christians' or 'regular Christians.'

"So, what's a fundamentalist Christian, at least in the eyes of the American media's theological experts?" Ackerman asked rhetorically, unable to resist the sarcasm. "Admittedly, I'm guessing here, but I think you folks use 'fundamentalist Christian' as a contemptuous term to describe someone who is truly a follower of Jesus. Someone who doesn't just claim to be a Christian, but who actually lives it. Such a person believes that Jesus is the Son of God who came to earth in human form and lived a sinless life, yet died a horrific, excruciatingly painful death on a Roman cross in order to pay the penalty for the sins of the world, and then rose from the dead three days later and appeared to hundreds of people. This person knows that he's done wrong, that he's sinned, and that he continues to do so sometimes, but he believes that God loves him so much that God is willing to allow Jesus's death to be the penalty for those wrongs. Because this person's penalty for sin has been paid by Jesus, he will spend eternity in heaven with God, and he's so grateful for that wonderful gift.

"This is a person who doesn't just read the Bible, but who studies it. This is someone who prays regularly and who isn't ashamed to invite you to come to church with him. He donates money to his church and the local Christian orphanage. His wife teaches children's choir at their church on Wednesday nights, and his kids listen to contemporary Christian music on the radio. This family bows their heads in prayer before meals, even in public restaurants.

"This guy sometimes quotes the Bible in the course of conversation, and this makes you uncomfortable. You don't understand why he and his family do these things or live this way. You assume that he's ignorant and uneducated and has probably been duped by a shady evangelist on TV. You think he's crazy to spend time, money, and effort to 'impose his religion on other people.' So, friends, is this a reasonably accurate description of what you and your colleagues in the media would call a 'fundamentalist Christian?'"

Ackerman paused here, waiting for a response from the gaggle of reporters crowded before him. After a few awkward glances at each other, rolling their eyes as if to say, *Who is this guy?* most of them nodded and mumbled words of assent.

"All right then," Ackerman went on. "If that's our working definition of 'fundamentalist Christian,' then count me as one of them. And, to close the loop by answering the gentleman's question from earlier, I do in fact believe that a fundamentalist Christian like myself can be elected to the presidency."

Ackerman could see the headlines now: Republican Candidate Admits to Being a Fundamentalist! Editorials laced with contempt for him and for Christianity, thinly disguised as concern for the well-being of the country, would soon follow. But Ackerman didn't care at this point. He might lose the election, but he wasn't about to renounce his faith, or even water it down, in order to keep his slim hopes alive. The candidate had no idea why this press conference had devolved into a theological debate, but he now felt the need to go on offense rather than continuing to play defense.

"In fact," Ackerman continued, "if we use this definition of 'fundamentalist Christian' that we've established here today as a guide, I would submit to you that nearly all of our past presidents have been fundamentalist Christians. For that matter, our current president may even qualify. I know President Landers says that he's a Christian, and I have no reason to doubt him on that. I'm sure that the press will take the first opportunity to ask him about the sincerity of his beliefs and ask that he inform the voters as to whether he falls into the 'fundamentalist Christian' camp—again, using the criteria we've described today—or if he's just sort of a cultural Christian who doesn't actually believe in the core tenets of Christianity."

More negative headlines sprang into Ackerman's mind. Ackerman Questions President's Faith! or Ackerman Doubts Landers Is a True

Christian! But he was having fun now. Time to bait the reporters one more time.

"Okay, with that topic put to bed, does anyone want to discuss any other religious topics? Perhaps you want to ask me about my views on transubstantiation? Or substitutionary atonement? The imputation of righteousness? How about the teleological argument? Maybe you're wondering whether I think a pre-tribulation, mid-tribulation, or post-tribulation rapture is more likely?"

A long, embarrassing pause followed. None of the reporters had the first clue what this madman was babbling about now. Some grinned at their colleagues. Others looked down at their feet, embarrassed for the candidate even though they didn't like him all that much. They fiddled with their cell phones and recording devices and tried to pretend that this sort of thing happened every day.

"What, no takers?" Ackerman asked in mock surprise. "All right. Since we seem to be done with our theological debate, perhaps we can discuss some actual public policy now?" The press conference went on for a few more minutes, but the reporters already had the material they needed for the next round of negative news stories about the Ackerman campaign. Adjectives like *testy*, *defensive*, and *prickly* would feature prominently in their stories. *This animal is vicious! It defends itself when attacked!*

The president's chief of staff, Richard Jordan, watched the Ackerman press conference live on television with a satisfied smile spread across his pale, thin face. It was fun to watch a plan work so perfectly. On the most recent semi-secret conference call for media insiders, Jordan had suggested that the media explore the angle of Ackerman's religious extremism. While the reporters hadn't used that exact phrase, the hoped-for effect had been achieved: Ackerman was now playing defense against the idea that he was a religious fanatic. Jordan was simultaneously amazed, disgusted, and thrilled to see further proof that the top reporters in the national media were nothing more than useful idiots. *Actually*, Jordan corrected himself, *the situation is even better than that: they are* my *useful idiots.*

Furthermore, Jordan knew that no reporter who valued his career would dare put President Landers on the spot with the "fundamentalist Christian" challenge that Ackerman had suggested. Jordan was quite certain that the media would continue to have kittens over Ackerman's genuine Christianity while ignoring the Christian-only-when-politically-useful aspect of President Landers' background. Yes, hypocrisy was the sin the media hated the most. But Richard Jordan knew from long experience that the press would never point out the hypocrisy of a prominent Democrat in the midst of a national election campaign against a Republican. In that circumstance, as far as the press was concerned, only Republicans could be hypocrites.

Jordan scribbled a note on his ever-present legal pad, reminding himself to push the phrase *religious extremist* once again on his next invitation-only conference call with like-minded reporters. He then flipped off the television and walked down the wide hallway in the West Wing to report the good news of Ackerman being on defense—once again—to his boss in the Oval Office.

Chapter 29

Austin Brant Column in the
New York Daily Ledger

August 2016

Austin Brant opened his copy of the *New York Daily Ledger* and flipped directly to the editorial pages. Although he was appreciative of online journalism and was always among the first to buy new phones and other high-tech gadgets, Brant continued to read the newspaper the way God intended: with a paper copy over breakfast and a hot cup of coffee. Though he'd never admit it, he still got a thrill from seeing his column published in America's most widely circulated newspaper.

But today was about more than feeding his ego while he simultaneously fed a bagel with cream cheese to his body. After having his superiors spike his column endorsing Jeff Ackerman for president, Brant was curious if they would run what he'd submitted for publication in today's paper. If not, he'd probably be out of work soon, either as a result of being fired or resigning in protest in an attempt to retain some semblance of personal honor. He found his column in its usual place on the opinion page and read it once quickly to see if it had been altered in any way. Seeing no changes, he read it a second time as he chewed his bagel, more slowly and with a deep sense of relief:

Jeff Ackerman Using Verbal Jujitsu to Defeat the Left-Wing Media

Jujitsu is a martial art form that teaches a smaller, weaker opponent to defeat a bigger, stronger opponent by use of technique, leverage, and manipulation. I confess that the previous sentence exhausts my knowledge of martial arts, but jujitsu offers an irresistible metaphor for the insurgent campaign of Governor Jeff Ackerman, so stick with me here. Ackerman, a heretofore unknown former governor of Mississippi, is winning hearts and minds in his campaign against the heavily favored incumbent President Upton Landers. And he's making the press look silly in the process.

In defiance of all political wisdom and precedent, the weaker Ackerman is using technique, leverage, and manipulation against the bigger, stronger, better-equipped mainstream media. Ackerman may not defeat Landers, but he has the president's left-wing media adjuncts on the ropes and in danger of being knocked out. Yes, those are boxing terms, but I already admitted that I know almost nothing about martial arts, so a little grace here, please.

In response to consistently poor treatment by the press, Ackerman returned fire at the Republican convention. Previous Republican nominees whined intermittently about media bias, and it got them nowhere fast. Ackerman learned the right lessons from those failures. Instead of repeating those tired tactics, Ackerman turned the momentum of the press against itself at the Republican convention. He used a portion of his prime-time speech to give voters a series of tips on how to spot the not-so-subtle left-wing bias of the media. The fact that this passage of the speech was omitted from the advance copy given to reporters, allegedly due to a "technical glitch," made the maneuver even more devastating.

He followed up by referring to network news anchors as "newsreaders with really nice hair." This backhanded compliment has the added advantage of being true, as these gentlemen get paid millions of dollars each year to do nothing more than read news stories (written by others) from teleprompters,

264

and, well, they all have really nice hair. Ackerman resisted the urge to say what didn't need to be said: these guys are incapable of independent thought and, absent their teleprompters, can do nothing other than regurgitate Democrat talking points. The voters—and, surprisingly, the news anchors themselves— clearly understood the unstated message.

This newspaper has been a favorite target of the Mississippi Republican. He recently stated, "If the New York Daily Ledger *editorial board ever agrees with me, I've done something horribly wrong." "In fact," he joked, "an endorsement by the* New York Daily Ledger *editorial board is grounds for impeachment. That's not in the Constitution, but it should be."*

My favorite Ackerman jujitsu move thus far occurred on a Sunday talk show this past week. The candidate was being interviewed as one half of a supposedly balanced pairing in which there is a give-and-take between left and right. When introducing Ackerman and his left-wing counterpart, Democrat spokesman John Silverman, host Randy Graham introduced Ackerman as "the Christian conservative former governor of Mississippi." When Silverman received no correspondingly partisan label, Ackerman interrupted the proceedings and helpfully supplied ideological labels for both Silverman ("radical anti-American leftist") and Graham ("liberal atheist who pretends to be non-biased when he's really just a Democratic Party hack who happens to have a TV show"). When they lapsed into stunned silence, Ackerman noted that he didn't mind being labeled as long as all parties to the conversation were similarly identified.

Recently, the media countered Ackerman by refusing to air footage of Ackerman's most effective attacks on the press. However, once again using the media's tactics against it, the Ackerman campaign responded by posting the full, unedited version of each press conference on Ackerman's campaign website. Ackerman's supporters quickly post the most, ahem, intense snippets on YouTube, Facebook, and other social media.

Each of Ackerman's jabs inspires a media response and additional media hostility toward Republicans in general and Ackerman in particular. The

Republican establishment is horrified at what they view as a deteriorating situation. But Ackerman understands what the Republican elders have never grasped: these verbal spats with the press are clarifying events for the voters. No amount of playing nice, no amount of courting reporters or liberal pundits, will earn Republicans fair treatment in the press, so why try? And neither loyal readers of this newspaper nor die-hard viewers of a left-wing news channel such as HBT (all sixteen or seventeen of them) will ever vote for a Republican in any event.

Ackerman and his team understand that each thrust by Ackerman lures the press into ever more outrageous and destructive behavior. This has caused the already-poor public reputation of the media to drop below that of plaintiffs' lawyers and used car salesmen. And it makes future media attacks on Ackerman and his fellow Republicans less credible. Jeff Ackerman probably won't win this election, but he's giving a black-belt-level performance on the media relations front. Hopefully, other national Republican figures can learn to engage in similar political jujitsu.

Chapter 30

Miami, Florida

August 2016

Jeff Ackerman delivered a solid, well-reasoned speech to the Miami Chamber of Commerce. He laid out his views on taxes, federal regulation, and economic policy in general. He expounded on a theme his campaign had been employing recently: the urgent need to reverse the economic decline of the United States.

In this speech, he likened the U.S. economy to a company being run by the third generation of owners. The grandfather founded the company and grew it. The father then built it up, solidified it, and made it a trusted brand. But now the grandson is in charge.

The grandson is on his fourth wife, and his children are drug addicts. His house is heavily mortgaged and his cars are leased, but he keeps on spending Granddaddy's money. He thinks his father and grandfather were small-time thinkers and that his new ideas will boost this family-owned business into a huge publicly traded, money-making machine. But he ends up ruining everything, bankrupting the business because he strayed from the wisdom and vision of the company's founders.

Yes, America was and is a great nation, Ackerman pointed out, but the current owners—namely, the Upton Landers administration—have strayed from the Founders' principles of individual liberty, property rights, and economic freedom. Landers had decreed his desire to "transform America," and, unfortunately, he was succeeding. Landers was now in the process of transforming America into a second-rate economy, slowly strangling American business by means of high tax rates and intrusive government regulation.

Ackerman then laid out his proposed solutions, which he contended would reverse the decay of the American economy. Tax policy would be a top priority in the Ackerman administration. Cutting individual tax rates would spur economic growth, job growth, and wage growth. Eliminating certain deductions would serve the twin purposes of helping to pay for the tax cuts and simplifying the tax code. Ackerman contended that tax implications should not drive the decision of whether to buy or sell a house, or whether or not to purchase an electric-powered car.

He pushed for a flat tax of 12 percent on all income over ten thousand dollars, with no deductions. He admitted that this might not be politically feasible, as Congress enjoyed fiddling with the tax code in order to encourage certain behaviors while discouraging others, but Ackerman made a strong case for the flat tax. Yes, Democrats would scream that it was "unfair" and that the wealthy should have to "pay their fair share." But what could be fairer than having everyone pay the same tax rate?

The wealthy hedge-fund manager would pay 12 percent of his five-million-dollar salary, while his administrative assistant would pay 12 percent of her fifty-thousand-dollar salary. After giving effect to the ten-thousand-dollar exemption, the hedge-fund manager would pay $598,800 in federal income tax, while the secretary would pay $4,800. Yes, he earned 100 times more than she did, but he would pay 125 times more in taxes.

Ackerman also argued for a significant cut in the corporate tax rate. American corporations paid a federal tax rate of 35 percent, which was one of the highest rates in the world. In a global economy, where businesses and capital can go anywhere, Ackerman said, we shouldn't let our exorbitant corporate tax rate motivate companies to locate elsewhere.

Cutting the corporate tax rate would not reduce federal government revenues, he argued, for two reasons. First of all, a lower rate would boost the economy, thereby producing more tax revenue even though rates were lower. Second, a lower rate would encourage foreign business to move to the U.S. and encourage new companies that would otherwise be formed overseas to incorporate in the U.S. instead. If the United States cut the corporate tax rate to, say, 20 percent, it would receive a 20 percent tax rate from these newly attracted businesses instead of the 0 percent that it was getting now.

In addition to cutting and simplifying taxes, the candidate pushed for significant reductions in government regulation. He noted that complying with the ever-increasing amount of bureaucratic red tape constituted a significant yet little-noticed cost on American businesses. The time, money, and energy spent dotting government-imposed I's and crossing federally mandated T's hurt the owners, employees, and customers of American businesses. Ackerman advocated a boost for all three of these constituencies by means of reducing and simplifying government regulations.

The speech was a success. His text was well written and smoothly delivered. His audience was friendly, attentive, and receptive. He took a moment to shake a few hands and bask in the group's appreciation of his economic proposals. But Ackerman dreaded the next item on his daily calendar: a press conference to discuss the items he'd just raised in his speech. He knew he'd face exactly the opposite of the warmth and goodwill he'd just experienced with the

Chamber of Commerce members when jousting with an increasingly hostile press corps.

Ackerman stepped into a meeting room adjacent to the ballroom where he'd given his speech. He forced himself to smile and greet the shabby, wrinkled throng of reporters assembled in front of him. No one smiled back. The press was ready for an argument, and they were in no mood for pleasantries.

The candidate had barely finished his brief greeting when a reporter from the *New York Daily Ledger* yelled out, "Governor Ackerman, aren't you concerned that your proposed tax cuts would benefit the wealthy more so than the poor and the middle class?"

"I'm not concerned about that at all," Ackerman responded calmly. He could envision tomorrow's page-one headline now: Republican Candidate Not Concerned About Poor and Middle Class. By way of explanation, he continued, "My proposed cuts to individual tax rates will benefit all taxpayers. None of the poor, and only about half of the members of the middle class, pay any federal income tax at all under our current system. You can't cut taxes for people who don't pay them. And so, since you can't pay less than zero dollars in income tax, any tax cut is going to benefit the wealthy more on a dollar-for-dollar basis.

"But you have to ask yourself," Ackerman went on, "whether it's somehow unfair or immoral to cut taxes for the wealthy. Your question and your tone suggest that it is, but I disagree. 'Cutting taxes' for people who don't pay taxes isn't a tax cut; it's a welfare program. We can discuss welfare programs and their sorry and sordid history if you like, but let's deal in reality here for at least a few minutes.

"Public Policy 101 dictates that if you want to get less of some item or some behavior, then you should tax it more and regulate it more. Conversely, if you want to get more of a particular item or a particular type of behavior, then you should tax it less and regulate it less. Income taxes are a tax on work, a tax on jobs, a tax on effort, a tax on savings and investment. I'd like to see us have more work, more jobs, more effort, more savings, and more investment in this country, and I'd like to think that even a reporter for the *New York Daily Ledger* could agree with those goals."

Unfazed, the *Daily Ledger* reporter snapped back, "But shouldn't the wealthy be obligated to pay their fair share?"

Working hard to keep the disdain he felt from being reflected in his tone, the candidate replied, "First of all, I note that 'fair share' is a vague term that liberals use to shift the goal posts. No matter how much the upper-income folks pay in taxes, it's somehow deemed by the elitist intelligentsia to be less than their 'fair share.' When the typical leftist whines about making the rich pay their 'fair share,' what he's really saying is that he's jealous of his next-door neighbor, who's a brain surgeon and earns ten times more than our typical leftist makes as a reporter for the *New York Daily Ledger.* The economically illiterate reporter wants the government to take that smug doctor down a few notches by forcing him to pay his 'fair share.'

"But let's put some numbers to your question and see if your argument makes any sense. Currently, the top one percent of income earners in the United States pay over thirty-seven percent of the total income taxes collected, and the top five percent pay over fifty-eight percent of the total. The top ten percent of earners pay seventy percent of the total dollars of income tax in this country. And the top fifty percent of earners pay almost all of our country's income tax: about ninety-seven percent. Under my flat tax proposal, those percentages will stay about the same. Accordingly, the wealthy already pay far in excess of their fair share. And they'll continue to pay much more than their fair share under my proposal. Moreover, what could be more 'fair' than having everyone pay the same tax rate?"

Ackerman hoped his rhetorical question would put an end to this line of questioning, but the *Daily Ledger* reporter wasn't willing to concede anything yet. After all, this twenty-seven-year-old reporter had a journalism degree from Columbia, by God, and this yahoo from Mississippi wasn't about to show him up just because he'd governed a state for eight years and could throw some boring numbers around. Facts didn't matter when someone's feelings, especially a liberal's feelings, were at stake. "But Governor, isn't it true that some members of the poor and middle class will actually pay more in taxes under your plan?"

"Yes, that's true," Ackerman conceded. "Mostly, it's due to the fact that a relatively small number of folks will go from paying zero federal income tax to paying a few hundred dollars per year. In a perfect world, that wouldn't happen, and I'm open to suggestions during the give-and-take with Congress on how to correct that as long as we end up with only one tax rate and no deductions.

"However, I don't think it's necessarily a terrible thing to cause someone to become a taxpayer. I think having more of our citizens with some skin in the game is good for our democracy. Folks that don't pay taxes have no problem with spending other people's money for increased government services. But if the government is planning to spend your tax dollars, instead of the taxes collected from the guy next door, you're much more vigilant and engaged in the public debate. Finally, please note that economic classification isn't permanent. If we stimulate and grow the economy, which my plan will do, we'll lift millions of poor into the middle class, and many middle-class folks will become wealthy."

The *New York Daily Ledger* reporter had one more card to play, and he thought it was a good one. "But sir, several prominent billionaire investors and businessmen have noted that their taxes are too low and advocated for higher tax rates, not the lower rates for which you're arguing."

"Yes, I've seen those stories. I'm embarrassed to see these smart guys voluntarily make themselves look dumb. If they really believe that they aren't taxed enough, there's nothing to stop them from voluntarily paying more in taxes than what's required. I'm quite confident that they've never done so. Instead, they go on television and plead for higher taxes as an act of virtue signaling. *Look at me! I'm a good person!* The press then writes about how wonderful and generous they are, all because of a few cheap words said in front of a camera."

The *Washington Chronicle* reporter in the first row was tired of listening to the *Daily Ledger* reporter monopolize the questioning, so she yelled out, "In light of our twenty-something trillion-dollar national debt, isn't it immoral to cut the tax rate on corporations?"

"Wow," Ackerman responded with a levity that he didn't actually feel, "the *Washington Chronicle* wins the award for the most loaded question of the day. Congratulations! Such a loaded question contains several incorrect assumptions that need to be debunked separately.

"First of all, your question assumes that our national debt exists due to a lack of revenue, and that we could make that debt go away, or at least cut into it, if we only taxed big, bad businesses a little more. This is not the case. Federal tax revenue has increased steadily over the decades, but, unfortunately, spending has increased even more. We don't have a revenue problem in this country; we have a spending problem.

"Second, you're wrong in your assumption that cutting the corporate tax rate from thirty-five percent to twenty percent will decrease federal tax revenue and therefore increase the national debt that you pretend to be so concerned about. Remember, we don't pay our bills in this country with tax *rates*, but with tax *revenues*. If we give American businesses the correct incentives, they will grow and become more profitable. My proposed cut in tax rates will lead to economic growth that generates more actual revenue than the higher rate.

"And, finally, you're most spectacularly wrong in your assumption that cutting the corporate tax rate is somehow immoral. Many liberals, especially those with journalism degrees who write for the *New York Daily Ledger* or *Washington Chronicle*, assume that American businesses have unlimited amounts of cash, and that the government could force those big, mean companies to pay enough money in taxes to solve all of our country's problems if only our politicians could summon the political will to do so. In the muddled minds of the American left, it is immoral to 'allow' businesses to make profits when they could be strong-armed into handing over cash to the IRS.

"But hear me clearly on this," Ackerman continued, forcing himself to speak slowly. "Corporations don't pay taxes. I'll say it again, hopefully slowly and simply enough so that even a left-wing reporter can understand it: corporations don't pay taxes. Have you ever seen Coca-Cola or IBM or General Motors write a check? Sure, those companies, and thousands of smaller ones all over this great country, send checks to the IRS with the corporate name listed as the payor. But corporations don't actually pay taxes. Individual people like you and me are the ones who actually pay corporate taxes.

"You see, tax dollars paid to the government by corporations come out of the pockets of real people. For each corporation that ostensibly pays taxes, these people fall into three main groups: the customers of the corporation, the employees of the corporation, and the owners of the corporation. Let's use Coca-Cola as an example.

Every dollar of federal tax paid by Coke is a dollar that could have been paid to its employees as increased wages, or passed along to its customers through lower prices, or paid out to its shareholders—its owners—as a dividend. And before you go all class-warfare on me, keep in mind that almost everyone in this room has a 401(k) plan or similar retirement savings plan in place, and it's very likely that you own some Coke stock whether you realize it or not. Therefore, you and I pay Coke's taxes, together with all of the other corporate taxes in this country.

"Thus, there's no moral distinction between corporate taxes and individual taxes. If Coke has a moral obligation to pay more in corporate tax, then you have a moral obligation to pay more in individual tax. I don't see how any reasonable person could make a rational claim that there's anything immoral about a democratically elected government decreasing tax rates."

Ackerman was pleased with his answer, yet frustrated by the knowledge that little or none of his rationale would appear in the inevitably one-sided news stories about the event. The reporters would find plenty of space on the front page for his critics to blast him, but they'd run out of room before laying out the arguments in favor of his policies. He made a mental note to brainstorm with his staff about how he could do a better job of getting his message out to the voters while avoiding the leftist filters imposed by the mainstream media.

"Okay, folks, any other questions?" Ackerman asked, hoping his rebuttal of the *Washington Chronicle* reporter would discourage the remainder of the mangy crowd.

But the BNI reporter who drew the dreaded assignment of following the Ackerman campaign would not be denied. "Governor Ackerman, President Landers has proposed an increase in the federal minimum wage to fifteen dollars, and opinion polls show strong support for such a measure. You didn't mention the minimum wage in your speech to the wealthy business owners earlier today. Do you agree with President Landers that we should adjust the minimum wage?"

Not for the first time today, Ackerman smiled at his questioner with his mouth but not his eyes. "For once, I agree with the president. We should in fact adjust the minimum wage."

A minor buzz went through the press corps as the BNI reporter mentally congratulated himself for making some news. Perhaps this Ackerman guy wasn't so unreasonable and so unenlightened after all.

The candidate continued, "However, I disagree with the type of adjustment needed. You see, I believe that we should adjust the minimum wage downward, all the way down to zero, because zero dollars per hour is the actual, true minimum wage."

The murmuring from the crowd of reporters got a bit louder, although it was now indignant rather than hopeful.

Ackerman plunged ahead, speaking a bit louder to overcome the noise from the reporters. "If someone wants to hire you for five dollars an hour, or ten dollars an hour, and you're willing to take the offer, you and the potential employer should be free to enter into such a transaction. But if the employer is able to pay a maximum of ten dollars, and the federally imposed minimum is fifteen dollars, he won't hire anyone. Both parties lose. The business owner has to find another way to get the task done, and the would-be employee has no job. Thus, the would-be employee ends up earning the true minimum wage: zero dollars per hour.

"Study after study provides real-world evidence to prove that increases in the minimum wage lead to job losses and economic stagnation. Yes, the minimum-wage earners who manage to keep their jobs get a small benefit from the increase, but many of these people lose their jobs, and many others never get hired in the first place. The real benefit to minimum wage increases is that it makes liberals *feeeeel* good, and it has the added benefit of allowing the typical leftist to *feeeeel* like he's helping the poor by means of taking money from someone else. You see, voting for left-wing, redistributive policies is so much easier than actually using your own time and money to help other people. But it's terrible economic policy.

"Again, in the economically challenged brain of the twenty-first-century Democrat, American companies have huge piles of cash that could be given to employees, or to the IRS, if only those business owners weren't so greedy and evil. But that's simply not the case. Business owners are willing and able to pay whatever salary is required to fairly compensate an employee for the value of his or her work, no more and no less."

Perversely, Ackerman reveled in the disapproving glares from the press pool. He decided to voice one more thought. "Now, you say President Landers wants a fifteen-dollar-an-hour minimum wage. Obviously, he believes there's no negative overall impact from increasing the minimum wage. Well, if that's the case, why be so stingy? Let's make the minimum wage one hundred dollars per hour. For that matter, make it one million dollars per hour. That way, we'll all be rich, right? I'm sure some of your colleagues who cover the White House will quiz the president on this at the first opportunity."

The reporter from the *San Francisco Record* was weary of all this boring economic mumbo jumbo. She didn't understand it or care about it, so she assumed no one else did either—at least none of the really enlightened people who read her newspaper. Thus, she sought to change the subject to something more relevant and important. "Governor Ackerman, are you willing to acknowledge and apologize for the grave damage wrought on our society by white males over the past three hundred years? And do you agree that white males remain a destructive force today?"

"I'd be glad to discuss that," the candidate responded soberly. "But please note that, for purposes of this conversation, I hereby self-identify as a female and expect you to treat me as such. My pronouns are *she* and *her*."

"But . . . but you can't do that!" the reporter whined from the front of the gaggle of reporters. "You're making a mockery of transgenderism! This is hate speech!"

"No, no. I'm simply playing by the rules that your sort has established. According to the transgender activists, gender is a fluid concept and can be changed on a whim simply by declaring it to be so. And we've heard repeatedly from those folks that one's self-announced gender identity cannot be questioned. I and I alone get to determine my gender, and it's all based on how I *feeeeel* at any point in time. We seem to have completely forgotten the fact that all societies in the world, for over five thousand years of recorded human history, quite reasonably believed that there were only two genders, and that gender was fixed at birth based on genitalia. Now, instead, according to certain enlightened Californians, we're told that there are actually about 4,317 different genders, and we all get to declare for ourselves what we'll be at any particular point in time.

"And I've also learned that you're not allowed to question or doubt or criticize my gender selection. If you do, you're intolerant and beyond the pale of polite society. Therefore, solely for purposes of answering your question about evil white males, I hereby identify as a female. And I want you to call me Loretta," he deadpanned as visions of Monty Python comedy skits danced through his head.

The reporter stormed out of the room as her colleagues chuckled at her self-imposed humiliation. Addressing the remaining throng of reporters, Ackerman continued, "Once I'm elected president, the left is going to hate playing by the rules they've established. Maybe I shouldn't even wait that long, though." He rubbed his chin thoughtfully. "I mean, why should it just be the leftists that get to create all of these new genders and assign their characteristics? In fact, I think I'll make up one of my own and identify as that going forward whenever it suits me. I hereby decree myself to be 'Warrior Poet Taxpayer Man Who Bears No Guilt for Previous Sins of White Males Who Have Gone Before Me'. I hereby insist that this gender be included on all governmental forms as a box that I can check. And it must be listed in at least thirty-three different languages, including Farsi, Arabic, and Hungarian. Otherwise, I'm being discriminated against and will sue everyone in sight.

"Now, ladies and gentlemen, please excuse me while I go find a left-wing baker and ask him to bake me a cake to celebrate my gender shift."

With that barb, the press conference concluded. As he walked to the waiting bus, Jeff Ackerman reminded himself that it was in fact possible to have fun on the campaign trail.

Chapter 31

Green Bay, Wisconsin
September 2016

J eff Ackerman sat in the black Suburban with Art Morgan and
Scott Williamson as the campaign's motorcade sped toward the
small airport in Green Bay, Wisconsin. It was a perfect late-sum-
mer day, with no clouds, bright sunshine, and temperatures in the
seventies. But the beautiful weather simply served as a reminder to
the underdog Ackerman team that they could be doing something
much more enjoyable than engaging in a doomed quest to get their
guy elected to the presidency.

Ackerman's adrenaline was still pumping from a successful speech
delivered to the workers at an auto parts manufacturing plant. Most
of them were union members, and Ackerman had worried that they
wouldn't be receptive to his free-market message. But he had calmly
pointed out that, while unions had their place in the early part of
the twentieth century, they weren't necessary any longer because
they had accomplished their mission. Employers now understood
the value of a stable labor force and the need to retain the workers
that they had spent time and money training.

The candidate had noted that the concept of organized labor

continues to exist because of the assumption that individual workers are incapable of negotiating their own pay and benefits. Ackerman told his audience that, unlike his counterparts in the Democratic Party, he trusted the average assembly line worker and forklift driver to look out for his or her own best interests. He also pointed out the numerous industries that were suffering because of union issues, such as auto manufacturing and steel. Tellingly, nonunion auto workers in right-to-work states, such as Mississippi and Alabama, were making as much or more money than their union counterparts without being forced to pay onerous union dues.

In short, he concluded, unions exist today for the benefit of union leaders and Democratic politicians who receive huge campaign donations from unions, while rank-and-file union members have little or nothing to show for their union dues and membership. Wouldn't they be better off keeping their dues in their pockets and deciding for themselves how to spend that money?

The speech went well. Ackerman was convinced that he had changed at least a few minds and won at least a few votes. But as the adrenaline wore off, the candidate was again beset by reality: he was trailing in the polls, and nothing he had done in the past three months had worked to close the gap between his upstart campaign and his incumbent opponent.

"This isn't working," Ackerman growled to his two most trusted advisors. "We have good events and receptive crowds. I say exactly what I want to say. And I do a pretty good job of delivering my speeches. I've even been able to win most of my debates with the media. But we're not getting results. Every good event is followed up by a negatively slanted news story or broadcast, and then by a highly critical opinion piece. And the polls don't move my way at all. We've gotta do something else, or do something different. Any ideas?"

Art Morgan was about to respond that the upcoming debate between Ackerman and Upton Landers would provide the type of boost the campaign needed, but Scott Williamson spoke first.

"Our problem," he said, "is that we're relying on the left-leaning media to get our message out. You speak to five thousand people at a time, which is nice, but then the media reports what you say—or what they incorrectly think you meant—to one thousand times that many people. Whatever you accomplished in your live event is therefore more than offset by the reporting on the event."

"Thank you very much, Mr. Williamson," Ackerman replied sarcastically. "That's pretty much what I just said. I think we all understand the problem. What I'm looking for is a solution. I need an end-run around the media's control of my message."

"I was getting to that," the young staffer answered. He wanted to add "before you interrupted me" but decided at the last nanosecond to say it with his tone rather than actually uttering the words. After all, Jeff Ackerman paid his salary, even if he used Hal Harrington's money to do so. "Anyway, a minute ago you said that in your speeches, you get the chance to say exactly what you want to say. The problem only arises when the reporters distort your message. So let's enter the twenty-first century and get your words directly to the public without media interference and without having to pay millions of dollars for TV or radio spots."

"How are we gonna do that?" Morgan inquired suspiciously, not liking where this conversation was going. Anything new, untried, or otherwise groundbreaking was automatically a bad idea, to his way of thinking.

"We'll have Jeff make a series of short videos, each of them two or three minutes long at most," Williamson said. "Each one will cover a single topic. We'll outline the issue, describe the Democrats' approach, why we disagree with that, and what we propose to do instead. Taxes, immigration, healthcare, defense spending, Israel policy, foreign trade, whatever topics we want the voters to hear about. And then,"—excitement brightened his tone—"in order to get it to the voters directly, we'll post the videos on YouTube, Facebook, and Instagram. We'll make sure to talk them up, and soon folks will be forwarding them to friends, family, and coworkers."

"Is it really that simple?" the candidate asked.

"What's YouTube?" Morgan snarled as he dusted a bit of dandruff off his fraying blazer that was older than most of the campaign staffers he supervised.

Ignoring Art the Dinosaur, Williamson said, "Yes, it's really that simple. I'm a little embarrassed that we haven't done this already, but better late than never."

Ackerman was intrigued and wanted to dig into the idea further. "And why do the videos need to be so short? Two or three minutes doesn't sound like much time."

"They need to be short so that the voters can process them," Williamson explained. "Our brains are wired to process information in small chunks. You could give a twenty-minute speech, but most people will zone out at some point along the way and miss the bulk of your message because of that. Give them the most important ideas, boiled down to their essence, that would otherwise be buried in twenty minutes of talking. And then do the same thing with another topic, and then another."

Scott Williamson was enthusiastic now, and the ideas poured out. "We could film several of these at once and stagger their release over time. If we do this right, people will be looking forward to their daily dose of Jeff Ackerman on social media, informing the voters on the issue of the day in an easy-to-understand, three-minute video clip. We can use graphics, music, and background images to convey even more than what the narrator's words alone say. Some will be very serious, others more light-hearted. We should definitely do one that highlights the racism industry."

Ackerman gave a quizzical look. "What do you mean by 'racism industry'?"

"You know, the Proud Black Brotherhood, the Law and Policy Group, pundits like Allen Bollman. These are groups and individuals that worked for a good cause decades ago: fighting real, actual racism. Now that racism is largely extinct here in the U.S., these people have to invent artificial racism in order to stay relevant. They 'manufacture' this racism and sell it in exchange for donations, campaign funds for Democrats, etc. Hence the rash of fake hate crimes and references to microaggressions, white privilege, systemic racism, and the like.

"I'm not even sure if they realize how stupid this makes them look. Take the ideas of white privilege and systemic racism as examples. These are basically the same concept. According to the racism industry, white people have rigged society in favor of whites and against blacks. Even if no one is burning crosses or bombing black churches anymore, and even if no one is refusing to hire a qualified black candidate, there's allegedly some secret force within our society that keeps blacks from making economic and social progress. This 'systemic racism' results in 'white privilege': they claim that whites are the privileged beneficiaries of this rigged society and thus enjoy 'white privilege.'

"But when you look at whites compared to Asians, this argument breaks down. Asians do better than whites on almost every statistical measure in the U.S. Did whites rig things to help Asians but hurt blacks? Seems pretty unlikely. Do Asians have the political and social power to organize our culture for their benefit? Nope. The whole argument breaks down when you think about it for about four seconds.

"You see, liberals won a lot of power and a lot of credit for the good work they did fighting actual, real racism back in the 1960s. Hats off to them. They did a good job, even if it was Republicans more so than Democrats doing the legislative heavy lifting. To keep that power, and to keep the money flowing in, liberals constantly need a dragon to slay. That's why they never celebrate our society's victory over racism and why they go to ever-more-ridiculous lengths to claim that racism is everywhere.

"Anyway," Williamson concluded, "these are the sorts of ideas we can explore on the short videos."

Ackerman and Morgan nodded along with the younger staffer, impressed with his concise, logical analysis of the racism-industry concept. They were even more impressed with his idea for circumventing the media monopoly on the Ackerman message.

Ackerman enthusiastically signed off on the idea of short videos and instructed Williamson to get it implemented as soon as possible. Two days later, the first three videos appeared on social media, with more to come. Facebook groups, Twitter, and email distribution lists were soon spreading the videos around the world. Ackerman feared it might be too little too late, but at least now the voters would hear from him in his own words.

Chapter 32

The White House

September 2016

C hief of Staff Richard Jordan chaired the meeting of the top
campaign staff for the president's re-election bid. They gathered in the Roosevelt Room of the White House, in blatant violation of federal laws designed to separate government activity from
campaign activity. Jordan didn't give this issue a second thought,
knowing full well that his loyal lapdogs in the press would ignore
the story. Besides, a first-term president's every word and deed was
designed to get him elected to a second term, and laws designed to
divide politics and governing were so silly that they demanded to
be broken. Thus, the Hatch Act could be safely ignored, at least until
the next time a Republican occupied the White House.

A meeting designed to discuss and predict the next leader of
the free world should have been exciting, but this one certainly
wasn't. Landers continued to hold a solid-but-not-spectacular lead
over Ackerman, somewhere in the 52–48 or 53–47 range. Normally,
such a lead less than two months before the general election would
be perfectly acceptable, but both Jordan and Landers wanted more.
Nothing short of a landslide would do. Jordan pushed the campaign

staff for ideas on how to expand the lead, how to generate the landslide that their boss deserved. Although they each spoke up with potential solutions, they might as well have saved everyone some time and admitted that they had no clue.

The meeting broke up, and most of the participants engaged in a coffee-induced race to the restroom. But Landers' campaign director Gretchen Lewis and political director Chloe MacKenzie hung back and asked Richard Jordan for a word. Jordan actually had plenty of time, but he wasn't about to admit to the pair he sarcastically referred to as the Dynamic Duo that he was anything other than extremely busy.

"We know you're busy, so we won't take up much of your time," Lewis began, needlessly wasting ten seconds of time to say that she wouldn't waste his time. "We wanted to give you a heads up on some recent developments we're seeing around the country."

Jordan just stared at her with a bored expression that urged her to just get on with it, for God's sake.

"We didn't mention it in the meeting because there's no statistical or numerical support for it, but we're starting to see some anecdotal signs that the race is moving in Ackerman's direction."

Frustration quickly replaced boredom on Jordan's face. "So are you going to tell me about these so-called anecdotal signs or just stand here wasting more of my time?"

Lewis glanced at Chloe MacKenzie as if to tell her that it was now her turn on the firing line.

"Yard signs, T-shirts, hats, and bumper stickers in favor of Ackerman seem to have popped up out of nowhere," MacKenzie reported. "His short videos on social media are getting a large number of hits, and most of the comments are positive. We don't have any statistically useful way to track this stuff or to tell how or if it translates into votes in November, but it just feels like Ackerman is getting a bump."

"But the polls don't show any changes in that direction?" Jordan asked.

"Correct," MacKenzie replied.

"And that's both the public polls and our internal polls?"

"That's right, although we haven't done much internal polling lately, especially in the blue states."

"So," Jordan summarized, "you're telling me that the data and hard information methods that we spent years perfecting and millions of dollars implementing show that everything is in good shape for a comfortable win but not a landslide. But in spite of all of that evidence, you have a feeling"—Jordan derisively emphasized the word—"that an upset is brewing?"

"You can call it whatever you like," Gretchen Lewis replied, with no effort to hide her exasperation. "We just thought you might want to know about these anecdotes, this gut feeling, this sense of ours, before it shows up in the polls, rather than after. What you do with the information is up to you."

"Well, that's sort of the problem, isn't it?" Jordan almost shouted with a derisive shake of this head. "You're not giving me any actual *information* here. There's no data, there's no numbers, there's no actionable insight. You're giving me useless anecdotes as some sort of CYA exercise in case this thing goes south down the stretch for some reason. Now, if you'll excuse me, I need to rush into the Oval Office to tell the most powerful man in the world that some redneck in Arkansas planted an Ackerman sign in front of his doublewide trailer, and that our campaign people are fretting about it."

The women stalked out of the room, angry but satisfied that they had done their jobs and alerted the chief of staff that trouble may—or may not—be brewing.

Left alone in the room, Jordan pondered this latest development, scribbling a flowchart on the pad in front of him. He set aside his frustration with what he viewed as a textbook example of useless Washington ass-covering and employed the logical, rational side of his mind to the situation.

Only a couple of boxes and arrows into his flowchart, he determined that whether or not the Dynamic Duo was correct about a possible Ackerman surge, his course of action was the same. If the political hacks were right, Landers might be in trouble of losing the election, so he needed something to change the momentum. But even if they were wrong, Landers still had only a decent-sized lead. In order to get the blowout he wanted, something significant had to happen to boost Landers' margin of victory. Thus, under either scenario, Landers needed something big to give him a lift in the polls, and Jordan had to figure out a way to make it happen. Understanding that he needed a major pre-election win for Landers or a significant blow to Ackerman was the easy part. The difficulty lay in engineering such an event.

A television in the corner of the room caught his eye. It was tuned to BNI with the volume muted. Jeff Ackerman was giving an impromptu interview to a BNI reporter, apparently in between campaign events. Jordan grabbed the remote control and turned on the sound.

"Sir, Upton Landers has nearly four years of presidential experience under his belt. How do you think your experience as governor of Alabama compares to what your opponent has learned during his time in office?"

"Interesting question. That's certainly the first time I've heard that I was governor of Alabama," Ackerman replied with a shake of his head. "The people of both Alabama and Mississippi will be rather startled to learn about that."

The reporter realized his mistake but didn't bother to correct it or apologize. Instead, he simply gave the candidate a slight shrug, as if to indicate that this was an insignificant detail that didn't merit further discussion. After all, who could be expected to distinguish one racist backwater state from another? And so, after an uncomfortably long pause, Ackerman continued on for a few seconds with his stock answer to this question that he'd already been asked about a dozen times during the campaign.

Watching from the Roosevelt Room in the White House, Richard Jordan certainly didn't think it was a cardinal sin to confuse Mississippi and Alabama. The punchline of a joke about the only difference between the two states was on the edge of his memory, but he couldn't quite grasp it. Something about whether or not you had to put on your best Sunday T-shirt in order to shop at Walmart. He thought the answer depended on whether or not your wife was coming with you and whether she was your first or second cousin, but the details were fuzzy.

The reporter then asked another question. "Governor Ackerman, you haven't had much to say about reproductive healthcare in the United States. What are your views on that topic?"

Jordan got out of his chair and walked over to the TV.

"Of course," Ackerman replied, "like all Americans who have considered the topic, I'm one hundred percent in favor of reproductive healthcare."

The reporter's eyes lit up and his grip on the microphone became noticeably tighter. He was making news! Visions of Emmy Awards danced in his head as he prepared to follow up on this stunning admission by a conservative Southern Baptist Republican that he was in favor of abortion! He was trying to think of an intelligent follow-up question, but he was just a little too slow.

Ackerman continued, "I'm surprised this is even an issue on people's minds. I love babies, and women need reproductive healthcare if they're going to successfully reproduce and give birth to healthy babies. Accordingly, I think all women of child-bearing age should seek out reproductive healthcare as soon as possible so that they can reproduce in a healthy manner. My goal is for every pregnancy in America to end with the birth of a healthy, beautiful baby who grows up to be a happy, productive citizen, and we need doctors to provide reliable reproductive healthcare in order to make that happen."

Ackerman was fully aware that the reporter was asking him about his views on abortion, but the candidate wasn't about to miss the opportunity to chide the reporter for using a euphemism as misleading as "reproductive healthcare."

Richard Jordan couldn't help but laugh as the slow-witted reporter stammered awkwardly for a few seconds and then stopped and took a deep breath in an effort to gather his thoughts. Jordan was certainly rooting for an Ackerman mistake, but he appreciated good politics when he saw it, and this was good politics by Jeff Ackerman.

After an awkward pause in which Ackerman simply stared at the reporter, waiting for the next question, the reporter finally said, "Sir, excuse me, but I think we're talking about two different things. What I meant was, what are your views on reproductive rights?"

"That sounds like a distinction without a difference to me," Ackerman responded thoughtfully. "Again, I love babies, and I think women are amazing. I've been married to a great woman for almost thirty years, and we have two amazing daughters. I can't imagine that anyone would want to prevent a woman from having a baby, and so I think it goes without saying that women have the right to reproduce."

The reporter was stupid, but he wasn't *that* stupid. He now realized that he was being played. Unfortunately for the hapless BNI reporter, his rhetorical skills were well below those of Jeff Ackerman.

"Governor, I'm sure you know what I mean. I'm talking about a woman's right to choose!"

Mustering the most innocent expression and tone that he could, Ackerman responded, "Choose what? The baby's name? What doctor she'll use to help ensure a healthy baby?"

Indignant now, the reporter said loudly, "Sir, this is a serious matter, and you know as well as I do that I'm asking you about your views on abortion."

"Oh. Well, abortion is indeed a very serious matter," Ackerman said with a dignified sadness. "It's so serious, in fact, that it shouldn't be cloaked in deceptive happy talk and misleading phrases such as 'reproductive healthcare,' 'reproductive rights,' or 'a woman's right to choose.'"

Staring gravely into the camera now and ignoring the reporter's attempts to cut him off, Ackerman spoke directly to the BNI audience. "Whatever you call it, we're talking about a sad, horrific, barbaric process in which a baby is chopped into six or eight pieces. Some of those parts are sold on the black market, and the rest are tossed into the Dumpster out behind the so-called 'clinic.' It's so sad, so bloody, so inhumane that those who promote it can't even bring themselves to accurately describe it. They're forced to use misleading euphemisms like 'choice' or 'reproductive rights' to keep the listener's mind off the baby who is being butchered. Unfortunately for millions of babies who never got a chance at life, the proponents of this grisly state of affairs have done a great job of hiding the facts in plain sight.

"Abortion is a bloody stain on the American conscience, just as great as slavery. Calling 'slavery' something else, like 'involuntary labor conditions,' for example, doesn't make it any less evil. The same is true with respect to butchering a baby: referring to it as an 'abortion' or as 'reproductive healthcare' doesn't wash the blood away. Fortunately, our nation had the wisdom and courage to end slavery, fighting a tragic war in order to do so. I hope and pray that we'll have the same wisdom and courage to end abortion. As things currently stand, over half a million American babies are slaughtered every year. This is largely the work of the American left and the Democrat Party. One wonders if their bloodlust will ever be satisfied, and I shudder to think about how many more babies will be sacrificed on the altar of leftism. But rest assured that the Ackerman administration will do everything in its power to reverse this tragic, sad situation."

Ackerman looked solemnly into the camera and thanked the viewers for their time and attention. He then walked away without another word, leaving a stunned and silent BNI reporter in his wake. BNI cut to a commercial in order to avoid embarrassing its employee even further.

Richard Jordan clicked off the television. His media allies would do the heavy lifting in denouncing Ackerman's extreme rhetoric, which was obviously inspired by religious bigotry and zealotry. Jordan didn't need to expend any effort in order to gin up a storm of criticism aimed at the Republican candidate. *That Neanderthal deserves everything that's coming to him*, Jordan thought, and then his nimble political mind moved a few steps further down the mental road.

Richard Jordan had a hunch. He quickly walked to his office to start the process of learning if his hunch was correct. If so, he already had some ideas about how to make the best use of it.

Chapter 33

Ackerman Campaign Strategy Memorandum

October 2016

**STRICTLY CONFIDENTIAL;
ANYONE CAUGHT LEAKING WILL BE TRADED TO
THE DEMOCRATS FOR A STAFFER TO BE NAMED
LATER**

To: All Campaign Staff
From: Art Morgan
Date: October 4, 2016
RE: Campaign Strategy Memo Number 44

Status of the Race: We've progressed from "likely landslide loss" to "they fought the good fight but came up a little short." The race has tightened enough to give us a puncher's chance, but we're still the clear underdog.

Internal Polling Data: Landers is up 49%–45% nationally. State-level polling has improved a little but still shows us with a gap that reinforces the national numbers. We've improved our standing with the voters to the point where we shouldn't lose any of the traditionally red states, but we haven't progressed enough to move any of the states that Landers won in 2012 into our column. On a more encouraging note, there is some evidence that our man is starting to win some hearts and minds. Our people in local offices are reporting a surge in Ackerman yard signs, bumper stickers, T-shirts, and the like. But none of this is showing up in the polling, and we all know that the guy who's shouting that the polls are wrong is usually the one who's making the concession phone call on election night.

Financial Update: No worries here. Hal Harrington's cash opened the door. Hal's contribution, combined with money from some other big donors plus the usual small stuff, means that money isn't really an issue. Yes, we're being outspent, but there's an upper limit to the effectiveness of campaign advertisements. We won't be able to use lack of funds as an excuse for losing this race.

Media Strategy: Yes, the media hates us. Yes, the media is rooting for Landers to crush us like a grape. Yes, the media's bias is showing up in their reporting. But all of this would have been true even if Governor Ackerman had played nice with the media. It's true that we haven't made any new friends in editorial offices around the country, but at least we're punching back. We'll continue to ridicule the press at every opportunity, largely because every thinking American can see that the press fully deserves to be ridiculed. Pointing and laughing at the media's stupidity and its leftism (but I repeat myself, because leftism is clearly stupid) is more effective than playing the victim and whining about liberal bias. It's also a lot more fun. Accordingly, we'll continue to chide the media and undermine what little credibility they have left with the public. Feel free to assume that any individual reporter is anti-American, anti-capitalist, and anti-Christian unless and until clearly proven otherwise, and don't hesitate to challenge the premise of any question you're asked by a reporter.

Strategic Plan: No major changes here. The press is pushing us to abandon our conservative message. The media is oh-so-helpfully suggesting that we "tone down our divisive rhetoric" in order to "appeal to moderate, undecided voters." Screw that. We've made significant inroads with the electorate by not only taking strong, traditional, conservative positions, but also by explaining the reasons and rationale for those positions. Even moderates who aren't sold on our policies are starting to express respect for our willingness to stand up for our principles and to thresh out the logical basis for our positions. We have logic and reason on our side, whereas the left can only sell the fact that their policies make their advocates feel good about themselves.

Operational Plan: Minority voters are our best hope for pulling off the most stunning political upset of the last two centuries. We don't have any hard polling data to support it, but subjective evidence suggests that our efforts with black and Hispanic voters are paying off. Black pastors are now freely inviting us to speak in their churches, whereas we had to bribe them to let us in the door just a few weeks ago. Hispanics are expressing a quiet respect and approval for our plans to beef up border security, which was unthinkable during the primaries. Therefore, we'll continue to hold rallies and give speeches aimed at these two groups.

The short videos starring Governor Ackerman and posted on social media have been a huge success. We'll post a new one today about our plans to eliminate the federal Department of Education. It will discuss the hundreds of millions of taxpayer dollars that will no longer be tossed into that sinkhole and why the elimination of this funding will not hurt our students or teachers in the classroom. Spoiler alert: federal education dollars are spent on bureaucrats, paper-pushers, and other apparatchiks, together with feel-good initiatives that don't work. None of these money-wasters helps little Johnny or young Sally learn to read or write.

Florida, Ohio, Iowa, Michigan, Pennsylvania, Wisconsin, and New Mexico are shaping up as the key battleground states down the stretch. Florida and Ohio are must-win states for us, but we'd need one more of the battleground states to win in the Electoral College. We think the media has overplayed its hand in attacking Ackerman for his Christian faith. This isn't selling well in Middle America. The left's anti-Christian hysterics, combined with the open-borders stance adopted by the Democrats, gives us a shot in Iowa, Michigan, Pennsylvania, and Wisconsin.

New Mexico is on the list due to the progress we're making with Hispanics. Landers won this state by only two points in 2012. It's not on the national radar yet, but we think we can flip enough Hispanic voters our way to put New Mexico into the red column for the good guys.

Messaging and Themes: Again, no change from our twelve key words: Cut taxes. Cut spending. Reform entitlements. Protect our borders. Appoint conservative judges.

We know many of you are fielding questions about Governor Ackerman's faith and its role in the campaign. Frankly, the governor and I are rather surprised that this has become such an issue this year. We haven't run an overtly religious campaign. Yes, the governor is a Christian, and yes, the governor is a conservative. But he hasn't really run as a "Christian conservative." Nevertheless, the press is painting him as the second coming of Jerry Falwell, and our good friends in the media are throwing a pearl-clutching fit because they're convinced we're trying to establish a theocracy here in America.

Our suggestion when dealing with the press on this issue is that you simply point out that Governor Ackerman has not initiated any sort of religious aspect to this campaign and that he should not be discriminated against as a man of faith. Every previous president has been a Christian, and this inured to the benefit of our country. Furthermore, our opponent, Upton Landers, also professes to be a Christian, so, unless he doesn't actually believe what he says he believes (which raises a different set of problems), then religion should be a non-starter in this race.

Conclusion: You're doing a great job. The governor and I understand that you're exhausted, running on fumes, and ready for this race to be over, regardless of the outcome. But we need one more push from all of you to make your hard work to this point pay off with an historic election victory. We've come this far, so we might as well win this thing. Press on!

Chapter 34

Berkeley, California
Mid-October 2016

J eff Ackerman and his campaign team saw firsthand just how difficult it was to negotiate against someone who has all the leverage.
As a relative stranger to the national political scene, Ackerman needed
as many opportunities as possible to introduce himself to the voters,
and so he and his staff pushed for at least five presidential debates. The
live television audience for the debates, together with a few days of
pre-debate build-up and another day or two of post-debate analysis
for each debate, would be invaluable to him. They also pushed for
conservative moderators and asked that the debates be held in locations where the audience was likely to be conservative.

Unfortunately for the Republican underdog, Upton Landers and
his handlers were well aware of Ackerman's need for national exposure and fought hard to deny him the opportunity. Landers already
owned the biggest microphone in the world: the platform afforded
to the president of the United States. He also had nearly every media
outlet in the world squarely in his corner.

Landers had little to gain and much to lose from sharing the
stage and the spotlight with Jeff Ackerman, so he simply said no to

everything: no debates at all, and therefore no conservative moderators or audiences. So sorry, the message went. The leader of the free world is simply too busy and too important to waste time debating a political upstart who is clearly not ready for prime time. Oh, and he's a religious extremist and probably a racist to boot. We can't possibly have the president lower himself to the point of sharing a stage with a freak from a crazy cult.

Ackerman then played the only card available to him: he claimed to every media outlet that would listen that the president was afraid to face him "man to man, no holds barred," as if the debate were a prize fight. Although the president's media allies downplayed Ackerman's taunts, the verbal assault on his manhood was more than Upton Landers' ego could take. Not for the first time in American politics, vanity triumphed over political wisdom, and Landers agreed to a debate.

But only one debate, and only with a trio of moderators that might as well have consisted of the Upton Landers fan club: a liberal columnist from the *Washington Chronicle*, a left-wing commentator from HBT, and the president of the ultra-left Law and Policy Group. For good measure, the debate would take place on the campus of the University of California at Berkeley, the epitome of left-wing campus radicalism, where Landers would be assured of a very friendly audience.

Prudence dictated that Ackerman decline such an offer, but he couldn't really do so after claiming so loudly that Landers was afraid to face him. Thus, he and his team had reluctantly agreed to tonight's debate. The Ackerman campaign then immediately began the task of trying to manage the public's expectations by pointing out the president's many advantages in such a setting.

The night of the debate finally arrived, and Jeff Ackerman was tense. He sat in the green room, wondering, not for the first time, why they called it that. He had done all that he could to prepare for this moment, his last real chance to swing the election in his favor. With the preparation and practice sessions behind him, he was just ready to get rolling. Unfortunately, he still had fifteen minutes before he took the stage. The TV folks had already applied his makeup—he wished they would call it something else—and affixed a microphone to his lapel. Ackerman made them swear that the mike wasn't on or active yet. He knew he'd need to use the restroom before going out on stage and had no desire to broadcast that event to the world.

Ackerman wanted nothing more than to be alone, sit quietly, and try to calm his nerves. Perhaps he could watch some of the World Series on television. Anything mindless before he appeared on TV in front of millions, possibly billions, of people. On the campaign trail, the candidate was constantly surrounded by people who all spoke at once and insisted on responses from him. He really wanted some peace and solitude right now. The last thing he wanted to do was to talk or to be forced to listen to someone else talk.

Unfortunately, his wife had other ideas. Michelle Ackerman insisted on sitting with her husband in the green room. Worse yet, she took the TV remote away from him, turned off the television, and placed the remote on the table to her right, out of Jeff's reach. "Let's chat," she said cheerfully. "You've been so busy that it feels like we never get to talk these days."

She then unleashed a torrent of words. Empty, meaningless words. Hundreds, and then thousands, of words. She commented on the frigid temperature in the green room, wondered aloud if she should try a new diet, and gave him a blow-by-blow account of the most recent developments on a television show that he'd never watch in a million years. She asked him questions but didn't pause for even a second for answers from him before pouring out yet another stream-of-consciousness monologue. Eight minutes to go.

Jeff had neither the heart nor the courage to ask her to leave him alone for a bit. She was obviously as nervous as he was, and he at least controlled his own destiny to some extent. She could only wait and watch. Besides, Michelle probably thought that she was being helpful and supportive by waiting with him. Sort of a stand-by-your-man kind of thing. And perhaps she thought that assaulting his ears with a million words about a thousand items of minutia would take his mind off of his upcoming audition for the most important job in the world.

Asking her to be quiet would only hurt her feelings, so he kept his mouth shut. But he used his eyes, posture, and facial expression to say it as plainly as he could without actually saying it: *For the love of God, please shut up, if only for just a few minutes.* But she either missed the message or was willfully ignoring it, and the words continued to pour forth. Six minutes until stage time.

Isn't the weather nice here in Berkeley I wonder if the leaves are changing color back home do you think we should paint the deck this spring I wish the girls could be here with us but they'd probably just be staring at their phones did I tell you I talked to my mom her car finally got fixed her neighbor was so nice to give her a ride to the repair shop because my dad was too busy watching golf to take her himself I'd be really mad at you if you made me get a ride with a neighbor to deal with my car instead of helping me yourself.

Jeff reached his breaking point. He was about to risk hurting her feelings by asking her to give him a few minutes alone when she abruptly shifted topics yet again. But now she was talking about the substance of the campaign, rather than everyday minutia.

"So are you going to bring up religion in the debate tonight?" she inquired.

He was surprised, first by the fact that she was now discussing the debate, and, second, by the fact that she actually paused and waited expectantly for an answer.

Jeff was still bothered by her mere presence during what should have been a time of solitude and quiet reflection for him. He wasn't sure where she was going with this new topic, but he was pretty sure he wasn't going to like it. Unable to mask the irritation in his voice, he replied somewhat harshly, "No, no, definitely not. The press constantly grills me on the religion angle, as if I'm trying to become pastor in chief instead of commander in chief. Then, no matter what I say in response, I'm portrayed in print as a religious freak, some sort of extremist evangelist who would reinstate Prohibition and send gays to concentration camps. They report as if I'm giving sermons instead of speeches. No, the last thing I want to do is raise the topic of religion myself, although it will probably get raised by one of the moderators, forcing me to deal with it yet again. Art, Scott, and I talked this through, and I think we have a good strategy for diffusing the issue."

He glanced at the clock for the seventeenth time in the past thirty seconds. Four minutes to go.

"Well," Michelle responded, "isn't that different from how you've handled other aspects of your campaign?"

"What do you mean?"

"For other issues, you've been very up-front and outspoken. You've raised controversial topics, sometimes before you're even asked about them, and you've spoken fearlessly about what you believe. Better yet, you've explained *why* you hold the positions that you do, and that's what's gotten you to within a few percentage points of the lead in the race. Why have you taken a different approach with respect to your faith?"

The candidate had no good answer for this, and he fervently hoped that this would be the last time tonight that he was stumped by a question. He wasn't ashamed of his religious beliefs. And he hadn't consciously decided to treat religion differently from any other aspect of the campaign. "I don't really know," was all he could muster in response.

"I've been giving this some thought over the past few weeks," Michelle began.

Well, why did you wait until three minutes before the biggest debate of my life to mention it? Jeff screamed the question with his eyes. Fortunately for him and for his marriage, he was able to keep his mouth shut while Michelle continued.

"I know you have a chance to win this election. When you first told me you were running, I didn't believe that, but now I do. I'm so proud of you and what you've done to close such a huge gap in the race, even if things don't go our way on election night. But . . ."

He'd known there was a *but* coming and braced himself for what might follow this small but most portentous of words.

Michelle went on, clearly nervous about broaching the topic with her husband, "What if the presidency isn't the really important opportunity here? What if the opportunity you've been given instead is the chance to share your faith on a huge stage, with the world watching? What if God got you this far in the race so that He could use you to accomplish something much bigger than winning an election?"

Because Jeff was mentally prepared to match wits with Upton Landers and the debate moderators—to argue, to debate, to question the premise of every question—his first instinct was to push back against Michelle's line of thinking. "Honey, I'm not a missionary. I'm not a preacher. Right now, I'm not even a Sunday-school teacher. I'm a politician. People aren't voting on who has the best theology or who can save the most souls. They're voting to determine the next president, which is obviously a secular office. And anyway, I'm running for president of all of America, not just Christian America."

Michelle answered with a gentle smile, "I know all of that, and your answer just now was perfect. You can explain anything you put your mind to, and I think you can talk openly and boldly about Jesus without alienating people. There are thousands of people who disagree with you on a lot of issues who will vote for you anyway because of how logical, reasonable, and courageous you've been. You've taken one unpopular stand after another and then made the case for it, changing minds and gaining votes in the process. How awesome would it be to use those same skills of yours for a cause bigger than yourself? Bigger than politics? Bigger than the country?"

His nervousness and adrenaline caused his thoughts to fly rapidly through his brain and his emotions to turn on a dime. In a span of less than a minute, he shifted from frustration with Michelle's meaningless gabfest, to puzzlement over her questions about the larger meaning of the election process, and now to anger. Anger at her for not recognizing his need to be alone with his thoughts. Anger at her for confusing him and distracting him with only one minute to go before he took the stage for an incredibly important debate. Anger over her having the audacity to contradict the advice of his expert political staffers.

Anger because . . . well, because she was *right*.

Chapter 35

Berkeley, California

Mid-October 2016

Voters expected professional politicians to set aside all emotion and ignore all irrelevant influences when performing on stage. This was true whether it involved something mundane like cutting a ceremonial ribbon at a newly opened hospital, or something momentous like putting your political career on the line in a hostile environment in a debate with the sitting president of the United States. Politicians were expected to smile and wave at the right time and to speak the exact words that the voters wanted to hear, using exactly the correct tone and volume. It didn't matter to the electorate if the candidate's refrigerator broke that morning or if his dog was sick.

The voters certainly didn't care if a candidate's wife challenged him to defy all political wisdom and commit political suicide by sharing his Christian faith in a secular environment with an audience that already suspected him of being a little too religious for the country's own good. The fact that said challenge was made just minutes before the debate was also irrelevant, at least in the mind of the mythical Average American Voter.

But Jeff Ackerman was rattled.

He was angry with his wife for strongly hinting that he cared more about the election than his faith. He was frustrated with his campaign team for failing to negotiate more even-handed arrangements for the debate. He felt hostility toward the audience, who had just cheered his opponent upon Landers' entrance but simply glared at Ackerman. He was fearful of the type of questions the moderators would use to try to make him look foolish in front of millions of viewers. Most of all, he was mad at himself for having the audacity to think he might actually be able to make the leap from forgotten former governor of a small, mostly insignificant state to become the leader of the free world. These emotions, when combined with the natural nervousness and fear over appearing on national television in a battle of wits with a capable opponent and hostile moderators, nearly overwhelmed him.

Ackerman was an emotional wreck. His emotional state began to manifest itself physically, and the effect was not good for the underdog Republican. His face was pale despite the orange stage makeup that was caked on. He fought a losing battle to keep from perspiring under the hot glare of the blazing TV lights. His knees were weak, and he suddenly wondered if he might become the first presidential candidate to pass out on stage during a debate.

The preliminaries were wrapping up and the debate was about to begin. Jeff Ackerman was desperate to get himself under control before humiliating himself with the whole world watching. But nothing was working. He tried deep breaths, in through the nose and out through the mouth, but these just made him feel more lightheaded. He tried jamming the fingernail of his forefingers into his thumbs, but this simply made him feel pain in addition to being lightheaded and sweaty.

Finally, he remembered a tip from his public speaking professor in college: if you get nervous, picture your audience members naked.

Desperate for a solution, Ackerman squinted through the glare from the TV lights and found the hostile, liberal audience scowling at him. As a general rule, leftists were a decidedly unattractive species, and this crowd was both more leftist and more unattractive than usual. A shiver went down Ackerman's spine as he thought of naked male hippies with scraggly gray hair hanging to their waists. The women were even more repulsive. He quickly decided with a barely suppressed grin that the evening would be a success if the number of votes he gained tonight equaled or exceeded the number of unshaved female armpits in the audience.

This did the trick. His body temperature dropped rapidly and his breathing slowed. He got that calm, cool, relieved sensation that followed a bout of nausea: *I felt really bad a few seconds ago, and I might feel really bad again in a few minutes, but for this moment at least, I'm okay. I'm okay. I'm okay.*

After the customary handshake between the participants, the debate began. President Landers got the first question, a softball from the HBT commentator asking him if he was pleased with the results of his efforts to end Israel's "occupation" of Palestine.

So, that's how this will go down, Ackerman thought. *There's never been a nation called Palestine. There is no Israeli occupation. Israel is surrounded by millions of Muslims that want to kill all Jews, drive them into the Mediterranean, and wipe the nation of Israel off the map. How can people not understand this? And what's Landers gonna say in response to this invitation to pat himself on the back? Will he say "I'm a dunce and I blew it?" Of course not. He'll say, "I'm very proud of the efforts of my administration to end the Israeli occupation of Palestine and to create peace in the Middle East, but we still have work to do. I look forward to continuing to provide leadership on this issue for the next four years, blah blah blah and blah."*

Ackerman managed to keep a somewhat straight face as President Landers uttered nearly exactly the same words the Republican candidate had anticipated, taking the easy question and turning it into a nice, relatively cliché-free campaign ad for the Democratic incumbent. Landers was polished, smooth, and confident. He appeared relaxed and well rested. The favorite smiled modestly as the audience enthusiastically applauded his answer.

The friendly tone of the debate changed abruptly with the first question to Jeff Ackerman. It came from the moderator from the Law and Policy Group. "Governor Ackerman, you haven't addressed the urgent problem of income inequality in the U.S. during your campaign. You haven't raised it in your speeches, there's nothing in the Republican Party platform about it, and your website ignores this pressing issue. In fact, many of your policies would exacerbate the problem by helping the rich at the expense of the poor. Will you continue to dodge the issue of economic inequality?"

A few audience members hissed at Ackerman, having found him guilty of the crime of being insensitive to the poor, or something like that. Ackerman ignored them and delivered a professorial response, assuming the role of the college professor calmly but firmly rebuking a wayward undergrad who had uttered illogical nonsense in class. "I certainly take issue with the assumptions and accusations underlying your question," Ackerman said bluntly. "There are at least three of them. First, you say that economic inequality is a 'problem,' and second, it's not just a problem, but an 'urgent problem' and a 'pressing issue.' Third, you falsely claim that I've 'dodged the issue.' But let's put aside your bad faith and rabid partisanship for a moment and examine the matter of economic inequality.

"Economic inequality is simply not a problem. Instead, it is merely a set of left-wing policy goals mislabeled as the 'solutions' to a 'problem' that doesn't actually exist." He air-quoted the emphasized words. "You see, in the muddled mind of the American leftist, the U.S. economy is a fixed, unchanging pie, and all the participants are fighting for a larger share of that fixed amount.

"Under this befuddled way of thinking, anyone who is deemed by the intelligentsia to have obtained too large a slice of the pie has, by definition, taken something away from others who have smaller slices. But never fear, your friendly neighborhood Marxist politician will soon ride to the rescue. He'll impose punitive taxes on those with larger slices of the pie, under the guise of helping those who only have a few crumbs. Unfortunately, these crumbholders won't be any better off. They'll still have only crumbs despite the promises from Democrats in Washington. No one will be any better off, except perhaps a few apparatchiks in D.C. All that will happen is that the upper-income folks will be pushed down a few notches so that they too can become mere crumbholders.

"In reality, however, our economy is not a fixed pie, and someone who earns an extra dollar is not taking that dollar away from someone else's salary. If it was a pie of a fixed size and amount, if our economy never grew, we'd all be fighting over the sticks we use to roast our dinosaur meat over the fire at the edge of our cave. You see, despite the best efforts of the left to tax and regulate our economy into a shrunken, shriveled mess, our economy—or our national pie if you will—continues to grow and expand. Almost every year, there are more dollars, more assets, more resources that make up our national economic pie. Let's take an example."

Ackerman raised his voice to be heard over the grumbles from the audience. "Imagine two neighbors who live in northern Virginia. We'll call them Bob and Stan. Bob has always been a real hard-charger, a high-effort guy. He majored in electrical engineering in college, a very demanding field, and Bob got a job as a web designer for the *Washington Chronicle* earning one hundred thousand dollars per year when he graduated.

313

"Stan, on the other hand, is lazy, both physically and intellectually. He majored in journalism because he wasn't smart enough to learn anything useful or substantive. The only job he could find when he finally graduated from college after six years was as a cub reporter for the *Washington Chronicle*, making twenty-five thousand dollars per year."

The *Washington Chronicle* columnist who was sitting in front of Ackerman as one of the moderators just happened to be named Stan, and he had spent six years completing his undergraduate degree in journalism. This particular Stan had taken numerous cheap shots at Ackerman in print during the campaign, and the candidate was enjoying the opportunity to retaliate somewhat.

"To the Democrats," Ackerman went on, "this is a problem. Bob is making four times more money than Stan! Oh no! Economic inequality! Bob must be punished for having the audacity to work hard and be smart, and he must pay for committing the crime of ambition so that the feelings of the Stans of the world won't be hurt. Unfortunately, the Democrats have no effective means of bringing Stan up to Bob's level, so their policies are designed instead to kick Bob down to Stan's level. They want to make the Bobs of the world poor and miserable along with the Stans so that we can all be poor and miserable together.

"But what's happening here in our example is simply the free market at work. Anyone with a fifth-grade education could do Stan's job, but it takes intelligence, effort, and talent to perform Bob's duties. There are a lot of Stans out there, and very few Bobs. And the Bob and Stan in our example each earn salaries that reflect this relative difference in supply and demand."

Ackerman continued, "Let's take it one step further. I know this sounds far-fetched in this era of dying media entities, but let's say that the *Washington Chronicle* somehow has a very good year in spite of its radical leftism, and profits increase significantly. Let's further assume that the increased profits are mostly driven by increased website revenue, and that Bob's hard work helped make that happen. And so Bob is promoted to be the chief technology officer for the *Washington Chronicle*. His salary doubles from one hundred thousand dollars per year to two hundred thousand. This is great for Bob, but has he hurt Stan by taking this increased salary? Of course not. Stan is still being paid a salary that is commensurate with his ability, or lack thereof. Yes, income inequality has increased, but so what?

"Now, perhaps, against all logic and expectations, let's say Stan also does pretty well at his job and is promoted to the position of opinion columnist for the *Chronicle*. His salary likewise doubles, going from twenty-five thousand dollars to fifty thousand dollars. Most sane, intelligent individuals would deem these raises and promotions to be a good thing for both Bob and Stan. But liberals pushing this income-inequality nonsense are neither sane nor intelligent. In their warped minds, we still have a huge problem, because income inequality has increased. Bob previously earned seventy-five thousand dollars more than Stan. Now, even after Stan's raise, Bob earns one hundred and fifty thousand dollars more than poor little Stan. How horrible! This cannot continue!" Mock horror punctuated his words. "Pass more laws! Enact more regulations! The Bobs of the world must be stopped! How dare they work hard and achieve great things!

"But the fact is, Bob isn't taking money out of Stan's pocket. They are both being paid a market wage, and each could leave for another job at any time if the *Washington Chronicle* ceased to pay him a competitive salary. Thus, contrary to the assumptions contained in your loaded question a few minutes ago, income inequality is not a problem, and it's certainly not an 'urgent problem' or 'pressing issue' as you claimed.

"Finally, and again contrary to the assertion contained in your question, I have not 'dodged' the issue of income inequality. I haven't dodged it because it's not an issue, and I haven't even been asked about it until now. I've held more press conferences than any presidential candidate in modern U.S. history, with no restrictions on the types of questions that can be asked. No one has asked me a single question about income inequality until just now. To claim that I've dodged the so-called issue is completely disingenuous, and I look forward to your public apology to me once you've had a chance to think about this for a few minutes."

The audience sat in stunned silence. Everyone knew that economic inequality was a real problem that must be addressed right away, because . . . well, just because. Surely there must be some reasons somewhere. These folks weren't accustomed to having their dogma questioned at all, much less as bluntly and directly as Jeff Ackerman had just done. And they weren't mentally equipped to process such a strange event.

Ackerman was fairly pleased with his performance in the early going. He relished the role of the underdog, one guy standing up for his conservative policy positions against a wily, experienced liberal opponent who had the moderators as well as the audience on his side. The debate continued along these same lines, with Ackerman handling himself well.

However, even though the Republican from Mississippi performed at a high level, he was unable to land a telling blow on President Upton Landers. Questions on tax policy, defense spending, illegal immigration, and the national debt all produced similar results. Each candidate gave predictable, almost scripted answers to these questions. The responses were almost verbatim restatements of positions that the candidates had already espoused in numerous speeches and interviews over the past few months.

Ackerman wasn't losing the debate, but he wasn't exactly winning it either. The challenger needed a clear, decisive win in the debate in order to keep his fading electoral hopes alive. Landers understood this fact and did an excellent job of dodging, weaving, and denying Ackerman the chance to score significant points with the voters. All Landers had to do was run out the clock. And in the mind of Jeff Ackerman, the clock was ticking faster and faster.

As the debate wound down, Ackerman began to despair, feeling that he'd missed his last opportunity. He also had his wife's gentle challenge in the back of his mind: was he man enough to openly discuss his Christian beliefs in this hostile forum? Unexpectedly, the topic of religion hadn't been raised thus far, and Ackerman hadn't been forced to engage in the tactics of deflection that he'd developed with help from his staff. But what if Michelle was right? What if he had been given this opportunity not to swing the election, but rather to tell people what he believed about Jesus and why he believed it?

Chapter 36

Berkeley, California
Mid-October 2016

After a commercial break, the debate entered its final stage. In this last segment, each candidate would have the opportunity to ask a single question of the other, followed by an answer, a rebuttal, and then about ten minutes of freestyle debate between the two on the topic raised by the initial question. The format for this concluding portion represented the only victory that Ackerman and his team had won during the negotiations with the Landers squad about the debates. Landers had used his superior leverage to win on the number of debates, moderators, location, and the like.

Landers' team had actually proposed this unusual freestyle candidate-on-candidate format in the early stages of the negotiations. They theorized that the poised, confident Upton Landers would easily dispose of the bumbling bumpkin from Mississippi. After all, Ackerman was a public-school product who was new to the national stage, whereas Landers held two degrees from Harvard along with the gravitas bestowed by the office of the presidency.

Ackerman actually relished the thought of debating Landers directly, as this would strip away the covering fire from the moderators that was sure to be aimed solely at Ackerman. As a negotiating tactic, his team had pretended to be horrified by the freestyle debate idea, and they agreed to it only at the very end of the process. They got what they wanted by pretending not to want it.

Landers went first, asking Ackerman an entirely predictable question about immigration, using clever, calculated phrasing along the lines of "When did you stop beating your wife?"

Ackerman was thoroughly prepared for this, both substantively and tactically. The Republican more than held his own in the give-and-take that followed. But nothing about the exchange served to make Ackerman the clear, decisive winner of the debate, which was what he had to have for a realistic chance of winning the election that was only two weeks away.

It was now Ackerman's turn to ask a question of President Landers. Ackerman had only a few seconds to make a decision that would likely determine not only his own future but possibly the direction of the country as a whole for the next four to eight years, and perhaps longer. While the implications were enormous, his choice was simple.

He could ask the question about income tax rates that he and his team had carefully formulated and then dutifully rehearsed. He had notes and flowcharts on the podium in front of him with hints and reminders about how to proceed, depending on how Landers responded initially to the scripted question. Ackerman was thoroughly prepared for this type of exchange. Unfortunately for Ackerman, however, President Landers had performed rather well during the debate thus far, and the incumbent was likely to be just as well prepared for this topic as Ackerman. Thus, the scripted question was unlikely to deliver the knockout punch that Ackerman's campaign so desperately needed.

The Republican challenger's other option was to go completely off script and ask Landers a question dealing directly with religion.

Landers and his media surrogates had worked hard for the past half year to paint Ackerman as a raving fundamentalist who was hell-bent on establishing a Christian theocracy in the United States. Although Ackerman had parried these charges, the polls showed that he had been damaged by them. Accordingly, Landers would almost certainly be caught off guard if Ackerman now raised what he had been trying diligently to avoid on the campaign trail. This latter option certainly offered both higher potential rewards as well as higher risk for Jeff Ackerman.

Not for the first time, the image of a Christian being fed to the lions, surrounded by a mob howling for blood, dashed through Jeff Ackerman's mind. He gave an imperceptible shake of his head to clear his mind, turned toward his opponent, and asked bluntly but calmly, "President Landers, what's your favorite Bible verse?"

No introduction or build-up to give away the topic of the question. No warning for Landers whatsoever. Although he was a seasoned political pro, Landers couldn't prevent a look of surprise from flashing across his face before he could regain control and employ his standard concerned-yet-thoughtful frown. His head even jerked back an inch or two, as if he had been struck by a physical blow. It all happened in an instant, but not fast enough for the TV cameras to miss.

The left-leaning crowd emitted a collective groan of disgust. They couldn't believe this Ackerman guy had the audacity to bring up a religious topic in a secular forum. Why should the most powerful man in the world be forced to pretend to believe in a two-thousand-year-old book of fables and fabrications?

Well, Michelle, I've just committed political suicide. I hope you're happy! Ackerman thought.

But Upton Landers was in trouble, and he knew it. He had no idea how to respond intelligently. Yet he had to answer quickly. An awkward pause was a sure prelude to defeat in this format. And so the president simply started talking, employing the age-old politician's trick of speaking for a few minutes without really saying anything, rambling on in an effort to buy time for his thoughts to catch up to his mouth.

Landers was trapped by his own tactic of portraying Ackerman as being too religious. The Democrat had always professed to be a Christian himself. This was because it had been good politics to do so, at least until the past few years. However, he knew that disowning Christianity completely at this point would alienate many voters, so he hadn't taken that step publicly. Instead, he hoped the public would view him as having a Goldilocks amount of religious faith: not too little, not too much, just right.

But neither Landers nor his advisors had ever thought this through. They'd never articulated just where the president stood on spiritual matters. And now he was being asked to quote the Bible! He hadn't opened a Bible in decades. He had never had a favorite Bible verse. And he was pretty sure that he didn't know anyone who did.

"Well, the Bible obviously offers a lot of good advice," Landers began in an effort to buy time. "We should certainly encourage people to gain knowledge and wisdom from many different sources, both secular and religious, including the Koran and the Torah in addition to the Bible." Landers, along with most of the audience members and the media who were covering the debate, was ignorant of the fact that the Torah was part of the Bible. So far, he was doing a decent job of winging it. The president was just about to say something silly and slippery, such as "The Bible has too many good verses for me to pick just one," when he finally dredged up a Bible verse from the depths of his memory.

Speaking faster and with more confidence now, President Landers continued, "The Bible, the Torah, and the Koran all have many truths to offer us and many passages that we would be wise to follow. And although it is difficult to pick just one verse of the Bible as my favorite, I would have to say that my favorite verse is 'God helps those who help themselves.' I'm not quite the Bible scholar that you are, Mr. Ackerman," the president said half-modestly and half-sarcastically, "so I can't say exactly where that's found in the Bible."

Chief of Staff Richard Jordan, the remainder of the president's entourage, the debate moderators, and the live audience in the auditorium all breathed an audible sigh of relief. Some version of *The Old Man's still got it* passed through many of their minds. He managed to pull a Bible verse out of thin air and avoided looking like a fool in front of millions of people. After all, some of those religious freaks in flyover country actually opened their Bibles occasionally. And those people voted. They'd be offended if their president couldn't offer a single quote from a book that they, in their unenlightened little minds, claim to be sacred. All Landers had to do at this point was run out the clock tonight and declare the debate to be a success, and then he'd cruise to re-election. But the relief of the president's supporters was premature.

"Congratulations, Mr. President," Ackerman replied, smiling ever so sweetly before bringing down the proverbial hammer. "You just managed to quote a favorite Bible verse that's not actually in the Bible. You see, 'God helps those who help themselves' isn't a Bible verse at all. It's from Benjamin Franklin in a 1757 edition of *Poor Richard's Almanac*, although Franklin took the phrase from an article published by Algernon Sydney in 1698 entitled *Discourses Concerning Government*."

Unfortunately for Upton Landers, Ackerman didn't stop there. "Now that we've established your lack of biblical literacy, Mr. President, I have to ask you this. In your previous campaign four years ago, you said that you're a Christian. It was on your campaign website, and you used your identity as a Christian to win votes on your way to the White House. And I'm certainly not questioning your faith or doubting your sincerity. But just four years after you publicly and freely identified yourself as a Christian, you and your media allies have strongly criticized me for my Christian beliefs. What's the distinction here? Why was your Christianity a reason that people should vote for you four years ago, and why is my Christianity a disqualifying factor now?"

"Oh my God," muttered Richard Jordan from his post just offstage, not appreciating the irony in his remark.

The reaction from the audience and the moderators was similar. Their guy was suddenly on the ropes, in danger of decisively losing the debate. While he would almost certainly still win the general election, any chance he had of a landslide victory would vanish unless he could somehow salvage at least a draw in tonight's encounter against this upstart Republican.

On the opposite side of the backstage area from Richard Jordan, Jeff Ackerman's advisors were also worried. Their candidate had not only gone completely off script, but had also raised the topic of religion that they had worked so hard to avoid. Did he really want to be elected? If so, why was he sabotaging his own slim hopes?

For his part, Upton Landers was on the verge of panic. He literally had no logical response to Ackerman's question other than the truth, which was that he thought religion was a waste of time, money, and energy. He had claimed to be a Christian four years ago merely out of political convenience. Now that Christianity was out of favor in the general culture, Landers had quietly dropped all references to his religious preference from his campaign materials. Of course, he couldn't admit this in the debate. But he had to say *something*, so he took a deep breath and plunged into the pool.

"Isn't the distinction obvious to anyone with half a brain?" Landers responded with as much confidence as he could muster. His tone and body language conveyed his contempt for this line of questioning, and he hoped that his mannerisms would be strong enough to overcome the weakness of his words in the minds of viewers around the country. "Mr. Ackerman, you are a fundamentalist who ignores science, evidence, and reason. Yes, I'm a Christian, but I'm also willing to admit that not everything in the Bible is true. And so, I have a reasonable faith, based on what can be proven scientifically, whereas you have no evidence for what you claim to believe. I've managed to keep faith out of the way of my duties as president, whereas you would turn the White House into the equivalent of a Southern Baptist church. And that, sir, is the distinction between our two approaches."

Landers drew half-hearted applause from the audience here, not because he sold them with his argument but because they wanted to encourage their man on the stage.

Knowing that he had his opponent on the ropes, Ackerman pushed further, to the chagrin of his campaign team. "Mr. President, you just said that part of the Bible is true and part of it is not. You've obviously studied this issue closely in order to determine which pages of the Bible are valid and which ones can be ripped out and ignored. Can you describe for us how you came to this conclusion and give us some examples of false doctrines contained in the Bible?"

"Oh, this is ridiculous," Landers fumed. "I'm not about to get into a theological debate with you over issues that no one cares anything about. Let's just say that you have no evidence for the most outrageous claims of Christianity and that I believe the parts of the Bible that science can prove to be true. Now, let's move on to discuss the many problems facing the American people."

Ackerman wasn't about to let Landers off the hook. "Mr. President, it's simply not true that there is no evidence for the claims of Christianity. The two biggest, and perhaps the most controversial, claims that Christians make are, first of all, that God created the universe and, second, that Jesus was executed on a Roman cross but then rose from the dead three days later, just as He predicted He would do. A thoughtful, rational, reasonable person can examine these two claims and come to the logical conclusion that they are both true based on the available evidence. In the interest of time, I'll summarize some of this evidence for you and our audience tonight, as you obviously haven't examined this for yourself."

Ackerman now turned slightly to face the audience and the moderators squarely. He was talking to the TV cameras now, rather than to his opponent. "Let's look first at some of the evidence for the belief that God created the universe. One of the strongest arguments in favor of this assertion is a formulation based on science and logic that goes like this: Everything that begins to exist has a cause. In other words, nothing simply pops into being, completely uncaused and out of nothingness. And science demonstrates that at a particular moment in time, the universe began to exist. That is to say, at some point in the past, there was simply nothingness, a complete void. There was no space, no matter, no energy, no time. But then, in a single instant, all of those things sprang into being.

"Scientists refer to this beginning as The Big Bang, but that's simply a name for an event, and naming it doesn't explain how the event happened. Because the universe began to exist, it must have a cause. What entity is powerful enough to create our universe, to create space, matter, energy, and time, and to cause these things to start to exist when they didn't before? You could call it anything you like. You could take the Star Wars approach and call it 'The Force.'

Or you could call it Bob or Sally or Juan. But this entity sounds like God to me, and that's what I and billions of others choose to call it.

"That's just one of several strong pieces of evidence for God's existence and His creation of the universe. But what about the Christian belief that Jesus was God in the flesh and that He died and then rose from the dead? Again, there is much evidence to support this, so I'll just hit the highlights here.

"Some modern-day skeptics say that Jesus never claimed to be divine and that His followers simply invented that idea after His death. This is clearly not true, because Jesus' claim to divinity, to being equal to God the Father, was the reason He was killed in the first place. The Jewish religious leaders and Roman government officials didn't kill Jesus because He was a great teacher, a criminal, or a military threat. They didn't kill Him because they were bored and wanted something exciting to do on the Friday of Passover week. No, they killed Jesus because He claimed to be God. Blasphemy was the charge for which Jesus was executed by being nailed to a Roman cross.

"Thus, we know that Jesus claimed to be God and was killed for it. He also predicted that He would rise from the dead after being killed. All of Christianity rises and falls on whether or not Jesus actually rose from the dead. The Bible itself notes that if Jesus didn't actually rise from the dead, then Christian faith is in vain. Therefore, we must ask ourselves: did this actually happen?

"Some skeptics say that Jesus didn't really die on the cross. Instead, they claim that He merely passed out and appeared to be dead but revived later. Almost no serious scholar buys this claim any longer. You see, the Romans were experts at killing people, and they got a lot of practice. The soldiers who handled the crucifixion would have been executed themselves if they had failed to kill Jesus properly. And there's no way a guy who had been flogged with a whip, then had his hands and feet nailed to a cross, and then been stabbed in the side with a spear, could have rolled a heavy stone away from the entrance to his tomb and then strolled out under his own power, with no medical attention. Even if he managed to do all of this, he wouldn't be in any condition to claim that he'd risen from the dead. He would be a bloody, crippled mess who no one would mistake for the Son of God.

"Thus, we know from both biblical and non-biblical sources that Jesus was killed on the cross. And we also know that His tomb was empty. If it wasn't, the Jewish religious leaders who opposed Jesus would have simply said, 'Look, here's the body. It's clear that this guy is still dead.' That would have stopped Christianity in its tracks, but it didn't happen because the tomb was empty.

"We now have a dead guy who claimed to be God, together with an empty tomb. But maybe the disciples stole Jesus' body so that they could plausibly claim He'd been raised from the dead. That was the argument that the Jewish religious leaders made from the beginning, but it doesn't hold water. You see, the disciples didn't initially understand or fully believe Jesus' prediction that He would rise again. They were terrified and in hiding. Their leader had been executed in a painful and humiliating fashion by the occupying power, the Romans, with the help of the Jewish leaders. The disciples were, quite logically, afraid that they'd be the next ones to be executed.

"Yet something happened to change their fear and timidity into great boldness, and that something was the appearance of the resurrected Jesus among them. They were transformed from cowering, uneducated fishermen into bold ambassadors for a new religion in defiance of the dictatorial government and all social norms. They traveled the known world proclaiming that Jesus rose from the dead and promoting the idea that Jesus, the Son of God, had died to pay the penalty for the sins of all mankind.

"In doing so, they faced imprisonment, torture, and death. They were social outcasts. All but one of them were executed, in a brutal and extremely painful fashion, because of his faith in Jesus. But if the disciples had stolen Jesus' body, they would have known that Jesus wasn't God, and that Jesus didn't rise from the dead, that it was all just a hoax and a big lie. And there's no way that these guys would be willing to die for a lie. From a worldly perspective, there was no upside for them in preaching about Jesus: no money, no fame, no political power. No book deals or movie rights. Just the chance to get flayed alive, or killed with arrows, or crucified upside down.

"The only reasonable conclusion, then, is that Jesus did in fact rise from the dead, just like He said He would, and just like the disciples claimed that He did. And those who believe this and accept His offer of salvation can rest in the knowledge that spiritual death has been defeated, and that Jesus' death on the cross serves as a substitute for the penalty that we all deserve for our own sins and shortcomings. This substitutionary atonement that Jesus made on our behalf means that our debt has been paid in full, and thus we'll be permitted to enter the presence of God the Father in heaven."

Ackerman paused for a deep breath and a sip of water before wrapping up. "Ladies and gentlemen, I'm sorry for the Sunday-school lesson that I just delivered. I recognize that you didn't tune in tonight to hear a discourse on religion. But the president and his media allies have worked hard to use my religious beliefs as some sort of disqualifying factor for the presidency, despite the fact that every prior president has claimed to be a Christian. Even President Landers says he's a Christian. But somehow I've been held to a different standard in this campaign. I'm not sure why that is, but I'm not going to whine about it.

"My only fear or regret is that perhaps there are people out there following this race who have been turned off of Christianity because they don't like my politics, or who have been turned off of conservatism because they don't agree with my religion. To those folks I simply say this: please investigate the facts of Christianity and conservatism for yourselves. I readily admit that I may not be the best politician in the world, and there's no doubt in my mind that I have a long way to go before I'm a good Christian. But please don't use any failures of mine to judge these two belief systems. If you give each an honest look, I think you'll find that conservative, free-market principles are the best way to govern our great country. And I also think you'll find that the Bible is trustworthy and that Jesus is who He claimed to be.

"I felt compelled to use this opportunity tonight to demonstrate that calm, reasonable, rational people can believe in God and believe in Jesus based on solid evidence, science, and logic. You see, I and billions of other followers of Jesus around the globe don't believe the Bible is true because we have faith. Instead, we have faith because we believe the Bible is true.

"Finally, please understand that I am running for president, not Pope or priest or preacher or pastor. My opponent has introduced religion as a campaign issue, not me. Before tonight, I have not mentioned religion at all except in response to questions from the president's media minions. I look forward to serving all of you, Christians and non-Christians alike, as your president, not as your preacher. Thank you for your patience and understanding tonight."

The debate concluded soon thereafter. No one was happy with the result. Ackerman was simultaneously relieved that he'd had the courage to defend his faith, angry at his wife for forcing him to do so, and disappointed that he'd missed an opportunity to make election night something other than a foregone conclusion.

Landers, on the other hand, was humiliated for reciting a Bible verse that isn't actually in the Bible and for failing to out-debate this

rube from Mississippi. Yet he was comforted by the fact that Ackerman's religious ravings had almost certainly offended most of the
nation. Each side claimed victory in the press but privately despaired
over a lost opportunity.

Chapter 37

Austin Brant Column in the
New York Daily Ledger

Late-October 2016

Austin Brant emphatically punched the *enter* key on his keyboard to transmit his weekly column for publication the next day. He'd received pushback from management regarding the subject matter of his piece, but all involved knew how ridiculous it would be to prohibit the paper's sole conservative columnist from writing a pro-Jeff Ackerman column with less than two weeks to go before Election Day. Brant threatened to resign if management didn't stop interfering with his writing. After all, he was paid to write an opinion column, and his opinions hadn't changed since he'd been hired. Management quickly folded, mumbling spitefully to their token conservative that he was free to support as many mouth-breathing morons for high office as he saw fit.

Brant didn't initially view the piece as his most hard-hitting work. It wouldn't have made his personal top ten list of the Best of Austin Brant. But he decided the column must be hitting pretty close to the mark for his bosses to get so exercised about it. He read it again from his computer screen before ducking out for lunch.

Ackerman Campaign Is Reclaiming the Language of Politics

Presidential candidates, their immense staffs, and their most fervent donors and volunteers can't afford to focus on anything other than the final sprint to Election Day at this point every four years. Similarly, with less than two weeks to go before the votes are cast, reporters on the campaign beat are rightfully zeroed in on the horse-race aspect of the election. If you've made your way this far through today's newspaper, you've already seen several stories noting that Upton Landers retains a significant (though gradually shrinking) advantage over Jeff Ackerman. Ackerman has narrowed the gap considerably but will likely run out of time before he can close it completely.

Thus, you don't need this column to tell you what you already know: Upton Landers will likely win re-election with a solid but non-spectacular margin over the unlikely candidate from Mississippi. But unlike those involved in the hectic frenzy of final-stage campaigning, your humble columnist has the luxury of looking beyond the daily tracking polls, instead seeking the long-term implications of seemingly small events. This column has previously applauded Jeff Ackerman's masterful handling of a hostile press corps. Today, I'd like to draw your attention to the battle over words. Here, too, Jeff Ackerman has waged a winning campaign in the battle, if not the war.

Words matter, and not just to opinion columnists and others in the newspaper trade. They matter to presidents and to congressmen and to judges and juries, to soldiers and policemen and to teachers and students and parents. For generations, the political left has dominated word choice in our political and cultural discourse. For example, the goals of the left are described as "progress," whereas the right is always accused of trying to "turn back the clock" on said progress, primarily because conservatives are so "reactionary."

Jeff Ackerman has taken note of this development and worked hard to reclaim the linguistic battleground largely abandoned by his fellow Republicans. The Mississippi conservative recently noted that Republicans are frequently described as "far-right," but the corresponding phrase "far-left" is almost never used by mainstream media outlets. In the eyes of the left-leaning media, Ackerman went on to say, only Republicans are ever painted as "hyperpartisan" or "divisive" or "dogmatic," whereas Democrats are much more likely to be lauded for being "moderate," "practical," "results-oriented," and "willing to reach across the aisle." Even the most radical left-wingers aren't described as such; instead they are "progressive" and, at worst, "quirky" and "ahead of their time."

The same concepts apply to legislation passed largely or completely along party lines. President Landers' signature tax increase bill didn't receive a single Republican vote in Congress, and yet, because it is liberal legislation, the law is never described as "partisan" or "divisive." Those terms have simply come to mean "anything that Democrats don't like." Jeff Ackerman has pounded these ideas home on the campaign trail to great effect.

In several speeches in the past two weeks, Governor Ackerman has ridiculed the notion that federal judges should treat our Constitution as an evolving document in order to achieve "progress." He's made liberal heads explode by asking what it is that we're supposedly progressing toward? A more Godless, less family-friendly society? Is that really progress? And if those devilish Republicans succeed in their fiendish plot to "turn back the clock" on this so-called progress, back to the bad old days when children were likely to be raised in stable homes by two married parents who loved and protected them, is that really such a terrible thing?

Perhaps the most vivid example of reclaiming the linguistic high ground was Ackerman's humiliation of a BNI reporter over the abortion issue. The candidate showed clearly that the ever-shifting euphemisms for abortion are not only highly inaccurate, but also cruelly contrived to divert voters' minds from an evil, cold-hearted, brutal, life-ending ritual defended most strongly by the new priesthood of the secular left. In response to such fearless treatment of the press, Governor Ackerman has been described as a "bully." He adroitly responded that the media's definition of "bullying" is "anything that makes a leftist snowflake upset." When derided as "angry," the jovial, ever-smiling Jeff Ackerman replied with the old joke that, "This animal is vicious; it defends itself vigorously when attacked."

Ackerman often employs his sense of humor as a sword, not just as a shield. He uses it well in service to his goal of taking the high ground on the linguistic battlefield. Earlier this week, a crazed left-wing activist yelled at the candidate while he was shaking hands during a rope line event. The activist called Ackerman a "Christian Nazi" and suggested ever so helpfully, "Why don't you just kill yourself before we have to do it for you?" Ackerman later joked that this lovely lady "probably has bumper stickers on her Prius imploring us to 'Coexist' and 'Embrace Tolerance' and reminding us that 'Hatred is not a family value.'" He went on to note that, unfortunately for normal Americans, there's no one more hateful and intolerant than a supposedly tolerant liberal.

Governor Ackerman's phrase "racism industry" wins the prize for the most brilliant new terminology during this campaign season. After the Democrats attacked him as a racist with no supporting evidence, Ackerman informed the public in one of his short videos that racism, sexism, and the like are all that the left has. Because they can't make effective, substantive arguments on policy matters, they hurl labels like "racist" and "sexist" at conservatives in an effort to take conservative ideas off the table. After all, they reason, even the most sensible policy idea must be ignored if propounded by a racist. And because Republicans aren't actually racist, the racism industry must manufacture fake racism in order to enable Democrats to continue demonizing their opponents. Ackerman went on to perceptively proclaim that the left has cried wolf far too many times: when all opponents are racist, no one is.

Ackerman also uses his sense of humor to show that liberals aren't the only ones who can make unfounded allegations of racism. For example, when confronted with the news that actress Suzanne Stratton had promised to move to Canada if he somehow won the election, Ackerman deadpanned, "Why Canada instead of Mexico? She's obviously a racist who's afraid of living among people who don't look like her. She must be very anxious to preserve the benefits of her white privilege."

Governor Ackerman threw a reporter for a loop by asking for a precise definition of the so-called "working families" that would be harmed by his tax proposals. After the reporter stammered incoherently for a minute, the candidate rightly noted that almost everyone who pays taxes in the U.S. works and is part of a family of some type. So wouldn't those "working families" benefit from the tax cuts he'd promised? He also silenced academics for a few minutes (no small feat) by wondering aloud why white professors, who are always scolding the rest of us about "white privilege" and "diversity" and "inclusion," weren't resigning in droves in order to free up tenured positions for "people of color."

Ackerman is winning the war of words and for words by saying things that most Americans view as rational, reasonable, and logical, such as "Build a wall" and "America is founded on Christian principles, and I won't apologize for that." But then the press treats them as outrageous, as beyond the pale of polite society. The media speculates that Ackerman has finally gone too far, and that his insurgent, unlikely candidacy will surely collapse now. Ackerman then points and laughs at the media, thereby creating a new rush of stories that gets his message out yet again, helping the reputation of the candidate and simultaneously hurting that of his media critics. Then Ackerman rinses and repeats with a new topic or issue.

National elections are very difficult affairs. It's possible for a candidate to do almost everything right and still lose the race. This includes reclaiming the language for the good guys. If Jeff Ackerman isn't able to pull off the upset of Upton Landers, he'll be one more piece of evidence for the proposition that the best candidate doesn't always win.

Chapter 38

Washington, D.C.
Late-October 2016

Richard Jordan pulled the piping-hot popcorn from the microwave in his upscale condo in the tony Georgetown neighborhood of Washington, D.C. A health freak who took no joy in consuming food, popcorn was the closest Jordan came to eating anything unhealthy. He punished himself for this dietary extravagance by omitting both butter and salt, which made eating popcorn the equivalent of munching on Styrofoam packing peanuts. But he wanted something to munch on while watching his favorite reporter ambush Jeff Ackerman on live television, and popcorn was the most appropriate snack.

Jessica Stone was the primary talking head on HBT, a hard-left TV news channel. At the suggestion of Richard Jordan, she had arranged for a live prime-time exclusive interview with the Republican nominee to be conducted ten days before Election Day. As a favor to Jordan, she had, of course, sought his input on the types of questions she should ask. To no one's surprise, Jordan just happened to have a list of questions typed up and ready to send to Stone as soon as her request hit his email inbox.

The fact that the interview was pitched to the candidate as being limited to his economic and tax proposals was deemed irrelevant by both Jessica Stone and Richard Jordan. After all, modern presidents were expected to be able to think on their feet, to respond clearly and coherently to the most unexpected situations. Thus, breaking the promises made to the Ackerman campaign was actually a service to the country. Those idiots actually thinking about voting for this whacko needed to be shown just how inept he was when hit with questions on topics for which he hadn't been prepped by his handlers.

Jordan had to admit that Ackerman had been brilliant with the press to this point in the campaign. But Jordan knew that this was because the questions asked by the befuddled buffoons on the Republican campaign beat were so easily predictable. They were the junior varsity at best, with their more senior and insightful media colleagues getting the more desirable assignment of covering the Upton Landers campaign. Jordan could watch an Ackerman press conference and correctly guess about 80 percent of the questions that would be served up to the Republican nominee, and he knew that Art Morgan and the rest of Ackerman's staff could do the same.

Accordingly, Ackerman had been thoroughly prepared for these surface-level questions and made the press—and, by implication, their Democrat puppet masters—look silly and incompetent. However, tonight's interview would restore the natural order, with Jessica Stone peppering a bewildered candidate with hostile questions for which he had not been coached. *Ackerman deserves what is coming to him,* Jordan rationalized as he sank into his expensive leather sofa, TV remote in one hand and popcorn bowl in the other. After all, any Republican candidate who was dumb enough to submit to a Jessica Stone interview on live television and trust her to keep her word about the scope of the questions deserved to have his naiveté revealed to the voters in prime time.

After greeting the live television audience and introducing her guest, Stone began the interview with what she considered to be a bombshell question. "Governor Ackerman, you've been widely criticized as a slightly nicer, less outwardly aggressive version of Adolf Hitler. How do you respond to that?"

Ackerman kept his cool, although warning bells were ringing in his head. "Well, Jessica, in a way, those ridiculous comparisons are somewhat of a backhanded compliment. You see, no one was comparing me to a Nazi dictator when I was polling in the single digits in the early days of the campaign. But I knew that I was being taken seriously by the Democrats and their media acolytes when I achieved the holy trinity of Republican presidential candidates.

"One, I was audited by the IRS, even though I pay my taxes, I'm not wealthy, and I don't have a very complicated tax situation. This always seems to happen to Republican presidential candidates, especially when running against a sitting Democrat president. Two, I've been compared to Adolf Hitler, which is obviously ridiculous. And three, I've been compared unfavorably to the last three or four Republican presidents and candidates. You see and hear the phrase *a strange new respect* applied to Reagan, Bush I, Dole, Bush II, McCain, and Romney when media types compare me to them. You have to understand that these fine gentlemen were all demonized as Hitler when they were running against Democrats, until the next Republican came along. And then, all of a sudden, the last guy didn't seem so bad when the media was trying to make a monster out of the current candidate.

"And so, I've now achieved this somewhat dubious trifecta. There's nothing fun about any of it, and it's hurt me and my family. But I take comfort in knowing that the harassment by the IRS and the crazy comparisons by the media are driven by fear and are part of the standard playbook for Democrats when they're in a tight race."

"But sir," Stone responded, "you haven't responded substantively to my question. Serious media outlets such as this network, the *New York Daily Ledger*, and the *Washington Chronicle* have compared you to Nazi dictator Adolph Hitler. With such widespread criticism, there must be some substance behind the comparison. How do you respond to that?"

"Well, Jessica, my understanding from the conversations between your team and my campaign was that you wanted to interview me about my economic and tax proposals. But if you want to run down this Nazi rabbit trail, I'll answer your question."

Taking a calming breath, Ackerman continued, "I have almost nothing in common politically or personally with Adolph Hitler. Hitler was an advocate of gun control, while I support the Second Amendment right of the people to bear arms. Hitler was an abortion enthusiast, whereas I strongly oppose it. And of course, Hitler was virulently anti-Semitic and killed over six million Jews, whereas I'm strongly supportive of Israel.

"Remember, the word *Nazi* is simply an abbreviation for Hitler's political party, which was the National Socialists. I'm on the opposite extreme from the socialists. Socialists like Hitler advocate government control of pretty much every aspect of life, whereas I have worked and I will continue to work to shrink the role of government. Hitler was a man of the left, just like Hitler's political kindred Joseph Stalin was a man of the left, and just like Hitler's fascist ally Benito Mussolini was a man of the left. I'm loudly and proudly on the opposite end of the political spectrum from those brutal monsters. In fact, today's Democrats are much closer ideologically to Hitler, Stalin, and the like than Republicans are. And now, with that out of the way, I'm hopeful that we can get to the economic and tax topics that I'm here to discuss."

But Jessica Stone wasn't willing to be dismissed so cavalierly. How dare this simpleton try to lecture her! Everybody knew that

Republicans were Nazis, because Nazis were bad and because . . . well, she might not know the actual reasons, but really smart people like her had been likening Republicans to Nazis for generations, so there must be something behind it. She fired her next bullet.

"How can you say that Hitler and Stalin were similar in their politics? They were bitter enemies. Millions of Germans and Russians died fighting each other. Is this the sort of historical ignorance that passes for wisdom in the Republican Party in 2016?"

"Hitler and Stalin were definitely political allies for a long time," Ackerman persisted, working hard to remain calm and speak slowly. "They were both totalitarians bent on world domination. They were both advocates of complete government control of all aspects of society. They were both extremely anti-Semitic.

"They differed only at the margins. Hitler emphasized the nationalistic aspects of socialism. He wanted socialism, but he wanted the nation of Germany to take over the world and impose it on everyone. Stalin was a step ahead. He wanted international socialism without the nationalistic aspect, but only after the Soviet Union conquered the world. Political observers in the 1930s and 1940s saw clearly that the two visions were similar and that Stalin's views were simply a logical extension of Hitler's. In fact, the phrase 'First brown, then red' was commonly used in Germany as shorthand for the idea that Nazism—the brown—was a precondition to achieving full-blown communism—the red.

"Of course, even though there was very little daylight between Hitler and Stalin politically, they were both megalomaniacs bent on personally ruling the world. That's why Hitler attacked Russia. It certainly was not because of any major left/right political schism.

"And by the way, this really threw American leftists for a loop at the time. They were simultaneously pro-Hitler and pro-Stalin until Germany invaded Russia. Until then, both communism and

National Socialism sounded like great ideas to America's left-wingers. They then had to turn on a dime and manufacture some reasons to oppose Hitler once Stalin needed ideological support against the Nazis. Without any evidence to support the idea, the default position became, 'Well, Stalin and the Communists are on the left and fighting against Hitler and the Nazis, so Hitler and the Nazis must be on the right.' This became the narrative that continues to this day, with Republicans like me being compared to Hitler and called Nazis, with no factual basis to support it."

Ackerman was rolling now, and Stone was on her heels, sputtering incomprehensibly. While she tried to form a semi-intelligent response, Ackerman took advantage of the opportunity to challenge another linguistic twist employed by the Democrats.

"And that's not all, Jessica. Democrats and their media allies aren't content to refer to me and fellow Republicans as 'Hitler' or 'Nazis.' We're also commonly referred to as 'fascists.' A lot of folks on the left, the Democrats, are eager to brand someone a fascist, but I don't think they know what the word means. To them, *fascist* simply means 'Someone I don't like.' What about you? How do you define fascism?"

Jessica Stone had completely lost control of the interview at this point. The candidate was now grilling her! This was not how this was supposed to happen. She managed to spit out some vague yet logically incoherent references to "right-wing" and "conservative" and "totalitarianism."

Calmer now after Stone had revealed herself to be nothing more than a mindless repeater of slanderous labels and Democrat talking points, Ackerman noted that fascism is the idea that everything in society is within the government and for the government and controlled by the government, and nothing is outside the scope or the reach of the government. "The Republican Party in general, and myself in particular, have been working very hard to reduce the role of government in our lives," Ackerman went on. "This is the exact opposite of fascism. If anyone is advocating fascism in today's politics, it would be the Democrats, who want more and more and more government control, more and more and more government power and coercion."

Stone appeared to be on the verge of having a seizure of some kind. Voice cracking and fighting back tears of rage, she shrieked, "You can't come on my program and call me a fascist!"

"I didn't," Ackerman replied with a poker face. "Unless, of course, you identify yourself with the Democrats. Surely, for an objective, non-partisan journalist such as yourself, that's not the case." Nod, nod, wink, wink. Now, after that body blow, the peace offering from Ackerman. "All of that aside, as you know, Jessica, I traveled here to New York in the midst of a very busy campaign to sit down with you, all because you told me you wanted to interview me about my economic and tax proposals. I hope we can move on to those topics now."

"I'm asking the questions here, Governor," Stone replied icily, beginning to regain her composure. Glancing at her notes, she selected another Democrat talking point provided by Richard Jordan, who was definitely not enjoying his flavorless popcorn while watching Stone's poor performance from his sofa in D.C. She soldiered on. "You've been a strong advocate of voter identification laws. Why are you so eager to suppress votes? And isn't there a racial motive there?"

"I'm only eager to suppress fraudulent and illegal votes, Jessica, as I've said many times. And I want to protect the valid, legal votes of American citizens from being offset by fraudulent, illegal votes cast by illegal aliens or felons or dead people. And no, there's no racial motivation to my preference for voter ID laws. I want all voters, regardless of race, to show a valid photo ID before casting a ballot.

"The fact is, Democrats can't win a close national election without committing voter fraud. Now, for a long time in this race, I trailed by more than the normal margin of fraud. But I've now closed the gap to the point that the Democrats will need to activate their election-fraud process in certain battleground states. Dead folks will be miraculously casting ballots in Philadelphia and Detroit and Cleveland. Democrat opposition to voter ID laws is based solely on their need to make voting fraud as easy as possible. When power is all that matters, the ends always justify the means, and power is all that matters to the left in America today.

"Think about our twenty-first-century society for a moment," Ackerman continued. "You have to show an ID to buy beer, wine, or cigarettes, to cash a check, to rent a car, to board a plane, et cetera. In fact, I had to show a photo ID in order to enter the HBT studio for this interview tonight. If we employ your so-called logic, then HBT must be a racist organization who is seeking to suppress access to news and information. Why do you work for a racist organization? And will you resign in protest of this blatantly racist effort to suppress the news?"

Ignoring his questions once again, Stone moved on to her next set of talking points. "Your strong, dogmatic, and inflexible Christian beliefs have been a major point of contention in this campaign. And I must say, you've done a very good job of debating the press about Christianity thus far." A little flattery of her guest, no matter how insincere, seemed like a good approach at this juncture. "But, frankly, most members of the media aren't well educated on religious matters, and they haven't pushed back on your arguments in favor of the validity of Christianity. And so, in the interest of giving the American people a more complete picture of your faith, I have a few questions for you in that arena."

"That's fine, Jessica, although, again, I accepted your invitation to appear with you here tonight on the premise that we'd be discussing my economic proposals. But perhaps," Ackerman concluded with a half-hearted smile, "you want to know how the doctrine of the Trinity relates to supply-side tax cuts."

"We'll get to your discredited views about trickle-down economics in due course," Stone replied, getting in a jab of her own by using the left's more derisive term for supply-side policies. "But let's get back to the topic at hand. As you've stated publicly, your Christian faith depends on your belief that Jesus was the Son of God and that He was crucified and rose from the dead. But the Bible is your only source for these beliefs, and it is obviously biased. Doesn't it bother you to have so little evidence for such an important claim?"

"Well, the first part of your question is definitely true. Christianity is a huge waste of time if Jesus wasn't who He claimed to be and if He didn't rise from the dead. But you're very, very wrong about the Bible being the only source of information about Jesus. In fact, every major first-century historian mentions Jesus, including the secular non-biblical writers. This includes writers who were hostile to Christianity as well as some who were neutral on the subject. I'm talking here about sources such as the Jewish historian Josephus, the Roman historian Tacitus, and the Jewish Talmud.

"Interestingly, there are at least ten known non-Christian sources that mention Jesus within one hundred and fifty years of His life on earth. For reference purposes, there are only nine such sources that mention Tiberius Caesar during this period, and Tiberius Caesar was the Emperor of Rome at the time of Jesus' life. Thus, the number of secular writers who mention Jesus exceeds the number who wrote about the ruler of the civilized world at that time."

Stone wanted to interrupt this discourse, but Ackerman was on a roll and didn't give her a chance.

"And it is very interesting to see the picture painted by these secular writers. Remember, these writers were not arguing in favor of Christianity. In fact, some of them were overtly hostile to this new religion. But if you take their writings as a whole, you can learn almost all of the important facts about Jesus's life as described in the New Testament.

"For example, these historians tell us that Jesus lived a virtuous life, that He was a miracle-worker, that He was acclaimed to be the Messiah, that He was crucified under the direction of Pontius Pilate on the eve of the Jewish Passover, that an unexplained darkness and an earthquake occurred when He died, that His disciples believed that He rose from the dead, that His disciples were willing to die for that belief, and that Christianity spread rapidly from Jerusalem as far as Rome. This sounds exactly like the Jesus portrayed in the Bible. In short, to claim that the Bible is our only source of information about Jesus is simply ludicrous."

Jessica Stone was not used to being embarrassed by her guests. In fact, the opposite was normally the case. She almost always finished an interview looking smarter and better informed than the poor slob who had foolishly agreed to be her next victim. Stone was angry in addition to being humiliated, but her anger was starting to shift from Jeff Ackerman to White House Chief of Staff Richard Jordan.

After all, Jordan had given her these talking points. And he had assured her that the information was solid and well researched, especially the material designed to poke holes in the fundamentalist faith proclaimed by the bumbling Baptist sitting across the table from her. But this was a live interview, and she still had about ten minutes to kill. Thus, she couldn't give up now, especially since she didn't actually have any questions prepared for the ostensible purpose of the interview: Ackerman's economic proposals. And so she pressed on.

348

"But Governor Ackerman, aren't you concerned about the contradictions contained in the Bible?"

"What contradictions are those?" the candidate asked reasonably.

This response by Ackerman was normally enough to dispatch this line of questioning, as many non-believers claimed the Bible is full of contradictions without actually having read it. When challenged to name a contradiction, they quickly retreated because they didn't have a clue as to what—if any—contradictions actually existed. But Jessica Stone was a little better prepared than most on this point.

"Let's look at the different accounts of the empty tomb found in each of the Gospels," Stone responded. "Matthew mentions one angel at the tomb. Mark says there was 'a young man' at the tomb. Luke mentions 'two men clothed in dazzling robes.' John mentions two angels." Stone was almost reading from her notes at this point. She certainly didn't have anything close to this level of biblical knowledge herself.

She continued, "In addition to the contradictions regarding angels, the Gospels are also inconsistent on the identities of the women who supposedly discovered the empty tomb, as well as the time of day the discovery allegedly occurred. Matthew writes that 'Mary Magdalene and the other Mary' came 'as it began to dawn.' Mark discusses 'Mary Magdalene, and Mary the mother of James, and Salome' and says they went 'very early on the first day of the week' and that they 'came to the tomb when the sun had risen.' Luke writes of 'Mary Magdalene and Joanna and Mary the mother of James,' as well as 'other women with them,' and Luke's crowd went to the tomb 'at early dawn.' John mentions only Mary Magdalene and says she came 'early . . . while it was still dark.'

"And so, Governor, if the resurrection of Jesus is the end-all-be-all of Christianity, don't these inconsistencies in the biblical accounts of the resurrection cast severe doubt over whether it actually happened?"

"No, no doubt whatsoever," Ackerman responded quickly. "There are several items to note here. First of all, these are not actually contradictions. Let's look at what you've mentioned: the identities of the women, the number of angels, and the time of day.

"None of the Gospels purport to give an exhaustive list of the women who were present, or of the number of angels present. For example, John's Gospel doesn't say that Mary Magdalene went by herself to the tomb, and there's nothing in his account to indicate that other women weren't with her. The same with the angels: yes, Matthew and Mark mention only a single angel, but that doesn't preclude the presence of others. They each write of an angel that spoke to the women and wouldn't have a particular need to mention whether there were other angels present. Therefore, for both the number of angels and the identity of the women, there's no reason to believe that the Gospel accounts are inconsistent.

"As to the time of day, again, I don't see any inconsistency. The four Gospels all indicate that women went to the tomb very early in the morning and reached the tomb just before or just after dawn. First-century writers weren't nearly as concerned with precise time references as we are today.

"In conclusion, there aren't any actual inconsistencies. All four Gospel accounts tell us that one or more women went to the tomb very early on Sunday, encountered one or more angels, and found that Jesus' body was not in the tomb. And the gist of the story is the same in all three: Jesus died on the cross and rose from the dead, just like He said that He would.

"Second, note that these slight variances in the description of the event are actually evidence for the truth of the Gospel accounts. Imagine for a moment that all four accounts were precisely the same, right down to the smallest detail. That would imply that Matthew, Mark, Luke, and John had conspired in their writing as part of a cover-up. Today, we would refer to this as getting their stories straight. Instead, the accounts vary on the fringes, just like the news reports would be slightly different if four different news networks were all covering the same event, live and unscripted.

"Finally, it is very significant that all four Gospels have women discovering the empty tomb. Women were second-class citizens, at best, in first-century Israel. They weren't even allowed to testify in legal proceedings because they were deemed unreliable. And so, if Matthew, Mark, Luke, and John were just making things up, there's no way they would use women as the primary witnesses of the empty tomb.

"Sorry for the long answer, but I hope I've shown that the substance of the Gospel accounts of the resurrection of Jesus are consistent and don't present contradictions." With a note of challenge creeping into his voice, Ackerman concluded, "Any other alleged biblical contradictions you'd like to discuss?"

"Well, unfortunately, that's all the time we have this evening," responded Jessica Stone. She was relieved to be done with this disaster of an interview and caught herself hoping, for the first time in her career, that her viewing audience was smaller than usual.

Back home in Washington, D.C., a dismayed but undaunted Richard Jordan flipped off his television and arranged the remote in precisely its appointed place on the corner of the coffee table. He admitted to himself that Ackerman had handled Stone remarkably well, even with the brilliant talking points that Jordan had provided to the reporter. But Jordan had one more card to play, and it just happened to be the ace of spades.

Chapter 39

Media Outlets Nationwide and
Rose Garden at the White House

Late-October 2016

Michelle Ackerman Had an Abortion! screamed this morning's front-page headline in Jackson's *Daily Dispatch*, the hometown newspaper of former Mississippi Governor Jeff Ackerman. Bold letters, all caps, in the largest font available. The paper reported that Michelle Ackerman had undergone the procedure at a Jackson clinic in 1985 at the age of nineteen. A photo of the first page of the clinic's record of the abortion accompanied the article. For any reader who had been living under a rock for the past year, the article made it clear that Michelle Ackerman was the wife of Jeff Ackerman, the anti-abortion Republican Christian conservative candidate for president.

Although not mentioned in the article, the impetus for the story was a hunch formed by Richard Jordan, chief of staff to President Upton Landers. Jordan dropped a hint or two to a *Daily Dispatch* reporter who was friendly to the Landers administration. The reporter took it from there. To the pleasant surprise of the reporter, the clinic in question was quite cooperative with his investigation. This, of course, was a breach of patient confidentiality and highly unethical. But Jeff Ackerman's vocal pro-life stance as Mississippi's governor had been a major detriment to the clinic's business, and thus the operators of the establishment were quite happy to slip a copy of Michelle's confidential medical records to the *Daily Dispatch* reporter. Off the record, of course.

The paper's editors and columnists were just as liberal and left-wing as those at major international outlets such as the *New York Daily Ledger* and the *Washington Chronicle*. But they had to sell papers and advertising to a largely conservative consumer base, so they had to at least pretend to be impartial politically, much to their chagrin. This story, however, gave them the chance to further the liberal cause by simply providing their readers with important information.

The editors were a bit embarrassed not to have uncovered this bombshell story sooner, such as when Ackerman was running for either of his two terms as governor. But this earlier professional lapse was far overshadowed by the enthusiastic praise and adulation heaped upon the newspaper from national media outlets, Hollywood stars, union leaders, and other left-wing organizations around the country. Pulitzer Prizes were surely on the way!

The Bible-thumping, far-right-wing Republican prude had loudly and proudly claimed to "love babies." He'd frequently called abortion a "barbaric" and "bloody" procedure. And now he had been knocked off of his high horse by the revelation that his wife had had an abortion.

The news flew around the world at light speed. BNI and HBT provided round-the-clock coverage of the story, complete with medical and psychiatric experts who couldn't wait to tell the viewers/voters how safe abortion was. They added the claim that those who were most vocal against reproductive rights were the ones most likely to have had—or facilitated—an abortion themselves.

The evidence for both of these assertions was dubious at best, but this was a chance to strike a blow for a woman's right to choose, dammit! The facts could wait! None of them paused to reflect on the invasion of Michelle's privacy that had occurred or the damage the story would inflict on Jeff and Michelle Ackerman and their two daughters.

National Republican figures were mostly silent in the face of the anti-Ackerman onslaught. Many of them had been embarrassed by Ackerman's blunt language about abortion during the campaign, and they were slow to defend their candidate publicly now that his hypocrisy had been exposed. The least conservative of them consoled themselves with the hope that perhaps this humiliating turn of events was the hard lesson needed in order to get the Republican Party beyond the abortion issue once and for all. Maybe this would silence those religious-right zealots and enable the more reasonable Republicans to once again get invited to the A-list dinner parties in D.C. and New York. They pretended to be disappointed to see Ackerman's always-slim chance of pulling off an upset be wiped out, but they let everyone who would listen know that they had been way too sophisticated and wise to get their hopes too high in the first place.

Richard Jordan was fully prepared to exploit the news for the benefit of his boss. A press conference by Landers on the topic would have been too obvious. Even a statement from the Landers campaign might be viewed as over the top. Instead, Jordan had arranged for a Rose Garden ceremony at which the president would announce the appointment of a new third assistant to the deputy undersecretary of the Bureau of Land Management, or something else equally meaningless.

The president's remarks would then be followed by a very well-planned and highly orchestrated "spontaneous" media availability in which the press would be free to ask questions of the president on any topic. Shockingly, because this just happened to occur late in the morning of the day the news about Michelle Ackerman broke, the president could barely complete his remarks about the important work being done by the Bureau of Land Management under his fearless and bold leadership before the reporters started shouting questions to him about the Ackerman bombshell.

Richard Jordan looked on from behind the reporters as they all performed exactly how he would have scripted it if given the opportunity. The reporters shouted questions all at once, repeating them at ever-louder volume while Upton Landers pretended to be surprised by the topic and their enthusiasm.

"Mr. President! Can you comment on the news about Michelle Ackerman's abortion?"

"What impact will Governor Ackerman's hypocrisy on the abortion issue have on the election?"

"Will Governor Ackerman have to withdraw from the race?"

"Will these events help you get more pro-choice judges confirmed to the federal courts in your second term?"

Upton Landers performed exactly according to Richard Jordan's stage instructions. The president allowed the media to shout their questions for the perfect length of time before assuming a saddened expression, raising his hands to ask for quiet, and bringing order to the chaos. "Ladies and gentlemen, please, I know you have a lot of questions regarding the latest news about my opponent. I don't have a lot to say about this right now, as I only learned of it when it hit the national news this morning." The president lied skillfully here. Jordan had informed Landers several days ago that the story was about to break. Now it was time for the president to act statesman-like, as though he were above such political pettifoggery.

"It appears that Jeff Ackerman has been lambasting American women and their doctors for making the same decision that he and his wife made in the past. It saddens me to see a candidate for the highest office in the land stoop to such levels of hypocrisy in a desperate effort to win votes. Mr. Ackerman and his wife will have to make difficult decisions about how to deal with this news, just like they did many years ago when they had to make a difficult decision regarding Michelle Ackerman's right to choose. I am certain that there will be a political price to be paid by my opponent," Landers hinted, "and I'm also certain that you and your colleagues in the press will work hard to get to the bottom of this story." *Go get him and tear him to shreds*, the president was signaling to his media stormtroopers.

In order to take the thoughts of the public beyond the actions of one man, Landers now speculated, "Perhaps the silver lining here is that religious extremists will now be less likely to throw stones from their glass houses. I truly hope that those on the far-right fringe of society will rethink the idea of turning back the clock on the right of women to control their own bodies. That's all I have to say for now, but perhaps I can answer more of your questions in the days ahead when more information becomes available." Translation: *Let's keep this story on the front page for the next week or two.*

Perfect, Richard Jordan thought. *Now, exit stage left.*

As if he could hear the thoughts of his chief of staff, Upton Landers gathered his papers from the podium, turned to his left, and strolled away with a quick departing wave to his good friends in the media while thinking, *Good luck talking yourself out of this one, Ackerman. Enjoy being asked about this by every reporter you see between now and Election Day.*

Chapter 40

Jackson, Mississippi
Late-October 2016

Storm clouds loomed ominously on the horizon this late-October afternoon at Ackerman campaign headquarters in Jackson, Mississippi. The weather matched the mood in the cramped lobby of the building, where media members from around the country gathered for a hastily called press conference. The story of Michelle Ackerman's abortion had broken early that morning and quickly reverberated around the country. The candidate had been campaigning in Michigan but abruptly made an unannounced return to Mississippi to deal with the fallout from the story.

This unscheduled trip home fueled speculation that Governor Ackerman was suspending his presidential campaign in light of the news about his wife's past. Some political analysts even predicted that he would drop out of the race completely. Pundits who specialized in forecasting election results updated their projections, and all now predicted an historic landslide for Upton Landers. This news and speculation was all conveyed to the voters by the media with barely suppressed glee. The anti-abortion hypocrite was now getting what he deserved, at least in the minds of those who shaped the news.

The reporters, camera crews, and other media types speculated among themselves as they waited for the candidate to appear at the podium. Bets were placed as to whether or not Ackerman would drop out of the race. Those who had wagered on an affirmative answer to this question were more optimistic as Jeff Ackerman walked slowly into the room, looking pale, haggard, and tired.

Cameras flashed and reporters shouted questions as Jeff Ackerman reached the podium and paused to arrange his notes. Holding up his hands in a gesture asking for silence, he began his address to the media in the same fashion in which he'd walked into the room—slowly, tiredly, sadly. "Ladies and gentlemen, today is a very sad day for American politics and for Americans in general."

Those in the audience who had predicted that Ackerman would drop out of the race nudged their colleagues and smirked confidently.

"This is a sad day because what we've all seen in our newspapers and on television is the publication of an outright lie and a political smear of the most detestable sort."

Murmurs wafted through the crowd of reporters. He was denying the story? How was that possible? They'd all seen the photo of the medical record with Michelle Ackerman's name on it showing that she had undergone an abortion. Now, the reporters who had wagered that Ackerman would not drop out of the race glanced at their counterparts. Some even rubbed their fingers against a thumb, indicating that their colleagues should pay up.

The candidate continued, "Today we've seen a complete and total abdication of journalistic standards by the *Daily Dispatch* in breaking this so-called news. And rather than seeking confirmation or real evidence of the truth of the allegations, media outlets all over the country simply assumed that the story was true and happily repeated it all day today.

"But I am here to tell you the truth and to set the record straight.

My wife, Michelle Ackerman, did not have an abortion in 1985. She's never had an abortion. She's never had an unwanted pregnancy. The *Daily Dispatch*'s story is completely and totally inaccurate and libelous with respect to my wife.

"I know you all saw the photo of the medical records that accompanied the article, so let me address that now. Yes, a woman named Michelle Ackerman did have an abortion in Jackson in 1985, just as the picture in the paper indicated. But that woman is not my wife. Let me say it again, very slowly and clearly, so that even left-wing reporters can understand it: the woman who had an abortion as alleged by the media is a completely different individual than my wife, Michelle.

"My wife and I were not married when the abortion in question took place in 1985, and her name was Michelle Jenkins until we were married in 1987. In case you're wondering if my wife might have used an alias for the abortion, please note that we didn't even meet until 1986, and so it is highly unlikely that she would have chosen Ackerman as a fake last name."

Gripping the edges of the podium tightly with both hands, Ackerman's disgust and contempt were evident in both his voice and his posture. "The *Daily Dispatch* thought they had a scoop on their hands, but what they did was humiliate themselves. Moreover, they gave the world just one more piece of evidence among many, that the American media is little more than a partisan army marching in lockstep with the Democrat Party and its leftist agenda. With just the slightest bit of research, the *Daily Dispatch* could have confirmed what I'm telling you here today and avoided this fiasco.

"There is one thing the paper got right. They wrote that, 'Governor Ackerman's campaign did not respond to a request for comment on this story prior to publication.' While that is technically true, let me give you some color on this 'request for comment' by the *Daily Dispatch*.

"Although the newspaper's writers and editors knew for at least a day, and probably longer, that the story would run in this morning's paper, no one asked my campaign for comment until eight p.m. last night. And the request for comment didn't come to me, or to my campaign manager, or to my communications manager, or any other senior staffer working for me. The paper has access to all of us via cell phone or email, but they did not contact any of us in that way. Instead, the newspaper called the general phone number of my Jackson headquarters at eight o'clock last night, knowing full well that no one would pick up the phone at that hour, and left a voice-mail asking for comment on their story. From this, I think we can safely conclude that the reporters and editors at the *Daily Dispatch* didn't actually want to give us a chance to refute their allegations prior to publication.

"Today, I call upon the *Daily Dispatch* to retract its story and to apologize to my wife, to the rest of my family, to its readers, and to voters all across America. While such an apology is necessary, it is definitely not sufficient. Accordingly, my attorneys will soon be filing a libel suit against the *Daily Dispatch*, and we'll also name as defendants each other media outlet that acted with reckless disregard for the truth.

"Speaking to the reporters that are assembled here today: I know that most of you are very disappointed that this story turned out to be fake. I know that many of you speculated that I would drop out of the race, and you hoped that I would do so because that would ensure a huge win for your man Upton Landers. While I wish we had a free and independent press in this country, I've come to understand that such is not the case here in 2016. But I hope all of you will learn from this episode that just because you hope a story is true, that doesn't make it true. And it doesn't absolve you of your obligation to verify its truth before reporting it or repeating it.

"And now, to the voters out there, I hope this sorry incident will serve as a reminder to you to carefully evaluate every word spoken or written by the American media. Almost all of them are ardent supporters of the ongoing slaughter of American babies that they euphemistically refer to as 'reproductive freedom' or 'a woman's right to choose.' In part because of this bloodlust by the media, they are avid supporters of my opponent in this election. Even on the rare occasions when they try to hide their bias, their stories are still shaped in a fashion designed to hurt me and to help him. What we have here today is nothing less than a complete fabrication by the media in an effort to influence the election. I encourage all Americans to ask themselves this question: if the media will lie about this, what else will they lie about?

"As an aside, I again urge the voters to not only evaluate what the media says, but how they say it. I note that the *Daily Dispatch* headline today and the first sentence of the story prominently featured the word *abortion*. They didn't celebrate a woman taking 'control of her body' or exercising her 'reproductive rights' or her 'right to choose,' which is how they normally speak about this terrible procedure when they are trying to sell it as acceptable and normal. In this instance, they wanted to paint my wife in a bad light and me as a hypocrite, so they used the harsher, more straightforward word *abortion*.

"Finally, just in case some of you still believe the story in the newspaper this morning instead of what I've told you here today, I'd like to introduce to you the real individual who had that abortion back in 1985. Her name was Michelle Ackerman then, and her name is Michelle Ackerman Stewart now. It took us all of about seven minutes of internet research to determine the falsity of the *Daily Dispatch* story and to identify Mrs. Stewart as the actual subject of the story. The *Daily Dispatch* didn't bother to undertake this sort of effort, and I think we all know why. Mrs. Stewart has a few words she'd like to say to you, and then she'll take your questions. Once that's done, I'll be available to you and answer any remaining questions that you may have. I'd also like to thank Mrs. Stewart in advance for appearing here today. She's truly an innocent victim in all of this and agreed to endure the significant public humiliation of appearing before you today in order to help set the record straight. My wife, Michelle, and I are both very grateful to Mrs. Stewart for her courage and decency."

Governor Ackerman strode away from the podium amid a decidedly different atmosphere in the room. The now-deflated and depressed media had assembled in order to gawk at the cratering of the Ackerman campaign, but instead they would now be forced to report on their own incompetence and bias. How would they shape these stories to make this mess look like Ackerman's fault? Surely their editors would come up with something. They couldn't allow this self-righteous jerk to be elected to the highest office in the land.

Michelle Ackerman Stewart stood nervously at the podium and recounted the story of her abortion back in 1985. She was a private person unaccustomed to the spotlight. But she had seen the newspaper story about Jeff Ackerman's wife and knew that she must come forward.

She deeply regretted the decision to terminate her pregnancy and mourned her unborn baby every day. But she felt pressured by everyone around her to have an abortion. Her parents, her high school guidance counselor, and especially the father of her unborn baby all acted as though abortion was her only option. The baby's father made it clear that he would pay for an abortion but would provide no financial or other support if she carried the child to term. Ironically, Mrs. Stewart informed the assembled reporters, all of the putatively pro-choice people in her life insisted that she didn't

364

actually have a choice at all. The only choice, according to them, was to kill her baby.

While Mrs. Stewart was speaking, Jeff Ackerman walked into the next room and called Austin Brant from his cell phone. The *New York Daily Ledger's* token conservative columnist had somehow gotten wind of the story and alerted the Ackerman campaign to it. Although it was not enough warning to allow them to stop the piece before it ran in the paper, the information had been sufficient to help them respond to the false story quickly and thoroughly. Ackerman thanked him effusively and then asked Brant how he found out about the piece in advance.

"Well, Governor," Brant replied, "I can't say too much without compromising a source of information. But I can say that I'm pretty certain that Landers' chief of staff Richard Jordan planted the story. I would also speculate that he knew it wasn't true, because otherwise he would have had the *New York Daily Ledger* or the *Washington Chronicle* run it. I have it on good authority that he asked his Beltway media contacts to spread the story with gusto, but he hinted to them that they should be very careful in their phrasing. In other words, to avoid any sort of legal liability, they should make clear that they were simply reporting on the *Daily Dispatch's* story, as opposed to vouching for the truth of the contents of that story."

After another round of thanks and pleasantries, Austin Brant hung up the phone, amazed that he'd been able to surreptitiously dial in to yet another of Richard Jordan's conference calls with his media allies. Brant's conscience was now clear. To his way of thinking, his under-the-table help for the Ackerman campaign offset the less-than-honorable bargain he'd made to get his position with the *New York Daily Ledger.*

Chapter 41

Brandon, Mississippi
Election Day

Jeff Ackerman pulled out of his driveway with Michelle beside him in the front seat. He'd insisted on driving himself to the polling place this morning, knowing that he'd better get used to being a private citizen again in light of the decisive defeat looming in today's general election. It felt a little strange to be behind the wheel, and he was trying to remember the last time he'd driven a car, when Michelle spoke up.

"So how much can I spend on my gown for the inaugural ball?" she asked with a grin.

Jeff gave a slight shake of his head. "Honey, there won't be an inaugural ball, at least not for me. Landers will have a big blow out to celebrate his victory, but I'm pretty sure we won't be invited."

"I don't know about that," Michelle answered. "I've got a good feeling about today. I think we're gonna win."

Jeff wondered if his wife had been completely oblivious to his uphill struggle over the past six months. Had she not read a newspaper recently? He was already depressed about his upcoming defeat, and having to explain the obvious to his wife wasn't on his to-do list for the day. The unlikely candidate reminded himself to be kind and gentle, and he took a deep breath before responding. "I appreciate your confidence. I really do. But we're going to lose today. It will be closer than most thought a few months ago, but I'm not going to be elected president."

"How do you know? No votes have been counted yet. Besides, I'm telling you I have a good feeling about this election."

Jeff was never surprised by Michelle's optimism, but this bordered on naiveté. Everyone with an ounce of political knowledge and experience knew that he was going to lose the election. It wouldn't be a landslide loss—probably not, anyway. But it would be a loss nevertheless. Was she really relying on her feelings and intuition in the face of so much expensive polling data and political wisdom to the contrary?

He really didn't want to argue with his wife. But he felt an obligation to manage her expectations. After all, he wasn't the only one who would have to deal with defeat and rejection. Michelle would have to go through the same ordeal.

He suddenly realized that his wife's method of processing the loss would be very different from his. She'd want to talk about it endlessly, discussing dozens of if-only scenarios in excruciating detail. He, on the other hand, wouldn't want to discuss the election at all. Talking about the defeat would make Michelle feel better, but it would make Jeff feel worse. He'd already been thinking about getting away somewhere, perhaps to a remote beach, where he could avoid newspapers and political talk shows and blogs. But he couldn't leave his wife behind, and her need to spend hours discussing his upcoming electoral humiliation would be a huge hurdle for him to overcome.

Being publicly humiliated by losing a national election was a risk that he'd willingly taken. However, he hadn't anticipated a potential adverse effect on his marriage in addition to political defeat.

The candidate's mood darkened even further, even as Michelle sang along to '80s rock on the car radio, seemingly without a care in the world.

She suddenly stopped singing and turned toward him again. "You never answered my question."

With lyrics from U2 running through his head, Jeff glanced at her. "What question?"

"Pay attention, Mr. Almost-President-Elect!" she said with a smile. "How much can I spend on my fancy dress for the inaugural ball?"

Tired of arguing with her and knowing that it was a moot point in any event, he replied, "Spend whatever you want."

Jeff pulled into a parking place at the local elementary school that served as their polling place. He was surprised to see a crowd of supporters in the parking lot, waving "Ackerman for President" signs and dutifully standing outside the invisible arc around the voting location in which electioneering was prohibited. Unlike other campaign events during the past several months, the candidate knew many of the names that went with these faces. These were friends and neighbors and fellow members of his local church. Many of these people had donated money to his cause and written him encouraging notes during the darker days of the campaign.

For the second time that day, the candidate was forced to contemplate the effect of his upcoming defeat on people other than himself. He fervently hoped that his candidacy hadn't embarrassed these kind, hardworking people. The media's months-long assault on Republicans, conservatism, Christianity, and Mississippi's past had certainly impacted these fine folks, even though the candidate himself was the primary target. Jeff and Michelle were each encouraged by the hugs and warm handshakes they received from this crowd, both before and after they cast their ballots.

The candidate fervently hoped that each of these dedicated people understood how sincere he was when he thanked them for their support and their prayers.

Chapter 42

Jackson, Mississippi
Election Day

After voting, Jeff Ackerman kissed Michelle goodbye and then joined his senior staff in a small office suite at his Jackson headquarters to begin the waiting process. There was no real reason to be at his headquarters, as he could endure the electoral drubbing that would most likely develop this evening from anywhere. The unlikely candidate could do nothing more to improve his chances, and the location from which he watched the votes pour in for his opponent wouldn't change the outcome. A tropical beach or a mountain retreat might be a bit more soothing. It would certainly be less hectic.

But he felt an obligation to endure the day with the team that had worked so hard on his behalf. Ackerman didn't think about it, but his staffers felt the same way. There wasn't much productive work for them to do at Ackerman campaign headquarters today, but they felt obliged to be physically present with their boss when their loss became official later this evening.

Jeff slumped behind his desk in his office. Art Morgan slouched in a soft leather wing-back chair across from the desk, but the ever-alert

Scott Williamson sat ramrod straight in a highly uncomfortable guest chair to Morgan's left. Each of the three men thought back to their first "staff meeting" eighteen months earlier in a conference room a few blocks away from this building. And they thought of all that had transpired since then. They had gone further in the race than any of them dared to hope at the time, but that was only a small consolation with defeat looming.

None of the three had any enthusiasm for the upcoming conversation. But the candidate insisted on this meeting to review and analyze the campaign they had just concluded. Ackerman knew such a review would be even more depressing after the results became official, and so he wanted to get it out of the way now. He could've skipped this process entirely. After all, he'd almost certainly run his last political race, because losing presidential candidates rarely got a second chance. But the leadership part of his brain insisted that there were more lessons to be learned in a loss than in a victory, and perhaps the healing process would be easier if they autopsied the race to see what they had done wrong.

No one wanted to speak first. Morgan and Williamson hid behind the boss's prerogative to begin the meeting, sitting quietly until he did so. After a deep breath, Jeff Ackerman kicked off his final meeting as a candidate for president of the United States. "So, men, where did we go wrong?"

Art Morgan and Scott Williamson glanced at each other. Williamson gave a slight nod to Morgan, simultaneously exercising the virtue of deference to the senior staff member and the vice of fearfully avoiding the deliverance of bad news to his boss.

Morgan surprised both of the others by being rather generous in his assessment. "It's hard to see how we could've done any better, Jeff. We started this race not just in the single digits in the polls, but in the very lowest of the single digits. You came from out of nowhere, won the nomination, and gave a sitting president all he wanted—and then some—in the general election."

He generously omitted any reference to the plane crash that killed Ackerman's strongest opponent in the primary, instead continuing with his analysis and projection. "We'll end up losing by less than three percent, and we were closing fast the last few weeks of the race. If we had had another two weeks, I really think we would've won. It's kind of a tired cliché, but it applies here: we didn't really lose; we just ran out of time."

Scott Williamson nodded along as Morgan spoke. "I agree with Art. You did a great job in this race. And your strategy was sound: peel off a slice of the black vote and the Hispanic vote by explaining why conservatism works for them, and bring the Reagan Democrats back to the Republican tent by promising to reverse the decline of America. Your speeches directed at these groups really spoke to them. And your claims and statements had the added advantage of being true, which we all know isn't always the case in politics. You accomplished these goals to a significant extent and just barely came up short of what we needed to win. You'll end up with more black and Hispanic votes than any Republican presidential candidate in the past thirty years. You showed that Republicans can compete for and win those votes. Moreover, you laid the foundation for the next guy to win even more of them."

Williamson continued, "On the Reagan-Democrat aspect, I think we can expect Wisconsin, Michigan, and Pennsylvania to actually have to count most of their votes before being put in the blue column tonight. The networks can usually declare the Demo-crat to be the winner of those states within about twelve seconds of the polls closing, but that won't be the case tonight. The Dems will probably even resort to having a few thousand dead folks cast ballots in Philadelphia and Detroit just to be on the safe side. That proves that you'll have won the votes of a solid number of blue-collar union types who are normally automatic votes for the left."

"It's amazing how many people who have been dead for years manage to show up at the polls every four years," Ackerman commented with a sad smile. "How does the joke go? Something like, 'My grandfather was a lifelong Republican. Since he died, however, he's voted Democrat in every election.'"

Williamson wrapped up his assessment of the campaign with one final note. "Jeff, I have to tell you that your approach of waging outright war with a hostile press was brilliant. I thought you were crazy to try it, but it worked. You ripped off the media's mask and revealed to the public just how biased the media has become in favor of far-left candidates and policies. That's another gift you've given to future Republican candidates."

By now, all three men had reached the same conclusion: their campaign strategy worked, but it didn't work quite well enough. No further analysis was needed.

Shifting the topic from the Ackerman campaign to the Landers campaign, Ackerman asked his senior staffers, "Why do you think the Dems were so thoroughly and openly anti-Christian in this cycle? They would've beat us by at least the same margin, and maybe more, if they just continued their prior history of pretending to tolerate Christianity."

Between Scott Williamson and Art Morgan, Williamson was the more theoretical, the one more attuned to big-picture themes and policy. Williamson was also a devout Christian and somewhat of an amateur theologian. Morgan's expertise, on the other hand, was more centered in managing the day-to-day grind of a campaign. As far as Ackerman and Williamson knew, Morgan was an agnostic who had never voluntarily darkened the door of a church. But when the younger staffer had nothing to add here, merely shrugging his shoulders in response to his boss's question, Morgan surprised the others by speaking up.

"You have to understand, gentlemen, that leftism is much more than a set of policy positions or mere political beliefs. Instead, leftism is itself a religion. This springs from the fact that all humans are naturally inclined to worship something. We worship God, or nature, or money, or sex, or a college football team, or our favorite rock star or actor.

"For over two hundred years, most Americans worshiped God primarily and then other things only secondarily. But the leftists now own and control the Democratic Party, and the left gradually killed off God over the past decade or two. Now that Democrats don't worship God, they've replaced Him with their new religion of leftism. They have their own religious rites and rituals: taxes take the place of tithes, and abortion is just a modern-day version of child sacrifice. Judges and justices wear priestly robes. You've probably noticed that Democrats are much more passionate about politics than Republicans, and this is why. To a Republican, it's just an election. He still has his religion and his family and his hobbies. But the typical Democrat places politics above all of those other things."

Neither Ackerman nor Williamson had ever heard Art Morgan speak so philosophically before, and each sat up straighter and leaned toward the older man, wanting to hear more.

Morgan went on, "Leftist Democrats, therefore, don't view Christianity as simply an ancillary topic, and they don't see Republicans or conservatives as their main opposition. Christianity is ultimately their main enemy, because worshiping God is antithetical to worshiping leftist politics. This is why we don't simply have political disagreements any longer, where the political players ultimately have a lot in common and actually like each other when they're not on the public stage. We also don't have straightforward, fact-based debates about which policy is best to address a particular problem. This is because politics is the equivalent of religion to nearly half the country, and left-wing faith trumps facts every time.

"To those on the left, Republicans who happen to be Christians aren't simply political opponents who share common values with the left and differ only in their political beliefs. In fact, there is no such thing as *only* politics with the left, no such thing as a *minor* political disagreement. No, for the left, Christian conservatives are religious heretics who must be metaphorically burned at the stake, not because they are conservative but because they are Christian.

"And so we see this generations-long effort by the left to destroy traditional religion, which in America effectively means destroying Christianity. They've largely succeeded in removing religion from public view: God has been kicked out of the schools, the workplace, the courts, sports arenas, and graduation ceremonies. Sharing your faith with a non-believer is now viewed not only as impolite but as a form of bigotry, almost a type of violence. God is now mostly confined to the church building on Sunday morning.

"This is why you hear Democrats acknowledge, begrudgingly, that we have 'freedom of worship' here in the U.S., which is a much more limited concept than the 'freedom of religion' that's actually protected by the Constitution. They'll tolerate Christians worshiping inside the church for an hour or so on Sunday mornings as long as Christianity doesn't spill into the workplace or the public square. And that, my friends, is why we just witnessed a months-long assault on Christianity during this election cycle. The Dems weren't just trying to win an election. They were trying to marginalize religion even further."

Ackerman and Williamson simply sat and stared at Art Morgan, stunned and impressed with this rhetorical tour de force. The candidate wanted to pursue this line of thought further, but he realized that he couldn't improve upon anything that Morgan had just said. So instead, he moved to the next agenda item on his checklist. "Scott, I'm gonna need a concession speech. As diligent as you are, it's probably already written, but I won't put you on the spot by asking you for it now. I want it to be gracious, polite, humble, and honorable. But, and this is a large *but*, I want to make it clear that humbly accepting the results of the election does not mean that we accept or accede to the Democrats' attacks on my religion or on conservative ideas. Republicans are almost always good losers, too good sometimes. But the Democrats, even when they lose an election, continue to push hard for their worldview and refuse to view the election results as anything other than a temporary aberration. They don't let a minor thing like being rejected by over half the country slow them down for an instant. We can learn from that and try those tactics ourselves. And so I want a speech that's polite about the election results but unapologetic and unshakeable on policy, religion, and culture. Okay?"

"You got it, Jeff," Williamson replied. He had in fact already written a speech along these lines, but he wouldn't embarrass his boss by saying that he'd long anticipated the need for a concession speech. Instead, he sought to encourage the candidate by asking, "Do you want me to rough out an acceptance speech also? You know, just in case we catch lightning in a bottle?"

"No, that's all right," Ackerman replied with a wan smile. "I've given several acceptance speeches and can wing it if we pull off a miracle. But I've never had to give a concession speech, so I need something pretty polished and complete from you on that front. I don't trust myself to get it right if I ad-lib it. Thanks for your help, guys."

As Morgan and Williamson stood to leave the meeting, a young staffer tapped timidly on the half-open door. When Ackerman nodded at her to enter, she rushed over to his desk with a sheaf of paper in her hand. "Sorry to interrupt, but we're getting some very interesting reports from our local offices in the battleground states, and I thought you'd want to see them as soon as possible."

Chapter 43

Washington, D.C.

Inauguration Day

President Upton Landers sat on the podium, bundled in a heavy trench coat, cashmere scarf, and custom-made fur-lined leather gloves, well-insulated against the cold on this blustery January day. He was as emotional today as he was on the same occasion four years ago, but the previous four years in the White House fish bowl had provided him with a graduate-level education in hiding and containing his feelings. Accordingly, he gazed stoically out at the massive crowd that filled the National Mall. He smiled and nodded at his friends—very few of these—and political supporters—more numerous—that joined him on the podium for the occasion.

President Landers noted the large number of American flags among the throng before him, whipping in the winter breeze and seemingly floating among the waves of people. He managed to suppress the sneer that nearly formed on his almost-frozen face. Every day for the past four years, at the insistence of his handlers, Landers had worn an American flag lapel pin on his suit jacket in what seemed to him a cheap attempt to proclaim his love of country. But now that he had run his last political race, he was free to discard that tacky accoutrement. *No more pretending to love God and country for me,* Landers thought, casually running a gloved hand over his now unadorned lapel. He would never face the voters again, so he was free to say, or not say, or wear, or not wear, whatever he liked.

His deepest contempt, however, was reserved not for the American flags before him, but for the dolts who held them, who gawked at them, who venerated them above nearly everything else. What possessed someone to drive—they certainly couldn't afford to fly—from Indiana or Missouri or Arkansas to Washington, D.C. just to wave a stupid flag in this freezing weather? A hateful flag. A flag that symbolized racism, imperialism, sexism, and . . . and, well, probably several other *isms* that he couldn't think of at that moment. Worse yet, his political fate was linked to the whims of these dullards, these overweight slugs who worshiped God, guns, and grub, although not necessarily in that order. At least, it used to be. Now that he had run his last race, these inbreds from nothing little towns in nothing little states in the middle of flyover country would have no power or sway over President Upton Landers.

But, to his bitter disappointment, he would only be president for another twelve minutes. After that, he would be a footnote to history, the answer to a trivia question: "Which American President lost in the biggest upset in U.S. political history?"

He cursed Richard Jordan under his breath, not for the first time today. *Jordan tricked me into a high-stakes campaign. I could've played it safe and would now be mentally rehearsing my second inaugural speech instead of sitting off to the side, freezing my ass off and watching a crowd of morons applaud the newly elected Moron in Chief. But no, Jordan talked me into running against God and country and conservatism as a whole, when all I really had to do was act presidential in an easy contest against a backwoods buffoon.*

Intellectually, Landers knew this criticism of Richard Jordan wasn't entirely fair. Jordan had clearly outlined the possible strategies and their corresponding risks and rewards. He had given Landers the choice between a safe, sure, easy win or running an aggressive race in an effort to completely marginalize both Christians and conservatives for a decade, if not longer.

Neither Jordan nor Landers had anticipated that their attacks on Christianity hurt, rather than helped, their chances with many non-Christian voters. It turned out that a sizable majority of non-Christians, although not believers themselves, had a neutral-to-positive view of Christians as a whole. After all, there weren't too many atheist groups in their communities running homeless shelters, food pantries, and orphanages like the Christian churches were doing. And the Michelle Ackerman abortion non-story was an unmitigated disaster. The voters quickly saw it for what it was: a political dirty trick and a completely unfair and unfounded attack on a candidate's wife and family.

Although Jordan nudged him into it, Landers had made the choice about his strategy. And now Landers would now pay the price in the history books. But nothing that had gone wrong during his presidency had been Upton Landers' fault to this point—at least in his mind—and he wasn't about to start accepting responsibility for his decisions now that his career and legacy had smashed into the proverbial brick wall.

Forty feet away, President-Elect Jeff Ackerman gazed at the flags and the crowd and the Washington Monument standing staunchly in the distance with very different thoughts and emotions. He was grateful, of course. Grateful to the voters and his wife and his daughters and his staff. Grateful to God for giving him this opportunity and for getting him through the meat-grinding electoral process.

But he was also terrified. He felt so small, so insignificant. *Who am I to think I can lead this great nation?* He would never say it aloud, yet he was acutely aware that he had spent the past fifteen months thinking much more about how to become the president than what he would do if by some miracle he won. Ackerman silently prayed a prayer of thanksgiving, along with a desperate request for strength and wisdom—the same prayer he had prayed at least five times each day since winning the election.

He comforted himself with the reminder that both his political philosophy and his prior executive experience taught him that his main job was to simply stay out of the way. He had promised during the campaign that he would scale back the scope, size, and reach of the federal government, to enlarge the individual by shrinking the state. Ackerman knew that he could succeed, in large part, by simply getting the government out of the way of the American people. A friend had made a plaque for him that read *Don't just do something. Stand there!* He planned to display it prominently in the Oval Office, and he looked forward to the media's horrified, pearl-clutching reaction.

The media. The memories of the collective gasp from the media when it became clear on election night that he would win warmed him more efficiently than his thick black overcoat. His staff had spliced together a montage of clips from all the major networks and the left-leaning cable news channels as Ackerman was declared the winner in Ohio, then Pennsylvania, then Wisconsin.

A narrow win in Michigan had put him over the top, securing a win in the Electoral College and completing the stunning upset of a sitting president who was expected by all to cruise to an easy victory. This triggered an epic wave of wailing and gnashing of teeth by the reporters and commentators on nearly every channel. Randy Graham, the former White House aide in a Democratic administration and current network news analyst, had literally cried on the air as he announced that Ackerman had won. Jeers of "Man up, snowflake!" echoed throughout the Ackerman campaign's election-night headquarters. Leftist tears were everywhere that night, and Ackerman quipped that leftist tears taste very, very good.

Almost as if they had all been on a conference call together or were reading from the same script, the commentators and columnists immediately began speculating fearfully about the president-elect. They fretted that Jeff Ackerman, the newly elected "Christian conservative" and member of "the far-right wing," would "make America into a theocracy" and "turn back the clock" on the rights of gays, African Americans, women, the transgendered, Hispanics, and perhaps even left-handed people. There was even talk of impeaching President-Elect Jeff Ackerman. Although the Democrats and their media minions had not yet agreed upon the rationale for such a step, they were confident that they could whip their followers into enough of a frenzy to get articles of impeachment introduced in the House of Representatives.

Just as they had done during the campaign, Ackerman and his team simply pointed and laughed at the press. Once again, this strategy paid dividends. Media mockery by the Ackerman team simply made the reporters and talking heads even more hysterical, thereby creating a virtuous cycle that boosted the reputation of the president-elect in the eyes of the public while further depressing the already-dim reputation of the press.

When he'd been asked by an interviewer about the possibility of being impeached, Ackerman simply shrugged, smiled, and said, "The Democrats have tried to impeach every elected Republican president since Eisenhower, so trying to impeach me would simply be par for the course. They aren't very good losers, which is strange when you think about how much practice they've had at it."

Time now to take the oath of office. President-Elect and Almost-President Jeff Ackerman walked toward the podium. He tried to keep his eyes turned toward the crowd but glanced down occasionally to avoid the embarrassment of tripping over one of the dozens of microphone and television wires that crisscrossed the stage.

The unlikely candidate and even more unlikely victor raised his right hand, placing his left on the tattered Bible he had inherited from his grandmother. With Michelle beaming at him from his left, and with the massive throng before him hushed into a reverent silence, he began the oath of office. In a slow, steely, Southern-accented voice, Jeffrey Clinton Ackerman echoed the words of the Chief Justice of the Supreme Court, swearing to "preserve, protect and defend the Constitution of the United States, so help me God."

So help me God. So help me God.

Acknowledgments

T hank you to Brad McBrayer, Matt McCook, and Barrett Johnson for reading early versions of this manuscript and providing valuable feedback and even more valuable encouragement and friendship. Thank you to my tireless editor, Christy Distler, who caught and corrected my many mistakes and improved the writing tremendously. Any remaining errors are my own. Thanks to designer Kristen Ingebretson for her hard work on the cover and to typesetter Laura Jones turning words on a page into a final product.

Thank you to Jennifer for being the best wife in the world and my best friend, for giving me two amazing daughters, and for being my partner and biggest supporter in all things, including this little venture.

About the Author

S tephen Palmer is from Jackson, Mississippi and a graduate of Mississippi State University and Emory University School of Law. He practiced law for twenty years before retiring early to focus on writing and public speaking. Stephen and his wife Jennifer have two daughters, Avery and Haley, and live in Marietta, Georgia.

Visit www.sdpalmer.net to learn more about Stephen's writing and speaking engagements.

Printed in Great Britain
by Amazon